Prescription for Justice

BOOKS BY VICTOR WARTOFSKY

Mr. Double and Other Stories
Meeting the Pieman
Year of the Yahoo
The Passage

PRE-SCRIPTION FOR JUSTICE

Victor Wartofsky

Lyle Stuart Inc./Irma Heldman

Secaucus, New Jersey

Published by Lyle Stuart Inc.
120 Enterprise Ave., Secaucus, N.J. 07094
In Canada: Musson Book Company
a division of General Publishing Co. Limited
Don Mills, Ontario

Queries regarding rights and permissions should be
addressed to: Lyle Stuart, 120 Enterprise Avenue,
Secaucus, N.J. 07094

Manufactured in the United States of America

Library of Congress Cataloging-in-Publication Data

Wartofsky, Victor.
    Prescription for justice.

    I. Title
PS3573.A783P7   1987   813'.54   86-23174
ISBN 0-8184-0423-X

Nobody in the world can be the judge of the criminal before he has realized that he himself is as much a criminal as the one who confronts him. . .

—Dostoyevsky, *The Brothers Karamazov*

Prescription for Justice

ONE

He saw her and whipped a U-turn across a space in the median strip and then over two lanes, braking to where she stood under a street lamp. Startled, she gasped and drew back but then sighed with relief when she saw who it was.

He leaned over to poke his head out of the passenger side window. "Good evening, miss. Just thought I'd remind you that it's pretty dangerous out here this time of night. Don't you have any other way of getting home?"

She shook her head. "The bus'll be here in about ten minutes."

He made a big show of concern by shaking his head and making clucking sounds with his tongue. "Well, I hate to take business away from the bus company, but if you want a lift, hop in."

She shrugged. "Well, I don't know."

He couldn't let her get away. He had been cruising for several hours without success and might not have another opportunity like this the rest of the evening. "Oh, come on. I'll have you home in a jiffy. No charge."

Still she hesitated, nervously looking down the road for the bus she knew wasn't to be seen yet, but hoping that her look would convey her preference for the bus and her reluctance to impose upon him.

Now he spoke with friendly exasperation in his voice, in the manner of a radio announcer gently berating listeners to forego one product in favor of another. "For gosh sakes, if you can't trust a public servant, we're in pretty bad shape."

She smiled. "Okay, I guess."

He returned her smile and flipped the door open. The light came on, illuminating the interior and causing him an instant of panic. For that moment he wanted to cup the bulb with his hand or hide his face, but then he realized the foolishness of his worry.

To begin with, she'd be seeing a lot of his face, morning, noon and night. And then she'd never be able to tell anybody what he looked like. After a few days she'd never be able to tell anybody anything.

The coroner's examining room, usually kept on the frigid side, was warm and close. The cooling unit had broken down, making Detective Sergeant Vincent Imperateri wish the medical examiner would quit gabbing so much and get on with the job.

Dr. Morris Cohen paused to comb the blood-matted pubic hair of the young girl's corpse and gathered up loose hairs which may have belonged to someone else. He placed them in an envelope. For a comparative study later, he clipped specimens of the girl's own hair and dropped them into a separate envelope.

A consulting medical examiner for the District of Columbia, Morris Cohen was an elderly man, so thin that he was as cadaverous as his subjects. As he now examined purplish cuts and indentations on both inner thighs of the body, he addressed Imperateri without looking up. "Hey, Vinnie, don't the Redskins open training this month? You think they're going to do anything this year?"

"Like always," Imperateri said, removing his jacket and tossing it on a chair. "Good start. Choke up in midseason." He suppressed a yawn. It wasn't as though he disliked professional football. It was just that the violence of real life so sickened him that he couldn't show interest in manufactured mayhem. He did, however, keep up with the sports pages. This way he was able to say the right words to any of his fellow officers who brought the subject up.

Cohen picked up saline-moistened swabs to remove stains

around the vagina. "What they need is more young players, Vinnie. An infusion of fresh serum." He smiled.

Imperateri shook his head and wiped perspiration from his face. "Doc, I'll tell you a secret. They had youth and speed a few seasons back but didn't even make it to the playoffs. Then they traded for age and experience. They made it to the playoffs but got clobbered. Some people just can't win." He wiped his forehead again. "For God's sake, Doc. What happened to the air conditioning?"

Morris Cohen looked up at the tall, blond detective as if surprised at his question. "I told you, compressor's busted."

Imperateri glanced around the autopsy room, not daring to breathe deeply of the odors of chemicals and a two-day old corpse. "How come these places never have any windows?"

Morris Cohen grinned. "Because we don't need them, that's why. Have a look. I've got plenty of light to see the semen." He bent his head low to examine stains on the skin which were easily detectable, appearing as glistening slug trails, yellow and scaly under the powerful fluorescent lights.

"I wasn't thinking about lighting, Doc. I think I'm going to pass out."

"Big tough-ass detective like you? If you do, I might be tempted to put you on the table to see if you have a heart. I already know you don't have a brain." Morris Cohen guffawed, stopping only to place the swabs in stoppered test tubes to be examined later for possible evidence. "If you think this is bad, you should have been around in the old days. I remember morgue work before refrigeration."

"You've been at this a long time, huh, Doc? Forty years?"

"Forty-five, including fifteen years of intermittent retirement. We used to be called coroners in the old days, but you didn't even have to be an M.D. Then they called us medical examiners. Now we're forensic pathologists." He laughed again.

"Why do you keep breaking your retirement?"

"I lend a hand weekends, holidays. The chief ME asked me to cover for the holiday week."

11

"A hell of a way to spend July Fourth. Everybody's at the beach this week."

Again Morris Cohen looked up. "Except maybe the killer of this kid." He returned to his scraping and sighed. "I can use the consultant fees. What about you, Vinnie? Haven't you put in your twenty yet?"

"Just about. But as long as I can still close a case, I'll stick around." Imperateri didn't know why he suddenly chose to lie. He wished he could leave the force and the work which he now disliked. There were many other opportunities around. He was still a relatively young man, just over forty, young enough to begin a new career. If he could have a lieutenant's salary he would be entitled to a higher annuity, enough to leave the Department, provide for child support, go to school and live fairly comfortably.

"Hey, Vinnie, guess what?" Cohen rubbed and sniffed something between his fingers. "This seminal stain isn't come juice after all."

Imperateri cocked his head to the side. "What do you think it is?"

"I *know* what it is, thanks to my poor old Jewish mother, may she rest in peace. It's dried chicken fat, that's what it is. Semen is white and looks starchy. This stuff here is yellowish, greasy."

Imperateri removed a notebook and pen from his jacket and scribbled Cohen's observation. "I wonder how it got there," he said, looking as if for the first time at the body lying on the slotted metal table. Cohen had explained that the wounds to the hands and forearms were defensive ones, shields to ward off striking blows of a knife or some other sharp instrument.

"What's strange," the doctor continued, "is that it looks like the killer attempted to wash the body with soap and water. Didn't do too good a job, though."

Although Imperateri had seen corpses at autopsy many times before, the naked body before him bothered him deeply. He did not known why. Perhaps because the victim reminded him of his own young daughter, Judy, now living with her mother on the other side of town. Perhaps also because the corpse of the young girl appeared alive. Each fold of skin, orifice and lump glistened in reflected light. Even the hair fluttered to life, moved by an oscillating fan brought into the room as a substitute for the faulty air conditioning.

Imperateri felt a wave of nausea. At the same time a burning pinpoint seemed to prick deep within his stomach. He put the notebook and pen away and took a deep breath. Why in hell did he have to show up here? he wondered. He could have waited until later to receive the coroner's report, all cleaned and nicely typed. But he knew that his impatience would not allow him. He was like that with every case he worked on.

Yet now all he cared about was just getting out of the autopsy room. Gone were the thoughts of the grieving parents who had demanded that their daughter's body not be violated by the coroner's knife. Nor did he presently care about the media people who would badger him anew for details about the rape and murder of the fourteen-year-old girl.

"Do you know what I'm doing now, Vinnie?"

Imperateri shook his head. "I'm not a doctor. It's tough enough being a cop."

"Do you much care what I'm doing?"

"Just hurry it up, Doc. Quit the bullshitting."

"Touchy, touchy. Well, I'm looking for contusions of the vaginal introitus," Morris Cohen said in a manner suggesting that he was only thinking out loud and did not expect Imperateri to understand. "The incidence of vulvar trauma is very high in pediatric patients. I guess you could still call her a pediatric case. She wasn't much over the age of puberty. What do you know about her?"

"Name's Kitty Burns. Missing since the beginning of the holiday week. She was found in a shopping center trash bin."

"Dead for about two days, I'd say."

Imperateri's eyes, blue and deepset within a squarish face, watched as the coroner continued to work, spreading the body's legs even further apart and slipping gloved fingers in and out of the vagina, like a plumber cleaning a rusty pipe. "How much do you have to go, Doc?"

13

"What's the matter, Vinnie? You anxious to get back to the crossword puzzles?"

"There's going to be another murder in here if you don't hurry up. I promised the girl's old man you weren't going to cut her up. He said we had a half hour with the body, and then he was going to claim it."

Morris Cohen shook his head and looked up. Anger blazed in his eyes. "Meddlers! Look, you tell the parents we have a homicide here and if I think it's necessary to have a full autopsy, I'll order one. It so happens right now I think I know what killed her."

"What?"

"I'll tell you, sonny boy, when I'm good and ready. And that'll be in about a minute."

Saying that, Morris Cohen ballooned his thin cheeks up with air and probed deeper within the vaginal vault. As he continued to speak, the vexation in his voice gave way to sarcasm.

"Well, Mr. Detective Sergeant Vincent Imperateri of the illustrious homicide squad, it looks like you're going to have to give up the racing form for awhile. We've got some work cut out for you."

"Number one, Doc, I've never looked at a racing form in my life. And two, I don't have to be a coroner-medical-examiner-forensic-pathologist to spot a rape-homicide." Imperateri hoped his own sarcasm would get to Cohen, but with the old man you never knew.

"Yeah, wise guy, but this is a particularly vicious one. We've got severe vaginal trauma here. Whoever's done it forced some blunt objects into her. Bottle, stick, maybe even a butter knife. She's had a laceration that pierced right through the peritoneal cavity. Believe it or not, that's not what killed her."

The medical examiner shook his head as he smeared specimens onto the glass slides for another pathologist to examine later. "Look at her neck, Vinnie. See those marks? Strangulation by hand. You can also see evidence of rope burns."

"He tried to hang her first?"

Morris Cohen shrugged. "The rope wounds aren't severe enough for that. Maybe he kept her tied up. Could have used a chain rather than a rope. I'll have to take a closer look." He paused and then shrugged again. "It's asphyxia by strangulation, all right. But I'm going to order the surgeon in."

"If you already know how she died, why bother?"

"I'd feel better about it, that's why."

"Damn, I promised the parents."

"I'm sorry, Vinnie. Maybe we'll find something else."

Imperateri shuddered at the thought that each of the girls organs would have to be cut and removed, weighed and examined, and the contents of the stomach and intestines analyzed. Of course after disembowelment the body would be put back together and prepared for a funeral, but the pathologist surgeon's work would be marked by telltale black thread which made no effort to mask the incisions.

"If you wish, Vinnie, I'll speak with the parents."

Imperateri drew a sigh of relief. "Thanks, Doc. I'm a coward when it comes to things like that."

Moments later the burning in Imperateri's stomach changed to a gnawing, empty feeling. Turning slightly so that Morris Cohen couldn't see what he was doing, he removed an antacid pill from a container which he kept in a shirt pocket and popped it into his mouth.

But the doctor noticed. "Still got that ulcer, huh, Vinnie?"

"Comes and goes."

"You've got to go on a diet and lay off the smoking. Take a couple of weeks. Go away somewhere."

"Thanks, Doc." Imperateri knew all that. It was one of those things easier said than done. He nodded towards the corpse. "Anything on her wrists, ankles?"

"Nothing. It doesn't look like she was tied by hand or foot."

"Those neck marks, Doc. My bet is that he kept her on a leash like a dog. Dragged her along for a couple of days to satisfy himself whenever he felt the urge. Then for one reason or another, killed her."

Morris Cohen grimaced, lifted the victim's hand and scraped under each fingernail, putting the scrapings in still another labeled envelope.

Imperateri edged closer. The victim could have scratched her

15

assailant in self-defense. Skin abrasions scooped up by her nails might offer information about the killer's skin and blood type. "Doc, you're right about one thing."

"What's that?"

"Viciousness. The killer's not your average find 'em, feel 'em, fuck 'em and forget 'em rapist. His MO's pure freak. We've got a very sick and dangerous man."

"What makes you so sure it's a man, Vinnie?"

"Oh, come on, Doc. It couldn't have been a woman."

"Everybody's a suspect, sonny boy. Didn't they teach you that in detective sergeant school? Look, there's no evidence of seminal stains on the body. But, as I've said, the killer cleaned it. I'm not one hundred percent sure, but it doesn't look like there was penetration and ejaculation. I took vaginal smears but I don't think I'll find spermatozoa."

Morris Cohen paused to wipe his brow with the sleeve of his white laboratory coat. "I'm sure about one thing, though. Whoever it was chewed up the kid's inner thighs."

"Those are bite marks?"

The coroner nodded. "We'll need a dentist. A forensic odontologist. We're going to have to take some real sharp impressions."

"That's the easy part," Imperateri said, removing his jacket from the chair. "The hard part is matching them with the right freak rapist."

Morris Cohen looked up and stared into the distance for a few moments before speaking. "They don't come around too often, thank God. I remember one back in '52 who killed some ten or twelve girls before we caught up with him."

"I hope we're quicker," Imperateri said, turning to leave. He stopped suddenly and looked back at the body once more. "Little Kitty Burns. Her parents and friends say she was a good girl, no drugs, no drinking, no slutting around. Just got good grades and held a part-time job at night. Just never made it home after work one night."

"That job's what killed her, Vinnie."

Imperateri shook his head. "No, not the job."

TWO

William Crawford waved his clipboard to signal the next waiting car forward. The automobile eased up to a white line and stopped, enabling a middle-aged man to get out. Crawford surmised that he was probably the father of the young girl inside.

The girl slid over to the driver's side, flashing for an instant bare white thighs against the dark leather of the seat. The sight did not escape Crawford. At that moment, he felt the familiar tingle in his groin. Confused, he bit his lip and stared down hard on the scoring sheet attached to the clipboard. A thought, more a worry than a fear, came to him. His own body had broken faith with him.

It was too soon. He shouldn't be getting those urgings for at least another few weeks.

Breathing deeply as if to steel himself against the unexpected awakening within him, he went to the window and asked to see her learner's permit. He studied her as she rummaged in her purse.

She had a round face and large eyes, and wore her glossy brown hair long and loose. Her nose, turned up, seemed to crinkle in anticipation, and her anxiety only fueled his own.

He examined the permit but his eyes strayed over the card and on to the girl's legs. A tight, short skirt fell far above the knees, revealing soft, fleshy thighs. The flesh quivered, and he imagined that it called to him, a silent mating call that only he could understand and fulfill.

Crawford handed back the permit and nodded to the father, still standing nearby. "We'll be about fifteen minutes."

17

Now squeezed inside the small car, he again forced himself to look down on the clipboard. Yet he could not erase the picture from his mind of her legs, the actuality of which was only bare inches away from him.

It was too soon.

Had not the overwhelming desire been satisfied, the propelling force dissipated? he wondered. Had not he been promised a period of rest by his recent salvation, so strong as to be likened to a drowning victim being lifted to safety?

Now, several days after that deliverance, William Crawford again thought about the pressures within him. He recalled that a psychiatrist at the state hospital had said they were an inner storm that occasionally sent out sudden lightning shafts of violence.

Nevertheless, William Crawford thought of the pressures as sweet urgings, even though he knew that they turned him into a savage satisfied only by blood. After one of his girls died, an incredibly liberating orgasm came to drive his inner devils away.

He knew that what he had done was wrong, was criminal, was murder, but he rationalized his guilt away. The girl could have died of a disease or in a traffic accident. The way kids drive nowadays and smoke and take drugs, it's a wonder she hadn't died before now.

He laughed to himself. At least she died helping her fellow man. Me.

True, he felt sorry for her. But he hoped that her last moments were enjoyable ones, giving her at least some of the pleasure that they gave him. And more important, providing him with the release he so desperately needed.

But now the animal urgings had suddenly returned, brought on by the sight of young, bare legs. He had to control himself. He could not risk being suspected of anything, especially in the shadow of police headquarters.

"All right, young lady," he heard himself say, "don't be nervous. I'd like to see you pass the test as much as you. Now just start it up and drive."

He could smell the wholesomeness of her perspiration, drawing him like a shark to blood. Be careful, he repeated, almost in a whisper.

"What did you say, sir?" The voice was sweet, high, pleading.

"Ah, nothing. Just continue up the next block and then take a left."

She slowed for a stop sign, her legs spread wide apart as she valiantly worked the brakes and clutch.

Why did she have to wear a short skirt instead of jeans? he asked himself. Why couldn't she have been in a car with automatic transmission instead of a stick shift?

The car lurched in fits and starts, coughing, staggering almost like a drunk. She sighed deeply and glanced at him to see if he'd take points off for poor clutch control.

He did not. He was too busy trying to keep his eyes away from her skirt which hiked up even further. She continued to breath deeply, constantly pushing her breasts forward and licking her lips wet.

He felt his perspiration building and his heart pounding. It was all that he could do not to take over the wheel and drive to his house and succumb to the new demand within him. He realized he'd probably be caught and punished, but the minutes with her would be worth it. A hungry tramp smashing a bakery window could not care for the consequences.

Yet he was not a tramp but a respected member of the police department's motor vehicle division. And he could not afford to be so careless, remembering the first time when he hadn't taken precautions and paid for his carelessness.

The girl's body had been found in a secluded lean-to William Crawford had built on his father's California chicken farm. The corpse was mutilated with numerous wounds around the breasts and thighs. Around her neck could be seen the mark of a thong with which she had been strangled.

There was no doubt who killed the twelve-year-old daughter of the town's feed merchant. William, a skinny, pimply-faced youth of sixteen, was found cowering under a small bridge where he had gone to hide after seeing the sheriff's car arrive.

He readily admitted stabbing the girl with a knife used to slit the throats of chickens, and then choking her. Under intense cross-examination, he broke down and confessed that the abrasions on her inner thighs came from his teeth and that he did have an orgasm while biting her. But with tears streaming down his cheeks, he denied having sexual intercourse with her. "She died a virgin," he exclaimed.

William Crawford was found not guilty by reason of insanity and declared a mentally disordered sex offender. He was sent to a maximum security state hospital for an indeterminate, open-ended sentence.

A new phase began in William Crawford's life. He learned that if he convinced his psychiatrists that he could be trusted with freedom, he could be freed sooner than if he had been sent to prison. But he knew that if the analysts saw through his scheme, or believed that he was incurable, he would be kept in the hospital or transferred to prison.

William cooperated. He eagerly went to counseling sessions with the analysts. For several years he observed how they sought to manipulate him to examine himself and his past behavior and to work on changing his attitude.

He reasoned that the first sign he'd have to show was remorse for his deed. He did, repeatedly telling the psychiatrists that he felt a need to pay for his sin. At times he told them he even wanted to commit suicide to erase his guilt.

"If I could with my life restore hers, I would gladly do so," he said several times, more taken with the poetic and humanitarian sentiment of his words than with their meaning. Nevertheless, he did not stress the taking of his life too often, realizing that he shouldn't lengthen his treatment by trading one psychosis for another.

The second sign he showed was a willingness to pour his innermost secrets, beginning with the chickens on his father's farm. He hated them because he just could not keep the feed and water troughs clear of their droppings and his father accused him of being lazy and whipped him. He hated the way they pecked at his legs and hand when he tried to feed them. He hated them because they were dumb and vicious, eager to attack in numbers and tear apart a weaker chicken. And he hated them because they died easily from disease, though they were difficult to kill.

Once, when he was twelve, his mother asked him to kill a chicken for dinner. Choosing a large hen who had pecked him several times, he tried to wring its neck but couldn't with bare hands. He found a thong which he slipped around the hen's neck, and pulled with all his might. Yet the fowl squawked and struggled, making William experience a strong and peculiar feeling of sexual pleasure. There was something feminine about a chicken, its feathers, its fevered panting when warm.

Leading the hen along with the thong, he then slashed at it with a knife and finally plunged the weapon deep into its breast. Furtively, driven by a compulsion he could not resist and would not question, he held the bloodied chicken to his member and achieved an orgasm.

Later at the dinner table, the erection returned when he ate the chicken.

He killed many chickens that way, explaining the carnage away to his father as the result of disease, or due to a dog or wild animal breaking into the coops. His drunk father never caught on. William killed his last chicken a few days before he lured the feed merchant's daughter into the lean-to.

The analysts, separately and together, scribbled voluminous notes and asked many questions. They learned that his mother was forceful and strong-willed and fought constantly with her husband. She refused sexual intercourse for fear of contracting venereal disease. His father, a brutal, philandering alcoholic, once raped her in front of William. The father often beat William mercilessly, accusing him of having sex with the girls of the town. The charge was not true. William had never had intercourse, either as a youth or as an adult.

For twelve years William underwent therapy in the hospital. When his analysts pronounced him cured, fit to return to society, and convinced a judge that he was no longer a danger to the community, William left that community for another in the East.

In Washington, D.C., he joined the motor vehicle department as a driving test examiner. On his application he lied about ever being in trouble with the law. His fingerprints and application were sent to the FBI for routine checking, but nothing surfaced. William Crawford had no record. Because of a privacy law, the sentencing of the mentally-disturbed juvenile to the California hospital was not programmed in the computer data system of criminal convictions.

Fourteen years. He could never go back to that hospital prison where his animal urgings could find no expression, building up within him and threatening to destroy him. Surrounded by male analysts and orderlies, he kept away from the other sex offenders, the rapists, the perverts, the child molesters, all of whom disgusted him. He sought solace only in looking at the photographs of women in magazines, or watching the images of actresses move on television.

His loins ached, waiting.

"Take another right and head back to the station."

The girl nodded and again her legs worked up and down, her knees calling to him. He felt his throat constrict, his mouth turn to sand.

If he tried anything, there'd be no end to it. He'd be traced and tracked down even before he'd reach home. An investigation would follow, the putting of two and two together, and he'd be sent away. This time perhaps forever. No, it would not work. He must wait and take the steps which have proved successful. A holiday and the use of a police cruiser.

She slammed the car to a sudden stop, throwing his head forward where it almost smashed against the windshield. Then she turned towards him, her eyes pleading.

"Did I pass?"

He nodded, stealing one more look at her thighs. Labor Day. Only two weeks away. It was going to be a long wait.

THREE

The alarm screeched. Vincent Imperateri stretched an arm and pushed the clock's button. With the other arm reaching out on the other side of the bed he flipped a switch on a makeshift wood box on the night table, energizing an ancient Victor Talking Machine set up nearby on a rolling tray. A scratchy 78 RPM record, already cued on the first groove, squeaked to life. The voice of Enrico Caruso, overpowering a tinny orchestra, was released.

"Vesti la giubba e la faccia infarina . . .

The Victor was a 1911 windup model, complete with a flower horn measuring twenty-four inches in diameter, and with a front panel showing the trademark of a dog cocking its head while listening to its master's voice. The side panels were missing, exposing a maze of wires and indicating that the once hand-cranked machine had been modified to run on electricity. An electrician friend had fashioned the switchbox and retooled the Victor to add an automatic turntable. Yet the machine and switchbox worked improperly, shutting off frequently and making Imperateri wish he'd given the relic to a museum.

His whole efficiency apartment and its furniture also belonged to the past. Square and spare, the room held old and mismatched furnishings scooped up from rummage sales or second-hand stores.

As part of the divorce settlement, Beth got everything, the child, the house and furniture, including the stereo and VCR. He got the Victor Talking Machine.

Imperateri, eyes closed, palms sheltering head on a pillow,

listened to the music and hummed snatches softly, dropping his chin to keep in touch with the lower registers. He lifted his head for the high emotional point and sang along with the great tenor.

"Ridi Pagliaccio, sul tuo amore infranta!
Ridi del duol che t'arvelena il car!"

The Victor was given to him by his grandfather along with hundreds of 78's, mainly Italian operas and Neopolitan love songs. Imperateri could not bring himself to part with the records and the machine. They were a remembrance of his grandfather and the little flat near Brooklyn's Sheepshead Bay area.

He remembered that as a child he used to sit by his grandfather's chair while the old man sang along with Caruso in a voice strong and full of gusto but grossly untrained. Imperateri smiled to himself as he recalled the image. A stunted, homely, spaghetti-gorging, brick-laying Sicilian with hands almost the size of shovel scoops. A gruff comedian, jack of many trades when there was no bricklaying to be done. A widower with five children, including Imperateri's own father, who raised them to understand the meaning of respect and honor, of family, country, church. Not like the bullshit of today, Imperateri often thought, which rendered those words meaningless.

Yet the old man had failed with his youngest son, Imperateri's father, a ne'er-do-well whose marriage failed and who packed off young Vincent to live with the old man.

Imperateri now wondered whether he was repeating his father's mistakes. Except for a soured marriage and such side aggravations as a daughter growing up without proper supervision and an ex-wife constantly bitching about child support payments, his life was stable. As stable as a cop's life could be.

The phonograph record came to an end and the old machine groaned as its automatic arm dropped the next heavy 78 platter with a loud thump on the turntable. A moment later a soft-voiced Caruso sang the Flower song from Carmen, accompanied by Imperateri as far as the opening notes.

"La fleur que tu m'avais jetee. . ."

The aria over, Imperateri shut the machine off. He sat up on the side of the bed with great effort, yawning, shaking his head, breathing deeply, as though trying to seek a hidden source of strength within him. He was tired, too old for this sort of thing, he thought. Too old to carry caseloads of up to fifteen cases and be dependent on the weather and the strength of the Department. The unending warm weather seemed to bring an increase in homicides. And the Department was going through another budget-cutting session, dropping younger officers from its rolls and not replacing retiring ones. All of this was reflected in his caseload, the most he'd ever had.

Like a baseball player long overdue for a hit, he needed to close out at least one of his standing cases. He'd even settle for a resolution of last week's Saturday night poker game stabbing which any police cadet could have easily shut on Sunday morning. Things were that bad for him.

Yet of all his active cases only one galled and frustrated him, the Kitty Burns murder. He was no closer to cracking it than when the girl's body had been discovered weeks ago. No leads, no witnesses. Dr. Morris Cohen reported finding no fingerprints but did recover hair samples. The good doctor, bless his insistence on a full autopsy, also found undigested food in the victim's stomach, indicating that the murderer had fed her during captivity.

Nevertheless, the case was growing stale. With the passage of time, the press cooled its lurid stories of the cannibal murderer, the child-killer whose identity remained a mystery.

Imperateri rose and stumbled to a nearby chair, on which his clothing lay where he had thrown it, ready like a fireman's garments for quick dressing but in reality showing the seedier side of lazy bachelorhood.

Again he shook his head. He needed a woman, not just a shack-up, but a companion, a wife. He was ready for the plunge again. Maybe with a good woman he'd learn how to live like he hadn't with Beth. Maybe he wouldn't work so much. Like today, another lonely holiday.

Time to go to work.

Labor Day Monday drew overcast skies and muggy air, much like most of the dog days that had preceded it. Vincent Imperateri, smug in the knowledge that by working he wasn't missing anything weather-wise, pulled up in front of the municipal building, an enormous edifice housing not only police headquarters and the district attorney's offices, but also the city's motor vehicle department. Today being a holiday, empty parking spaces beckoned invitingly like free coffee and doughnuts at a reception for freeloaders. Normally, street parking was rarely available.

Imperateri felt little sympathy for the cops who cursed a new Department order that officers observe parking regulations, just like any other citizen. No exceptions. Meter Maids, the ubiquitous mini-skirted officers, were ordered to ticket any cop's official or private car on an expired meter. The fine was to be paid out of the offender's own pocket.

Sure it was tough, Imperateri had told the complainers. But the law applied to all, even the enforcers.

The parking now reminded him of his need for more money. Though he deserved a promotion and had passed the written examination, the head of the homicide division, Captain Terence Anderson, had turned him down.

Anderson had admitted that a promotion was certainly in order, but gave various excuses for holding it off. At first, because the division's table of organization called for only six detective lieutenants and those slots were filled. But when one of the lieutenants retired, Anderson then claimed that budgetary constraints called for a reduction in expenses, starting with promotions. "We're just another city agency fighting for crumbs," he often repeated.

Another time Anderson confided that he was under pressure to promote a black officer and didn't want to give Imperateri a leg-up now for fear of creating internal squabbles.

Too many excuses. The real reason? Imperateri could only guess that the captain had to have something of value to be produced as either a reward or punishment when the time came.

Though he often lied, Anderson was not a bad man. Deep

down, Imperateri held a certain respect for the captain, whom he considered a good cop but a poor administrator. Anderson, everyone knew, was a living example of the principle stating that one rises to one's level of incompetence. As a cop on the beat in the city's worst precinct, he was promoted to plainclothes by dint of having the best collar record on the force. He gained further promotions by repeating his arrest rate, and by seniority achieved by remaining while his colleagues retired or resigned.

Smiling to himself, Imperateri parked his eleven-year-old car in Anderson's reserved space. The captain would probably be at the beach now, guzzling beer far away from routine worries.

He entered the building and ran up to the fourth floor, two steps at a time, his way of trying to stay in shape. Passing by the desk lieutenant's office, he waved to the officer at the chest-high counter with the arrest book on top.

"Holiday business, Freddie?"

The desk officer shrugged. "The usual. Couple robberies. Calvert Street Bridge suicide. One homicide. Not to worry. A pusher. We got him."

Imperateri nodded and continued striding down the hall, greeting other officers in shirtsleeves with guns riding their belts who escorted various suspects, one of whom had a head swathed in a bandage.

At the entrance to the homicide squad room a large, handprinted sign was posted on a pillar to impress visitors.

HOMICIDE CASES THIS YEAR	292
CLOSED	243
STILL OPEN	49

The sign, yellowed and aging, was more than five years old, but nobody wanted to change what represented one of the squad's best years.

On the walls were tacked wanted posters and menus from nearby restaurants. Greasy pizza cartons and ash-filled trays shared desk space with manila report folders.

The squad room was a jumble of gray metal desks and file cabinets purchased by the city during a hand-me-down sale of federal government surplus. The equipment, battered and rusted, looked as if it had gone through several generations of civil servants. As if appearances were not bad enough, every drawer stuck and every chair squeaked.

Imperateri strode in on the linoleum floor and headed straight for his desk. He waved at only the two other detectives present, Dave Noseworthy, standing by the metropolitan police wire, and Bob Perkins, who pecked anxiously at a manual typewriter.

Imperateri's desk was laden with the manila folders, all marked *Report of Investigation*. Each had a subtitle for a particular case, such as *Kitty Burns*. At a corner of the desk was a large framed photograph of Judy, showing waves of blond hair like her father's and eyes so blue that they looked artificial.

The telephone rang and Perkins answered it. "Homicide."

Imperateri sat down, shoving the .38 caliber revolver strapped to his hip a bit forward so that the chair would not jab it into his back. He sighed as he looked at the pile of photographs and wondered how many times he had examined the blow-ups of the Kitty Burns strangling scene, each time hoping that he'd notice something, the minutest detail, which had escaped him before.

"Yes, ma'am," Perkins spoke into the telephone, "we're open holidays. As a matter of fact, we're open twenty-four hours a day."

Almost all of the photographs were of the victim, dead and mutilated. Artless, revealing, taken by a police photographer, they showed her clothing, neatly packed in a transparent plastic bag near the body.

"Well, ma'am, I really think you ought to speak with our Missing Persons desk if you don't know where he is. Just a moment, I'll transfer you."

A moment later Perkins hung up and turned to Imperateri. "Christ! Her husband doesn't come home one night, and she thinks he's been murdered."

"Maybe it's her hidden wish," Imperateri said, grinning. "Better check her out."

"Shit, Vinnie. If I checked everything I'd be working a ninety hour week instead of a seventy. For the same goddamn pay, too."

Imperateri allowed a half-shrug and returned to the photographs. He leaned back on the swivel chair, putting his feet up on the desk. He hated this kind of case where there were no leads and no witnesses. So far, only two people were involved and one of them was dead.

He again thought of the safety of Judy. Beth was far too lenient, too permissive with her. Somehow he'd have to do something about that. But what? Anything he'd recommend or suggest she would reject out-of-hand. He wondered whether he'd dare withhold child support until Beth saw things his way, such as not permitting Judy to ride the city's transit system at night and forbidding her to use the jogging trails alone in Rock Creek Park.

Sighing once more, he arose from the desk and took the elevator for the food dispensing machines in the basement snack bar. Returning with a cold cheese on rye and a bitter but hot black coffee, he was greeted at his desk with a sight that almost took his breath away.

He was struck first by the long, bright red hair, visible like a burning bush in a darkened arena. Coming closer, he saw the chalk-white skin, devoid of any kind of makeup. No, he corrected himself, there was just a touch of eye shadow and a soft lipstick. The rest was aristocracy, a thin nose and high cheekbones. And like a feudal royal lady, she had preempted his desk, using his typewriter and smoking a cigarette.

What the hell was this, he wondered, a dream? A glance at Noseworthy and Perkins told him it was not. The former grinned widely at Imperateri's good fortune while the latter made an obscene gesture behind her back.

"Miss," Imperateri began, "is there anything I can do for you?"

She shook her head without looking up. "No, thanks. I'm waiting for someone."

"That's fine, but you're occupying my duty station, such as it is."

29

She looked up and smiled and blinked several times. She damn well knows how beautiful she is, he thought, marveling at how well her deep green eyes complemented her fiery hair.

"Then you must be Sergeant Imperateri, just like it says on the name plate. Hello, I'm Marie Mackay, filling in for Bob Preston who's been reassigned. You're just the man I want to see."

"A reporter from my favorite newspaper," he said, again glancing up at Noseworthy and Perkins who still stood in the background out of Marie Mackay's line of vision and who still were behaving like schoolboys.

"I'm sorry for grabbing your, ah, duty station, did you say?"

"I won't charge you with unauthorized use of city property."

Again she smiled. "Actually, it looks like a slow news day and my editor asked me to do an update on the Kitty Burns murder."

He nodded, once more noting his two colleagues, grinning, leering, acting now like absolute asses. He had to get her out of the squad room. "Look, why don't we talk somewhere else over lunch?"

She looked at the cheese sandwich and coffee which he still held. "Oh," he said, "this is an emetic for a suspect who swallowed the evidence."

Laughing, she gathered her notebook, the paper from the typewriter, and a pocket tape recorder. "Do you mind if I bring along my recorder?"

"Only if you promise to turn it off when I get romantic."

Again she laughed, prompting Noseworthy and Perkins to stop their foolishness and look at each other as if wondering what charm Imperateri had that kept the young lady so amused. As Imperateri winked at them on the way out, he was stopped by the booming voice of Captain Anderson.

"Who in hell parked that shit wagon in my space?"

Anderson, possessor of a hulking body to match his blustery manner, noticed Marie Mackay and mumbled an apology for his profanity. He then looked at his three detectives and immediately addressed them in the same loud tone, as if trying to draw attention away from his graceless manner in front of the woman.

"Ah, so you three are my loyal, dedicated men hard at work while the rest of us sons-of-guns play."

Anderson had been drinking. The captain's face, flushed redder than usual, and his slurred speech revealed that a lot of liquor had been consumed.

"What are you doing here today, captain?" Perkins asked. "I thought you said you're taking the day off."

"Just checking to see who really gives a damn about the division. Now I know who really comes in and works on a case until it's closed. Give me three white men, good and true. That's all I ask."

Imperateri looked at Marie Mackay, raised his eyes in mock horror, and then introduced her to the captain, hoping that would shut him up. Anderson studied her for a few moments, shaking his head in disapproval.

"So you must work with old Weepin' Willie, the best friend of every mugger and murderer in town."

Imperateri flinched. Weepin' Willie was the police epithet for William Fisher, a local affairs columnist for the newspaper.

"Look what that son of a bitch wrote today," Anderson continued. "Crocodile tears over that black bastard Carson. A goddamn killer of two people and the Weeper is making a hero out of him in the Black ghetto. Even the goddamn white liberals are now saying he didn't get a fair trial because of some technical bullshit."

"Diminished capacity was what the lawyers argued," Perkins said. "Whatever that means." He accented his words in a manner suggesting that the term was nonsense.

"It means," Anderson said, "that he didn't have the brains to kill those two people."

Imperateri shook his head. "The Weeper said Carson was unable to form the necessary malice to commit murder."

Anderson made an angry, sweeping motion with his huge arm. "What the hell's the difference? Old Let 'em Go Joe is only going to give him fifteen years. You can bet your ass on that. And I'll bet he'll be out on the street in three."

"Who?" asked Marie.

31

"Carson," replied Imperateri.

"No, I mean, who's Let 'em Go Joe?"

"District Court Judge Joseph Baldwin, friend of the felon, confidant to the convict."

"Ah," she said, lifting her head and smiling like a little girl who was just told of a secret.

Imperateri found it difficult to keep from staring at her. "Shall we leave now?" he asked.

Anderson moved quickly to block their way. "So you're a reporter looking for a story," he said, glancing at both Noseworthy and Perkins as if to seek their approval. They grinned, and he continued. "Ain't that something? Why don't you write that old Let 'em Go Joe is responsible for half the crimes in the city?"

She smiled broadly, showing an even set of strong, white teeth. "It's the judicial system."

Caught up with the enthusiasm of his own words and with her daring smile, Anderson continued. "Right, and it stinks rotten. The son of a bitch is making my job impossible. Read your own newspaper. We arrest them, lock them up, and they're back on the streets so fast they beat us home."

"Doesn't every officer say that, Captain?"

"That's because it happens to be true. Let 'em Go Joe is a disgrace to the whole criminal justice system. How many more murderers and rapists is he going to turn loose before the community gets wise? That's where you reporters are failing to do your job. Telling the public that judges are protecting the criminals."

"Quit preaching, captain," Imperateri said. "It won't do any good."

"Can't do no harm, neither," Anderson said, looking with envy at the departing news reporter and detective sergeant.

He chose a restaurant that was a little more than he could afford, what with the child support and other expenses he paid out from a cop's salary that wasn't that large to begin with. But he told himself that this was a special occasion being with a very special lady, in another class from the courthouse secretaries he'd dated since his divorce.

32

"I'm afraid I brought you here under false pretenses," he said struggling not to stare at the blue starbursts around the pupils of her eyes. "There's absolutely nothing new on the Kitty Burns case. We're looking for a very sick person. Kitty seems to have been his first victim. I hope to God she was his last. So that's your story for tomorrow's papers."

"That was the story in last month's paper. I've got to come up with something new. But let me ask you this. Do you agree with your captain's view on the criminal justice system?"

"It's the only system we have."

"That's not what I asked."

"What do you want me to say, that there's no respect for the law, for the cop and fireman and schoolteacher and anybody who represents authority? And that the parole boards and their advising psychiatrists and the courts and judges are ruining the country?"

"You just said it. And your Captain Anderson certainly doesn't help the case."

"Don't let his big mouth throw you. He's a good cop."

"You're loyal as well as articulate, Sergeant. Tell me, you do your best to put someone behind bars while the system does its best to set him free. How do you handle that?"

He shrugged. "My job is seeing to it that nobody hurts anybody else. I operate within the legal framework. I guess you could compare me to a doctor. He doesn't go off practicing what isn't established, isn't in the textbooks."

She nodded agreement. "But suppose that doctor found that a certain drug wasn't helping the patient. Helping, hell! Let's say it was hurting the patient. Wouldn't he make changes?"

"He'd be a fool not to. But it's not up to the cop to make the changes. If and when people ever get fed up with the emphasis on criminal rehabilitation that threatens them, they'll demand a change."

She said nothing for a few moments. When she spoke again, her voice was low and steady but indignant. "I'm just thinking of what would happen if someone raped me and then got a sentence no longer than some drunk would have who punched out the bartender. What would I do? Maybe I'd kill him. And then you'd hunt me down, being the super law enforcer that you are."

Imperateri didn't like the tone of their conversation. They were close to having an adversary relationship, hardly what he had in mind. "Marie, can't we change the topic to a more pleasant one? Such as, are you married or otherwise spoken for?"

"Spoken for? That sounds like I'm some kind of chattel."

From the frying pan into the fire, he thought. "I'm sorry. These days a man has to walk on eggs when inquiring about a woman's availability."

"I don't even like the word *availability*."

Disgusted with his heavyhanded approach, he tried to recoup. "I didn't mean availability in the sense of a long-term commitment, but rather for a specific . . ." He paused, and then was grateful for her interruption.

"You're asking for a date?"

He nodded.

"Wow!" She raised her eyes. "I hope you're more direct when questioning suspects." She looked at him as if for the first time. "You may call me."

"Now with that out of the way," he said, "let's order."

FOUR

When he returned to the squad room he found a message from Beth. It was in Perkins's handwriting and it was long, detailing, it seemed, every grievance she ever had against him. All boiling down to money and more money.

Imperateri crumpled the note and threw it into a wastebasket. That bitch. She couldn't wait for him to return the call. She had to embarrass him in front of Perkins. Now the whole squad room will have a field day with gossip.

He snatched up the telephone and dialed. Before his hello faded, she began, her voice a baritone from whiskey and cigarettes.

"Judy wants to go on a ski trip. She's going to need some new outfits. You know, boots and a parka. Bib pants. She doesn't even have the equipment. Skis and poles."

"How much?"

"I don't know for sure. There's also ski lessons and transportation. I'll just charge and you'll pay."

"That's all I've been doing."

"I don't like your tone. She's your daughter, too."

"If she's my daughter, too, then how about letting me have a say in what she's doing? You're letting her run wild with freaky friends, staying up all hours of the night. She's not even sixteen, for God's sake."

"You take her, then."

"You know I can't. You know my job, my hours."

"Then shut up."

He shut his eyes tightly. "Okay, just send me the bills. You

35

might want to cut back on her dancing and modeling classes. At least until the pinch is over."

"The pinch is never over for me. Just be grateful that I'm able to take care of her."

"You could also contribute a little to Judy's welfare. She's your daughter, too."

"I'm an emotional wreck!" she screamed. "You made me what I am!"

She slammed the telephone, causing him to jerk the receiver away from his ear. He held the telephone out in midair for several moments, studying it as if it were responsible for all of his misfortune with Beth. Finally, he replaced it in the cradle and again examined the photographs of Kitty Burns in the repose of death.

The next morning Imperateri dreaded going to work. He knew that Anderson would be on the warpath, and was not surprised when the captain summoned him before he could even get to his desk.

"Good morning, Sergeant," Captain Anderson said. "Please have a seat."

Imperateri detected the stiff, dour look of the morning after, when a man in a responsible position is ashamed of his previous drunk and attempts to compensate by surplus sobriety and somberness. Despite the austere appearance, the homicide commander tried to smile. Imperateri knew the Captain had little to smile about.

On Anderson's desk were Tuesday morning's newspaper and a folder. The Captain picked up the paper and opened it to the metropolitan section which he spread for Imperateri to see.

"I've already seen it," Imperateri said, glancing at the now familiar article which he had read and re-read in disbelief over breakfast. Over the byline of Marie Mackay was the story head in large black letters that even the visually impaired couldn't miss.

HOMICIDE HEAD BLASTS JUDGE

It was all there in the lead. No one needed to read the whole article to get its message, Anderson's attack on the rights of felons, the criminal justice system, and his reference to race and criminality in the city.

At first, Imperateri was angry with Marie for a betrayal of trust. Then his anger turned to annoyance when he realized that she had never pledged confidence, nor had he the presence of mind to ask her to. He couldn't have anticipated that she apparently considered everything fair game, on the record. Finally, when he'd finished his breakfast, he saw her point of view. She was doing her job, and to ignore what she had heard and seen would be as if he were to see a bank heist and turn his back.

"I'm sure you've seen it, Sergeant. I'm sure everyone in the division, in the whole Department and in the mayor's office has seen it. I lodged a protest with the editor, but he's sticking with that woman, your, ah, friend. It doesn't look like there'll be a correction."

You can't correct the truth, Imperateri thought. To Anderson, he said, "There'll probably be an investigation by an Internal Affairs panel."

Anderson nodded gravely and looked down on the folder, which he opened. "Sergeant, I've been reviewing your record along with your new promotion request."

"I've got the best close out record in the division, Captain." Imperateri paused, wondering when to stop blowing his own horn. He decided that if he didn't do it himself, nobody else would. "I've got the time, experience and the recommendations going for me, too."

Anderson shuffled some papers within the folder as if to provide instant verification of Imperateri's claims. "The promotion warrants serious consideration," he said, then fell silent for several long moments. When he continued, his voice was lower and his words came slowly.

"Sergeant, I'm going to do something that I've never done before. Well, you're damn right there'll be an investigation." He paused again, rising to pace the office. "I'm going to ask you to support my testimony. In other words, tell the panel that I didn't say what that girl wrote."

"In other words, lie?" Imperateri said quickly.

Anderson leaned his head back several inches, clearly an expression of displeasure. "That's a pretty strong word, Vincent."

The use of Imperateri's first name sounded strange coming from Anderson's lips. It was the first time the Captain had said it, always preferring *Sergeant* or *Imperateri*.

"I'm asking your help for the good of the division," the Captain continued. "If anything happens to me because of this horseshit, the division will be torn apart. I've built it up from the days when it was nothing. Because of a couple of stupid things I may have said while I had a few drinks all of my efforts will go down the tube."

Imperateri's lack of response, either by voice or facial expression, prompted Anderson to continue speaking in a louder, almost pleading voice.

"Look, there's all kinds of horseplay going on. You know what I mean, ethnic kidding. Everybody kids everybody else. I just happened to have said something to a stranger, an outsider."

Imperateri shrugged. "You couldn't have picked a worse stranger. Next time make sure a visitor isn't a reporter."

Anderson laughed his embarrassment away. "Let's you and me be honest for a change, huh, Vincent?" Now his voice dropped several octaves and Imperateri knew that if they weren't in the privacy of the captain's office, Anderson would be continually looking over his shoulder as he spoke in confidential tones.

"Between you and me, Vincent, ninety-nine percent of the crime in this town is committed by Blacks. It's a fact of life like there's a night and there's a day. Right?"

Imperateri shook his head. "Well, not quite. You've got to realize that this is a Black town. It's like saying a hundred percent of the crime in an all-white city is committed by whites."

Anderson smiled. "Okay, but let me say this. If the panel censures me and subsequent action by the mayor and his council forces me out of this job, you can bet your ass that they'll appoint a Black captain in my place. And then you'll see who'll get the next promotion to lieutenant around here. It won't be a wop with the best close out record."

Imperateri grimaced. "I'd rather you don't use that word, Captain."

"What word?"

"Wop."

"Oh, sorry. But look, Vincent. If it bothers you about fibbing a little bit about what I said, just say you didn't hear anything. That's a little less of a lie, isn't it?"

"What about the other guys, Perkins and Noseworthy?"

"Don't worry about them. They're family."

"Does that mean I'm not?"

"That's up to you, Vincent."

Imperateri left with the feeling that no promises had been exchanged. He would think about it. Yet when he returned to his desk he realized that by not refusing outright he'd given Anderson tacit approval.

He made a move to turn back but then stopped himself. There was time to say no. He'd wait to see if the matter could clear up without hurting either Marie Mackey or the captain. Or his own chances for promotion.

Vincent Imperateri looked forward to the evening with Marie. He had no intention of getting into an argument with her. But when she opened the door, instead of hello, he said, "How could you have done it?" He immediately felt like kicking himself.

She shrugged at his question and walked to a small bar in her living room. "What will you have?"

"Vodka on the rocks," he said.

She fixed a vodka for him and a cognac for herself. Only when she handed him his drink and sat down did she speak.

"How could I have done it? Simple. Just type it up and pass it along to my editor."

"It was wrong," Imperateri said.

"Anderson knew damn well I was a reporter."

"Even if he didn't say his remarks were off the record you should have realized it. Besides, he was drinking."

"Diminished capacity, huh?"

"Marie, he's not a bad guy. He's a bit thickheaded, but he does the job the taxpayers pay him to do."

"He's a drunken oaf and a racist, to boot."

Imperateri wanted to stop talking about Anderson. He wanted to stop playing a hypocrite's role, for wasn't he going to betray her in order to get his promotion? Right then, he despised himself for even harboring the thought for a moment.

Smiling now to ease the tension, he held out both palms as if in a plea. "Okay, Marie. But can I expect to see an account of our meeting here in tomorrow's paper?"

She returned his smile. "That depends on what happens."

"You're inhibiting me. Publicity could turn me into a neuter."

"I doubt that," she said.

They exchanged a long look. It was all in the look, he told himself, the most tangible of the intangibles. He had heard of another hint, that a woman's pupils dilate when she is attracted to a man. He stared into her eyes. Did they give permission? He wasn't sure.

She noted his intense look. "Never saw an Italian with eyes so blue and hair so fair."

"Half Italian. My mother was German. She and my father split after I was born. I guess their cultural differences got in the way. And I suppose I inherited something from each of them. My German genes are constantly doing battle with the happy, easy-going Italian ones."

She threw her head back and laughed, barely getting out her next words. "Who raised you?"

"My grandfather. A Sicilian-born mason who never really learned English and was never corrupted by New World ways in his sixty years here." He studied her face. "What about you?"

"You haven't finished telling me about yourself."

"Me? The same sad old story. Divorced. One child, a teenage daughter who's being spoiled rotten by her mother. Now, your turn."

She shook her head. "First tell me how you got into police work."

"High school," he replied. "It began there. I had all of those great social ideas of helping people and improving society. But when I finally got into it, it was much different from what I'd thought. There's only so much you can do for people. Too often they hurt themselves and don't want to be helped."

"Do you remember your first case?"

He thought for a moment and then leaned back and grinned. "I was riding patrol and we had a call about a burglary in a big department store downtown. At first, it looked like a typical smash and grab case, you know, where the burglar breaks the window and makes off with whatever's in the display, all within thirty seconds or so. That's about the time needed to respond to the window alarm. But there was something odd about this one. All the display clothing, fur, jewelry, were still on the mannequins. All except one, which was stripped clean and lying on the floor, surrounded by its clothing. We didn't know what to make of it until we examined the mannequin and found sticky stuff around its lower parts."

She cocked her head to the side for a moment, grinned, and then roared with laughter. He, too, laughed, but stopped to continue.

"Some pervert broke in and violated the mannequin. I guess he pretended it was alive and more or less willing."

"What amazes me," she said, "is that he did it all in thirty seconds, including the breaking of the window entering and the ripping off of the clothing. The poor mannequin. I hope she made it back into show biz."

Imperateri nodded. "We passed by some time later. She was no worse for the wear and was modeling a swimsuit. But we never found the intruder. The MO was never repeated." He paused and patted her hand. "Now, aren't you going to tell me about yourself?"

"You're a detective. Go figure me out."

He ran his hand along her arm. Why does one person's skin feel better than another's? Vibrations, he replied to himself. Now he squeezed her shoulders like a carnival huckster guessing occupations. "Married once. Didn't work out."

"That's not saying much. Almost half the population can make that claim."

"You're from the midwest. Came here to get away from your ex and to find a new challenge."

"Cleveland. That hardly midwest. As for the other, well, good but no great work of detection. I hope you're better at your job."

He shook his head. "Almost all of my cases got solved despite my efforts."

"How so?"

"By dumb luck, serendipity. By leads supplied by the public."

"What's police work really like?"

"Not like television, where the cops solve a crime in less than an hour with commercials snuck in every few minutes." He leaned back, gulped the remainder of the vodka and told her about the long hours, the unrelenting pressures, the danger. And how the agony and despair of real victims could never be duplicated in the movies, no matter how good the actors. Nor could film ever capture the iron, sickly smell of blood or the odor of a week-old corpse alive with maggots.

He stopped suddenly, realizing that he was destroying the mood again by all the serious talk. He had to get back on the track. He picked up her hand.

"Strong. Do you play tennis?"

She nodded.

"How about going a couple of sets with me tomorrow night?"

"You're on. I belong to the Linden Hill Tennis Club over in Bethesda," she said, reaching for the ringing telephone. She answered and handed it to him. "It's for you."

He shrugged. "Nobody knows I'm here." Taking up the telephone, he paused a moment before speaking. "Imperateri."

"I had a hunch I'd find you there," Noseworthy said, his voice more nasal-sounding over the wire. "Been looking all over."

"What's so important that it couldn't wait?"

"Something from Arlington. Looks like another Kitty Burns."

FIVE

The two-man Arlington County evidence team had already sketched the crime scene on legal pads, outlining the body in crayon. Now they examined the ground for evidence while other detectives canvassed the neighborhood, seeking witnesses.

Vincent Imperateri waited until the police photographers were through before looking around at the scene lit up by portable lamps and cruiser spotlights. He felt a strong sense of *déjà vu*, of seeing another Kitty Burns in another parking lot. Another girl, nude, cut up, battered. This one a petite blonde with hair matted like muddy straw on a barn floor, lying peacefully with eyes closed.

During his career, Imperateri had seen many corpses, parts of bodies and mutilated victims, but he was constantly amazed at the varieties of sexual perversion. He had attended an FBI sex seminar and learned about the personality of sex criminals and what deep compulsions drive them to commit such acts, but he nevertheless hated them despite their illness.

"What do you think, Vinnie?" Lieutenant Arnold Lewis of the Arlington homicide squad asked. He was a thin, nervous man, with darting eyes and hands which constantly clasped and unclasped. "She's been missing since the beginning of the holiday."

"Looks like the same MO," Imperateri said. "Down to crossed t's and dotted i's." He bent low and looked at the neck of the corpse. A groove had been formed by a rope or a chain.

Lewis also crouched down. "We've rousted the medical examiner out of bed. We ought to know something pretty soon."

43

"You people work fast," Imperateri said, rising to his feet. "Our coroner works only on other people's lunch hour. But now I've got to get some sleep. Call me, would you?"

An hour later Imperateri was back in his own apartment. Dead tired, he flung himself into bed and fell asleep with his clothes on. What seemed to him only minutes later the telephone began ringing.

Though deep in sleep and lying on the opposite side of the bed, he rolled over and snatched the telephone before the first ring had ended. His quickness in scooping up middle-of-the-night calls before they could awaken anyone else in the household was part of his early training. But in his sleep he'd forgotten that both daughter and ex-wife were no longer with him.

"Hello, hello!" an insistent voice repeated. "Is that you, Vinnie?"

Recognizing the voice of Lieutenant Lewis had the effect of a cold water awakening. "Yeah, Lew. What's up?"

"Got that information you asked for."

Imperateri glanced at the night table clock. It was four in the morning. "Tell me about it."

"The thighs on the victim. Chewed up, just like your case."

Imperateri took a deep breath. "How long has she been dead?"

"About twelve, fourteen hours. The subject suffered multiple incised wounds. . ."

"Incised?"

"They're cuts less deep and more narrow than actual stabbings," Lewis explained, telling Imperateri something he already knew. "She caught some blows on the head, back, face, all over."

"Cause of death?"

Lewis paused, as though to look for something. "Okay, I'll read this to you. 'The injuries caused separation of several cervical vertebrae and hemorrhaging of the brain and perforation of the jugular.' "

"Did your man find anything in the vagina or evidence of rape?"

"No penetration at all, except maybe by a broomstick. But we found something like soup on her, like she spilled it all over her lap before she died."

Imperateri bit his lip. "Do me a favor, Lew. Don't mail the report to me. I'll pick it up on the way to work."

He hung up and lay his head on the pillow, thinking of catching another two hours of sleep, but sleep did not come. His mind raced.

The murderer had simply tired of the girl and had killed her. He had no choice but to get rid of her after a few days of captivity. Not only because he was afraid of her identifying him but maybe for some other reason. Maybe because he had to return to work after keeping her somewhere during the holiday weekend. Holiday? Kitty Burns also on a holiday, the Fourth of July.

Vincent Imperateri arose from bed once again. There'll be no more sleep now. He believed that he had put together the first pieces of a puzzle. Except for the chicken soup.

With coffee steaming in a styrofoam container, Imperateri studied the autopsy report and photographs. Just as in the Kitty Burns case, the second victim had been sexually abused but there was no penis penetration and no seminal stains on the body. And sometime before death, the killer had chewed on the inner thighs of both victims.

Imperateri held up one of the photographs, a color close-up of the victim's inner thighs. He could see purplish indentations, as clear as those made on a hard apple. He shivered, more in anger and frustration than in fear. What kind of man was he up against?

He went over in his mind what he knew about the cases. Two similar murders in a period of a couple months, both on holidays. The first had set up a model of abduction, sexual assault, brutalization, and murder without witnesses. The victims, both forced or lured into a car. The killer kept them prisoner at least for a couple of days. And he used them. *Used.* An instrument of pleasure to be employed until consumed. And then had strangled and mutilated. He thought it strange that a rapist-murderer could run the spectrum from all-consuming sexual passion to murderous rage, all perhaps within a few moments.

45

Staring blankly at the photographs, he tried to guess why the killer would take the trouble to dispose of the body in a certain way. The position was one of complete sexual acceptance, legs spread wide apart frog-like fashion, with the vagina grotesquely exposed. Was this the killer's way of showing that the victim had finally accepted him in death, if not in life? But this was for the police psychiatrists to determine. His job was to find the murderer, and plumbing long-range the psyche of the killer could or could not help locate him.

In the meantime one fact gnawed at him. The absence of leads and witnesses meant that the killer couldn't be found unless he struck again.

The next evening after several vigorous sets of tennis during which they discovered that they were quite evenly matched, they showered at the club and returned to Marie's apartment for coffee and brandy. While they nursed snifters of brandy, he spoke about what was foremost on his mind. Though he got her sworn promise to keep it off the record, he had a nagging doubt he might not be able to hold her to it in the long run. Yet it was a relief for him to tell someone else the lurid details that had not been made public.

She listened intently, occasionally shaking her head in disbelief or in disgust. When he was through, he managed a wry smile.

"You know, Marie, everyone says that cops rely heavily on motive to solve a crime. Well, we've got a motive. He wants their bodies."

"Sick, sick, sick," she repeated. "He really needs to be locked up and examined."

"I'll tell you something again, off the record, if you don't mind."

She smiled acceptance of his wish.

He got up from the couch and gazed from the window. Below, the rush hour had come to an end and now the beginnings of traffic flow built up in the other direction, towards town, for an evening's entertainment.

"The shrinks say," he began, "that a sick mind can be helped. Probably many can. But I disagree with them about one thing.

There are some sick minds that can't be helped. There are pure and plain evil people who are completely without consciences."

"Oh, Vinnie, you've been a cop for too long."

He spun around. "There are people in our society who can look you right in the eye, smile sweetly, and then shove a knife in your ribs for no other reason than that you didn't tell them the time fast enough."

She raised her hands in mock surrender. "Okay, Sergeant, I won't argue that point. If I really did want to do battle with you over something, it would be letting me write up those off the record details."

"You got enough for an article. You could do a story right now and on November 11 warning young women."

"November 11?"

"Veterans Day." He paused to shrug. "But who knows for sure? The holiday murders could be pure coincidence. Two cases don't really make a pattern. But let's assume that he acts only on holidays. The question is, why?"

"He's off from work, naturally."

He gave her a playful sock on the arm. "Get serious."

"I'm not kidding, Vinnie."

"He's probably off evenings, weekends and vacations, too," Imperateri countered. "So why haven't we heard from him on those days? And why suddenly only during the last two holidays?"

"Maybe he's new in town. And maybe he's got something going for him on holidays that he doesn't have otherwise. What you do now, sergeant, is check the records of every moving company during the past year."

He walked over and bussed her on the forehead. "Thanks, Captain Mackay. We'll do it and you'll do your article."

"You really want us to scare the pants off little girls about going out alone at night?"

He smiled. "Yes. You know what I want to get across. A story about mothers telling their daughters not to speak with anyone they don't know."

Marie's eyes widened. "But Vinnie, the killer may very well be someone they do know."

SIX

Imperateri awoke earlier than usual Sunday morning, his day off. Whistling a melody from *Rigoletto,* he looked forward to the day's activities like a young man in love. Today was to be the annual Italian festival picnic and Marie Mackay was to be his date. He quickly showered and shaved, and then picked up the Sunday paper outside of his door to read while breakfasting.

Two stories bylined by Marie were featured prominently in the metropolitan section. The first one she hadn't told him about, and it raised anew his concern over her loyalty to him.

The story was about a special Saturday meeting of the city council which ended with a demand that an outside investigation be made of the Anderson affair. The council members, almost all of whom were Black, resolved that having the police investigate themselves would result in a whitewash.

Why hadn't she told him about the meeting when she saw him last night? She knew he'd be involved in any investigation and was deeply interested in any aspect of it. Yet she made no mention of it.

Momentarily, he felt as if a support had been pulled from under him. Then he decided that she had kept it from him in order to avoid a new argument over Anderson. Besides, didn't he keep certain matters from her? Anderson's playing up to him, for example.

As far as the council resolution was concerned, he believed that the investigation now would be delayed while behind-the-scenes powers played. The House of Representatives District of Columbia Affairs Committee recommended appropriations to the city. It was made up mostly of Southern conservatives who would press for a police internal affairs probe. In the meantime, the Congressional Black Caucus would exert pressure from another side.

Imperateri drew a breath of relief. It was just as well there'd be a delay. He had enough on his mind without having to worry about lying for Anderson.

His eyes shifted to the other article. Though he'd asked Marie to write it, he wasn't pleased with the printed outcome.

She reviewed all that was known about the rape murders. But she also gave wrong information. A break in the case was imminent, the article stated.

That was not true. Nor was identifying him as leading the investigation, with no mention of Arlington County's Lieutenant Lewis, with whom he collaborated closely.

He tossed the paper aside and finished eating, but he remained at the table, thinking about their relationship. Desspite pite what he felt were minor faults in her newspaper reporting, he considered her somewhat of a superwoman. She was better educated than he, knew more about books and even the opera, which he loved. He realized now that he was infatuated with her and wanted her totally for himself. Yet he understood that she behaved as though he were just a friend, nothing more. After all, she hadn't demonstrated any real affection for him.

How to make his feelings known to a fiercely independent woman without turning her off? He'd find out at the picnic.

The public address system blared tarantella music as couples struggled to keep up with the whirling rhythm. At another end of the picnic grounds, children attempted to skimmy up a greased pole while their elders tried to win at bingo. Further away, under tall oaks, Vincent sat alone with Marie at a picnic table. In front of them were mugs of beer and thick, six-inch squares of pizza.

Earlier, she had shamed both him and several other men on the softball field by hitting safely all of her three times at bat. Now he studied her as she munched and looked out at the remaining softball players.

She indeed was a beautiful woman. She had everything. Brains, beauty, and if you considered her athletic ability, brawn. The genetic jackpot. So many common people robbed to make a Marie Mackay. She was a gift, and he swore to himself that he would fight for her.

He leaned over and whispered, "I like you a lot, Marie."

The thwack of a ball against a bat sounded. Nearby, old widows watched, their black shawls covering woolen coats to protect against the vagaries of early November weather.

Marie gulped down a mouthful of food. "What did you say?"

He repeated it, sliding over closer to her. She smiled and kissed him gently, as if to reward him for his admission.

"You're sweet," was her only reply.

He would sound her out. "Have you ever thought of marrying again?"

She guffawed and shook her head. "Good heavens, no! I don't want to go on that trip again."

"What's the problem? People marry, divorce, marry again."

"And divorce again. So much damn trouble. Look, my work occupies almost all of my time. What's left is for the good times."

Imperateri grasped his hands in a woebegone fashion. "Oh, if my poor, old Sicilian grandfather could hear you now. The times, they sure have changed."

"Times haven't changed," she said. "People have."

"People? I don't think so. The elite, the trend-setters say that it's exciting, sleeping with each other without any obligation, knowing you can split and that's that. Well, Marie, I'm old-fashioned. People should have something formal, a document stating that they belong to each other."

The tarantella music stopped and a man spoke into the microphone, causing a jarring feedback that nevertheless failed to alter a strong Brooklyn accent. "Ladies and gents! Enjoy yourselves. *La dolce festa Italia!* Plenty of fun and good food left. Don't nobody leave."

As if to lend support to his words, laughter filled the air and the smell of roasted chicken basted in olive oil carried to where Vincent and Marie were sitting.

50

"Vinnie," she said, pushing the food away from her, "you're not living in nineteenth-century Sicily which, if I recall my history, was hardly the ideal society, with its feuds and famines and where women were treated like the cows they were."

"That was the bad side," he countered. "There was also a positive side."

"Listen, Vinnie, I know something's on your mind. If you're thinking of rushing towards a deep commitment, please stop. I'm not sure I'm ready."

"What do you call deep?"

"Marriage."

"What about something with fewer strings? Like living together?"

She turned once more to look at the ballplayers. "Let me think about it."

Imperateri felt unhappy in his role as a prospective lover. Without the binding tie of marriage, it was like taking something for nothing. Even though she said she'd think about it, he felt dejected. He realized that single women now enjoyed sex with the same abandon as men. He reasoned that he was indeed hopelessly old-fashioned, as outdated as a flatfoot on a beat.

Smiling to himself, he recalled his days when he walked a beat. He never could swipe a fruit off a stand, repaying the vendor with a wink. He had thought it was wrong. He still did.

Maybe it was time he grew up.

SEVEN

William Crawford snapped the cabinet door shut, opened it again to peer inside, and then slammed it once more with a bang. The scissors were nowhere to be found, even though he was certain that he had cleaned and replaced them in the cabinet.

He doubled his hand into a fist and smacked the palm of the other several times as he tried to think where else the scissors could be. Then with a frustrated shrug, he turned back to the kitchen table where he had been reading the newspaper.

It wasn't so much that he absolutely needed the scissors now that angered him. It was the thought that he'd always been so careful with everything, especially anything connected to his secret life. At least until now. Was he slipping? he asked himself, sitting back down at the table where the newspaper lay spread open. Again, he shrugged, this time biting his lip as well.

Picking up the paper, he ripped out the article by Marie Mackay. That'll do for now. When he'd found the scissors, he'd clip it evenly and neatly for keeping.

Still the fact that the tool was missing gnawed at him, forcing him to set the clipping aside and make another quick inspection of the house, this time to determine if anyone had broken in, looking perhaps for evidence linking him to the rape-murders.

Finding nothing to feed his suspicion, he returned to the table and to the clipping, which he read for the third time, voicing aloud certain portions as if to memorize them.

"'If the psychological profile drawn by experts who have studied the murders is accurate, according to Sergeant Imperateri, the killer is of above average intelligence with a compulsion for cleanliness. He is a Caucasian who is believed to be a white collar worker, possibly in a position that suggests authority, someone whom women would trust.' "

Crawford chuckled. "Close. Sergeant Imperateri. Too close. I'd have to say." He read aloud further.

" 'The murderer probably lives and works in the Washington area, rather than being a transient, Imperateri added, and has a schedule that allows him freedom.' "

Now Crawford guffawed. "Not that much freedom, Sergeant!"

If the police only knew that he was an associate of theirs, a uniformed member privileged to take home a police cruiser on holidays. He laughed at what he considered the irony of the program allowing off-duty police local use of official cars on holidays and weekends. It had been initiated a few years ago to keep police visibility high and crime low. Crawford, low man in terms of seniority, couldn't get one for weekends. However, for holidays cruisers were available since many off-duty officers used their own automobiles for out-of-town trips.

He rapidly skimmed over the rest of the article, about how the whole area was frightened, and about warnings and advice to women living alone. That didn't interest him. What did was the news that Imperateri was close to breaking the case.

Was it a lie to calm the public? Crawford wondered. If it were, it would soon be evident. The risk of ridicule would be too great for the police to allow such a statement.

For the second time in the past few minutes, Crawford felt the beginning of a crack in his world. The lost scissors seemed to be an omen.

And now there was Imperateri, who bragged about being close to a solution. How close?

To gain freedom from fear of being caught, Crawford now believed that he'd have to kill Imperateri. That would slow down the investigation and enable him to obey one or two more of his recurrent urgings before moving on to another location. It should be easy to find out from the timekeeper's office the work schedule and home address of Vincent Imperateri.

Crawford arose from the table and paced the kitchen floor. There would also have to be changes made in how he found his women, of that he was convinced. Secondly, he'd alternate between using a police cruiser and his own car for the Veterans Day and Thanksgiving holidays. And for Thanksgiving, he'd change his MO. Maybe he'd start a few days before the holiday to find his next girlie. After that, he'd move to another part of the country.

A glint of steel from among china in the sink caught his eye. He looked closer. It was the scissors, just where he had mistakenly placed it in a moment of forgetfulness.

Already things were looking up. Now all he'd have to do was to eliminate Imperateri as a factor in his future.

The call came on the morning after the Veterans Day holiday. Detective Robert Burtell of the Montgomery County police department telephoned Vincent Imperateri in the squad room.

"Vinnie, it looks like we're the lucky ones this go-round. She's white, about fourteen. All cut up, just like the other two."

Imperateri listened to his colleague from the Maryland suburb north of the city and felt a sinking in the pit of his stomach. "This one reported missing?" he asked. "I've been watching the ticker but didn't see anything."

"No," Burtell said. "We don't even have an ID on her. Do you want to look it over before we clean?"

"Yeah," Imperateri sighed. "Give me the address."

On his way out Imperateri stopped at a machine and traded a handful of coins for a pack of cigarettes, thus ending a year-long effort to quit smoking. In the half-hour it took to drive to Montgomery County, he went through three cigarettes.

The MO was repeated, a large shopping plaza and a trash dumpster behind one of the stores. The usual scene greeted Imperateri, swarms of cruisers with top lights blinking like fireflies after a summer's rain, and three or four television news trucks unloading equipment.

Cordoning off the lot were signs proclaiming *Crime Scene Search Area—Stop!* And within the lot were dozens of uniformed and plainclothes officers prowling, searching, measuring, photographing.

How many times had he seen the same familiar setting? For the civilian spectators gathering at the perimeter and gaping at the police investigation, it was live theater. For him, it was the same play performed by different actors. He wondered how it felt to be a civilian office worker, arriving at a quiet work environment in the morning, perhaps chatting with a fellow employee or having a cup of coffee before actually sitting down to work. Perhaps he'd never know.

He approached, and was promptly challenged by a state trooper, to whom he showed his District of Columbia police badge. The trooper nodded and stepped aside grudgingly. Back in Washington, when he would arrive at a scene, the police and detectives from the precinct stations would hurriedly make way for him. There was an unspoken assent as to who was in charge. He was. He was from downtown.

Imperateri sometimes exulted in the power that the badge bestowed upon him. It was a superficial compensation for the long hours and low pay, he realized, meaningful only to younger officers new to headquarters.

Detective Burtell greeted Imperateri by slapping his back and shaking his hand, acting as though they just happened to have run into each other at a neighborhood bar. But soon the smile disappeared on Burtell's florid face as he filled Imperateri in on the details.

The young girl had been found by a food store employee emptying a load of trash. According to the medical examiner, there were knife wounds all over the body, but only two were fatal. They were in the chest, filling the cavity with blood and collapsing the lungs.

"What about the thighs? See any teeth marks?"

"That's why I called you. Lewis from Arlington is coming up, too."

Imperateri reached for the pack of cigarettes but put it away without taking one. It didn't seem right to be puffing while looking at the body. "Can I see her, Bob?"

Burtell nodded and led the way through the evidence team milling around the dumpster. The two detectives climbed up to a dock and peered down into the trash bin. There the body lay, arms and legs spread wide apart, mouth wide open in a silent scream.

The victim was slashed almost beyond recognition. Blood, dried black, caked the body's rents like an incredibly bad plaster and paint job. But this was no wall, not even a mannequin. Imperateri shut his eyes and opened them again. It was, or had been, a living thing, a being, a child like his own, filled with love and ambition and the joy of living.

Imperateri turned away, muffling a groan and stifling a gag wrenching his throat. He had seen enough.

On his way back to the squad room he spotted Anderson at the end of the hallway. The Captain beckoned him forward with a forefinger.

"Step into my office for a minute, huh, Sergeant?"

Back to *Sergeant*, Imperateri thought. It was just as well. He didn't care for Vincent, anyway.

Anderson retreated behind the desk, plopped his massive bulk in a chair, and pointed for Imperateri to sit down. The Captain wasted no time in getting to the point.

"If it's not too much trouble for you," he began, a half-smile lending support to the sarcasm in his voice, "I wonder if you might favor me with a report."

Imperateri could smell the liquor wafting across the breadth of the desk. "Report on what, Captain?"

Anderson gripped the edge of the desk, as though to steady his own temper before it got out of control. "On the rape cases. What else? That's where you've been spending one hundred percent of your time."

"Not quite, and you damn well know it," Imperateri said, proud that he was able to keep the anger from showing. "I'm carrying a super-full load of other cases."

Anderson suddenly relented. "I know, I know. But all I hear or read about is the rape-murders. Third case just reported and everyone's comparing him to the Boston Strangler."

Anderson pushed himself up from the desk, turned to look out of the window and then clasped his hands behind him in the classic contemplative pose. "Sergeant, I think that maybe we ought to have a lieutenant, maybe Gibbs or Massey, heading up this investigation. It'll look better. This is a pretty big case. Three jurisdictions involved. You only being a sergeant. You know what I mean?"

"No problem with the other agencies so far. We've an agreement that all disputes be resolved at a low level. No bureaucrats. Anybody above the rank of sergeant we consider a bureaucrat."

The captain showed his own up-from-the-ranks origins by laughing loudly. He turned to face Imperateri. "Can't argue with that. No, sir. But seriously, I know you want this plum. You want to close the case all by your lonesome. If you do that, you could go over my head and ask the chief for a directive making you a provisional lieutenant, getting the pay, too. And when there's a vacancy, you'd be made permanent, regardless of anyone else's standing and with or without my okay."

"Captain," Imperateri replied slowly, once more controlling his temper, "I hadn't thought of it, but now that you've mentioned it . . ." He paused, grinning.

"I've got nothing against you doing that. Believe me, I'd like to help you out. We have to stick up for each other."

Here it comes, Imperateri thought. Still another pitch to lie for him before the trial board.

"As a matter of fact, Vincent, maybe I ought to just put Noseworthy and Bork full-time on the cases. Of course, you'd be in charge."

Imperateri nodded assent. He got along fine with both men, especially John Bork, a young detective, eager to help and to please.

"Remember, Vincent, you scratch my back and I'll scratch yours." He squinted as he watched Imperateri shake his head. "What's the problem?"

"One thing, Captain. Could you call me Vinnie?"

Back at his own desk, Imperateri immediately brushed

Anderson's heavyhandedness from his mind and concentrated on aspects of the new case and the old ones.

The murders, all in the Washington metropolitan area, but all in different police jurisdictions. One in his area, one in Arlington County across the Potomac River in Virginia, and now the latest in Montgomery County, north of the District Line in Maryland. The killer didn't play favorites. He wanted to make sure he confused the police.

Why, Imperateri wondered, did the killer choose trash bins in shopping centers to dump the bodies? Such conspicuous sites were an unnecessary and a considerable risk. Even though he acted late at night, the killer stood a chance of being discovered. But then, he may have had a motive, perhaps a subconscious one. Was he making a plea to be caught swiftly? Imperateri recalled the case of the Chicago murderer who scrawled on a toilet cabinet mirror with his victim's lipstick, *Please stop me before I kill again.*

Thanksgiving Day was a little over two weeks away. There was no doubt in his mind that there would be another murder. And there was nothing anyone except the killer himself could do to stop it.

The front door to the apartment building was unlocked. Inside, no receptionist greeting him. William Crawford, a believer in signs and omens, was filled with a sense of easy success. He quickly cautioned himself, however, about an opportunity.

The mailboxes imbedded in a side wall showed Vincent Imperateri's name. Apartment 412. And the building superintendent's, apartment B-1.

Moments later he knocked on B-1. A slight bespectacled Oriental man answered, speaking in heavily accented English. A recent Vietnamese immigrant, Crawford guessed, pleased at the prospect that, if ever questioned, the man might have difficulty describing a Caucasian suspect.

Crawford's good feeling was erased by the sight of a ring of keys attached to the super's belt. Were all the apartment keys hanging there?

"No vacancy. Come back in month."

"What about a waiting list?"

"Come," the super said, stepping aside to permit Crawford entry to the foyer. "You wait."

Crawford watched him leave for another room. Just then, an aroma of deliciously-spiced cooking wafted to Crawford's nose, but it was a wall panel that made his stomach churn. Hanging on little hooks were spare keys.

Just as he'd expected. Every super had an arrangement like that. The only drawback was an opportunity, which he now had.

He lifted the key to 412 and let it drop into his pocket. Then he left. There was no reason to give the super another look at his face.

So easy.

The strains of a lilting waltz pierced through the dream of examining a corpse. From the morgue he was suddenly thrust into a ballroom. Omm pah-pah omm pah-pah omm pah-pah went the orchestra. A lusty song came from his lips.

Libiamo, libiamo ne' calici, che la belleza infiora . . .

Within moments a crackling noise that sounded like small sticks being broken accompanied his song. And then the words came out along with lung-bursting coughing.

. . . e la fuggeval, fuggeval (achem, achem, achem) *ora ora s'innebril e volutta . . .* (achem, achem, achem)

His eyes flew open. A flickering flame lit the surroundings, showing a veil of smoke shadowing the whole room as Enrico Caruso continued Alfredo's aria from *La Traviata*.

Libiamo ne dolci fremiti che suscita l'amore . . .

Imperateri jumped from the bed and raced towards the window to open it, but his feet tangled with a blanket, tripping him. He reeled to catch himself, hands flying, clutching for something to break his fall. Nothing solid came between the floor and him and he tumbled with a resounding crash.

He lay there for a few moments, gasping for breath as the drowsiness of a deep sleep departed quickly. A sudden realization came to him that lying sprawled on the floor was the best place to be until he got his wits about him.

Poiche quell' occhio al core onnipotente va . . .

His apartment was on fire, or rather something was burning in a corner next to the snack tray holding the Victor Talking Machine which still spun out the merry waltz. That something, he could now see through sleep and smoke-dazed eyes, was the armchair he'd picked up at a second-hand store only weeks ago.

Libiamo, amore, amor fra i calici pui coldi baci aura . . .

Scraping along the floor on hands and knees, he made it to the bathroom where he kept a rubber shower hose. He jumped to his feet and ripped off the metal sprinkler head and turned the faucet on full blast. Pulling the hose as far as it would go, he directed the sharp and steady jet of water at the armchair until the flames were extinguished. Now the room was again plunged into darkness.

Libiamo, libiamo, the enthralling voice of soprano Alma Gluck joined that of Caruso's on the record.

Imperateri crawled under a curtain of smoke back to the living room where he managed to throw open the window. Holding his breath, he dashed to the apartment door. To his dismay, he found it already ajar. He pushed it wide open and stepped into the hallway to catch his breath.

Coughing, gasping, he tried to remember if or why he'd left the door open before going to sleep. Was he so tired that he didn't know what he was doing?

A door down the corridor opened and out stuck a man's face, bloated with sleep. "Mr. Imperateri," the man said, "have some regard for others. Would you mind lowering your record player?"

Imperateri mumbled an apology just as the man saw the smoke.

"A fire! I'm calling the fire department!"

"No, I already did," Imperateri lied. He didn't want any clods with their boots and axes and watery overkill mucking up his apartment.

The open door and window soon ventilated the apartment. Within minutes, Imperateri was back inside. He switched on the lights and tried to turn off the Victor but found it already in the *off* position. He followed the wire from the switchbox to the Victor where he could see that heat from the flame had fused two wires, somehow starting the machine. He recalled that he had cued the tone arm at the beginning of the record so that the music would start as soon as he would flip the switch.

His eyes traveled to the armchair. Under it an object smoldered. He bent down, saw that it was the remains of a bunched-up rag, and then sniffed the unmistakable odor of gasoline. Without touching anything else, he telephoned the arson and explosion duty officer.

As he waited, he absentmindedly placed another record on the turntable. It was *Una Furtiva Lagrima* from *L'Elisir d'Amore*, but he paid no attention to the music. He could only think that someone had broken into his apartment as he slept. Someone had poured gasoline on a rag and ignited it. Someone had deliberately tried to kill him. But why? He knew that prosecuting attorneys and district attorneys were often threatened and sometimes attacked. Last year, he, himself, had collared a suspect who had shot an attorney on the courthouse steps. But who'd want to wipe out a detective? He had no more than a dozen active cases, and any one of them had collected two or three suspects who might try to stop him if they felt he was getting close to something. But which case and which suspect?

He checked around the apartment, wondering whether to run down to his car for the evidence kit. Instead, however, he reached for his pillbox and swallowed an antacid. Then he turned towards the Victor as if hearing the music for the first time.

"Thanks, Enrico."

The building cafeteria was alive with noise and movement, none of which distracted William Crawford. His eyes busily ran up and down news columns while his fingers squeezed each page, ready to turn. Finally, he lay the whole paper aside and stared off in the distance, still unmindful of the men and women around him in police uniforms.

Now he looked at his lunch of a sandwich and soup, but his

mind remained on the newspaper. There was not a word about Imperateri in it, nor even mention of a fire.

Again he felt as if he were losing control of the situation. Things were not working out. He was sure he'd left a fire blazing in the apartment. Why wasn't it reported?

He could only guess that the police sergeant was not harmed and was holding back publicity on the fire until an investigation was made. He knew that conventional police wisdom sometimes dictated that no mention be made of a crime in hopes that the criminal might become frustrated at the lack of recognition or encouraged by the anonymity and make a mistake. A psychological gambit that wouldn't work with him, he was sure. But he also knew how police got emotionally fired up when one of their own is attacked, sometimes working a sixteen-hour day until an arrest is made.

Nevertheless, his earlier feeling of unease dissipated. He felt confident that nothing could be traced to him, not even his examination of the work schedules. Nobody saw him in the personnel office looking over Imperateri's round of duty, shifts on, shifts off, and finding his home address which was unlisted in the public telephone book.

William Crawford was determined to seek some later opportunity to get at Imperateri. Now the detective was sure to be on his guard. Crawford even decided against checking out the detective squad room to learn what his adversary looked like and whether he was hurt. Instead, he would outplay Imperateri and the rest of them in their waiting game.

A soft voice with the lilt of a Southern accent interrupted his thoughts.

"Mind if I join you, Bill?"

His eyes raised, his heart jumped. It was the woman cashier from the motor department who always winked and smiled when their paths crossed. Standing, he pointed to an empty chair. "Please."

He studied her carefully, taking advantage of her involvement in sitting and with removing the food from her tray. She wasn't bad-looking he decided. A little too plump, perhaps, with too much makeup which couldn't even hide the fact that she was well over thirty years of age.

"My, Bill, you don't eat very much. I guess you keep your shape up that way."

He shrugged. He didn't even know her name, yet she knew his. *Bill*, yet. He guessed that the rumor had reached her about his being an available bachelor. "This is embarrassing," he said. "I seem to be blocking out your name."

"Mary Ann Austin. We've never met formally."

"My regret, Mary Ann.' He was pleased at her advance, but he had no intention of getting involved with anybody from work. Yet as they spent the hour together he was strangely attracted by her small town girl ways. She seemed to be genuinely interested in him, hanging on his every word. Before he knew it, he was inviting her for a drink after work. It was all right, he reassured himself. Mary Ann Austin would provide a good cover of normalcy for him. Now he wouldn't be considered an oddball by co-workers and subject to suspicion. He was behaving like a good, red-blooded American boy.

William Crawford smiled to himself. And in another few weeks his appetite will take another direction for a good American holiday. Thanksgiving.

EIGHT

An infant in his mother's arms wailed, triggering a like response from another baby who surpassed the original crier in intensity if not sincerity. Nearby, a pre-adolescent boy, pale with dark rings under his eyes, sat disconsolately between his parents. Scattered around the waiting room were several other children in their middle teens who sulked at having to be found in the same place with a bunch of babies.

Eva Barlow, her starchy white nurse's uniform rustling, passed by the reception counter near the front door. She whispered to the office receptionist, Betty Gruff, and laughed before continuing on her way. Again she paused, this time to speak with a man sitting alone. He was well-dressed in a custom-made suit. A heavy briefcase rested against the legs of his chair.

"I'm sorry you have to wait so long," she said. "Doctor is extremely busy, as you can see. Seems that everyone gets sick right before a holiday."

She left without giving him a chance to acknowledge her concern and continued her stride into a hallway where a suite of examining rooms held more children and anxious parents. She poked her head into one room and addressed a man sitting at a desk.

"The Payson boy is next, Dr. Stone. In the first room."

Dr. Julian Stone nodded and looked through a folder marked *Payson, Michael*. As he quickly skimmed the boy's past illnesses, inoculations, allergy shots, he yawned and then rose from the chair just a fraction of an inch before he sat down heavily in an exhausted manner.

He was tired, and he glanced at the clock even though he knew it wouldn't offer much solace as to how much longer he'd have to see patients. Only the lessening pile of patients folders on the corner of his desk told him. It was four-thirty but at least ten more folders remained. At an average time of about ten minutes per patient, he would be able to send his nurse and receptionist home at six-fifteen or so, barring any last-minute office drop-ins.

Stone leaned back and breathed deeply, preparing to make another effort at rising. He'd have to stay long after they left, though. There were still the telephone messages, some eight of them at last count. All of them would have to be returned. Though he tried to be brusque and to the point, each call used up about four minutes, even the ones to the pharmacists who had called to ascertain whether a prescription could be refilled.

He was reminded that he also had a drug detail man in the waiting room. Drug company representatives were accustomed to cooling their heels, but today Stone felt sorry for the man who was probably anxious to return home to his family for the Thanksgiving vacation.

Susan, his own daughter, was due to arrive at any moment for the holiday. He picked up the framed color photograph from a corner of the desk and smiled a greeting, as though she were standing before him.

He missed her. She had been away from home for less than three months, attending her freshman year at George Washington University in Washington, D.C. He often worried about her, not only because it was her first time away from home, but because she was an only child and represented the all-to-human urge to leave something behind after one's own passing.

Rising to his feet once more, he moaned with the effort. He was a large man with oversized nose and ears, and tried unsuccessfully to detract from their size by wearing his hair bushy.

In the first room the little Payson boy sat barechested on the examining table, his face already screwed up in fear. His mother stood by the side and immediately blurted out all that was on her mind as soon as Stone entered.

"He's been acting real sick, Doctor. He doesn't eat or sleep and his color is bad. Last week he had a rash and I wanted to call you but it went away before I had a chance."

Stone nodded understanding. This was their second visit that week. He could find nothing wrong with the boy. "Well, Mrs. Payson, we've checked out his blood and urine. Completely normal."

As he continued speaking, Stone poked into the boy's ears and mouth. "It's natural for a five-year-old to lose his appetite once in a while. There's nothing to worry about. Right, Michael?"

Michael shrugged and eyed suspiciously the stethoscope Stone picked up. The doctor placed the instrument's resonating bell against the chest, drawing a shiver and then giggles from the boy, who tried to push it away.

Stone rubbed the stethoscope on the back of his palm and replaced it on the boy's back. After shifting it around, he announced, "Lungs clear as a bell."

"Then why doesn't he eat?"

"I guess he's not hungry, Mrs. Payson."

The intercom buzzed. Nurse Barlow told him his wife was on the telephone. He hesitated for a moment. He did not encourage her calls, those little interruptions that could wait until he got home. She just needs more things to occupy her time, he thought. "Tell her I'm with a patient."

He again turned to Mrs. Payson. "Michael certainly doesn't look undernourished. As a matter of fact, he's a tad overweight."

"Maybe that's what is making him sick," she said.

Again the buzzer sounded. Annoyed at the second interruption and at Mrs. Payson's stubborn insistence, he snapped at the intercom. "What is it now?"

"Mrs. Stone, Doctor. She says it's important."

Stone pressed down on the flickering button. "Yes, Lois?" His tone was sharp.

His wife's own voice had a touch of urgency, but he suspected that she put it on after detecting vexation. "Julian, I'm at the bus station. Susan wasn't on the bus."

A lightning stab of worry shot through him. Quickly, silently, he chided himself. What was there to worry about? Susan missed the bus and would catch the next one. He expressed this thought and then asked Lois to meet the next bus due from Washington.

He turned to Mrs. Payson and was about to end the visit when he heard a distant wailing coming from the parking lot. Both he and Mrs. Payson as well as Michael stared at each other and listened as the sounds grew closer, first in the hallway and then in the waiting room. It was not a cry of pain or simple fear so much as one of sheer terror, prompting Stone to fly out of the examining room and into the outer office. There, flanked by his parents, stood a little brown boy wrapped in a multi-colored blanket.

Puerto Ricans, Stone thought, judging that they were recent arrivals from the island because of their light and colorful clothing.

The parents, short and dark with wide nostrils, and with eyes and hair black and shiny like wet coal, looked with pleading eyes at Stone. The father then pointed to the child and whispered, so as not to be heard by the other parents. "Ear-margencia."

Betty Gruff plunged in to do her receptionist duty. "You all haven't been here before, have you? Well, I'm going to have to ask you to fill out some forms."

Stone was appreciative of her concern to protect the office by ensuring proper payment from new patients, but he wished that she wouldn't be so efficient about paperwork in the face of an emergency. "Ah, Betty. Let's get the pedigree later."

He motioned the visitors towards a vacant examining room. There the father carefully removed the blanket, revealing trousers open at the fly. Peeking through was a small penis, red and ragged and bleeding slightly. It was ensnared in the zipper like a rabbit's leg in a steel trap.

"Why didn't you run to the hospital emergency room?" Stone asked the father.

"Ees bad there. Butchers. Better here."

Flattered, Stone gave orders quickly. The father was asked to pin the boy's arms down and the mother to secure the legs. As soon as Stone bent to examine the entrapped penis, the boy screeched anew.

"Now, now . . ." Stone began, and then looked up to the father. "What's his name?"

"Fernando. He no English speak."

Stone nonetheless spoke in English, relying on the soothing tones of his voice to calm the boy. "Now, Fernando, I'm not going to hurt you."

Without touching anything, he examined the prepuce in the zipper pincer. Had the child been circumcised, he thought, this wouldn't have happened. He could perform the surgery now, but for the father it would be like sacrificing a leg. Better not to argue *macho* and ethnic beliefs now. The child was suffering.

Although inured to the sound of crying children, Eva Barlow seemed upset at the boy's screaming. She kept her arms hanging, fists tightly curled. "Shall I prepare for anesthesia, doctor?"

Stone shook his head and rushed out to his own office and desk, from which he retrieved tools he never used in his practice, a wire cutter and two pairs of needle-nosed pliers. They were forgotten by some repairmen who never bothered to return even after Stone had called.

"You look like you're going to sacrifice a perfectly good pair of trousers," Eva Barlow said when he returned with the tools. "All you have to do is give it a good, fast unzipping."

"If it were your whang in there," he said, "you wouldn't be so eager to do that."

He saw the nurse return his smile, and then continued speaking to her in a loud but even voice above the boy's screams. "Nine times out of ten you can't safely get a piece of cloth caught in a zipper, let alone a foreskin."

"That does it," the nurse said. "No more penis envy for me."

He laughed and continued speaking. "The trick is to know the anatomy of the zipper, something they don't teach in medical or nursing school."

With a pair of scissors he cut away the garment cloth, leaving only the zipper tape. He carefully snipped through the tape and zipper above and below the captured skin.

New and louder shouts came from the boy. The father looked up and shook his head. "No, no more! Stop! I take him to hospital now. It is too hurting for him."

"Almost done and I haven't even touched him," Stone said. He cut the upper bar of the zipper slide with the wire cutter and removed the slide. Using both hands he next grasped the top ends on either side of the zipper tape with pliers and used a circular motion to rotate the two sides from each other, unraveling the track. The skin was freed.

The parents hugged each other, and then the boy, who now stared at Stone in silent awe. He screamed anew when Stone swabbed the wound with an antiseptic solution.

Just then Betty Gruff knocked on the door and poked her head in. "Mrs. Stone again on three."

"Tell her I'll call back. I'm right in the midst of something."

"She says it's very urgent, Doctor."

The same lightning charge struck at his insides. News about Susan? he wondered. No, a defensive mechanism told him. It was another of Lois's exaggerations. He really had to get her to stop acting like a doctor's wife. She had no interests except for a daughter who was away at school. Despite attempts at charitable work, at women's club activities, at desultory courses in college, Lois remained the same as when he married her. She was seventeen, product of a middleclass family, barely out of high school and overjoyed to marry a medical student while her girlfriends still dated fast food help and movie ushers. A year later she became pregnant with Susan.

Stone nodded to the receptionist. "I'll take it in my office." To the nurse he said, "Put some ice on his pecker. That should bring down the swelling."

Lois made no attempt to hide the fear in her voice. "Julian, I called Marcie Simkin. Susan's roommate. She says Susan hitched a ride with someone. A man. That was Sunday afternoon. This is Wednesday. Julian, it's only a four-hour ride from Washington."

Another stab of pain tore at his insides. No, he thought. Rationalize. Reason. No emotion. "Lois," he said, trying to keep his voice even, "it was probably somebody she knows. They stopped off somewhere for something to eat, a picnic, maybe. Visiting mutual friends. I really don't know."

"Marcie says Susan accepted the ride because she wanted to come home a few days earlier to surprise us. Marcie saw her enter a man's car. A complete stranger."

"It'll be all right, Lois. Let's just be patient. I'm sure she'll reach us soon."

He hung up and stared blankly. The worst thing, he told himself, was that Susan and the stranger stopped off at a motel.

No, that wasn't the worst thing.

Lois was waiting at the door when he arrived at seven in the evening, his normal time. He planned it that way, not wishing to send his patients home to show Lois his own worry by coming home early. One of them had to be strong. At least to appear strong.

"Any news?" he asked, fully knowing by her look that there wasn't. She shook her head and seemed to be making an attempt to hold back tears. He led her by the elbow to the living room and wondered how she was going to last the evening and night. She might need a sedative, perhaps 400 milligrams of meprobamate. He was glad that he had recently stocked his bag.

"Where could she be, Julian? She's never done anything like this before."

He couldn't tell her that Susan may not have had much choice in what was happening to her. "We'll have to call everybody. All the relatives, all of our friends, her friends. Everybody we know." He paused for a moment and gulped air almost like a drowning man. "Lois, please, you make the calls. If I did, everybody might think it's really serious."

"Isn't it?" she replied, glaring at him angrily. "You are such a

. . . . such a . . ." She stopped searching for the word. "Going merrily on with your work in the office and leaving me here alone to suffer."

"Do you think it was easy for me, too? I couldn't concentrate on what the hell I was doing." He shut his eyes tightly, despising himself. "Of course, Lois, you're right. We'll both make the calls."

"I've already made some. Nobody knows anything."

"Have you called the police?" He watched her shake her head before picking up the telephone. After three referrals, he finally spoke to someone at the missing persons bureau who identified himself as Officer Fisher.

"Well," Fisher began, speaking in the stilted manner of a third-grader reading a difficult passage aloud. "I think there is no cause for alarm at this juncture in time. I know teenager persons very well from long experience. They disappear for hours on end, sometimes days, thus creating worried parents such as yourself and Mrs. Stone. The teenagers nowadays, Dr. Stone, they seem to lose track of all time when they're enjoying themselves. I wouldn't worry at this juncture in time if I was you, Dr. Stone."

Stone imagined that this was the police equivalent of a doctor's advice to take two aspirins and call in the morning. "Can't you do anything now? We're going crazy just sitting around and waiting."

"If you want, Dr. Stone, I'll issue a call to the patrol cars to look out for your daughter."

"And that's all?"

"For the time being, sir. Oh, you can check back in the morning with Lieutenant Kirkland. He's in charge of Missing Persons."

Tonight, Stone wanted to ask what we are going to do tonight, all night? Instead, he said, "I'd appreciate that, Officer. You'll let us know as soon as you hear something?"

With Fisher's assurances ringing in his ear, Stone hung up. Then he realized that he hadn't given a description of Susan to Fisher, nor had the officer asked for one.

Long after midnight, with stomach growling reminders of its emptiness, and eyes stinging from fatigue, Julian Stone pulled the car to stop in the center of the bus station's parking lot. He closed his eyes and rubbed his neck, aching from constantly twisting from side to side as he scanned movements and shadows while driving across town.

The night's darkness did not dissuade him from counting his search. Lois had remained home, in the event Susan showed up or telephoned.

He leaned his head back on the headrest and pulled certainly into his thoughts that things would soon be all right. Susan would have an explanation, a good one or a crazy one, but something to explain her disappearance. For the Stones, things always turned out right. Considering all of life's tragedies, car and airplane crashes, accidents and sicknesses, he and his family and relatives and even his close friends had remained relatively unscathed. For him, it was only the names of strangers in the newspapers and on television news programs.

He'd had a small share of minor mishaps. Such as the time his automobile, a new and fancy Lincoln he'd persuaded himself to buy, had been stolen. It was an unnerving feeling coming to the place where he thought he'd parked it, only to find it gone, and wondering whether he'd left it somewhere else. Searching other areas of the lot, he then began to think that perhaps he hadn't driven it at all, and had left it home and taken the other car, an older Chevrolet. It was not until quarter of an hour later that the realization came to him. The car was never recovered. Nor was a valuable coin collection which was burglarized. But both car and coins were inanimate metals, their replacement assured by insurance. There was nothing to replace Susan.

How many times had he warned her, pleaded with her to be careful? *Careful*, she'd repeat, that's the most used word in a parent's vocabulary.

"Susan," he had once addressed her before she was to drive alone at night for the first time, "you have to be careful, extra careful. A girl has to be. Not just today, but every day you're by yourself."

"Why?" she asked, fully knowing the reason, for hadn't he clipped newspaper articles for her about rapes and murders to heighten her awareness? He constantly placed them on her dresser where she was sure to see them.

He looked at her with amazement. "You know darn well why," he replied, pulling out from a pocket a freshly-clipped article about a brutal rape and beating which had left a young woman paralyzed. "Here, now you see why I worry."

She glanced at it and frowned. "Daddy, you're upsetting me with all of these. I wish you'd stop."

"I'm doing it because I love you."

"You're smothering me."

"A reminder now and then won't hurt."

"Dad, I'm sixteen years old. Don't worry about me. I can always run, you know."

"There are maniacs in this world. And they can run too."

Lois Stone refused to take any medication and stayed up with Julian Stone to watch television talk shows and old movies until five in the morning. At dawn, they had a light breakfast, showered, and dressed. At seven o'clock, he called Betty Gruff at home and told her to cancel the day's appointments, explaining that he was ill. Moments later, he regretted not telling her the truth. Where was the shame in having a missing daughter?

Next he found the telephone number of Marcie Simkin, at home in Philadelphia for the holiday. He apologized for the early morning call. She repeated what she'd told Lois, that Susan had accepted a ride after advertising to share expenses to New Jersey, and that the driver was a stranger. When Marcie began to cry, Stone consoled her and they promised to exchange any new information.

The police in Washington had no information. He recalled that Washington was an enclave surrounded by a jumble of independent police jurisdictions in Maryland and Virginia. When he telephoned the Washington police again to get the names and numbers of the counties, he was told that they kept each other informed via a metropolitan area ticker.

73

He hung up and racked his mind about what to do next. He had to be methodical. There were hotels, motels, hostels, bus and train stations, airports. He couldn't call them all now, yet they had to be looked into.

Although Lois wanted to be near the telephone, he insisted that she accompany him to the police station. It was better for her to take an active role rather than stay home alone and worry.

Lieutenant Kirkland was a handsome man who spent much time in making himself more attractive, Julian Stone guessed. Long hair was heated and treated to wave luxuriantly, and fingernails were manicured professionally. The doctor did not have full confidence in the police officer, nor in anyone who was obviously consumed with personal appearance. Stone felt it could only detract from performance. Nevertheless, he listened carefully as Kirkland spoke.

"You have my full sympathy, Mr. and Mrs. Stone. Ah, Dr. Stone. We are doing all we can under the circumstances."

"Under the circumstances?" Stone repeated. "A lack of interest in a missing girl?"

Though Kirkland was obviously of Anglo-Saxon origin, he continuously pressed the fingers of both hands on his breast as he spoke and then pulled them away to show open palms, in the manner of an Italian or Jewish immigrant. "I'll level with you. We have absolutely no reason to treat this as anything but a routine missing persons case. There's no evidence that a crime has been committed. Was your daughter kidnapped, or did she go off with that guy? We have no witnesses, no hard facts."

"You have a witness," Lois said. "The roommate saw her enter that man's car."

"Yes, but your daughter is an adult, over the age of consent. Now, if she were younger . . ."

"She just turned eighteen. Besides, since when does age have anything to do with a kidnapping crime?" Stone asked.

"Look, folks, I don't make the law. If we had clear evidence of foul play, we could jump right in. There are thousands of people across the country who disappear every day, but who turn up a few days or weeks later. New York City has more than thirty thousand missing person cases a year. Look, maybe there's some reason for Susan to run away like that. School problems, for instance. Or a boyfriend."

"She didn't run away," Lois began, tears brimming up in her eyes. "My daughter's a straight kid. If she was going to be late coming home from somewhere, even ten minutes late, she'd always call."

Kirkland pointed an accusatory finger. "Then why didn't she call when she changed her plans and left a few days earlier?"

Lois paused, giving the matter some thought before continuing. "I don't know. Maybe because she wanted to surprise us. Or maybe because she didn't think it was important enough."

"She'd call for being ten minutes late but not for three days early?" Kirkland looked at Stone quizzically, hoping that the doctor would offer a better explanation. When Stone shrugged, the officer smiled knowingly before continuing.

"In addition to a lack of evidence, we're laboring with a multi-jurisdictional matter. We're not even sure it's a matter for New Jersey police. She may have never left the Washington area. And if the driver headed north from Washington, the authorities in Maryland and Delaware should be alerted. Maybe Pennsylvania, too. We'll put it on the ticker."

"Alerted?" Stone repeated, frustrated at the unwillingness of the police to mount an active campaign. "What exactly does that mean? Are they going to be looking for my daughter or only stopping her by accident, maybe because her abductor ran a red light? What's wrong with a full-scale search, round-up of known perverts, sex offenders?"

"Well, Dr. Stone, to be quite truthful with you, it's police policy not to enter a missing person case if it involves an adult who's been gone for less than forty-eight hours. That's because so many turn up after a day or so."

"Forty-eight hours!" Stone exploded. "Two full days? Well, my daughter has been missing since late Sunday. This is Thursday. When did you start counting?"

75

On Thanksgiving evening instead of turkey Julian Stone pre-pared cheese sandwiches and tomato soup while Lois slept. She had drifted off to sleep after returning from the police station.

Realizing that she hadn't eaten in almost twenty-four hours, he awoke her. She sat up with a start, her eyes darting to the telephone. Her face betrayed anger, and Stone guessed it was inwardly directed, perhaps for allowing herself the pleasure of sleep.

"I'd have awakened you, Lois, if there was a call. Now let's eat something or we'll both get sick."

She shook her head back and forth. "No, you go right ahead."

"You're going to eat," he demanded, handing her a sandwich.

She looked at it and turned her head away. "How can I eat at a time like this?"

He knew that she also meant how could *he* think of food at this time. So, she had now reached the point of striking out at any-thing.

"Lois," he began slowly, "don't you know that no news is good news? If Susan were hurt or something like that, the police would have found out and let us know about it." Liar, he told himself. Susan could be hurt, maybe dead somewhere, her body undiscovered. Lois was right. He shouldn't be home eating. He should be doing something. But what?

"Lois," he continued, "please eat something. We've both got to keep our strength up. Listen, I'm going to ask your sister to stay with you for a couple of days. I'm driving down to Washington tomorrow to check some things."

Taking two steps at a time to use the telephone extension up-stairs to arrange for the visit of his sister-in-law, he returned a few minutes later. Lois, staring at the floor, looked up at him.

"Oh, God," she said. "I hope she is all right. I hope someone is taking good care of her."

NINE

In the days that followed, the arson and explosion squad could only confirm what Imperateri already knew. Somebody had broken into his apartment and lit a gasoline-soaked rug. The arsonist apparently had worn gloves. Fingerprint dusters came up with no prints other than Imperateri's. There were no witnesses, no one who saw anybody loitering around the apartment house at three in the morning.

Obviously, Imperateri thought, it was not a random act of vandalism. He could only guess that any of the most likely suspects in his homicide caseload must have done it in order to slow or stop an investigation. The question was, who? He reasoned that it might be just as productive to track down the actual killer rather than be sidetracked by an attempted homicide by fire. On the other hand, working back from the fire to the homicide suspect might be just as easy and productive.

Imperateri did not rule out the possibility that someone else might have been the intended victim, perhaps a previous occupant of the apartment. He'd only been in the apartment for a little over a year ever since his divorce.

A sudden thought came to him. Only a few people knew of his change of address, unlisted in the telephone book. His daughter and ex-wife. Marie Mackay. The postman and a few friends, mostly cops. It wasn't going to be easy. It seemed that nothing he touched these days was.

Imperateri took a deep breath and looked around the apartment. It could happen again. He would have to install a chain on the door and sleep with the .38 under the pillow.

In the meantime, Thanksgiving was here and still no new victim of the lust-murderer had been found and no person reported as missing. Imperateri would celebrate by inviting Marie out to Thanksgiving dinner.

The thought of her jolted him. Of course. It was her news story about his being hot on the trail of the lust-murderer. The killer had obviously believed it.

Imperateri realized that he himself was now a prospective victim.

Marie eagerly accepted Vincent's invitation. She was slightly apologetic that she had to work on the holiday, else she would have prepared a homecooked meal for both of them.

Later he wondered what kind of life they would have together. Since being virtually rebuffed at the picnic, he hesitated about bringing up the subject of living together again. And despite his straitlaced notions, he was getting used to the idea. He wanted Marie and if those were the terms he'd accept them. Nothing too binding. That almost sounded good. Maybe it was wise to take it slow. After all, he had promised himself never to get involved again.

Partly because of his police work his life with Beth had been impossible. She couldn't abide his frequent holiday and weekend duty. She didn't understand his depressions while working on particularly brutal cases. She expected him to leave his haunted memories at the door, to come home happy and smiling. Yet afterthoughts intruded, perhaps of a young boy sodomized and thrown from a roof, or an elderly widow whose life's savings and intestines were equally ripped off and out.

With Marie it would be different. She saw the same crap on the streets. She had her own career with a work schedule as topsy-turvy as his. They'd be too busy, too caught up with their own work to be at each other's throat. The times they could scrape together would be restful, loving ones.

He was torn between feelings of affection for her and a raw suspicion that she had little interest in him as a man. Could she be using him as a ploy to get exclusive stories for her newspaper? More than a few times he'd wondered about that, fueled by her devious behavior in getting the Anderson story.

He made up his mind to be a bit more careful about what he said to her. He hadn't told her about the attempt on his life and had asked the other detectives to keep quiet about it. What kind of life would that be, he wondered, not being able to trust a woman you cared so much about? Maybe there would come a time when she wouldn't feel compelled to prove herself better than any of the other correspondents in town.

Yet he knew that there would never come the time when he'd be able to take home every detail of his work. In the lust murders, the press and public only knew that all of the victims had been stabbed, strangled and sexually assaulted. The lurid and gory details were never provided. It wasn't a question of their being too shocking to print. Much bloodier descriptions had appeared in the press. But in a working homicide, police held back information to be known only to themselves and the murderer. This not only eliminated phony confessions by publicity seekers, but gave police a valuable tool. They could pounce on a slip of the tongue by a suspect under questioning who dropped a fact that only the guilty person could know.

Marie and Vincent enjoyed a cozy Thanksgiving dinner in a quiet little bistro he frequented. They managed effortlessly to avoid talking about the lust murders. Over dessert and Irish coffee, she broached the subject.

"People," she said, "are comparing the case to Jack the Ripper and the Boston Strangler."

He nodded wearily, tired of hearing that speculation. "There are similarities but more differences. Jack the Ripper didn't rape his victims. He chose only prostitutes, slitting their throats and dismembering them. The Boston Strangler sexually mutilated but didn't rape all of his victims, about a dozen or so, I think. So far our killer has three, with one due right now."

"I should have known you couldn't relax, today of all days. And the way you keep glancing at the waiter. He knows who you are and the station knows where you are."

79

"You've done the same, I bet."

She nodded and laughed, and then fell silent for a few moments in thought. "Listen, Vinnie. I've got an idea. Suppose I talk my editor into publishing an open letter on the front page to the killer. We'll beg him not to kill again and not to take an innocent life. We'll promise not to hurt him, only to help him. We'll ask him to think of his own loved ones, perhaps his mother."

Imperateri emitted a low whistle. "That could be counterproductive. That guy could have a mother-hatred intense enough to have driven him to kill in the first place. One of the psychiatrists suggested that."

"It's worth a try, Vinnie. I read in the old files about the Mad Bomber in New York, the guy who set bombs all over the city long before the political terrorists thought of it. *The New York Journal American* wrote an open letter to him. Do you know what happened?"

Imperateri reached for a cigarette. "Didn't he respond with an unsigned letter? He said he had some kind of grudge against a utility company."

"Right. It seems he'd been fired or something like that. From there on it was only a question of checking everyone who ever had an argument with the utility company and tracking him down. They found the Bomber."

"We should be so lucky," Imperateri said. "Look, you don't need permission from me. Go ahead and do it. I really don't know if it'll help or hurt. Certainly your article warning girls about strangers didn't accomplish a hell of a lot."

"Apparently the murdered girl didn't read my article." She paused to sigh. "I just don't understand. Did the girls go willingly into his car? If so, how did he get them to do that?"

"The usual possibilities, Marie. The guy could be posing in a trustworthy position. A cop or clergyman. Even a friend of a family member. Maybe he has a taxicab, or is some kind of rich kid who drives a fancy wagon no girl could turn down."

"Taxicab?"

"Now don't go and panic the hack-users, Marie. We computer-checked all cabs, company and privately-owned, working on the nights of the reported abductions. No results."

Imperateri didn't bother telling her how painstaking a chore that was, more typical of police work than ticket-writing or accident-reporting. Young John Bork, the detective assigned to help him, also used the computer to search for interconnections among the cases of the three murdered girls. It was an ambitious task, creating a program that included schools, camps, and workplaces, even churches, and the names of classmates and fellow employees. The printout was beginning to get out of control, with computer stacks so high on Bork's desk that they provided a curtain of privacy for him.

Marie broke his thoughts. "Listen. Suppose the killer is so sophisticated that he uses hypnosis to lure the girls."

"Anything's possible, including the idea that there's more than one killer involved." He thought of telling her that she might next write something about the staggering number of psychos and oddballs running loose in town. But that would only panic the good citizenry.

The check paid, they rose to leave. "Where to now?" he asked.

"My place," she replied. "Our people know where to find us."

At her apartment he joked how his ancient furnishings would go well with her modern decor. Marie shook her head rapidly and rose from the couch.

"You're going too fast for me. I got sucked into a bad arrangement my first time around. I told you that I don't want to make that mistake again."

"You don't feel anything for me?" he asked.

"Of course, I do. I sincerely like you a lot. You don't have any of that *macho* crap that cops reek of, even the female ones. But we've only known each other a few weeks. If there's anything between us, it's just instant desire. One set of glands exchanging signals with the other. Not enough reason for shacking up. Or marrying."

He remained silent for a few moments and then tried to hide

his disappointment by feigning hurt. "I guess I expected too much. Me, a lowly cop. . ."

She cut him off. "Don't lay that self-pitying stuff on me. I've turned down network executives and real estate magnates."

"Hey, I'm only kidding!"

She sighed. "Well, I'm serious. It's just not time yet. Things have to take root and grow."

"Right now I feel like a hungry boy pressing his nose against a pastry shop window."

She giggled and popped off the couch, dancing lightly to the bathroom and closing the door. When she emerged, she was draped in a large bathroom towel. She sidled across the room and put on the stereo, releasing soft, dreamy music reminiscent of the '50's. Then she danced to where he sat and suddenly let the towel drop to a heap at her feet Looking at him through slitted kittenish eyes, she placed her hands on her hips and slowly rotated her body in the manner of a model exhibiting a new line. Her breasts swung tautly, like dual mountains beckoning and daring an explorer to conquer them before continuing on to a lush valley beyond.

"This is one pastry you're not going to do without," she whispered.

It had been a long time for him. For the last few months Beth had been with him he hadn't touched her, for their constant quarreling reduced his sexual desire to naught. And when they had separated, there had been no sexual frustration, no especial longing for the female body. He attributed this to the demands of his job and his reluctance for one-nighters with women he hardly cared for. Sex was no longer a driving force in his life. The thought caused him no worry. He knew that when the right woman came along, when there'd be love as well as sex, he'd respond.

And respond now he did. Ripping off his clothing with a wild abandon that surprised him, he felt his heart hammering with pneumatic intensity. He pulled her towards him, now feeling her own throbbing throughout his body.

They fell on the thick carpeting next to the coffee table and he permitted her to land on top of him. He loved the feel of her weight, her quivering abdomen and thighs, the smell of her perfume.

When he entered her, her eyes squeezed shut. Soon her head turned from side to side and she began murmuring softly, all the time digging at his back. Minutes later, they lay perspiring like sprinters, gasping to pay the oxygen debt.

He looked over at her and then squeezed her hand. "You said I'm rushing you. When would it be time? How will I know?"

"I'll know," she replied. "When I do, so will you."

TEN

Early Friday morning under fog and a fine drizzle Julian Stone drove the deserted New Jersey Turnpike. It was intermission for holiday travelers, long at their destinations and sleeping late while digestive systems completed the previous evening's turkey dinner.

Now and then a lone car sped by, causing Stone to look sideways at the vehicle's interior. Each time he knew he wouldn't lay eyes on Susan, but he looked anyway, more in reflex than in expectation. Yet he hoped against laws of average and probability. With a gambler's passion he stopped at every restaurant and rest area to examine faces at booths and counters, at entrances and exits. There was always the chance, no matter how slight, of an improbability becoming an actuality.

He drove slowly, preoccupied with his horror-dreams, permitting every passing car to speed by. Soon a large tractor-trailer roared up and tailgated him for a few miles. Suddenly and without warning, it quickly shifted to the center lane to pass. The driver glared over at Stone, raised his middle finger and mouthed the words, *fuck you*. At least that was what Stone at first thought he meant. Or could the trucker have said, *fifty-five*, suggesting that Stone was a fool to heed the speed limit?

The very idea of his own vindication of the truck driver bothered Stone. There he was, always trying to look for the best in people when there was so little to look for. When would he learn that?

He watched the tractor-trailer gain speed and pull further ahead. "Bastard," he murmured, recalling the incident last year

84

on the Turnpike, not too far from where he now drove. It was Christmas and he, Lois and Susan were heading south to Florida for a winter vacation. Then, like now, it had rained. Susan, just turned seventeen, had wanted highway driving experience and Stone let her take the wheel.

She chose the center lane and followed the maximum speed limit like the neophyte driver that she was, anxious to do well and obey the law. Stone, sitting in the rear and confident in her driving, settled back and soon drifted off to a sound sleep.

What seemed like moments later occurred a good hour after he had dozed off. The blast of a truck's horn shattered him to instant and fearful wakefulness. He looked through the rear window. There, a few feet behind was the hood of a tractor-trailer, snapping at their rear bumper like the jaws of a pursuing behemoth.

"Let him pass, Susan," Stone said.

"He has the outside lane," she replied coolly. "He can use that. Besides, he belongs in the right lane."

"He's insane," Lois said. "Don't argue with a truck."

The horn blasted again. Stone stuck his head closer to the window and looked up to see the trucker, a massive hulk who filled the cab with his arms and shoulders. He wore a cap and mustache as if to achieve anonymity. Instead of a face contorted by indignation, or at worse, anger, the trucker's lips were parted in a half-smile, an expression of amused expectation.

Stone jerked his thumbs in either direction, indicating to the trucker to pass on the right or left. The only reaction was an up-raised middle finger, jabbing up and higher into the air like a slowly rising rocket. Then the hand dropped to the horn to let loose a long, loud burst.

"For God's sake," Stone shouted, "jump over to the right and let him pass!"

"I can't, Dad. I can't see around the truck if the lane's clear. I can't even see the outside lane."

"Then speed up and then switch."

Tramping the pedal to the floor, Susan easily accelerated ahead, but seconds later, before she could change lanes, the truck was once again upon her, closer than before with horn blowing anew.

"He's gone mad!" Lois shrieked.

"Relax, Mother. He's playing a game."

"What kind of game is that?"

"He thinks he's punishing me for being a slow driver and not sticking to the inside lane. Well, I'm going the maximum allowable speed."

"I don't care! I want you to stop now, Susan!"

"Stop what, Mother?"

"Quiet, both of you!" Stone snapped.

"Dad, please don't get all uptight."

"Pull straight ahead again."

Susan again obeyed her father, and accelerated to sixty, seventy and then eighty miles an hour. This time, however, the trucker kept right up with her, not attempting to pass but roaring behind with his big engine and blaring horn.

Stone peered out of the window. The tractor-trailer was barely inches away, its driver hunched over the wheel, the smile now a wide grin.

It was murderous, suicidal, Stone thought. If they'd slow down, the trucker would ram right into them. And if they'd keep that speed up or even go faster, they stood a good chance of going into a skid and losing control.

His fear and anger caused him to perspire as though he were in a sauna. His hands shook uncontrollably, like those of a person with advanced Parkinson's disease.

He looked at Susan. She kept her eyes on the road, her hands steady on the wheel. She was calm, driving as if headed for a Sunday picnic with time to spare.

What advice could he give her? Speed up even more? Slow down? Sheer off to the side? If she swerved off to another lane at that speed they would certainly go into a skid.

Suddenly, in a spurt of raw speed he didn't know large vehicles possessed, the tractor-trailer pulled into the left lane and rolled alongside their car. Again from the cab came the grin and the upraised finger. Then the trucker roared further ahead, passing them and cutting sharply in front, so close that its tail end scratched across their front bumper.

Stone raised a fist and cursed. Lois screamed and put her hands over her eyes. Susan slowly lifted her foot from the pedal, apparently knowing that to hit the brakes might send the car reeling and maybe fishtailing off the road.

"Police!" Stone shouted. "Where are the police?"

"Whenever you need them . . ." Lois began, her composure returned.

If only I had a gun, Stone thought, I wouldn't need the police. I'd go after that murdering bastard and shoot him between his dumb eyes. He tried to kill us. He deserved to die, and I'm entitled to kill him.

Later, stopping at a restaurant and gas station, they found a state trooper who listened to their story while stifling a series of yawns. The trooper then went through the motions of writing a report and a description of the tractor-trailer in a little notebook. He also promised to locate the driver for questioning.

Stone, aroused from his reverie by another passing truck, reminded himself that nothing had been done by the trooper to catch the trucker, else Stone would have been asked to testify. Another thought was more encouraging. Susan was cool and responsible under great pressure. More so than he could ever hope to be.

Julian Stone was hungry and he was tired, but he knew what had to be done before eating and before checking in at a motel. He had to see for himself. It was more important to him than creature comforts.

Coming off the Baltimore-Washington Parkway, he knew the exact route to George Washington University, a city campus located several blocks west of the White House. He'd visited there with Lois and Susan when they were casting about for a good school not too far from home.

He exited on the Beltway and then picked up Connecticut Avenue going south to the downtown section. Soon he approached the campus, a mix of old buildings and modern, glassy structures. All looked deserted, as were the streets, instilling in him a strange feeling of forlorn loneliness though he knew that everything was closed for the holiday.

The thought struck him that he might not be able to enter her dormitory and might have to wait until Monday when the school re-opened. He decided he wouldn't wait and would get in even if he had to call the college president or break into the place like a common burglar.

Susan's dormitory lay in a cluster of newly-renovated buildings at the far end of the street campus. It was a nine-story former apartment building resembling a giant red brick standing on end.

The front door was unlocked, but he was challenged immediately by a janitor, a Black man wearing a castaway Army uniform with darker areas where insignia and stripes had been stripped away. His voice was deep, gravelly.

"Hey! Building's closed."

"I'm Dr. Julian Stone. My daughter is a student here. She's missing and we don't know what happened to her. Could I take a look at her room?"

"Nobody's here now, mister. Everybody's gone home. Gives us a chance to clean up. Fumigate the roaches and bugs. That's because the kids cook and eat in their rooms. They not supposed to."

"Her room is on the third floor. Three-four-seven. I just want to take a quick look."

"Against regulations. Nobody's allowed in. Security."

"You could come along with me. I just have to see her room."

"You say you don't know where she's at?"

"I'm telling you, she has disappeared. Nobody knows what has happened to her." Stone pulled out his wallet to single out a twenty dollar bill which he pressed into the janitor's hand.

Susan's room gave evidence of a hasty departure. Clothing was strewn over the two beds and on every piece of furniture, a bookcase, night tables, lamps. Even a cheap rug in the center of the room was partially hidden by dropped jeans, shorts and blouses. Here and there balled-up, fast-food restaurant wrappers lay like rocks on a lunar landscape.

Stone couldn't tell which items belonged to Susan and which to her roommate, Marcie Simkin. He easily identified his daughter's side of the room by the family snapshots taped to the wall.

"Sure is a mess, ain't it?" the janitor said.

Stone nodded and looked under a sweater on Susan's night table. Perhaps there was a scribbled address, something that could tell him where she was. He examined notes for a term paper in English and other papers dealing with some of her courses. The table drawer revealed cosmetics, more notes, paperback books and several ballpoint pens.

He pushed the drawer in and next looked at the closet. Hangars dangled with clothing. Books lined the bottom, boxes the top shelf. A huge trunk which he had purchased especially for college took up most of the space.

"You find what you looking for, mister?"

Stone whirled around. He'd almost forgotten that the janitor was still there. "What I'm looking for is my daughter."

The janitor nodded. "She just took off? Right? Just like that?"

"She got a ride with some stranger last Sunday. We haven't heard from her since."

The janitor whistled. "Man, that ride must have come off the bulletin board in the Student Union. They asking for trouble, kids who do that."

"Could you please show it to me?"

The bulletin board was covered with three-by-five cards listing needs and offerings under the headings *For Sale, Wanted, Room for Rent, Rides, Announcements.*

His eyes darted back to *Rides.* Would he find the card that enticed Susan? He searched out those which would have some bearing on her trip.

Ride wanted to N.J. Leave Tues nite or Wed morn Joe x0125

Rider needed to North N.J. near GW Bridge Tues. Share expenses and conversation. Rick 742-6114

Need ride to Newark area. Will share expenses. Susan x2347

His heart raced as he re-read the last card. It was Susan's. Her name, her telephone number.

He regretted that it had been Susan who had advertised and not the driver. Now he was left without a clue as to the identity of the person who had stood right here, read the card, called her and was responsible for whatever had befallen her.

Stone's eyes fell to the floor and then raised to the wall surrounding the board, as if expecting to see more evidence, a footprint, an item of clothing, even another note. He removed the card, if only because he wanted something of hers. Then he slowly pinned it back, believing that it was evidence, not to be tampered with, a matter only for the police.

Looking at the card once again, he felt a wave of emotion sweep him, knotting his stomach and squeezing his throat. Before he could control himself, he began sobbing in front of the janitor.

"Hey, man. It ain't that bad. She turn up. Give her some time."

Stone nodded and turned to leave.

"Here," the janitor continued, pushing something into Stone's jacket pocket. "I don't jack me up on someone's hurt."

Outside, Stone saw that it was the twenty dollar bill. He crumpled it and held it in a balled-up fist. Moments later, he traced the steps in front of the building where Susan had been picked up, according to her roommate. Was it possible that a little child, a milkman, even a sidewalk sweeper, may have seen something?

Across the street were private, two-story dwellings, a row of red brick houses with abbreviated plots of lawn surrounded by chain link fences. The grass, winter brown and lacking care, bore refuse strewn by students.

He shook his head sadly. There couldn't have been any gardeners outside. But the windows, could anyone have been watching from them at the time? A retired person, a widow with time to sit and gaze at passersby? He would visit each house, explaining what had happened and asking for their help.

Crossing the street, his heart sank. Greek letters adorned the doors, proudly denoting fraternity and sorority turf.

So they were not family houses. There was little likelihood that any student would gaze from a window right before a holiday while his or her friends were having a good time. Besides, unlike a one-family residence, each house was probably full of students. It would take him an unreasonably long time to corner and speak with each one once they returned to the campus.

Perhaps he ought to prepare a flier and circulate it. And then print up thousands of posters with Susan's photograph. He'd have them sent to every house, store and school for miles around. The cost would come out of his own pocket. He doubted whether the police had either the funds or motivation to do it.

The *police*. So little tangible help had come from them so far. His helplessness and frustration were too much for him to bear alone. It was time to go to them again. Time to drag them into doing the job they were paid to do.

Vincent Imperateri heard the shouting at the other end of the squad room but largely ignored it. Shouting, crying, arguing and general bedlam were part of the ambience. If the noise didn't come from suspects, it came from the detectives, from vice or narcotics, from robbery or homicide, arguing over cross-jurisdictional matters.

Imperateri continued to shut out the disturbance until Chris Daley from Missing Persons came over. Daley, recently promoted to plainclothes work because of a shooting injury, looked annoyed and amused at the same time.

"I've got this guy giving me a hard time, Vinnie."

"So what else is new?" Imperateri replied.

"I think you ought to see him."

"I've got enough headaches without trying to work your end of the street."

"Vinnie, this man's got a daughter, a GWU student who's missing after hitching a ride. She may be another one of your girls but so far there's nothing that looks like foul play."

"Okay, Chris, I'll do your job for you and assure him that we're working hard on the case."

Julian Stone immediately liked what he saw. Sergeant Imperateri, although tall with good features, wore a suit that not only was off a budget store's racks, but was also ill-fitting and long out of style. The officer seemed to be in absolute harmony with the meager office with its old furniture.

The two men eyed each other for several moments before Stone began speaking, repeating all that he knew of his daughter's disappearance. He also mentioned the lack of police involvement and his just-completed visit to the college dormitory.

"From there I went to FBI headquarters," Stone continued, "and got ushered in to see a very young agent. I asked him about FBI interest, in view of the interstate and kidnapping aspects. He asked me what evidence I had of that and I told him that was his job, gathering evidence."

Imperateri suppressed a laugh. "I guess there's not enough glamour in a mere missing person report for those glory-seeking guys. You can't blame them. They have to go to Congress for their appropriations each year and have got to put on an exciting show and tell."

Stone managed a smile before continuing. "The agent then asked me if I had a ransom note to show evidence of kidnapping. I said, no, but suppose my daughter's abductor doesn't want a ransom, just wants her. The agent then stood at his desk and said there's nothing they could do now but work with local law enforcement agencies."

The anguish was evident in the doctor's face, his voice. But Imperateri could not let himself be influenced by that, nor by putting himself in the doctor's shoes and imagining that it was his own daughter, Judy, who was missing. He understood all that, yet he knew he'd wind up empathizing, as usual. And, of course, the girl had disappeared over a holiday. Was she the victim he'd been expecting?

Imperateri pulled out his cigarettes, offered one to Stone who declined, and then held one in his hand without lighting it, the classic pose of one who is trying to cut down or quit. "Dr. Stone," he said, "first let me apologize for the apparent run-around you've been getting. Second, let me say that we will enter the case immediately, with all of our effort. You have my personal assurance on that. Now, how long are you going to be in town?"

"I'd like to stay until I learn something. I don't want to step on your toes, but I'd like to do my own investigating. I've got a medical background and I want to approach this scientifically."

Saying that, Stone produced a stenographer's notebook. "I've begun to write down everything dealing with Susan's stay in Washington. Names, addresses, telephone numbers of people she knew. I've got a list of places to visit, hotels and such. Transit stations. I'm going to check all unclaimed luggage, talk to drivers, ticket agents."

Imperateri raised a palm. "Hold it, Doctor. All that's fine, but it'll take you months. First go to the newspapers in town and tell them your story. There are three million people in the Washington area. One of them must have seen something."

"And one of them must have done something to my daughter."

Vincent Imperateri waited patiently for Marcie Simkin's sobs to subside. Tears were a byproduct of his trade. He was accustomed to them, and generally ignored outbursts as a carpenter disregarded flying sawdust. He had the time to wait, though Julian Stone in the car downstairs might grow a bit impatient. Imperateri had asked the doctor to wait outside, preferring to question Susan's roommate alone. He had a hunch he'd learn more without the presence of the father.

The detective wondered whether he was going to kick himself when it was all over. The Susan Stone case did have a few of the trappings of a runaway affair. Was he wasting time interviewing a witness when every moment should be on the rape murders? The Thanksgiving connection was a tenuous one, since she was reported missing several days before while the previous cases occurred on a holiday or an adjunct weekend.

Imperateri's eyes wandered about the dormitory room, hoping to pick up some clues as to Susan's personality. There was nothing to indicate that she wasn't an ordinary girl, albeit caught up in extraordinary circumstances now. He had to determine exactly what those circumstances were. If she were a runaway, he'd lose interest as fast as a shot put dropping. If she wasn't, that was something else. The key lay in Marcie's memory and truthfulness.

Again he addressed the petite girl with the large dark eyes. "Marcie, I know it's hard for you, but if you could help as much as possible, we may be able to find Susan. First of all, tell me about her. Did she seem to get along okay with everybody here? And what about her parents, did she have any problems with them?" He watched her wipe her eyes and shake her head. "Did she have some fight with her boyfriend?"

Marcie stopped crying suddenly. "Why do you ask me questions like that? I told you she was kidnapped by that man."

"I just want to know if she had any reason to get up and get away from it all for a few days. Okay, now tell me about that man. You actually saw him?"

"Not too well. He never got out of the car. He didn't look like any of the students here."

"You mean he was too old?"

"No, not that old. He was in his late twenties, I guess."

"How do you know he wasn't a student? Do you know the faces of the thousands of students here?"

She quickly shook her head. "That isn't what I meant. You know, when you go in one of the avenue bars near the school, you can tell who's a student and who isn't. The way they look and dress. Even the expression gives them away."

"Describe your non-student."

"He was bald in front but had long, light brown hair and sort of a common face. Nothing unusual. I could recognize him if I saw him again."

"Good, Marcie. I'm going to let you talk with our artist and see if you two could work up a likeness of the guy. Now, what kind of car did he drive?"

"An old one. Beat up. It didn't look like it could make it to Baltimore, much less New Jersey."

"Can you recall the color, year, make?"

She thought for a moment and then shook her head. "All I can remember is that it was dark and old."

"Maybe you'll recall later. Sometimes memory has a way of slipping and then returning. But let's get back to the boyfriend. Did she ever stay out all night with him?"

When Marcie hesitated to answer, Imperateri rebuked her. "Look, Marcie, you're not helping her by being loyal and closemouthed."

Marcie nodded understanding. "She never stayed out with him, but with another guy that she met at a bar. He's one of those motorcycle creeps, with a black leather jacket and all. She didn't want her boyfriend or her parents to know about him."

So it comes out now, Imperateri thought. A Romeo-Juliet runaway bit. Well, he'd talk with her boyfriends, both of them, and wrap this one up for Missing Persons before too long.

As he thanked Marcie and left, two questions bothered him. According to Susan's parents and her roommate, she was too anxious to go home. And who exactly was the driver in the old car?

If the stranger were the lust-murderer, police now had a witness. But Imperateri wasn't too optimistic on either count.

Marie Mackay sat at the small motel room desk with her notebook open. A sheepish look appeared on her face when she pulled out her taperecorder, switching it on. "I hope you don't mind being taped, Dr. Stone."

Julian Stone, seated across from her, shook his head and looked over at Lois sitting on the edge of the bed. Inasmuch as she didn't react to the reporter's question, Stone nodded assent.

Marie positioned the recorder and faced Lois. "Mrs. Stone, from a mother's viewpoint, how are you coping from day to day?"

Lois shrugged at first, and then began hesitatingly. "We try our best." She paused and wiped away a tear. "Just please write,

Miss Mackay, that someone just snatched my little girl off the streets as if she didn't belong to anybody." Saying this, Lois turned towards the wall and sobbed with great heaving thrusts of her torso.

Marie, taken aback by the outburst, swallowed and then addressed Stone. "Maybe I ought to come back some other time."

"She's taking it very hard, Miss Mackay. The only time she'll be herself is when we'll see Susan again."

"You still have great hope, then?"

Stone's voice trembled and then trailed off as he spoke, forcing Marie to lean forward to hear. "We have no illusions. We know about the series of rape-murders you've had down here. If Susan were alive, we'd have heard something. She would have let us know something. That's the kind of girl she was. . . is." He paused for a few moments, shaken by his own words, before continuing.

"Most of the time I think of the protective childhood Susan had. It seemed to have been my goal to build a wall of security around her, around Lois. But for Susan, the wall was stifling. For her, the other side represented excitement and adventure, not pain and evil. And then the day came when I had to let go. It was one of those agonizing times in a father's life when he has to decide just how far he should interfere in his daughter's life."

Lois turned around to face Marie. "Miss Mackay, you don't have a child for seventeen years and lose her without being changed. We'll never be the same. You asked me how I'm coping. I'm not. If Susan's dead, I just can't put her in the grave and make the best of it. There is no best of it. Nothing will ever make me feel good about it. No one can tell me anything positive about it."

She rose and took an uncertain step forward. "I feel sorry for the people who have to live in that animal world. I'm supposed to pity and understand the animals who beat and rape and kill. I don't. I hate them." Lois once more turned to the wall, staring at it as though it held a secret.

Stone, watching her, shook his head and spoke in whispers to Marie. "You have no way of knowing what we're going through.

How would you like to go to a home which was a warm and vibrant one and which now is dead? We had a lovely, beautiful child. Now her life is snuffed out."

"But we don't know that for sure, Dr. Stone. It's only been two weeks since her disappearance."

"For us, an eternity," Stone said, rising to touch Marie lightly on the arm. "You have to be careful, very careful," he said in a conspiratorial tone. "There are savages in the streets waiting to harm you."

ELEVEN

The time had come. Tomorrow he'd have to return the cruiser and now he'd love his girlie for the last time.

Like so many times in the past, William Crawford looked forward to the end with mixed feelings that ran deep and caused him much anxiety. On one hand he found it hard to suppress the excitement he knew he'd feel at the very end. Yet he regretted having to lose her. He had kept her the longest and she'd shown more spirit and fight than any other girlie he'd ever had. And he liked that. Except for her, all of them had whimpered and cried for most of the time they were in his care.

Feeling smug about his accomplishments, he smiled to himself at how he'd outfoxed the police by a modification in his tactics. Instead of a cruiser, he had used his own car in broad daylight and had simply found the name of a girlie on a college bulletin board. And when he'd be through with her, he'd then use the cruiser, now sitting in his garage. He'd also steer clear of shopping centers. He guessed that they were being watched by police and by everybody who read the newspapers.

William Crawford believed it was changes such as these and the dropping off of the girlies in different police jurisdictions that would throw the authorities off his trail. The fact that he'd failed to kill Imperateri and thus slow down the investigation did not bother him as much as at first. He had nothing to fear from Imperateri in the immediate future. If all worked out well, he'd have a couple, maybe three more girlies, and then pull up stakes.

Stretching now, he felt the thrilling tingling in his loins and breathed with pleasure as it seemed to spread all over his body like ripples on water.

Now.

He retrieved the scissors from the cupboard and ran an exploratory thumb across the snipping edges. The blades were getting dull and needed sharpening, but that would have to wait. They should be good for at least one more session, he thought, tucking them into a back pocket of his trousers.

With basement door swung open, he flicked on the light at the top of the stairs and stood watching her for several moments. She blinked in the sudden light and shaded her eyes with an arm. Then she looked up at him from where she was chained by the neck to a steel pillar embedded in the center of the floor. The chain was only long enough to permit access to a toilet a few feet away in the windowless basement with walls of poured concrete.

She lay nude on a waterproof air mattress. The beauty of her nakedness almost took his breath away even though he had satiated himself with her just bare hours ago. Again he felt sorry that it was to be the final time with the girlie with the long dark hair and the olive complexion. Nevertheless there would be others, many others, perhaps some just as beautiful and wild.

He began to descend. Seeing him, she shivered and shook her head with fright. For a moment he wondered why. She hadn't shown such fear before, just anger and hate. Could it be that, like an animal, she sensed that the end was near? How could she tell? She certainly couldn't see the scissors in his back pocket.

"You look a little bit scared, my sweetheart," he said softly, unbuckling his belt and letting his pants drop to his shoes. He took care not to let the scissors fall out where she would see or hear them.

"When are you going to let me go? You've kept me long enough. I promised you I wouldn't tell anybody."

"You're whining. I don't like that."

"You said you'd let me go."

"I will, in good time. Just cooperate a little, that's all I ask."

99

He hastily pulled off his shirt and removed shoes and socks next, leaving only his undershorts on.

"You're lying."

"I'm not. This will be the last time you'll do a favor for me. I'm going to love you like before. And if everything goes all right, I'll let you go."

She shook her head. "You've lied to me before. You said you'd only keep me for a few hours, then a day. You said you'd let me call my parents. You promised to let me take a bath, but you wouldn't let me go upstairs. Look, I'm all sweaty and I stink from your old chicken fat you greased me up with. Please let me wash."

"I will, I will. Look, I'm even going to take off the chain. Now don't you try anything foolish because I'll have to hurt you. And goodness knows, I don't want to do that."

He bent over and pulled two keys from a front pocket of his pants lying on the floor. Then he twisted them into the two locks binding the chain.

She rubbed the soreness around her neck and glared at him. "You've taken the chain off before. So what? It means you're just going into your perverted act again."

"Now, come on. You don't have to say that." He tossed the chain away and pointed to an alcove housing the toilet. "If you have to make wee-wee or do-do, now's your chance."

"Oh, fuck off, you miserable creep!" She lashed out, trying to strike him, but he caught her arm and twisted it hard, making her cry out in pain.

"I'm only trying to be nice. And you don't have to use that kind of language with me. I told you that I don't appreciate it."

Scowling, he pulled his undershorts off and stood before her stark naked, his member limp as cooked spaghetti. "All right, girlie, lie down on the mattress just like before."

"Where's the broiled chicken?" she asked.

He hesitated for a moment. "Ah, maybe later. Tonight's something special, really special."

She laughed. "More special than dripping chicken fat over me and licking it off?"

100

"That's right."

She pointed at his penis. "Will it finally make your flag wave?"

"That's disgusting talk! You've got some kind of problem, don't you, you with your foul mouth?"

"I have? What about you?"

"I'm really not such a bad guy."

"So I see," she said, forcing a smile. "I have to admit that at first I was petrified of you. I thought you were that maniac who's been killing all of those girls."

He knitted his brows and nodded. "Yes, I've read about him. They ought to lock him up and throw away the key."

"Then I realized that you're just a kink. Instead of whips and leather, you're into chicken fat. Talk about sexual perversion. Wild!"

"I really don't appreciate that. You keep that up and you'll be sorry."

"I think you'd better see a doctor. Maybe he could help you with an erection and having full intercourse, instead of masturbating over a woman."

He shook an angry fist at her. "It's none of your damn business!"

"Look," she said, her eyes darting in new fright, "I happen to be a psych major and I'm interested in your case."

"I am not a *case*."

"In you, then. Why are you so hostile to women? I read in a textbook about people like you, about their childhood. Want to hear about it?"

He said nothing, looking at the pile of his clothing and gently nudging it with his foot.

"I bet you had problems with your mother," she continued. "Sexual ones."

He shut his eyes and opened them rapidly. "Damn it! I'll bust your dirty, lying mouth in if you're going to talk like that. I've had enough of it. There was nothing wrong with my mother."

"I didn't say anything was wrong with her."

"I hate that kind of nonsense stuff. It's all intellectual crap that doesn't mean a damn thing."

"Did you also wet your bed? Enuresis is an overt expression of retaliation against parental rejection. That's what the textbook says. The child repudiates bladder control on his mother's terms because he feels he'd lost her as a love object."

"Oh, shut up, will you! You couldn't be more wrong. That's what too much education does to you, filling your head with stupid stuff that no one can prove."

"What about animals? Did you torture and kill them when you were young?"

"You really make me sick."

"There was a case of a man who crawled under the seats in movie houses and kissed the legs of women. As a boy, he torched kittens."

He stared at her quietly for a few moments before breaking out in laughter. "I know your game. You're trying to talk me into forgetting why I'm down here. Sort of like that Arabian princess telling stories night after night so that the king won't kill her."

"Scheherazade. She was Persian. A Thousand and One Nights."

"You're so smart. You know everything, don't you? But you're mistaken about one thing. I've no intention of killing you, like in the story. Let's begin. We've wasted enough time."

"And then will you let me go?"

William Crawford screwed up his face as if in deep decision. "Well, since you've been a decent girlie, how about right now?"

She gave a burst of joy and clapped her hands as he turned away. With his back towards her, he bent to remove the scissors from the pocket. Whirling now, he faced her, holding them in an arc over his head.

For a moment she stared in disbelief. Then she screamed, a high, shrieking shout that reverberated throughout the basement, pounding against his ears like ocean waves.

"Stop that!" he shouted back.

"Don't! Please don't kill me."

"I said I wouldn't do anything like that. What do you take me for? I just want a lock of your hair. You know, a souvenir." He held out an empty hand in friendship. "Come on, I promise I won't hurt you. Honest. Here, shake my hand."

She backed away, holding her palms up for protection. Laughing wildly, he lunged forward and thrust the scissors into her neck. Blood poured through the puncture like water from a burst hose. Gurgling sounds came from her throat as she went into shock, losing strength and falling to her knees with head bowed.

Standing like a crazed matador over a wounded, prostrate bull, he struck her again and again with the blades, in the back of her head, the shoulders, the buttocks. With abnormal strength he turned her over on her back and pierced her abdomen, releasing a fresh torrent of blood which cascaded from her body to the mattress and then to the floor.

Breathing heavily, fatigued with the exertion, he fell on top of her, making sure his flaccid penis did not come near her vulva. As he pumped against her, their bodies made sticking, smacking sounds drawn from the blood covering them both.

Eyes closed, she moaned and twisted spasmodically under him as she struggled instinctively against pain and death.

"Fight, girlie," he murmured, pinning her harder like a wrestler. "Try to get away."

The flowing blood excited him. He wanted to tear open her body and drink it directly from her heart. Instead, he sat up, straddling her and rubbing her blood over the clean areas of his own body as if the liquid were a lotion. Then he picked up the scissors once more and snipped pieces of skin from about her breasts. Using both hands to force the blades to slide past each other, he cut off the nipples and held them in his hands as if they were marbles. Finally, he stuffed them into her vagina, pushing the pieces of flesh as deep as his fingers would allow.

Now she lay absolutely still. He felt for a pulse. There was nothing, no beating rhythm, not even the slightest flicker of an eyelid, to signify life.

His own heart pounded with a triphammer beat. In a frenzy, he dropped his head between her legs and licked her inner thighs, again taking care not to brush against the vulva. Of a sudden, like a hungry dog over a chunk of meat, he bit deeply into the flesh, shaking his head violently from side to side.

An electrifying bolt shot through his body. He growled, he screamed and flailed his arms and stiffened his legs. Semen poured forth from his limp penis. He shuddered over and over again with relief and then reached out for the scissors lying next to him. With a final paroxysm of pleasure, he plunged it deep within her vagina.

Now he rested for a few minutes, his head reposing against her bloody thigh and facing the floor where he could see the semen mixed with blood on the gray concrete. He rubbed the liquids with his fingers, playing as a child would with wet sand.

It was time to clean up, wash the body and put it in a large plastic bag so that it wouldn't dirty the car. And then, with his new cautious method, avoid shopping centers for an out-of-the-way place.

He rose to his feet a little wobbly and stared at the body for a few moments. Again he felt sorrow that he would no longer have her for himself.

The telephone upstairs rang with a sudden sharpness that froze him in his tracks. For several moments he stood listening to the ringing, wondering who could be calling him. Then he dashed forward to the steps, if only to silence the noisy intrusion on his secret.

He slipped and slid on the wet surface. He flew in the air and screamed in pain even before he landed, sprawled on his back on the basement floor. He lay still, groaning. The telephone continued ringing. He felt his naked body, groping all over to determine whether any bones were broken. If so, he wondered how he'd be able to get rid of the corpse and return the patrol car.

Still the telephone rang, ten, twelve, fourteen times. Who was it?

"Stop!" he screamed.

With pain so severe he cried out anew, he struggled to his feet but crawled up the stairs, dripping her blood in his wake. At the top of the stairs, he rested for a moment, holding his head in his hands. Then with a great effort, he lunged for the telephone.

"Bill," the voice said, "I was worried about you. You haven't been at work for the past couple of days.

Mary Ann Austin, you crazy Southern bitch, he wanted to shout. Why don't you leave me alone? Instead, he breathlessly greeted her, explaining that he'd been ill.

"Not so much that you couldn't sign out for a weekend cruiser," she joked.

He joined in her laughter. "I picked it up Friday night, Mary Ann. You know my own car. I've got to save wear and tear on it."

"I was hoping you'd take me for a ride in either one, Bill."

He paused, now hating the very sound of her voice. "Give me a couple of days. I'm still a bit woozy."

When he hung up he deliberated how to drop Mary Ann before anything started. He believed that he no longer needed a cover since he made up his mind to leave town soon.

First things first, he thought. There was the pressing matter of taking care of the body in the basement. But he was in too much pain to move it tonight. Tomorrow would be soon enough. That meant he'd have to keep the cruiser another day. He'd call the motor pool, explaining that he was sick and in a lot of pain. After all, it wouldn't be as if he were lying.

TWELVE

"Vinnie, on four," Perkins shouted from across the squad room.

Vincent Imperateri looked at the telephone bank light blinking impatiently. He knew that whatever it was, it couldn't be good news. He never seemed to get any good news, or good feelings anymore, except when he was with Marie. Now he felt that he just couldn't take on any more responsibility, any more worries of the world.

He reached for the telephone but stopped, his hand suspended in midair while his mind debated. Suppose he didn't answer it, got up, put on his jacket and walked out. For good. What would happen? Suppose everybody did that, what then?

Sighing, taking a deep breath as though readying for a dive in water, he snatched up the receiver to hear the voice of Dr. Julian Stone. Good, Imperateri thought. He'd been meaning to contact the doctor to talk over a continuing problem with him and his wife.

"Sergeant, your police have arrested my private detective," Stone said, his voice brimming with indignation. "Instead of working on murder cases, they're harassing law-abiding citizens."

"I'm sorry, Dr. Stone. I just heard about it myself. It seems that your man doesn't have a license. Under the law, private investigators have to be licensed and undergo a security check. But look, I'm glad you called. I have to see you."

A moment later, Imperateri rang off, glad that he was going to deal with the Stones directly now rather than drag it out. As he left headquarters building and drove to the Stone's motel, he turned over in his mind the points of friction he had with them.

It was not as if he had ever expected a good working relationship to continue for long. Misunderstandings and differences of opinion were sure to arise. But it was time to tell them to get off his back. Of course it wasn't their problem that he considered himself out on a limb, meddling in Missing Persons business when there was no evidence of foul play. Nor did they know that he was in trouble enough with Captain Anderson and hardly needed any more headaches.

The Department had decided to conduct its own investigation of Anderson, and a day hardly passed that did not see the Captain drop subtle hints about the sergeant's support before an Internal Affairs hearing. It appeared that Anderson had already rewarded Noseworthy and Perkins for their pledges of silence. Both men had received merit pay increases and departmental commendations for breaking two routine homicides.

As for the Stones, Imperateri was perturbed by the way they had proceeded on their own, ignoring him and other police and detectives. They had hired a private detective and sought out the services of a psychic. Then they went on a media blitz, with newspaper and television interviews and with taping advertisements making a direct appeal to the public for help.

Imperateri believed that it was not beyond them to keep valuable information to themselves. It was, he felt, a combination of Jewish aggressiveness and a doctor's wealth. Who else could afford such a campaign, including the posting of a reward for $100,000 for information leading to the return of their daughter?

He felt that the Stones were also unpredictable. At first they wailed their belief to the press that their daughter was dead. And then they did a complete turnabout, suddenly undertaking the search for her, an unspoken denial from them that they had ever given up hope.

Imperateri's own best hope, questioning her worlds-apart boyfriends, one a preppie and the other a beer-guzzling motorcyclist, led nowhere. If Susan were indeed the lust-murderer's

107

latest victim, all Imperateri could hope for was that someone had witnessed the body-dumping.

He now pulled his car into the court of the motel where the Stones had converted a room into a combined command post and home since coming down from New Jersey more than three weeks ago. Had it been that long since the girl had disappeared? Imperateri wondered, shaking his head.

Several times he had brought up the possiblity that Susan had run away, and each time they had rejected it angrily. Last week he had pursued a line of questioning with them. beginning with whether she had ever run away before. Each question brought a denial, abrupt, imperative. No drugs, no problems at home or school with anybody or anything. Miss Perfection herself.

He knocked on their door and entered. They greeted him too coolly, he thought, then quickly chastised himself for looking too hard for a reason to quarrel with them.

The motel room, brightly lit and inexpensively furnished with imitation leather chairs, had been turned into an office. A collapsible cardboard file cabinet stood on top of a credenza, sharing space with papers, notebooks and a portable typewriter. On a corner of the floor was a pile of posters and flyers.

Imperateri had seen the flyers posted all over the city, but especially in the Foggy Bottom area where George Washington University was located. They were quite familiar to him, appearing daily in newspaper notices and showing a photograph of a smiling young woman with dark, model-pretty features. In large block letters above were the words, MISSING PERSON. Below, she was described as being five feet four inches tall, one hundred ten pounds, green-eyed. Following in smaller print was a description of the clothes she was last seen wearing, blue jeans and a bright yellow rain slicker.

Imperateri noted that the listed telephone to call with information was the Stones' motel room, not a police number as was the usual practice. It seemed as if the Stones had really given up on the police, he again thought, reminded of his mission.

He looked at the Stones, both of whom were seated on their respective twin bed. They were gaunt and their skins sallow. It amazed him how great stress could age the face, atrophying muscles around the eyes and mouth and causing sagging and wrinkling within such a short period of time. He decided to soft-pedal his remarks, keep his criticism low-key.

"Looks like you're becoming more and more organized," he said cheerfully. He pointed to a large loose-leaf binder on Mrs. Stone's lap. "What's that?"

"Everything," she said. "I've jotted down the names, addresses and telephone numbers of everyone who knew . . . knows Susan. The referrals have really accumulated. I'm now working on the possibility that she's in a hospital somewhere under another name."

"It's possible," Imperateri agreed, picking up a pile of photocopy sheets lying on a chair. He sat down, placing the pile on the floor, all the time wondering about the choice of words to use so as not to offend them.

"Dr. and Mrs. Stone," he began, "I understand why you're doing all that you can, but now things have become more of a hindrance than a help. That private detective you hired is an alcoholic who can't even deal with an errant husband in a divorce case."

"He came highly recommended, Sergeant," Julian Stone countered. "I'm sorry that you feel that way."

"And then there's that psychic. Let me tell you something. I've been in this business a long time and I've dealt with dozens of psychics. I never got any kind of a good lead from any of them. One time we had a missing rich kid, a suspected homicide. Three psychics got in on the act. They gave three different locations in town where the kid's body would be found. None panned out. The boy was picked up later in Hollywood, trying to break into show business."

Lois Stone burst in bitterly. "And what help do we get from the police? All of them, from Washington south to Virginia and north to New York, won't even bother to look for Susan because she's over eighteen. And the FBI doesn't want to become involved because there's no evidence of kidnapping or an interstate crime. Even the college campus police, bless their souls, have washed their hands of the matter. So who's going to help, Mr. Imperateri?"

"I'm sorry, Mrs. Stone. On top of the mental anguish, I know that all this is costing you so much money."

"My husband's a doctor and earns a great deal, but believe me, we're not rich. That reward money we put up we had to borrow."

"Mrs. Stone, I know the hell you're going through."

"Do you?" Lois Stone shot back. "Have you ever lost a child this way, or any way at all?"

"I've seen a lot of anguish, Mrs. Stone."

"But you've never felt it."

"Lois, he's only trying to help."

"A lot of help we've had so far."

"Lois, that's enough! It's not going to help, antagonizing him like that."

Imperateri raised a palm. "That's okay, Dr. Stone. Just let me say again that we really need more evidence than a parent's gut feeling and an eyewitness who saw Susan leave voluntarily. We just can't go off on a massive cross-jurisdictional search on that alone. The FBI demands good proof that a person is missing before it will put out something on its network."

Lois forced a short, smileless laugh. "The proof is that she's nowhere to be seen and nobody knows where she is. Thus it would seem that she's missing. What does the FBI want, a signed affidavit from her declaring her own disappearance?"

"Now, look, Mrs. Stone, you just can't dismiss the runaway business from the realm of possibility. Even if she weren't the type, suppose she became disenchanted about something and decided to travel around to sort out things. Happens to a lot of runaways."

Lois shook her head vehemently. "Even so, she would have called us. She wouldn't have wanted us to suffer. She'd have confided in me. Please believe me when we say she's in trouble, serious trouble."

Now it was Julian Stone's turn, speaking in a low but emotion-filled voice. "When we hear the word 'runaway' we feel like tearing out hair and screaming. The facts just won't bear out her running away. She had no clothing with her other than what she was wearing. Nothing is missing from her dormitory room."

"If she were going to visit you, she must have been carrying a suitcase," Imperateri said.

"No, Sergeant. She often came home without luggage, not even a toothbrush. She has everything at home, extra toothbrush, cosmetics, clothing. She said it didn't make sense to *shlep* stuff back and forth. And something else. If she was going to run away, she didn't do much planning, money-wise. She just had a few dollars."

"Credit cards?"

"We checked into that, Sergeant. Mastercard and Visa. We called their main offices and explained the situation. They promised to keep us posted. Up-to-date, no charges have been made."

"Susan is a nice girl," Lois Stone said, her voice close to cracking, her eyes tearing. "She took piano and voice lessons. She made good grades. She wrote poetry. Never a problem in high school with dope or sex or anything."

"Don't take offense, Mrs. Stone, but sometimes it's that kind of kid who takes off for the tall timber. Frankly, it's my feeling that if she'd just call you and let you know she's all right . . ."

"If," Lois interrupted, repeating the word in a sarcastic manner as though the thought were ridiculous.

". . .she could stay where she is for as long as she wants until she's ready to come home."

"I appreciate, Sergeant, your trying to make us feel better by insisting on your runaway theory. But why doesn't she call us?"

Imperateri looked down at his hands and studied them for several moments before he spoke. "She could have met somebody whom she feels is more important to her at this time. No matter how much you train a kid at home, an outside influence could change him or her from an obedient kid into a rebellious one." He hesitated once more before he continued, telling them about the motorcycle bum Susan had been seeing without their knowledge.

Julian and Lois exchanged a long look. Finally, Stone shook his head and began pacing the room. "What's this FBI network you mentioned?" he asked abruptly, changing the subject.

"The National Crime Information Center. It's a computer system that covers the fifty states."

"The FBI," Lois blurted out, "they should all take a long walk on a short pier."

At that moment Vincent Imperateri knew that it would be useless arguing with the Stones about the conduct of the case. He also knew that it was time to turn the whole matter back to Missing Persons, where it belonged. He rose simultaneously with the first ring of the telephone.

Stone snatched the receiver and listened quietly for several moments, his jaw dropping and his face draining of color.

"What's the matter, Julian?" Lois asked.

Stone cupped his hand over the receiver mouthpiece. "Sergeant," he whispered hoarsely, "this is a private call. I would appreciate . . ."

"I was just going," Imperateri said, heading for the door but willing to exchange a month's pay to learn what the call was about.

With Imperateri gone, Julian Stone spoke directly into the receiver. "I'm sorry. Would you mind repeating that?"

The voice on the other end was thick and deliberate, as though the caller made an effort to disguise it. "I'll be brief. If you want to see your daughter again, listen carefully. Take fifty thousand dollars in one hundred dollar bills to the Lincoln Plaza shopping center at twelve noon tomorrow. You will use a shopping bag for the money. Drop it in the trash can in front of the five and ten. Then leave. One hour later, you will have your daughter, safe and sound. No police and no tricks, or you will be sorry."

The telephone clicked and a dial tone came on. Stone still held the receiver to his ear, if only to feel closer to Susan. The telephone for the briefest of moments had been a link to her, albeit through the man who was her captor. The only barrier now to having her back was money. A simple solution.

"Lois!" he shouted.

"I'm right here."

He twirled around. She stood holding on to a dresser for support, almost like a lifeless statue, drained of color save for the redness around the eyes.

He told her about the call and of his plan to follow the ransom demands to the letter. When he was through, instead of the enthusiastic support he expected there was only silence and a continuous shaking of her head.

"What's wrong with you, Lois?"

"The police. What about them? Aren't you going to tell them?"

He waved a hand in an abrupt manner. "You're the one who's been ranting about them. Who needs them now?"

"But this is different, Julian. A new element . . ."

"Their main interest is catching the criminal. Ours is getting Susan back safely."

"No, Julian. It's not the right way. We need help from the police. Advice on what to do. And protection."

"You've changed your tune. I'm saying they're lazy public workers just like all the rest of the civil servants. If we just follow the kidnapper's wishes in a calm, rational way, we'll see this through."

He watched her continue to shake her head and again tried to convince her. "You read about it in the newspapers. Too many times the police panic the kidnappers into killing their victims. I don't want Imperateri mucking about when Susan's life is at stake."

"*You* don't want?" she repeated incredulously. "What about me?" Did it ever occur to you to ask what I want?"

He was taken aback. He hadn't expected opposition from her, at least not about something like this. "Please let me handle this alone. I don't think you ought to be worrying about all the details. God knows, you've been through enough."

"So have you."

Her reply was said with bitterness, and he accepted it as a rebuke to mean that *I'm no less a person than you and if you could take the pain so can I.*

He walked over to her and placed a hand on her shoulder. "I promise to call the police as soon as Susan is safe at home."

She turned away, shaking her head.

"All right, then," he said, his tone caustic, accusing. "Have it your way. Let her death be on your head."

Julian Stone drove into the shopping center at ten minutes to the noon hour and pulled to a stop about a dozen yards from the five and ten. When he saw the trash can he couldn't suppress a sigh. The can was overflowing with newspapers, empty cartons and beer and soft drink cans. There seemed to be no space for the bulky shopping bag stuffed with five hundred crisp one hundred dollar bills.

He had spent the previous hours feverishly rushing to several banks, waiting until they verified his account at his New Jersey bank, and then exchanging checks and monies to gather enough of the century notes to satisfy the ransom. That was the easy part. The hardest was dealing with Lois, convincing her that the police would be more of a threat than anything else. He knew that he hadn't persuaded her to believe that, only frightened her into letting him have his way.

And now he was faced with the problem of an overstuffed trash can. Ridiculous, he thought, not amused at the lightness of the situation after all that he had been through.

Should he remove some of the trash to make room for the bag? Suppose someone saw his curious behavior and investigated and found the bag with its contents.

Carrying the bag, Stone got out of the car and approached the can. Around him mothers marched with rebellious pre-school youngsters. He waited until he was absolutely sure no one was observing him before he thrust an arm into the receptacle and pulled out a soggy sack of beer cans which he carefully placed on the ground. Then he took his own bag and shoved it hard into the can, not too deep but high and visible enough so that the kidnapper could spot it.

Returning to the car, Stone waited, a new concern occupying

his mind. The trash removal company could come well before the kidnapper showed. On the other hand, Stone couldn't stay to protect the money because the kidnapper might be waiting for him to leave. He realized he had no choice. He twisted the ignition key.

THIRTEEN

When he returned from the motel Vincent Imperateri saw the note that Captain Anderson wanted to see him on urgent business. Imperateri had an inkling that it had to be either one of two reasons, another scolding about the rape case impasse, or another entreaty to remain silent before the Internal Affairs panel. If the former, Imperateri could expect a frown followed by an oral dressing down, while the latter could bring obsequious grins and whining tones. So when Imperateri entered the captain's office he studied his boss's face for some sort of a clue, but could find nothing. Anderson's face, usually a barometer of his feelings, was totally blank. Imperateri wondered whether both reasons cancelled out each other's expression.

"Sergeant," Anderson began, "I just wanted to tell you I'm in your corner. The bastards wanted to ream your ass but I wouldn't let them."

Imperateri's head tilted back in an inquiring manner.

"The chief's meeting," Anderson explained. "The rape cases came up for discussion. They wanted your head on a platter but I wouldn't hear of it."

Sure, you lying bastard, Imperateri said to himself. He was convinced that the captain was now going into his windup for the pitch asking for support.

"Look, Vincent. You remember what I asked you a few weeks ago? Well, the chief went ahead and ordered Internal Affairs to move fast on those phony charges against me. Someone's going to come around to talk to you. I hope you're not going to forget what you promised."

Imperateri stood at the desk, his palms pressed hard on it for support, and his body leaning over so far that his face was a little more than a foot away from Anderson's. "Captain, I'm afraid I gave you the wrong impression. I never said I was going to lie for you."

Anderson, jaw set like a belligerent bulldog, pushed his face even closer, forcing Imperateri to jerk back to avoid the sour smell of alcohol. Anderson spoke, his voice harsh, aggravated, though barely above a whisper.

"You know what's going to happen? The whole department's going to be torn apart over this. Worse yet, I'm going to be made a scapegoat for all the racial tension here. They've got an excuse to kick me out and put a Black man in my place."

"Oh, come on, Captain. You're getting paranoid."

Anderson shook his head rapidly. "The newspapers, the television, they're always trying to stir up some racial bullshit. It sells papers."

The captain shook his head several more times and closed his eyes. When he re-opened them, they appeared bloodshot, tired. "Vincent, I'm asking for a favor."

Imperateri stood straight and stepped back several paces. "If I don't tell the truth this time, how are you going to believe anything I'll tell you next time?"

Anderson guffawed. "I don't give a sparrow's shit about that. Look, if you play the role of a miss goody two shoes, the homicide squad will lose, the department will lose, and the whole goddamn city will lose."

Now it was Imperateri's turn to laugh. "The whole republic, too?"

Anderson shook his head sadly, failing to see any humor. "Just think about the repercussions, Vincent. Everything hangs on what you're going to say. All right?"

Imperateri backed still further away, almost like a subject leaving a royal presence, only the sergeant had absolutely no respect for the captain. Without saying anything further, he left.

Noseworthy greeted him in the squad room with eyes bulging

and jaw hanging low. "Get your coat on. We got that Thanksgiving homicide you've been looking for."

Even in the wind and cold, the odor was overwhelming. Acrid and fierce, it dominated the alley like another element of the weather, forcing a visitor to hasten through any business and leave lest he fall victim to its force.

Vincent Imperateri fought a strong impulse to hold his nose. He wished he could close his eyes as well, shutting out the garbage strewn about, the fish heads and tails, the broken shards of winos' bottles, the offal of cats and rats, and the dog droppings slowly decomposing in the pools of water.

"For Christ's sake," Noseworthy said, "doesn't the sanitation department ever come here?"

Imperateri shrugged. "Would you?"

The two men made their way through a knot of Black children and nodded to a single uniformed officer stationed at the entrance to the alley. They trudged forward to where another officer stood, about twenty yards away. Nearby a patrol car idled, its top light whirling and flashing impatiently, as though unaccustomed to a stationary role.

"The medical examiner's on his way," the second officer said.

"Where's everybody else?" Imperateri asked, already knowing the answer. If this had happened in white Georgetown, or affluent Chevy Chase, the place would be crawling with dozens of cops and reporters. And if the victim were a white girl, TV crews would have shot every conceivable angle and interviewed dozens of neighbors, just as they'd done in the Kitty Burns case. But it was only a little Black kid, dead in a poverty pocket of the inner city, most likely killed by another Black. This wasn't news to the white folks of Washington. Nor were the Black ones particularly interested. Crime was so prevalent and ubiquitous that only the absence of it was news to them.

It would be welcome news only for the Stones who would be relieved to know that it wasn't their daughter who was the victim of the lust-murderer.

But was it the lust-murderer this time?

Imperateri drew a deep breath as he looked. Stuffed in a wire barrel brimmed with trash was the body, drooping over slightly like a limp jack-in-the-box. The child's head, twisted to one side, and part of the naked torso were visible at the top of the can, and the arms dangled over the rim.

Imperateri guessed that she had been dead for only a short time and that death was due to stab wounds he could see near her undeveloped breasts. Leaning still closer, he noted the darker bruises barely visible on the dark skin. Even the face, strangely frozen serene in what must have been a terrifying death, bore marks of a beating.

"Same MO as the rape maniac?" Noseworthy asked.

"I doubt it," Imperateri replied, looking at the ground around the can. Grooves, some deep in the dirt soil and some smudged over, appeared as if someone had stood and struggled with a weight. Some of the grooves had a distinctive look, chopped vertical lines on the soles and unbroken horizontal ones on the heels.

Imperateri jogged back to the cruiser and searched in the trunk. There were several attache cases containing rape kits, crayons for outlining bodies, body shrouds, plastic bags for evidence and to pack bloodied clothing, glassine envelopes, and ropes for cordoning off crime scenes. But the shovel was missing. Taken, he guessed, for some officer's personal use.

Back at the site, he addressed Noseworthy. "See if you find a shovel at some neighbor's. I want as much of this ground as possible before anyone tramples on it." He turned to the officer. "Give me the name and address of the boy who found her. I want to look at his shoes."

Andre Jones turned out to be more of a man than a boy. Although lean, his folded arms, expressing hostility, were large and sinewy. He wore a black T-shirt which also revealed massive shoulders and chest, and a floppy hat that seemed to accentuate rather than mask his sullen mien.

Imperateri had radioed to learn that Andre Jones was sixteen years old and had a rap sheet which included everything from housebreaking to rape of a minor. Before arriving at the Jones home, the detective had told Noseworthy that the case would be closed by the end of the day.

Both detectives sat with the youth in a once-proud single family house now carved into a multiple family dwelling. The living room had a grimy, worn-down cast, with furniture fissured by age and use.

Imperateri began by questioning Andre about details of his finding the body. All of the time the detective glanced at the youth's shoes, expensive running ones, new and with padded collars, tongues and Achilles. Finally, Imperateri pointed to them.

"Where'd you rip those off, Andre?"

"Shit, man, I bought 'em."

"I know you don't have a job, Andre."

"My mama give me some green."

"We want to talk with her," Noseworthy said. "Is she here?"

"She working."

"Got a call about stolen shoes," Noseworthy continued. "You hand them over to me, I take them back. No questions asked. You don't, I book you on suspicion."

Andre Jones looked at Noseworthy, then at Imperateri, and finally at his shoes. He sighed and bent down to unlace them. "Take the motherfuckers."

Outside, Imperateri told Noseworthy to watch the house. "I'm running over to the station to match his shoes with the grooves. I'll get a warrant, too."

"Andre's our man?"

Imperateri nodded. "But he's not the lust-killer. We're still overdue another victim."

The arrest warrant for Andre Jones completed, Vincent Imperateri looked up from his desk to find his daughter staring quietly at him. How long she had stood there he didn't know, but he knew that something was wrong. Judy never visited him unless it was important, her last crisis being a temporary expulsion from school for smoking in the girls' room. For a fifteen-year-old, that offense wasn't too serious. He'd been thankful that with all of the drug and sex outrages, it could have been worse.

She smiled and plopped down on his desk, her long jean-covered legs dangling over the side. Her hair, much lighter than his, framed a round, pretty-girl face that wouldn't age too noticeably until she was well into her fifties.

"Hello, Judy." He rose to kiss and hug her. "No school today?"

"It's some sort of teachers' meeting," she said, looking down at the floor, as though to avert his disbelieving look.

If she'd merely skipped school, let that be the worst of her transgressions, he thought, again grateful for a minor sin. But her running around with freaky types was a different matter. He'd talked to her about that in the past, but the talks always came out as lectures, pious, sanctimonious, ignored at best, self-defeating at worst. He'd once told her that it was harder to live a bad life than a good one. She had laughed at him, and then apologized, saying that he sounded like one of those over-enunciating ministers on Sunday morning television.

"Everything all right at school?" he asked.

"Everything all right at headquarters?" she relied, more in a teasing than smart-alecky manner, and then laughed. "It's a real drag, Dad." She smiled again. "Catch any big criminals lately? What about that sex fiend? You on that case?"

Imperateri hesitated before answering. He'd never taken his work home to Beth, feeling a kinship with jurors who are sworn to silence. He now saw no reason to tell Judy anything. Maybe that was why the marriage with Beth didn't last. She never understood what his work entailed, never appreciated why he had to skip dinners and work extra shifts.

He lit a cigarette. "Well, honey, I'm not the only detective working on the case."

Her eyes widened. "But I bet you'll be the one to find the killer. Wait 'til I tell my friends."

At first he wanted to ask her not to, having a vague feeling that some harm could possibly come to her for having that knowledge. What the hell, he decided, let her brag about her old man. Christ, but there was nothing to brag about.

She pointed to his cigarette and then to the overflowing ashtray on the desk. "Dad, you smoke too much and I bet you're still drinking coffee all day. It's not good for you, for your ulcer."

"Your mother told you about that, huh? Well, Judy, it's like this. The more exhausted and frustrated I get, the more I do it." Then why do you do it? he asked himself. You've already ruined your family and your health. What next? It's not for nothing that cops are offered retirement after only serving twenty years.

"Hey," he said, "how's your mother?"

Judy said nothing, turning her head away. A tear formed at the corner of her eye. Imperateri reached out to dab it gently, now guessing the reason for her visit.

"I bet you two aren't getting along."

"Oh, Daddy," she blurted out, "let me stay with you."

He laughed and shook his head. "Honey, you know why you can't. What kind of father would I be to you? You know about cops."

She ignored him, spilling out a litany of words against her mother. "Since all of those rapes, she's made a virtual prisoner of me. She's on my back all of the time. She wants a timetable of where I'm going and who with."

"With whom," he corrected. "How're you going to go to college if you ain't talking good?"

"You're always joking around. Just tell Mom that I'm smart enough to take care of myself."

"Maybe, but your mother just happens to be right. There's a psychopathic killer loose. When he gets the urge, he kills. Young girls happen to be his weakness." Imperateri paused, and with sigh of resignation, continued. "I just know he's got the next one planned right now." Again, he paused, chilled by his own words, by the seeming deliberateness of the lust-killer's morbid drive.

Judy stepped back, wiping a tear away. "You can't wrap every girl in a cocoon. You can't keep your kids in the house and behind closed doors. You can't have a policeman with everyone all of the time."

Imperateri lit another cigarette and puffed a couple of times before replying. "I don't know what words of wisdom you say to parents to protect their kids. But what I can say to a kid is just to be careful. And sometimes even being careful isn't enough. You've got to be scared. Look, I'll talk with your mother about it. Maybe there's a middle way."

She smiled and pecked him lightly on the cheek. "I knew you'd see things my way. You're so understanding, just like you were when Rusty died. Do you remember how terrible I felt? I couldn't eat or sleep or do anything."

"You were much younger."

"I cried all of the time. I wanted to die, myself."

"That's because you felt guilty. You let Rusty outside and he was hit by a car." He recalled how he restrained himself for criticizing her for violating the law by allowing the dog to roam at large. No legal punishment could have hurt her as much as the consequence of her action.

Judy stared blankly as she spoke. "I was the one who found him lying in the street, dying and moaning. You should have heard him whine. That sound will never leave me." Now she looked him squarely in the face. "You offered to get me another dog but I didn't want one to take Rusty's place. And you talked to me all of the time, trying to help me. I must have been in pretty bad shape."

"Judy, when a family pet dies, it hits a kid the hardest. It's usually the first time a kid has to face up to the death of someone loved."

"Oh, Dad, you're so smart. Let's have some more talks, okay?" Once more she kissed him. She bid him goodbye and disappeared before he could turn to watch her leave.

He was left with Andre Jone's warrant and the stack of death photographs at the edge of his desk, a constant reminder when he didn't need one.

Andre Jones stared in shocked surprise at the two detectives standing in his doorway. When he recovered his senses, he turned to call out in the direction of the kitchen.

"Ain't nothin', Mama. Just a coupla friends."

"Glad to know you think of us like that, Andre," Noseworthy said, pushing past the youth and setting a brief case down on the floor. He looked at Andre's stockinged feet. "Didn't have time to rip off another pair?"

"Shit, man. My closet's full of 'em."

"Andre," Imperateri said, "you'd better call your mother in. We've got some important business to talk about." The business was a reading of Andre's rights before the arrest, based on incriminating evidence the detectives had found.

Andre's mother already stood at the living room entrance. She was a large woman, obese to the point of grotesqueness but she moved with the lightness and grace sometimes seen in the over-weight. She looked the detectives up and down, and then glared at her son.

"What you do now, boy?"

"Nothin', Mama. They just visitin'."

"Mrs. Jones," Noseworthy said, "we checked Andre's record with the juvenile division. He beat and raped a four-year-old girl last year and was ordered to undergo psychiatric treatment. Did he ever go?"

Mrs. Jones beamed, "Oh, is that all you want? Well, sir, Andre went for a while, but I'll get on him to go back. Ain't no problem at all. Sorry to see you come all this way for that little trouble."

Noseworthy glanced at Imperateri and then looked back at the youth. "Andre, tell your mother what you did to little Francine."

The mother's eyes flew open with rage. Her mouth widened to say something but all she could do was to fall down on a chair. When she spoke, her voice carried tears of anger and shame, rising to a wail.

"Andre, you do that? Tell me you didn't do that to that poor little Francine. Tell me, Andre."

"Didn't do nothin'. Somebody puttin' out shit."

"Andre," Noseworthy said, "your shoe treads were found around that trash can."

"Sure. That's because I take out the trash. Don' I, Mama?"

Noseworthy opened the briefcase and pulled out a child's underwear, boots and tan leotards. "Look, Andre, we found these buried in your backyard. And this, too." Out came a lunchbox and several books. "They belonged to Francine but your fingerprints are all over them."

Andre guffawed and shook his head back and forth. "Shit, that don' mean nothin'. Somebody put it there. Somebody set me up."

"Where's the knife, Andre?" Imperateri asked.

"What knife you talkin' about?"

"The one that you used to stab Francine nineteen times in the chest."

Andre shook his head again and slunk into his chair. Of a sudden, his mother jumped to her feet, swept across the room and walloped him on the side of the head.

"Answer the man why you stab Francine nineteen times!"

Andre, shocked by the blow, screamed back. "Because she wouldn't stop yellin'!"

Imperateri and Noseworthy exchanged glances, knowing that their work was over. It had been a piece of cake, a small boost to compensate for the lack of progress on the lust killings.

As they hustled the shoeless Andre into the back seat of their car, a radio message from Perkins elevated their mood even further. A witness claimed to have seen someone, maybe the lust-murderer, carry off a body in a deserted area.

FOURTEEN

Holding the shopping bag with one hand and the motel room key with the other, Julian Stone pushed his way in and found Lois sitting listlessly at the television. On the screen a contestant on a game show held up her hands to her face and squealed as she was being declared a winner.

"He didn't call?" Stone asked.

Lois looked at him in a disgusted, knowing way for several moments and then returned her eyes to the set. "Of course not."

"Bastard, filthy bastard."

"I could have told you that. We've been taken by some con artist."

"No, I got the money back."

"The money," she repeated, her voice ringing with sarcasm. "I could have told you it was a hoax."

"Please," he snapped, "no second-guessing, no lectures. You were just as anxious as I to go through with this."

"I wanted to go to the police. And I didn't want to be stuck here, going crazy out of my mind waiting to hear something from you, or from *him*. Mr. Imperateri could have handled the whole thing. He could have spared us some more misery."

Stone shook his head wearily, not in disagreement with her, but in disgust and anger with himself for allowing himself to be taken in by an obviously phony ransom call. After he had left the shopping center, he raced back to the hotel to await the expected telephone call. For three hours he and Lois had paced the room, too nervous to sit, or to do anything else. But still no response had come from the unknown caller.

Stone had worried. Did he get the instructions mixed up? Was he supposed to hang around the shopping center or return to the motel? Try as he had, he couldn't recall what the kidnapper had said, or whether the man had ever said anything about the matter at all.

With hope fading fast that he would hear from the kidnapper, he had instructed Lois to remain by the telephone while he returned to the center. Speeding there, he had spent another hour lurking discreetly not far from the trash can, anxiously eyeing each approaching vehicle and pedestrian. Finally, when he had realized that nothing was going to happen, he retrieved the shopping bag. The money was untouched.

Now he looked at Lois from across the room. She appeared shrunken, shrivelled, looking much older than her young years. He knew that he looked just as bad to her. How long could they go on like this?

"If only this thing could be resolved one way or the other," he said suddenly, without thinking. "We could go on with our life and our work. Right now we're in some sort of limbo."

She stared incredulously at him. "What do you mean, one way or another? You've already given up?"

He closed his eyes and nodded, blinking away moisture that had gathered under the lids. "I think she really is dead."

"Oh, Julian, don't say that. I couldn't go on if that's really so."

"Lois, Lois, she may not be alive anymore. Maybe if we think that, and it turns out to be so, the pain may be less for us. And if we should ever find her alive, we'll have that much more reason to be overjoyed."

"You're giving up!" she shouted. "You want to abandon her. It's your fault she's in trouble in the first place. You didn't want to buy her a car for her use. You said it would spoil her, hurt her school grades. So she had to go begging like a pauper's daughter for a ride home."

Stone knew that Lois would take offense at anything he'd say. Her nerves were shot. He understood. But he couldn't let her fall further down a hopeless abyss. "Lois,' he said, "we've got to face reality. We can't go on living in this motel forever, chasing down phony tips. Soon it'll be time to go back home and pick up with our own lives."

She shook her head violently. "Never! I'll never give up!"

He approached her with arms outstretched. "Lois, I promise you. I won't give up, too." He held her close, rocking to and fro, whispering words of support and encouragement.

The sudden jangling of the telephone made them both tremble with renewed expectation. He scampered to the end table and stopped, now fearful of lifting the telephone. He looked at Lois, as though asking for permission to answer. With a perspiring hand, he picked up the receiver and heard the muffled tones of the kidnapper's voice.

"Did you follow my instructions?"

Stone shook his head rapidly as if the caller could see him. "You didn't pick up the bag. I came back after three hours and it was still there."

"That's because there were too many people around."

"What the hell did you expect in a shopping center at high noon, Death Valley?"

"This is too serious a matter for jokes. I'm going to give you one more chance."

"And I'm going to give you a chance to prove that you have my daughter. Either let me talk with her or you pass on a question that I know only she could answer."

There was a pause, and then the man cleared his throat. "I'm afraid I can't do that."

"You can't because you don't have my daughter. Don't tie up the line. The real kidnapper may be trying to reach me." Stone slammed the receiver into its cradle.

Lois looked on with shock. "Julian, how could you be so sure he wasn't the kidnapper? Maybe he just couldn't arrange to put Susan on because she's with an accomplice some place else."

"If I'm wrong and he's telling the truth, he'll call back again."

"Then you could string him along and have the police put a tracer or something on him."

The pressure finally exerted its toll on Stone. He exploded.

"I'm not interested in tracking down some sick-minded bastard. I'm only interested in finding my daughter."

Lois retrieved her coat from the closet and picked up her purse. "Up to now," she said, "you've had things your way. Well, I'm going to see Mr. Imperateri and apologize. I'm going to tell him what happened and beg him to come back on the case."

"If that's what you wish . . ."

"After all, Julian, you wouldn't want him to practice medicine on your patients."

A knock on the door sounded loud and insistent. Stone, his anger still boiling over, shouted, "Who's there?"

"Imperateri."

Stone flung open the door, but it was Lois who greeted the detective. She then quickly poured out words recounting the episode about the ransom.

Imperateri nodded knowingly. "Forget about that cheap extortionist. We can also forget about the runaway business. Somebody saw a man carrying away a girl dressed like your daughter."

As dusk began to submerge daylight, lights could be seen flickering from living room windows in the development far across the field. At another end of the field, a densely-wooded area had already surrendered to the encroaching darkness. Despite the lack of light, dozens of men and women equipped with whistles and walkie-talkies swept alongside the woods. Another team made up of dogs and their handlers pierced through the woods, accompanied by news reporters and television crews.

At a makeshift command post, consisting of a cardtable, folding chairs and a portable water canteen, a man flapped his arms repeatedly to keep warm. He was Prince Georges County Sheriff Elwood Garth who wore only overalls and a flannel shirt to protect himself from the bitter cold. He did not wear his topcoat or uniform on dirty assignments inasmuch as the county would not reimburse him if the clothing were torn or soiled.

Nearby, a fire burned in a metal barrel but frequent changes

of wind direction blew smoke unpredictably, forcing him to
sacrifice warmth for cold but fresh air. A rope, tied to one leg of
the table and to a sapling about twenty-yards away, held a sign
proclaiming NO ADMITTANCE CRIME SCENE SEARCH AREA.

Julian Stone, approaching with Vincent Imperateri, looked at
the sign and wondered how it was going to stop anyone from entering the massive tract of land at other points. As Garth beckoned them to the fire, Stone listened to the man's peculiar
Maryland country accent, a strange mixture of Southern
inflection and the harsh urban consonants of Baltimore.

"After a couple, three days," Sheriff Garth said, "it's awful
hard to pick up a scent. And what you got here is a subject been
missing for, what, a couple, three weeks?"

"Our witness sighted her two weeks ago," Imperateri said.

Stone bit his lip. Fourteen whole days. What would be left of
her? He tried to recall pathology courses taken what seemed to
be a lifetime ago. Would he be able to recognize her through the
decomposition, the weathering? But there had been no heat and
no rain to burn away or molder the flesh. No ants this time of
year to hasten nature's way. The ravages of animals? Raccoons,
maybe. Magpies? No, not around here.

Again Stone bit a lip, drawing blood this time from the wind-
chapped lip as he visualized large black birds feasting on a human body. His Susan. Or was it?

If only the police would have acted sooner. If only that woman
witness would have reported immediately to the police what she
had seen. It was only after widespread circulation of the flyers
that she did recall the incident.

While picking wild plants and walking her dog, she saw a man
in the distance carrying an unconscious girl. The girl wore a
bright yellow slicker.

All he could hope for was that it wasn't Susan.

"What the shit, it's worth the try," Garth continued. "This
place is pretty thick, even in winter, and you could easily miss
seeing something, especially now it's getting dark, but my dogs'
noses, they're damn sensitive. Anything's out there, they'll pick
it up."

Stone said nothing. He began to amble away, towards the woods. He wanted to be by himself. He wanted to be far from their slips-of-tongue, and their embarrassed, apologetic mumbling. He thought of what Garth had said to his officers and volunteers at the beginning of the search:

"We have information that the missing subject may be in this area. If you should encounter a gravesite, it is incumbent upon you to preserve said gravesite until experts have perused. Now, don't leave no square foot uncovered until you know there's nothing there."

Saying that, he had split them off into two groups, marching east and west. He then turned to Imperateri and Stone. "Good thing there's no snow to cover the stiff," he said, immediately noting the pained expression on Stone's face. "Sorry, Doc."

Stone might have forgiven him that but for another statement he'd made bare minutes earlier. "Good thing it's been ball-freezing cold. Might preserve the stiff."

Imperateri had looked at Stone with an expression begging him to ignore the sheriff. At that moment, Stone had realized how much he liked Imperateri. The detective's sheer force and support seemed to flow into the doctor like an electric wave, giving him strength.

Now he heard Imperateri call after him as he shuffled away.

"Don't go too far. We may be finished here at any time now."

Still facing forward, Stone waved a hand over a shoulder to indicate that he'd heard the advice. As he strode, he did not poke through the overgrown weeds nor peer along the pathway through screens of bare scrub oak branches. The area had already been combed by the searchers. Besides, he did not want to be the one to find the body.

He recalled being with her once in a similar field, only then the soft breezes of spring blew as he and Susan walked off the effects of a large picnic while Lois was content to read under a tree. Approaching the edge of a wood, Susan, then thirteen, spoke of how the trees reminded her of a story she had read about a poor little orphan lost in a thicket.

"You have to stop reading those sad, sentimental stories," he told her. "You're getting too big for that sort of thing."

"They're only stories," she replied.

"But you take them too seriously. You know, there comes a time when you have to grow up."

"I know, Daddy, but what's the sense of rushing it? You can never be young again."

He laughed heartily.

"Do you really think my tastes are immature, Daddy? After all, if anyone should know, it's you. You're a pediatrician."

"Don't give me credit for things I may not know. If you prefer to hang posters on your wall of little cartoon animals rather than rock stars, I guess that's a matter of taste. There are plenty of grown-ups who'd prefer to look at Bambi rather than painted-up freaks."

She looked up at him. "I know you're trying to make me feel better about being immature. But you're right. I guess I should begin growing up."

"You're mature enough," he replied. "Keep loving your cartoon characters, your teddy bears and Prince Charmings. Life is hard and sometimes cruel. If you can find a bit of softness and kindness somewhere, hold on to it as long as you can. Just remember that some people aren't too nice and some downright wicked, just like in your stories. If you could be tough to handle the tough people, and soft for the nice ones, you'd have learned a lot."

She said nothing in return. It appeared to Stone that she was deeply impressed by what he said. In the years to come, she continued being a warm, gentle child. Yet there were times when she would turn into a cool, hard person, as shown by her handling of the insane trucker on the turnpike. He had hoped that this combination of traits would enable her to survive whatever befell her.

His meditation was broken by the sound of his name being called from the distance by Imperateri. He turned slowly, disturbed by the interruption. The detective beckoned by waving an arm quickly and repeatedly.

Stone felt a surge of fear and excitement grip his inner body like a vise. They found something. What else could cause Imperateri to shout so and signal so frantically?

Stone ran, skirting the ground holes and leaping small bushes with the determination of a young track hurdler. And while he ran, thoughts raced through his mind.

They found someone. Susan. Pray God that she is not the unconscious girl in the yellow slicker seen by the eyewitness. And if she is, could she have survived the weeks of bitter cold in the open?

With Imperateri and Sheriff Garth, he followed the cackling walkie-talkie near the banks of a frozen creek. Several volunteers holding lanterns circled around a spot covered with underbrush. Already a police photographer snapped a camera, recording a body wrapped in a yellow rain slicker.

Stone, his breath coming in gasps, pushed through the circle. He fell to his knees.

FIFTEEN

It was a sound that Vincent Imperateri would not forget. Animal-like in its intensity, human in its emotion, the cry emitted through the lips of Julian Stone was so long and sustained that it seemed to freeze the marrow in Imperateri's bones.

The detective stood transfixed for several moments, unable to tear his eyes away from the sight before him. Sour spittle pushed between his teeth, and his hands trembled at first with tearful emotion, and then with fury, and finally, with fear. He could not help picture the face of his own daughter upon the body lying so helplessly, all twisted up like a ragged doll with a yellow slicker for a shroud.

Judy, it could have been her. Maybe next time it will be her.

Imperateri shook the thought from his mind and watched as Stone knelt over the body, at first cradling and rocking it, murmuring soft words that were hardly intelligible. Then the doctor began treating the body as if it were a live patient in his examining room. With a silent scream of anguish on his face, he frantically felt for a pulse, squeezed and shook the lower jaw, and then pulled back the eyelids to reveal filmed-over marbles.

"She's gone, Dr. Stone," Imperateri said, pulling gently on Stone's arm. He thought that the doctor shouldn't be doing that. He was ruining possible evidence. But what evidence? The killer never left any. Let the poor father be with his daughter.

Stone now smoothed the body's tangled hair, combing it with his fingers. Imperateri now realized that the doctor was in shock. Turning towards Garth, he spoke softly.

"He's gone off the deep end. Could some of your people take him to the Washington Hospital Center?"

A few moments after three officers bodily lifted and dragged Stone away, Imperateri hunkered down to study the body. It was lying on its left side, half-ridden by dried-out leaves.

Carefully removing the raincoat, he noted the defensive wounds on her hands and forearms, just like in the other homicides. He knew that she had suffered the kind of excessive violence the psychiatrist called a rage type of reaction.

The body was fully dressed. That, and the fact it wasn't left in the usual froglike position in the trash bin, suggested to Imperateri that the killer sought to change his MO. One similarity to the other cases was that she had already been dead when dumped.

Imperateri swallowed several times, trying to force the sickness within him from erupting. Concentrate on the problem, he ordered himself. It was his job. Note and analyze every detail, and if you don't understand it, memorize and think about it until you will.

The gruff voice of Garth interrupted his thoughts. "Don't nobody touch nothing," the sheriff ordered, pushing everyone away with the dedication of a young traffic cop the first day on the job. Garth turned toward the news reporters and addressed them before any of them could say anything. "We've got nothing to report at this point in time. No leads, no motives, and no suspects. You guys got any questions at this point in time, don't ask me because I got no answers."

Imperateri shook his head in frustration over Garth. The detective would have preferred that the body had been found in his own territory. Now he'd have to contend with Garth and conduct a cross-jurisdictional investigation, a difficult, frustrating chore in the best of circumstances. The FBI would also have jurisdiction in the case because the girl had disappeared in Washington and crossed a state line. He'd have to check with a dozen guys every time he'd make a move. If he could at least get Garth off his back, things might be a mite easier.

"Sheriff," Imperateri said gravely, "looks like the subject was dumped here after the homicide in Washington. See, no blood, splotches or anything on the ground. I guess we could take full responsibility. Of course, if that's okay with you."

Garth nodded quickly several times. "Absolutely. No sweat. It's all yours. I'll be glad to help all I can." He was delighted to have the case taken away from him and it showed on his face. "Everybody get the hell out the way and give Sergeant Imperateri room to work."

"I'm all through here," Imperateri said, rising from his crouch. "If you could just ask your people to check the immediate area, I'd be deeply appreciative."

Even as he spoke, technicians using metal detectors began going over the terrain. Some scooped up soil samples from around the body, hoping to pick up hair and skin not from the victim but from the victimizer.

Imperateri took another look at the corpse, again visualizing the face of Judy. He regretted telling her that he'd talk with Beth about excessive strictness. Maybe that was exactly what the kid needed. As for Susan, he whispered the hope that she had lost consciousness long before the end came.

Julian Stone, physician, was accustomed to seeing the physical destruction of flesh, to witnessing dying and death. Yet he was not prepared for viewing the outrage against his own daughter's body. Stone was ashamed of being a male, of being the same sex of the person who had done this, and of being a member of the human race along with him.

Chain burns showing like dark scars appeared on the wrists and neck. Deep cuts marred her once smooth skin, leaving jagged gash marks. And worst of all to his mind were the bite incisions such as he had never seen before, impressions so deep that they appeared as if her killer had indeed intended to rend and devour her inner thighs.

I must try to keep Lois from seeing her like this, he thought. But he knew, of course, that was impossible.

Alternately filled with rage and grief, his anger was not dissipated by the rabbi's words at the funeral parlor chapel.

"The Book of Isaiah wisely admonishes those who have suffered the loss of a family member by violence. We are told that punishment must be left to the authorities to decide and to carry out. The aggrieved party, those closest to the violence, should not be tempted to acts of vengeance, of vigilantism."

Pressed tightly together with him in the first pew were Lois and relatives and friends sobbing and staring at the coffin resting on a bier flanked by two burning candles. He had asked that the coffin be closed so that no one could view his daughter's remains. He wanted to hide from the world and from himself the marks of her suffering. He believed that she would have preferred that secretiveness.

Only he and Lois knew how the body looked inside the poplar coffin, with a Star of David carved in its lid. Only he and Lois knew that she lay with head wrapped in a white turban and with body draped in the traditional white gown of Orthodox Jewish funerals. But only he knew that a white chrysanthemum lay across her breast, placed there by him early that morning.

On the way to the cemetery Julian Stone felt that his sanity would break unless he were to overcome his grief. He would not, he ordered himself, dwell upon the method of her death. But again he could not help wondering what manner of beast would do such a thing. He wished that he could meet this man, not to harm him or seek revenge, but to learn why he had savaged a fellow creature. In learning why, Stone believed that he would then be able to understand her death and perhaps to finally accept it, as one would accept an inevitable death from terminal disease.

Now it was time to bury the dead and to begin anew. Yet when the coffin was lowered into the ground, he felt a loss so profound and emptiness so deep that he wished he had not been so quick to bury and forget. He shut his mind out and listened to the rabbi's graveside words.

"Eternal God, our Creator, who makes and takes, You have given, now You have taken away Susan Stone, may she rest in peace."

Uncontrollably, Stone's cries joined Lois's wailing, so loud that they drowned out the chilling sound of the shovels grating on the gravel and the thud of the earth falling on the casket. Soon it was over.

Vincent Imperateri, attending the funeral, took Stone by the shoulders. "Dr. Stone, I know people are supposed to think that cops are tough and hardboiled and that nothing seems to bother them. That's not true. I just want you to know that Susan's case has affected me deeply." He paused, afraid that tears would show if he continued, but he did.

"I've handled hundreds of homicides, but this is one of the ones that hurts the most. If she were in the business with the hookers and the pimps, it would be one thing. You live that way, you pay the price. But she was a total innocent. She had no right to die."

Now a tear came to the detective's eye. "Look, is there anything I could do for you?"

Stone stared at him for several moments before replying. "Yes. Just let me know if you ever come across the killer. You could do this favor for me, couldn't you?"

Imperateri nodded, wondering what Stone would ever do with such information.

For days the telephone did not stop ringing. Visitors flocked to offer condolences. To all callers, Lois repeated a litany.

"Oh, you should have seen what he did to her. She was tortured. Her mouth was split open. I couldn't recognize her. Oh, you should have seen what he did."

Then the calls and visits stopped and Lois fell into a deep silence, as though struck speechless. Her lack of communication was then followed by a refusal to eat.

Through a psychiatrist friend, Dr. Carl Miller, Stone had her admitted to the psychiatric ward of a hospital where he had privileges himself. He was able to visit several times a day to see her and drop in on his own patients.

He watched helplessly as she appeared to lose weight daily. Soon she looked like a small, frail creature. Her breathing hardly stirred the blanket, and the only movement seemed to be the liquids from the IV tube.

When he spoke to her she looked at him and smiled, and then her eyes darted away in fear, as if she thought that only bad luck could come from his visit.

Stone recognized the psychological reaction to their daughter's death. It will pass in a couple of weeks or so, of that he was sure. He often spoke softly to her, reminding her that there was nothing more wrenching than to survive an only child, and that Susan would have wanted them to carry on and to brush away the longing and the guilt and the pain.

Despite his attempts, she continued to sit and stare. Where he had helped himself, he had failed her. He would seek help.

SIXTEEN

The wall of the psychiatrist's office was laden with framed evidence of education, experience and excellence. There was no desk, for Dr. Carl Miller believed it served as a barrier between the patient and himself. The only furniture on the gold-colored shag rug were two brown twill chairs and a coffee table holding a box of tissues and an ashtray.

Julian Stone stared at his friend with whom he had gone to medical school but who had opted for a career as a mind rather than flesh healer.

Stone couldn't recall Miller ever saying that he found psychiatry as intellectually rewarding as Stone found his own specialty, pediatrics. Nevertheless, over the years Miller's reputation grew and he was now considered to be one of the country's best analysts.

Now, sitting together, the pediatrician found it difficult to listen to the psychiatrist drone on, giving reasons why Lois had to remain in the hospital for an indefinite period of time.

"Don't you hear what I'm saying, Julian?" Miller said, noting Stone's faraway look. "She's in a catatonic state, unable to function."

"For how long? Don't tell me indefinite."

The psychiatrist shrugged and shook his head. "Weeks. Maybe longer. It won't be an overnight comeback. Gradual."

Stone shook his head slowly and rose in his seat to leave. Then, almost involuntarily, almost as if an invisible hand shoved him, he fell back into the chair. His voice now was deeper, more deliberate.

"How could anyone do something like that, Carl? I think I could guess what the pathological reasons are, but when it comes right down to it, right down to it happening to your own kid. . ." He broke off, squeezed his hands into fists and pressed them tightly against his eye sockets, as though to stem the flow of expected tears.

"Terrible things like that happen, Julian. When they do, you've got to. . ."

Stone dropped his fists. "Cope? I know, I know. I tell my patients the same crap. Well, Carl, I can't handle it. You have no idea what she meant to me, to Lois. I've just about stopped eating, sleeping. I can't practice medicine anymore. I'm finished as a person."

Carl Miller shook his head in sympathy, but said nothing. The two men looked at each other for a while without conversing, seemingly able to read each others thoughts. Stone finally broke the silence.

"You haven't told me who could do such a thing."

Miller breathed deeply, clearly reluctant to go into the matter. "It's male hypersexuality at its worse, at its most pathological state. There aren't too many cases like that around, thank God. But even one once in a blue moon is too many."

"There are dozens of rape cases every week in this town alone, Carl. What about them?"

"I'm not talking about your run-of-the-mill rapist. You know that the majoirty of rapists don't murder their victims. The rapist-murderer is the guy who'll kill in most cases to prevent discovery. Sometimes he'd kill in a panic, after being overcome by pangs of guilt. I'm not even talking about the sadistic or thrill killer who will murder and then mutilate his victims. That's a serious psychopathy of another nature. It may or may not have sexual aspects."

"Carl, quit talking like a shrink and get to the point."

"What I'm referring to is the lust-murderer who ends up killing his victim as a sexual climax."

"You mean he kills during penis penetration?"

The psychiatrist shook his head. "These guys don't bother

141

with intercourse. As a matter of fact, they may or may not have an erection or ejaculation. That's not important to them. They get their kicks, show their potency by killing and mutilating their victims. We know that the lust-murderer needs to perform this act as a stimulus to his entire central nervous system. He's compelled to cut, or stab, slash breasts, genitals. There may also be acts of cannibalism."

Carl Miller paused and studied the look of intense interest on Stone's face. "Look, Julian, this isn't helping you."

"Let me decide that. Tell me more."

"Most of them are able to suppress this murderous tendency, but occasionally all hell breaks loose. A lust-murderer can have a periodic outburst of paroxysmal sexual hunger which he can't control. But once his appetite is satisfied, he's completely normal."

"Until the next time," Stone added.

Miller nodded. "They're really sick people."

"Yes, Carl, but that doesn't give them a license to commit murder."

"I agree. They must be punished, but they must also be treated. They're patients as well as criminals. As a physician, you should appreciate that, Julian."

"I should, but right now I don't. I feel like cutting off their balls."

Carl Miller looked at him shrewdly and then stood to look for a book in a bookcase that took up a complete wall of his office. "In all seriousness, that's been tried in some countries, but it doesn't work."

Stone lifted his eyebrows. "I can't believe that. It physiologically has to stop their sex drive. Every kid knows that the source of androgen and testosterone is the testicles."

Miller pulled a large, beige-colored volume. "No, I don't mean that sex criminals can return to their previous sexual drive and criminal state. I mean it doesn't work as far as the man who's been castrated is concerned. At first it's okay, he feels liberated. He's free from the yoke of his sexual curse."

"So what's the problem?"

"Misery sets in, Julian. The man suffers considerable mental and physical changes. He can't accept the thought that he's inferior as a man. Some castrates can't take the effeminizing effects. It's tough for a former *macho* type to walk around with that eunuch look, the female hair patterns, the enlarged breasts and hips."

"I'm not concerned about how they feel," Stone said, almost shouting. "I'm concerned about their future victims. Their past ones are beyond the stage of feeling."

Miller leafed through the book. "That's a hard point to argue against, Julian."

Once more Stone rose to his feet, this time to gaze through the window. "Why is it we don't hear much about these monsters?"

"Now and then a case bursts on the front pages. In recent years we've had Theodore Bundy, tried and convicted for the murder-rape of three college girls in Florida."

"I read about that. Wasn't he also a suspect in some two dozen other murders all over the country?"

Miller nodded. "An otherwise charming and presentable young man. And then there was John Wayne Gacy in Chicago with a couple of dozen young boys he'd done it. So you see, not all lust victims are female."

Miller paused now to read and paraphrase from the book. "There's that other case of that man in Texas who allegedly murdered and buried twenty-seven young boys before he himself was murdered by an accomplice. And then there was the infamous Albert Fish, who murdered up to fifteen little girls before society caught up with him back in the mid-thirties. All of these stories are lurid, sensational. But what the press doesn't print is what the killer does. The cutting up of breasts and vaginas to be cooked and eaten. The drinking of cocktails, made with the blood of victims."

Miller stopped suddenly, studying Stone's face. "But you don't want to hear any more, Julian. Especially not now."

Again Stone raised his voice. "Especially now, Carl. Don't patronize me."

Miller slapped the book shut and sat down, rubbing his jaw contemplatively before continuing. "What more can I say? Unfortunately, each lust-murderer strikes many times over a wide geographic area before he's caught. And there are many women and children who've been declared missing and whose bodies may never be found. And whose unknown killers are still seeking new victims."

Stone turned from the window and spoke with words that fell heavily upon the sounds of his breathing. "What's the answer, Carl? Not just for the lust-murderer, but for all sex criminals. Catch them and keep them locked up forever?"

"Ah, but there's the rub," Miller said, once more opening the book. "They seem to be able to get released from prison after serving short sentences. It says here in this study that their relapse rate, recidivism, for rape, incest, child molestation, is pretty high. It ranges from twenty-five to eighty-six percent, depending on the type of crime."

"What about recidivism of the lust-murderer?"

"No published figures on that, but the odds are that any sex criminal, if released, will do it again."

"I repeat, Carl, what's the answer?"

"I'll give you the standard answer of a life-long liberal. Rehabilitate them, teach them the ways of normal behavior. Or try to. But the dreadfully sad news is that it doesn't work too often. They're prisoners of their hormones."

"You mentioned castration."

"Ah, bilateral orchidectomy. Removal of the testicles. I knew you were going to bring that up again. Listen to what it says here."

Miller looked at the book as he continued speaking. "Here are reports by Europeans about their experience with the sex crime repeater. I mentioned the high relapse rate in this country, up to eighty-six percent. Well, in the countries that castration has been tried, Sweden, Norway, Holland, Switzerland, Denmark and Germany, the relapse rate went down as much as two percent."

Stone permitted himself still another outburst. "For God's sake. Why haven't we tried it in this country?"

"A lot of reasons. The act is repulsive to many people who ordinarily wouldn't blanch at giving a life sentence or frying a guy in the chair. And then there's the potential for abuse. We still have memories of what the Nazis did."

"I understand that," Stone said impatiently. "The Nazis also ate breakfast. Do we have to give that up, too?"

Miller ignored the crack. "I believe there have been cases where some sex criminals had actually volunteered for the operation, either in hopes of being cured or of getting a reduced sentence. And that brings up another reason why castration isn't accepted here. Lawsuits by the castrated against those who advised or performed the operation."

"Ah, Carl, but that's voluntary castration. I'm thinking of the involuntary kind, a law making it mandatory for dangerous sex criminals."

Miller shrugged and replaced the book on the shelf. "Several state legislatures have tried unsuccessfully to pass castration bills. But opponents say such a law would be unequal because what do you do about female sex offenders? Snip away their clitoris? Also, suppose you castrate someone who's later found to have been innocent."

"But if the overwhelming evidence is incontrovertible, even if his own mother testifies against him. . ." Stone paused to collect his thoughts before continuing. "Maybe then and only then. . ."
Again Stone's voice trailed off, as if he realized that his argument were weak. But it was only his thoughts which intruded upon his speech.

Castration stops with near-perfect certainty the problem of sex offenders repeating their crimes, he thought. Only the death sentence and life imprisonment were more effective as a preventive. He'd always been against capital punishment. As for life imprisonment, he reasoned that sex criminals would rather face castration than a life behind bars.

"Julian?"
Stone snapped out of his thoughts.
Miller stared at him for a few moments before grasping him by the shoulder. "Look, Julian, you need a rest. Maybe a long

145

vacation. Mary and I are going to Europe soon for a long holiday. She's been after me to take a sabbatical. Perhaps Lois and you . . . The change would be terrific for her."

Stone rose to leave, shaking the psychiatrist's hand. "Thanks, Carl. I think we'll just stay home."

"Let me give you something to help you sleep, make you feel better."

"You forget I'm a doctor, too. I've got my own bag of tricks."

Miller laughed, but with a look of deep concern.

"I'll take a brisk walk before bedtime," Stone continued. "Exercise has always helped me with my tensions in the past."

Julian Stone left the office, knowing full well that neither exercise nor drug could make him forget, could erase the consuming hatred he felt for the man who took away Susan's life. He could never dig deep enough into his bag of tricks to get over his grief.

Vincent Imperateri wished so hard that his hands trembled and his gut ached with anticipation. He wished that the short, dumpy woman with glasses thick like beer mug bottoms would provide him with the key. All it took was one good lead, that lucky break homicide detectives often dreamt about. He recalled that in the Son of Sam case, it was an eyewitness who saw a man running for a parked car in the residential neighborhood where a victim had been gunned down. That car, along with others, had been ticketed earlier for a parking violation. For police, it was then just a matter of checking the citations issued to non-residents.

The lucky break. Every murder case that had been cracked had one.

With some homicides, the breaks came from a source, a street snitch or a paid informer, who could point a finger at a grudge killer, or at one involved with gambling, sex, or drugs. Imperateri knew that in these types of cases, a detective was only as good as his sources. You could operate without them, but it was like trying to row without oars. And without them, it was back to old-fashioned detective work. However, romanticized, it meant settling into a tiring routine of checking and tracking down every aspect of a case, juggling facts and nuances, hoping that something might turn up which hadn't occurred to an investigator before.

With luck, pieces were provided for a puzzle. But it was the lucky break that brought the pieces together. Sometimes it was someone who got careless and sloppy or who had got drunk and said something.

Sometimes a bystander, a random passerby, came forward.

Mrs. Gertrude Forbes had come forward. She was a retired schoolteacher, a widow who took her collie out daily to exercise in that Prince Georges County field where she studied and collected wild flora. Since providing information which led to the finding of Susan Stone's body, she had been questioned several times. Yet her story never varied, and never revealed the one important detail that could lead to the killer.

The break had come, but it wasn't lucky enough. On top of that, Mrs. Forbes was fed up with the incessant questioning and threatened to hire an attorney unless the police from four jurisdictions and the FBI stopped badgering her.

"Please, Mrs. Forbes," Imperateri now begged in the Prince Georges County substation, "this is positively the last time." He looked at Sheriff Garth as if to seek confirmation, but all he got was a blank stare. Obviously, Imperateri thought, the sheriff was to eager to believe that the homicide took place in another jurisdiction. It cost the county money, manpower and time to undertake an investigation and to prosecute. Imperateri could appreciate Garth's concern, for the county's budget according to the sheriff's lights could be better spent on pay increases, bonuses and promotions for the county's finest.

"I'm sorry," Mrs. Forbes said, regret evident in her voice. "I can't tell you anything new. He was just too far away for me to see his features clearly."

Imperateri was not altogether unhappy that her story never varied. Too often under long questioning a witness would change short into tall, dark into light. So far, the suspect was described as Caucasian, of average height and build.

"And I know what you're thinking," she continued. "I'm not going to be subjected to hypnotism because it's not going to help for the simple reason that his image never really entered my mind. I haven't forgotten anything. I just didn't see him. All I can say is that he had light brown hair and wore khaki pants and shirt."

"No coat in the cold?" Imperateri asked.

She shook her head. "He didn't have one when he carried the girl. She had a yellow raincoat on. You could see that from far away. It was only some time later, as I've mentioned time and again, that I went to the post office and saw the poster about the missing girl and the raincoat."

"Didn't it occur to you that it was rather strange, his carrying someone in the woods?"

"Look, Officer," she smiled, "if I told you about all of the strange happenings that go on in there, you wouldn't believe me. There are sex orgies and dope parties and drinking and fighting, to say the least." She looked accusingly at Garth. "And the police won't do a thing about it."

"Lady," Garth said, "we don't have the manpower to patrol every place where there's trees and bushes."

Imperateri cut him off by addressing her impatiently. "You didn't see either of them leave?"

"No. I didn't hear anything either. I was just too far away."

"What did the car look like?"

"Well, it was well off the road and it was mostly hidden by bushes. I couldn't see too much of it."

"You couldn't tell me its color or make or whether it was American or foreign?"

"To tell you the truth, officer, I don't know much about cars. They all look the same to me."

"Could you see the tags? Do you remember the color of any of the numbers?"

"All hidden. I'm sorry. May I go now? I'm sure if you'll look over the transcripts of my earlier questioning, you'll find the same answers and questions."

Garth lifted a finger at her. "That vehicle didn't have a sticker showing it was from Prince Georges County, did it?"

She stared blankly at the sheriff without answering.

"You know," he persisted, "the inspection sticker. Ours is green."

Imperateri spoke for her, careful to keep the scorn out of his voice. "We can assume that if the car was somewhat hidden and too far away to describe it would also be difficult to pick out a two-inch window sticker." He turned to Mrs. Forbes once more. "The man's khaki outfit, did it look like a soldier's?"

"No, more like a repairman, I guess."

Imperateri rubbed his hands, forced a smile and nodded in defeat. No new nuance, no uncovered fact. Nothing. "Mrs. Forbes, thank you very much. We really appreciate your helping us like this. If only I could see you later for just a few more minutes of your time. We'd like to see if you could identify some pictures of men we have."

She shook her head vehemently. "Officer, I can't take it any more. I told you all that I know about it. I'm a sick woman and all I do is answer the same questions."

Imperateri stood to gain the advantage of height. "Mrs. Forbes, we're imposing on you, we know. But if citizens like you won't help us, we might as well pack it all in and leave the streets to the criminals."

She said nothing, closing her eyes for a few moments. Then she emitted a deep sigh of aquiescence and nodded. Rising, she squinted, looking for the door.

Imperateri bit his lip. What the hell was the use? he asked himself. She'd have a hell of a time as a witness for the prosecution. Even with her thick glasses, she appeared to have trouble seeing. A defense attorney could tear her apart.

At the door she paused for a moment, then turned to Imperateri. "Oh, Officer. One thing I remember now—the sheriff's asking about that sticker brought it back. I could make out the top of his car. It had one of those bubble lights that flash. You know, just like a police car."

SEVENTEEN

With Lois under treatment in the hospital, Julian Stone plunged into his work, putting in long hours at the office and volunteering as a physician at a clinic for the poor. Still the day held too many hours for him.

At home, the telephone calls, the solicitous visits from friends and relatives, had largely ceased, and the stillness and loneliness tore into his soul. He could neither read nor watch television and often sat and stared into space, mourning.

At times he would enter Susan's room, standing in the middle of the floor and looking without touching anything, as though he were in a museum. Posters of rock stars, disco dancers. Books and magazines overflowing a bookcase. Stuffed animals, teddy bears, bunnies on the bed and on a dresser. Plants, many varieties, which he had promised to look after when she left for school.

He had enough presence of mind to realize that perpetual grieving for Susan wouldn't bring her back, nor would it return him to a sane, normal life. At the same time he felt that he would never be able to cope with what happened and would spend his days running from his thoughts until they would catch up and destroy him.

On one evening, he dwelled deeply upon the horror of it, the kidnap, the rape, the murder. A renewed rage surged within him. His property had been taken and destroyed. It was a feeling of helpless rage remotely similar to one he had had after his automobile had been stolen. His car, nobody else's.

Soon his anger turned inward. Susan hadn't been his or anyone's property. She had had a life, her own. And how dare he compare the loss of his car with her agony? He answered himself immediately. It was a psychological defense mechanism, beyond his control, designed to suppress his anguish, silence his torment.

Julian Stone wondered why he couldn't be an emotional, uncivilized man and tear his hair out and grab a shotgun and look for the killer of his child and then shoot him down. Shoot first in the groin to give pain and then later in the heart to take life.

Shuddering at the thought, he reasoned that there was a pool of angry vengeance in every human waiting to be tapped by tragedy. Vengeance, a relief valve, individual satisfaction to provide peace of mind. He now appreciated the ancient law of retaliation, an eye for an eye, a tooth for a tooth. He, the closest surviving male relative, holding the right to avenge his daughter.

He recalled what the rabbi had said at the funeral.

"Fuck him," Stone said aloud, feeling better for it, and eager now for his usual walk before bedtime.

The walk was not relaxing. He found himself constantly looking at the faces of the men he passed, wondering if any of them could possibly commit rape and murder. Could he determine by their looks?

He tried to think like a young girl, a woman, an elderly lady. How would he/she feel on an elevator alone with a strange man, or being brushed by a male on an empty street? He knew that it was improbable that he could experience a woman's panic at footsteps behind her and brute strength on top of her. Of course, he, a male, could also be mugged, but being beaten and robbed was not the same as being beaten and raped. And murdered.

He turned off the main street and strolled down a narrower, darker place. After a few minutes he heard the sound of footsteps behind him. A man's footfalls, heavy, menacing. Stone stole a glance over his shoulder.

A large man, a full head taller than he and with shoulders like football pads, strolled behind. The man's pace appeared purposeless, as though he looked for something to do.

Stone felt a flicker of anxiety. He tried to calm his fears by telling himself he was overreacting, letting his imagination seize upon his thoughts and run wild. Concerned though he was with his own safety, he played a game with himself. He tried to imagine how a woman would feel in his place now.

Could the man grab me, toss me into a car? Or drag me off into an alley, rip off my clothing, force his filthy prick into me? And then smash my face and choke or slice me apart? He could very easily.

Quickening his pace, Stone's worry built to a real fear. Yet he seemed to realize that if he were a woman, that fear would now be absolute terror.

The streets, the countryside, any place where a man-stranger and a woman-stranger were alone, still belonged to the male. There was no equality, no women's liberation.

He felt a hatred of men, a deep fear of their power, and an angry frustration at his—a woman's—powerlessness.

Stone broke into a trot. When he reached the end of the street he turned to look back. The stranger was just entering a private house. Stone sighed with relief but his thoughts continued.

He must prevent the real criminal from stalking and raping a helpless woman. Only by doing this could he make Susan's death meaningful.

He couldn't believe that he was thinking about revenge again and wondered whether he was following Lois into some sort of mental collapse. But he didn't care, for he now felt an expression of satisfaction that he hadn't ever experienced before.

Returning home to his study, he questioned whether society had the right to snatch away vengeance that actually belonged to him. That right, primitive, elemental, was his, and only through exercising it could he purge himself of the frustrated rage within him.

Julian Stone held his head in his hands. It was wrong to think such thoughts. He was an educated man, a physician, a thoughtful person not given to fancies, much less precipitate action. The same cannot now begin to mimic the psychotic.

Vigilantism, vengeance, not for him. It was the State's role, the function of his representatives, those whom he had legally helped elect and appoint to fulfill that duty. By killing his daughter, the murderer had committed a crime against the State, and it would be the State that would bring him to justice.

Even if he were to seek his own eye-for-an-eye justice, he could not hope to track down singlehandedly the assassin. His daughter's murderer was not known, and might never be known. There might never be a recipient of Stone's rage or of the State's justice.

Stone laughed to himself. Suppose the rapist were to be found. Would Stone then act to strike at him? Stone, the mild, forgiving person, the ardent pacifist and dedicated opponent of the death penalty. He had often argued with his conservative friends about the inhumanity of capital punishment, feeling that murder by the State was hardly better than murder by the individual.

As a physician, the idea of the State executing its most heinous criminals was barbaric to him. Murder by the State reduced society to the level of the criminal it sought to punish. He favored life imprisonment, with no chance for parole, unless some medical miracle was evolved to excise the evilness from the criminal body.

He recalled his dialogue with Carl Miller on the question of castration. Like capital punishment, it violated the criminal's body. But then, did not surgeons invade the diseased body to rid it of disease?

In some, malevolence and viciousness were like a disease. In the vampire rapist and the habitual rapist, there was the uncontrollable desire to harm other people for no other reason than the nasty thrill of it. Such dark deeds could be prevented by a relatively simple and safe procedure.

Castration.

He rose from his chair and turned to the wall bookcase, jammed with medical textbooks and journals. From a seldom-used shelf he pulled a heavy volume entitled *Textbook of Surgery, Volume IV Urology*. For several moments he balanced the book in one hand, staring at the cover as though it contained the salvation to all of his problems.

Dropping himself back into the chair, he quickly found the chapter dealing with castration. He glanced at the drawings and photographs and then read the text slowly.

It was all vaguely familiar to him. He had taken postgraduate courses in surgery and had watched many times as surgeons performed castrations, euphemistically renamed bilateral orchiectomy, on gonadal cancer patients.

The procedure was not all that difficult. He recalled that the ancient Greeks and Chinese castrated males without benefit of modern medicine, and that castration continued well into the nineteenth century to provide adult male sopranos for the Vatican. Since time immemorial, castrations were performed to convert a potentially dangerous young bull into an ox.

Nodding his head slowly, he was convinced that castration was the only answer to the habitual criminal rapist. The removal of a rapist's testicles was an act of mercy not only for future innocent victims but for the transgressor himself.

Julian Stone inhaled deeply, his mind churning with thought. What was there to stop him from performing the operation on criminals? The law? Sometimes the law ignored justice. His own temperance? For this operation, he would suspend it.

He would do it, seek out the rapists and remove their malfunctioning organ. They would suffer, yes, but mildly in comparison to the anguish they had caused.

Rising in excitement, he dropped the book but didn't bother to pick it up, for now he thought only of obstacles to his plan. Discovery by the police might not only thwart his plans but ruin him for life. But detection could be avoided by meticulous planning. As for finding candidates for surgery, that should not prove difficult. All he need do was to peruse old newspapers.

He'd have to be absolutely sure of his patients. There could not be the slightest doubt concerning their guilt. Too often he'd heard stories about a person found guilty of a crime and subsequently sentenced to a jail term. In time, another person confessed to the crime. Stone couldn't allow himself to remove a man's testicles unless guilt were evident beyond doubt. Any apology would hardly suffice if the man later proved to be innocent.

His patient would have to be convinced to undergo the operation, and that would be unlikely. No murderer-rapist was going to submit willingly. And then there was always the risk that the rapist might overpower or kill him.

Sighing, he picked up the textbook and strode to his desk where he looked through a bottom drawer. There, in a large envelope covered by a ream of paper, was the weapon he would use. It was a small, silvery pistol, effeminate and toy-like in design, but lethal in practice. He had bought it long ago to protect himself when he made house calls in bad neighborhoods, but had never fired it.

The pistol was a Beretta, less than five inches long. By its weight, he was reminded that he had never unloaded it. Unlike a revolver, which held bullets on a rotating tumbler, the Beretta was loaded by inserting a clip of ammunition into the handle.

With one hand he held the book. With the other, the pistol. He smiled at the irony of the symbolism. Humankind's most potent convincers, knowledge and force.

The time had come to use both.

The next evening, Julian Stone visited a Newark public library and found his way to the stacks holding out-of-town newspapers. Current issues of *The New York Times* were shelved prominently in front. From the rear and bottom of a second pile he pulled out older copies and carried them to a reading area.

He scanned the columns. His eyes sought out just the reports of crime, and of these, he read only the news of rapes. There were many, not solely reported in the city of New York, but in upstate cities and in surrounding communities in Connecticut and New Jersey. The assaults ranged from barroom pickups and hitchhiking attacks to rapes along bike and jogging trails. Few suspects were arrested.

He devoured each detail of the news stories yet could not find what he was looking for. He was not interested in the acquaintance rapes, those one-time incidents where the assailant, the boy next door, the doctor or minister, the family friend, is known to the victim.

Returning to the shelves, he replaced the perused papers and pulled out a half dozen of more recent editions. His eyes, slightly more practiced now in seeking out the crime stories in the metropolitan section, fixed on a possibility, a rape suspect in Yonkers who was identified as the man responsible for attacking four women in less than a month.

Stone read and re-read the story, memorizing the details when his eye caught another report on the same page. A teenage youth in Rochester had been formally charged with the rape of a seven-year-old girl, daughter of a neighbor for whom the youth had performed chores.

This wouldn't do, Stone thought. Neither story suited his needs. The suspects, even after a formal arraignment, still had to be tried and convicted. Even so, the youth he would not touch. With good therapy perhaps there was hope. The mass rapist, however, was a different matter.

Stone realized that he couldn't get to the rapist while the man was in custody. And if the suspect were to be released on bail bond, there still was the question of his innocence.

Sighing, Stone carried the papers back, convinced that his idea had no practical merit. Once the suspect had been convicted and sentenced, he would be out of Stone's reach.

At the stacks he noticed a section devoted to out-of-town newspapers and came across old copies of the *Washington Post*, some dating back several months. Here was the newspaper which served the area where Susan's killer probably still roamed. With a foot-deep armful of the papers, Stone trudged back to the reading room.

For a long time he leafed through the sheets, again reading only about rape cases. Tired now and feeling he was getting nowhere, he was about to return the papers when his eye fell upon an item which struck him like a shock. His breath almost stopped with the excitement he felt. He read it slowly, mouthing the words and moving his lips as though afraid to trust only his mind.

Larry Wilson, convicted for the rape and murder of an

Annapolis housewife, is being paroled today after serving nine years of a life sentence.

The 36-year-old former Marine will leave the Maryland State Farm following a parole board decision yesterday to free him for exemplary behavior. He worked in an automobile shop while in prison and counseled youths at the correctional facility. Wilson has been promised a job by a Rockville gas station and his counseling for the State will also be continued.

In a highly-publicized trial nearly ten years ago, Wilson was convicted of killing Mrs. Agnes Bethea, the mother of three young children, after beating and raping her. Earlier, he had served three years of a five year term for the rape of a hitchhiker. While in the Marine Corps, he was courtmartialed and sentenced to five years' hard labor for the robbery and rape of a commissary employee.

Larry Wilson would make a fine patient, Stone thought, surreptitiously using a fingernail to snip out the article. He looked around to see if anyone were watching. No one was, but he still felt pangs of guilt. He rationalized that the old paper would soon be burned anyway and that nobody would miss the clipped piece.

Suddenly, he laughed to himself. Here he was, contemplating a major crime according to society's lights, and he was concerned about snitching some worthless scrap of paper.

Worthless? No, not to him, he said to himself as he read the remainder of the article before pocketing it.

"If I could just tell the people I've harmed how sorry I am," the ex-Marine said, *"I would. Right now, I'm at the point where I want to start a new slate, become a new personality."*

"You will," Stone whispered.

EIGHTEEN

The styrofoam cup of coffee resting on the dash steamed up balloons against the windshield. The night was one of the coldest of the year, yet Julian Stone kept the heater turned off. He didn't want to run the engine, fearing that the noise and the spewing of exhaust fumes might draw attention to him, sitting in a parked car alone and across the street from a gas station. Passersby might consider him a lookout for a robbery or even a holdup man contemplating his move.

So he shivered and blew on his hands when they weren't tucked into his coat pocket, feeling the coldness of the Beretta. And all of the time he kept watch on the station where Larry Wilson worked.

Tracing Wilson had not been difficult. A call to the parole board provided the whereabouts of his employment, a gasoline station in Rockville, Maryland, a suburb of Washington. Stone then arranged to refer patients to another doctor for a few days, claiming to his nurse and receptionist that he needed a rest. To Lois he also lied. He told her that he was needed for a consultation in Baltimore.

He drove to that harbor city, skirting the downtown area and going directly to the Baltimore-Washington Airport. There he parked his own car and paid cash for a rental car after using false identification he had prepared. Then he checked into a motel, again avoiding the use of credit cards and his own name. That same afternoon he leisurely cruised the thirty miles to Rockville and located the gas station without any difficulty.

The immediate problem Stone faced was to identify Larry Wilson without raising suspicion and attention to himself. A telephone call solved the dilemma. He identified himself as Wilson's friend wishing to contact him. The manager replied that Wilson worked nights alone.

Alone.

The word sent shivers of anticipation and excitement through him. Was it going to be that easy, or was there to be some hidden element, a last hitch which would sabotage his plan and place him in jeopardy? He'd have to make a dry run, get the lay of the land, see for himself before taking action.

A feeling of frustration came to him when he had first arrived at the station. There was not one, but two men who pumped gas and attended to customers.

Which one was Wilson?

Again, there was no easy way to find out without drawing attention to himself and alerting Wilson that a stranger was curious about him. Stone tried to think, his eyes casting about as if seeking a visual solution.

A public telephone cubicle stood before a corner drugstore closed for the night. Stone stared at it for a moment before digging across the dark street as the taller of the two attendants jogged to the office to answer the ringing telephone.

"Hello," Stone said. "Larry Wilson?"

"Just a sec. I'll get him."

Stone hung up and returned to the car where he continued his waiting. The tall attendant left promptly at ten o'clock, leaving Wilson alone. At eleven, Wilson switched off the overhead arc lights, locked the pumps, closed the garage and office doors, and drove off in an old green Ford.

Stone followed at a good distance. It was not difficult tailing the Ford with its profusion of bright bumper stickers plastered on the trunk and rear window. Finally, the car pulled in front of a bungalow and sounded the horn. A young man sprung out, slamming the door behind and hastily pulling a jacket on.

No doubt they were going drinking and whoring, Stone thought, not bothering to follow. For a long time he sat in the car, his mind racing with what faced him.

How and where would the actual operation take place?

Wilson's home was out of the question. He may share living quarters with friends, Waylaying Wilson on the way home and forcing him at gunpoint to the airport motel was also inappropriate. Even more dangerous, at least from a medical viewpoint, was taking him to a dark and out-of the way place in the country. No, the entire procedure would have to be done at the gas station, amidst the grease and dirt, tools and tires.

The next day Stone gathered from different variety stores in Baltimore a wig, false mustache, and a pair of plain glass spectacles. He reasoned that such a disguise would be safer than using a ski mask, which might provoke Wilson to think he was being held up and to try something rash.

In his motel room Stone practiced putting the disguise on. He was amazed how much further his face changed when he stuck cotton into his mouth to pad his cheeks. Still another change came when he slipped on a pair of built-up shoes he'd also purchased that morning. The addition of several inches to his height would make later identification even more difficult.

The rest of the day, cold and blustery, passed slowly. He watched television, went out to eat, and then called Lois at the hospital to tell her that the consultation would keep him tied up another day. He was encouraged by hearing her speak. She sounded more alert and cogent.

At eight o'clock, he grew impatient. He left the motel and cruised aimlessly in the cold for another hour before returning to the gas station where he waited as the previous night's performance repeated itself. At ten the tall employee left as Wilson began cleaning up the station.

Again Stone drove off, picked up a hot coffee and sandwich at a nearby convenience store, and ate in the car while snapping on the wig with its thick, blond hair, and fixing the rest of his disguise. Then he returned once more to the station.

Now he watched as the coffee steamed window designs. He argued with himself about calling the whole thing off as a wild and stupid idea, born of a grief-stricken mind. He even cursed the white color of the rental car, so bright and shiny that it could be seen for miles, even by moonlight.

Before he knew it was time, the arc lights of the station shut off. He hurriedly took a last sip of coffee, inserted the cotton into his mouth, and eased into the station.

Wilson shook his head and jerked a thumb. "Closed, buddy."

Up close, Wilson, though light and blond, resembled an ape with his low forehead, deep set eyes and prominent jaw.

"I don't want gas," Stone mumbled through the cotton. "There's something wrong with my car. The engine's making strange noises."

"Bring it back in the morning. There's a mechanic on duty then."

"Oh, aren't you a mechanic?"

"Yeah, but I don't have time to mess with your car now."

"Well, look, could I leave it here and pick it up tomorrow after your man worked on it? I'll just take a cab home."

Wilson rubbed a jaw with a hand that was thick and dirty. Stone looked at it. Could this have been the hand that fondled and squeezed Susan's breasts, that shoved sharp knives into her, that choked her delicate neck until life left her?

Now Wilson shrugged a pair of thick shoulders. "Suit yourself." He pointed to the garage. "Put her in the second bay while I finish closing up. Be right with you."

Stone's eyes followed the man's peculiar swagger, gorilla-like with arms bowed and legs spread apart. It was almost as if the rapist followed the memory of a primeval force over which he had no control.

Maneuvering the car into the open bay, Stone felt his heart beating wildly, the perspiration building all over his body. How could he operate, he asked himself, feeling like this?

With clammy hands, he reached to the back seat for the bag containing the equipment. Working quickly and expertly now, he unwrapped a disposable hypodermic syringe and pushed its needle through a thin plastic cap over a vial containing sodium pentothal.

Again Stone hesitated. Without proper medical equipment to monitor life signs during the operation and without resuscitation apparatus, he would have to administer a lower dosage than what someone of Wilson's age and weight required. The only problem would be if Wilson awoke before the operation was over.

He measured off two milliliters. Then he pulled the barrel back and retracted the hypodermic.

He was ready.

With the instrument in hand, he levered himself out of the car and then pulled the Beretta from his suit pocket. He waited, holding both needle and gun behind his back like a teasing child hiding a toy. Moments later Wilson showed with a clipboard in hand.

"Give me your name and address."

"Thanks, and, ah, could you tell me your name? That's in case something happens to my car." Stone had to be absolutely sure he had the right man.

"No problem about that. Larry Wilson." Saying that, Wilson narrowed his eyes and moved his head back an inch, perhaps waiting for a sign of recognition as the notorious rapist, but Stone kept a cool exterior until seconds later when he swung the gun around.

Wilson took a breath and exhaled in an exasperated fashion. "Fucking holdup, huh?"

"Roll up your sleeve and lean over the hood of the car. Make any move and I'll blow your head off."

The injection was quick and neat, all over seconds after Wilson complained about the stinging jab. Still the precious moments counted. Stone could not risk having the patient gaining consciousness suddenly, nor could he chance police or passersby noticing something wrong.

Leaving Wilson draped momentarily over the hood, Stone pulled down the suspended bay door. From the car trunk he retrieved a cot mattress and dragged his patient on to it. A mechanic's trouble-shooter light attached to the car bumper provided enough illumination.

Stone worked feverishly. He began to pull off Wilson's dirt-and-grease stiffened dungarees. The underwear was torn and hadn't been washed in days. A strong odor of old semen, of a woman's dried vaginal secretions, of unwashed sweaty skin, was so overpowering that Stone reared his head back to catch his breath.

The doctor paused once more. There may be a problem with sepsis. Wilson was incredibly filthy.

Putting on sterile gloves, he took extra care in swabbing the whole groin area with an antiseptic solution. Then he reached for another disposable hypodermic for a local anesthetic. Next, he removed a sterile scalpel from the bag.

It was time to begin.

The operating area now lay before him, a flaccid cannon resting on ball wheels. He could not help wondering if this was the member which had penetrated his daughter's every orifice. No, because his daughter's murderer did not penetrate her.

Wilson was not quite an abnormal monster, merely a rapist-murderer and a repeated rapist. Still Stone was tempted for a moment to sever the offending instrument. He smiled to himself. Better still, remove all of the outdoor plumbing, restructure the penis into a perineal cavity, a vagina. Turn Larry Wilson into a transsexual. A fitting end for a sex criminal.

Now Stone shook his head. If I knew enough about urological surgery, would I still perform the transsexual operation? Am I here to punish or to cure?

No matter what he'd do, castrate or try to perform sex conversion, it would be illegal. Monstrously so, he told himself, akin to Nazi experimentation in the concentration camps.

What gave him the right to render the man harmless? He answered his own question. Why, the right of the aggrieved. Or perhaps the same right given a jury and judge to convict and sentence.

Once more he wondered if he were insane, transformed so by Susan's death and Lois's mental collapse. Or had he been insane long before, indifferent to crime, impassive to criminal trespass when it had not affected him?

Stone sighed audibly. He was wasting valuable time.

He dropped to his knees on the hard, cold floor. It was going to be difficult to operate in this way, but he had no other choice.

He shrugged off his own discomfort, thinking about that of his patient.

Holding the scrotum firmly, he gently stroked the knife through layers of tissues until the incision was complete. Then he stuck a gloved finger through the slit and felt the testis slipping away, trying to escape his grasp as if it had a life of its own. He milked it upward from the outside with his other hand until it appeared, covered by a thin membranous sheathing, which he carefully snipped away.

Shorn and forced out of its refuge, the testis was pinkish, the size and shape of a small hen's egg. It reminded Stone of a miniature planet, with its tiny arterial branches showing like rivers to irrigate the countryside.

With a sharp pair of scissors, he separated the blood vessels and vas deferens that connect to the testis, applied hemostatic clamps, and cut the testis free. He repeated the process with the other testis and then ligated the pedicles. After spraying an antiseptic, he stanched the bleeding and stitched up the scrotum, now a shriveled, wringled, burst balloon.

It was over.

"Now, Mr. Wilson, you should enjoy a near normal life without hurting anyone with your pecker any more."

Stone twirled some protective gauze around the wound. But that wasn't enough. He'd have to make sure the patient had immediate hospitalization. With good postoperative care, Wilson should be back at the gas pumps in a few days.

His instruments all packed and returned to the car, Stone made a final check for anything left behind. The slightest item could be incriminating, a wrapper bearing a Newark hospital address, a label which could be traced to him.

There was nothing, save the gonads in a transparent plastic bag, looking like some exotic tropical fish just purchased from a pet shop. These he would also take with him. There was always the possibility, albeit remote, of reimplantation by surgeons at the hospital.

It was time to leave. He glanced outside at the empty street. With the sterile gloves still on, he picked up the office telephone and called for an ambulance. Seconds later, he sped away, tires squealing and engine roaring.

Less than two hours later he was in his own car crossing the Delaware Memorial Bridge, more than halfway home. He edged over to the right lane and leaned to roll down the passenger side window.

A moment later the bag of balls flew out like an oddly-shaped Chinese kite to plunge into the cold dark waters below.

NINETEEN

With both man and machine, Mrs. Gertrude Forbes had failed. She couldn't finger any of the photographs of sex perverts. Nor could she ascertain that the common-faced composite picture conjured up by Marcie Simkin resembled the man she had seen on the field that day. To make matters worse, she couldn't even identify the car driven by that man.

Vincent Imperateri, alone now, stared at the pile of photographs. He had gone through great trouble and expense getting a picture of almost every type car having a flashing roof light. There were dozens, from the various police jurisdictions, fire departments and private security businesses.

Now his only substantial lead had come to a dead end. The lead had fit in so neatly with his earlier theory that the lust-killer could be a police officer. How else could the killer have gotten the girls in the car unless he were a man in a blue uniform, a trustworthy officer of the law? Otherwise, anyone entering a stranger's car was difficult to understand in light of the widespread publicity and warnings.

Maybe the killer used a taxicab. Maybe old Mrs. Forbes mistook a cab's top marker for that of a patrol car's top light. With her eyes, it was more than possible.

Imperateri shook his head in frustration. He was stumped, at a loss by the failure of his eyewitness. Normally, homicides were solved in one or more of three ways. A reliable eyewitness, a confession, or an abundance of physical evidence. He had none of these, not even the latter. The girls had disappeared and their bodies were later found somewhere else. He didn't have a crime scene to work with.

Noseworthy passed by, carrying a tear sheet from the metro wire and chuckling loudly. "Hey, Vinnie, here's something from Rockville. Somebody cut off a guy's balls. Suspect is middle-aged. White male. No holdup, no apparent motive."

"Drug deal?" Imperateri asked without looking up. He knew that revenge stabbings and body mutilations were common in the underworld of drug dealers. "Maybe a homosexual falling out," he added.

"Not with this ball-less wonder. He was out on parole after serving time for rape and murder."

Now Imperateri looked up. "No big mystery. A lot of people would have liked to take away his manhood. All Rockville has to do is check out every middle-aged, white male friend of Wilson's victim."

"Maybe a contract job," Noseworthy said as he spiked the tear sheet. He looked up to watch a stranger, a uniformed police sergeant approach.

"Where can I find Sergeant Imperateri?" the man asked.

Noseworthy waved an outstretched arm, palm upward, toward Imperateri, in the manner of an Old World waiter showing an available table. Then he stepped aside and left, allowing the heavy-set, red-faced sergeant access.

"Sergeant Imperateri, I'm Tom Gibson. Our paths have crossed a couple of times."

"I thought you looked familiar. You're from Chevy Chase."

Gibson nodded happily at the instant recognition. "Best precinct in the city."

Imperateri grinned. "That's because you've got a population of government workers and shopkeepers. Last entry you had was a stolen hubcap back in '72."

Gibson roared with laughter. He held a forefinger across his lips in a mocking plea not to give the secret away. Then he assumed a serious mien. "How're you doing on the rape cases?"

"Hit that brick wall," Imperateri said, not eager to talk about it. "What brings you here?"

Gibson screwed up his face and ran a finger along his collar. "Well, I got this job nobody likes but somebody has to do. Going around talking to people and pushing papers around. Believe me, I'd rather walk alone through niggertown at night than do this."

Imperateri wondered what the *this* was about that made it so terrible. Gibson certainly did not look any the worse for wear. His belly protruded, and his full face was capped by silvery hair. In short, he looked like a very rich man or someone who did not have to worry about working.

"They got me over this here barrel," Gibson continued. "I hurt my back and tried for disability. I was a week too late. The city council already tightened up on retirements."

Imperateri sat impassively, refusing to show any sign of sympathy. The old disability program had been a minor scandal. That many police and fire officials won disability retirement with eighty percent of their income as pension was not the problem. What forced the city council to act was the fact that almost all of the retirees immediately found other, more physically demanding jobs. Now not only had disability pensions been reduced, but retirees couldn't seek physically-demanding employment for several years after signing out. It had been a department joke how many officers with bad backs suddenly got better. In Imperateri's eyes, Gibson looked strong enough, with a healthy glow and non-stop chatter.

"Yeah, the bastards took me off the inactive duty roster while my papers were being processed. When the council ruling came in, instead of retirement they gave me limited duty. I begged them, put me back on the streets. They wouldn't listen. Shit."

Imperateri guessed that the man lied. No desk-bound cop ever wanted street patrol. Once you sit in a swivel chair with your hot coffee and danish and morning newspaper, the back alleys and the long knives held little charm. And then older cops like Gibson realize their fragility. Nobody can pay anybody enough to get hurt, or killed.

Gibson waved a notebook and pencil in front of Imperateri's

eyes, as if showing proof of his fate. "I've been detailed to an Internal Affairs panel."

The purpose of Gibson's visit at last dawned on Imperateri. The hearing on Captain Anderson had finally come up. Witnesses were now being asked for depositions.

Imperateri leaned back, trying to think fast. What the hell was he going to say? If he lied, Anderson would be off the hook and that long-awaited promotion might come through. *Might.* Suppose he'd support Anderson and the captain then reneged on the promise. It was possible. But if he didn't back Anderson, the promotion would surely die and the name of Imperateri would be cursed by every cop.

Gibson flipped over the pad cover and produced a miniature tape recorder from his coat pocket. "You know why I'm here, I bet. The Anderson case. You've been named a witness. I am required to take a preliminary statement. That in no way would prejudice your subsequent testimony before the actual hearing next month."

Gibson spoke his last sentences awkwardly, like a schoolboy reciting by rote poetry he didn't like. But it didn't matter to Imperateri, who thought again about the incident in the squad room.

Anderson had made a stupid remark. Everybody does now and then. Empty, ephemeral words that really didn't amount to much, except to produce regret. Yet a promotion to detective lieutenant was real, tangible, his ultimate goal before retiring to a new career.

No one would be hurt if he'd lie. No, that wasn't true. Marie Mackay would, terribly. But she was young and smart and ambitious and would go a long way, whether or not he lied. Of course, he'd lose her if she ever found out. And she would.

"Let me think about it, Sergeant. I'm really trying to recall exactly what happened. Sort things out. Can I get back to you later?"

Gibson switched off the recorder. "Take your time. You can send your statement in or make it directly at the hearing. No sweat."

Imperateri rose to shake hands and then watched the sergeant depart. He thought that Gibson was right about one thing. No sweat. At least, not now. Later, for sure. He hoped later would never come.

Though the seats were in third row center, Vincent Imperateri had a hard time concentrating on the opera. The stage, dimmed so that it was difficult distinguishing the characters, combined with the long German dialogue to send him drifting off with his thoughts.

He first reflected upon Marie and how she'd become strangely silent on the way to the opera. He questioned whether it had been wise to tell her about the upcoming Internal Affairs board hearing, and then to joke about the dilemma in which he found himself.

She had hardly considered it amusing. She'd replied that telling the truth was no dilemma, and then had said very little until the curtain rose for the first act. That she had no sense of humor concerning this bothered him almost as much as her implicit distrust of his testimony.

During the latter part of the opera his thoughts turned to Mrs. Gertrude Forbes, her old and weakened eyes, and the apparent dead end in the investigation after a short-lived euphoria.

Was it really a police car that the old lady had seen? With her eyesight, it could have been a tank. The possibility was also strong that she had mistaken a cruiser's dome light for a taxicab's roof marker. There were thousands of cabs in the Washington area, and a computer check had already been made after the murder of the second victim.

Nothing unusual, no sex record of any of the hackers, had been uncovered. He'd guessed nothing would turn up since any successful applicant for a hacker's license had to have a clean record. After that, what law a cabbie broke and got away with was anybody's guess.

He sighed, looked over at Marie sitting next to him and saw that she had dozed off again, minutes before the end of the opera. She had hardly enjoyed the earlier acts. Throughout the performance she had fidgeted in her seat, left it at least twice for a walk in the lobby, and finally fell asleep early in the last act.

He let her sleep, thinking that she'd had a long and tiring day. However, when her head began to roll from side to side, accompanied by heavy breathing heard by those sitting nearby, he shook her gently.

Now he awoke her again and they joined the opera lovers pouring out of the Kennedy Center to the lower level parking garage. They split off the main stream and left via the front entrance for the leisurely walk to her apartment a few blocks away.

Both strolled quietly on the plaza making up the Center's superblock. When he glanced over at her he could see her unhappy expression and could only guess that she was disturbed about the hearing. Did she actually believe that he wouldn't support her when called to testify?

He was glad that no date had yet been set for the hearing. During the past few days he'd gone over his options and possible consequences. If he lied, he'd lose Marie. That was plain and simple. But there were always other women around, police groupies who loved the hard erection-like sensation of snub-nosed .38's pressed against their soft tummies.

Yet none of these women came close to having Marie's style and class. As far as her integrity was concerned, that was a different matter. If and ever he'd support Anderson, it would be to get back at her for her initial deception with the tape recorder.

If he told the truth, he'd lose the promotion and throw a hefty retirement increase away. He'd also incur the undying enmity of Anderson and a lot of police officers.

If he lied, he'd lose his self-esteem. This would be difficult to regain. Once dishonest, the way to other deceits for a cop would become too easy, too tempting. The common wisecracks. *Show me an honest cop and I'll show you a dumb one. An honest cop, that's a mutually exclusive term. A dishonest cop, a redundancy.*

"Quiet, aren't we?" he said, immediately regretting his sarcastic tone. He quickly asked a genuine question. "Did you enjoy the opera?"

She replied at once, as though without thinking. "I can't stand

171

Wagner. Much less his *Siegfried*. Too long, too slow, too damn dull. And too damn stupid."

He was taken aback by the vehemence of her reply. Surely something else was bothering her, and no doubt it was his earlier teasing about his Anderson testimony. He wanted to confront her about this, but came to Wagner's defense first.

"Look," he said, "Wagner grows on you. His stuff isn't easy to like at first hearing, like *Carmen* or *La Boheme* are. He didn't write lyrical grand opera, but music drama."

She forced a laugh. "Ha! That's just it. He has characters standing on stage yapping forever in a foreign language completely unintelligible to ninety-nine percent of the audience. In romantic opera, all you need is a knowledge of the plot. The exciting music does the rest."

Imperateri shrugged. "Granted. Wagner has his painful moments, but stick with him. There's compensation. Great orchestration, great music."

She fell silent again, thrusting her lips out in displeasure. It wasn't until they reached her apartment house that she turned and spoke to him at the front entrance.

"Vinnie, do you mind if I don't invite you up? I've got a headache."

"And it's name is Anderson," he said, finally vexed with her attitude.

She glared at him and entered the lobby, leaving him alone. Moments later, he sought a cab, peering into the traffic for a lighted roof hump. At that instant an idea struck him.

He now knew how to get around the problem with old Mrs. Gertrude Forbes.

TWENTY

Julian Stone found barely any mention in the Washington papers about Larry Wilson. A one-paragraph story on a back page merely stated that a gas station attendant has been assaulted during an apparent holdup attempt. A description of the suspect followed.

Stone threw the paper aside. He felt cheated, let-down. He had failed. Only he knew that Wilson had been cured of his disease. The news reporter did not identify Wilson as a multiple rapist, did not write that it was unlikely that he would commit any more rapes.

Stone would have also liked to have seen in the news story hints of possible vengeance by an aggrieved party. But there was nothing like that, no explanation and no speculation. The police were apparently playing the case close to the vest, Stone gathered. Perhaps this was their way of trapping the perpetrator somehow by holding back on details.

He dismissed the idea that Wilson may have covered up the emasculation for private reasons. While not impossible, it was unlikely that a semi-comatose Wilson would have been able to hide the surgery from an ambulance crew and inquiring police. In any event, the deed was done, but it was hardly a complete success.

It was apparent to Stone that he may have to find another patient. Quite coincidentally his eye fell upon a news story with a Boston dateline. The report was of an appeals court overturning the conviction of a man found guilty of a double rape murder. The court ruled that the man, Charles Warren, had been denied a speedy trial.

173

Stone read further.

Warren was denied his constitutional rights because of "unreasonable delays" and the State's "calloused and lackadaisical attitude," the appellate court said in a 3–0 decision.

Warren was convicted last June of raping and murdering two teenage hitchhikers almost two years ago. Their bodies, mutilated so badly that it took dental charts to identify them, were found in a roadside ditch. Warren was indicted for the crime. However, it took prosecuting attorneys almost twenty-four months to convene a grand jury to hear the evidence.

The appeals court ruled that Warren's guilt and sanity were established to the satisfaction of the trial jury beyond a reasonable doubt. "Nevertheless, this court absolves him of the crime and lays his release solely on the failure of the State to prosecute within a shorter time than it did."

The State of Massachusetts will decide within the next few weeks whether it will appeal the decision.

Warren, a carpenter, is free pending a resolution of any such appeal, but must remain in the area.

He was convicted six years ago in another rape case and served twenty-eight months of a ten-year sentence at the state reformatory. At that trial, he entered a plea of guilty, but maintained that he had not understood what he was doing.

Stone shook his head at the thought of the prosecuting attorneys. "Damn your lazy bureaucratic asses," he cried aloud. He then cursed the appeals court for freeing Warren, a double murderer, because he hadn't been tried fast enough.

A sudden remembrance about Boston came to him. He examined a calendar of professional medical meetings. The American Academy of Chest Physicians was holding a Boston meeting in early January. Although Stone was not a member, he could attend as any physician could by merely registering. It was a good reason to be in Boston.

He dialed Boston telephone information and got the number of the local carpenters' union. A moment later, he dialed the union and spoke in what he hoped was a bureaucratic tone.

"This is the post office. We have a registered letter for a Mr.

Charles Warren, care of your union. Do you want it or do you have a local address where we can forward it?"

The apartment was in the run-down Dorcester section of Boston. Population shifts combined with economic change left dilapidated streets with storefront churches and half vacant apartment buildings. It was such a building that Julian Stone approached, grateful for the blustery cold wind that kept the street empty of people.

With heart pounding and stomach seemingly twisting into knots, he entered the sour, urine-smelling hallway and quickly found the apartment. He lay his medical bag on the floor and pressed an ear against the door. From within came the sounds of a television sitcom, a joke, laughter, a joke, more laughter.

One perspiring hand gripped the Beretta in the topcoat pocket while the other knocked on the door. He listened again. No sound now came from the television. Only silence remained.

Again, as immediately preceding the Larry Wilson operation, fear and uncertainty gnawed at him. Suppose Warren wasn't alone. What then? Excusing himself and then returning later would only alert Warren that something was wrong. On the other hand, assuming he was alone, there was always the possibility that he could become violent after seeing the needle. A man who was a carpenter by trade could be expected to be in fine physical shape.

Stone knocked again. Still no reply. He breathed deeply, swallowed, and rapped loudly, shouting at the same time.

"Open up, Warren! I know you're in there."

"Who's there?" a deep voice called out.

"Tucker, from district court."

"What the hell you want?"

"The judge says I got to get you to sign a release form."

The door cracked open. A pair of dark eyes peered through. "Shit. What the hell's that? Let me see it."

Stone was about to pull out the Beretta when he realized that someone else may yet be in the apartment. That wouldn't do.

He'd have to make sure. He smiled, then laughed. "Someone with you, Warren? Is that why you won't let me in?"

The door opened wider. "Nobody here but me."

Stone jerked the gun out and shoved in into Warren's face. "Then step aside before I blow your head off."

Slamming the door behind him, Stone locked it. Warren, standing shirtless with sinewy arms straight up in the air, stared at the gun with his eyes bulging. He was a tall man, well-defined musculature rippling on his torso.

"What the hell's this all about? You a cop?"

"Turn around fast," Stone ordered. He didn't want Warren to see his face any longer than necessary. Even with the disguise, later identification might be possible.

"I demand the right to see my lawyer."

Seeing Warren cringe, hearing his frightened voice, Stone lowered the gun. His hands shook uncontrollably. He could not continue. How could he mutilate still another man? In doing so, would it be another sign that he had indeed lost his power of reasoning. His sanity?

Despite his concern that unnecessary talk might make voice identification easier, he had to speak with the man. He had to find a new motivation, something to prod himself to continue with his plan.

"I read about you, Mr. Warren. I got interested in your case. But I want you to tell me about it."

Warren turned his head. "Who are you?"

"Don't look at me!"

"You're going to shoot me, ain't you? To get even for them letting me go. I know about guys like you. Vigilantes."

"No, Mr. Warren. I want to help you."

"Funny way of doing it."

"I want to know all about what you did to those two girls. It's for a report I'm doing for a rape crisis center." Stone was amazed at his new-found ability to lie with such ease.

Warren turned once more. An amused look flashed across his face. "They was whores. That's all."

"You turn again to look at me and it'll be the last thing you'll ever see. Now, you're going to have to tell me the truth, Mr. Warren. You know damn well they were just a couple of kids trying to get home when you picked them up."

Back and forth shook Warren's head slowly. "Hookers, I'm telling you. But I felt sorry for them, all alone at night on the road like that. They asked me right off if I wanted to fuck the two of them for the price of one. I laughed my head off. I said I never paid nothing for fucking in my life. Then one of them, the one sitting in the back seat, you see, one was in front. The one in back holds this here knife at the back of my neck. She wants money. She said she was going to kill me. I was lucky to swing the car and throw her off balance. Then I grabbed the knife away. And that's all."

"I see," Stone said. "And then you raped both of them and cut them into pieces. That's how you got even with them, right?"

Warren was silent. His shoulders lifted in a shrug.

"Mr. Warren, if you don't tell me the truth, I'm going to have to shoot you in your lying mouth. They weren't hookers, now, were they?"

Again Warren shrugged.

Stone took a deep breath. His mission needed no more reinforcing. He was a doctor who treated disease. A doctor, nothing more. But now he had to lie again, not for his patient's sake, but for his own. Telling Warren what was going to happen would make him unmanageable and dangerous.

"Yes, Mr. Warren, I read about you in the papers. I figured you could be one of my new customers. I lied to you about the other stuff. I push horse and am always looking for customers. Thought you might want a free sample. Just for starters. After that, you pay."

Stone reached into his bag and loaded a hypodermic syringe. Warren watched from the corner of his eye. He grinned and lowered one arm as an offering.

"Hey, man. Let the good times roll."

"They will, Mr. Warren."

The field was the same. Wild bush and scrub pine stood as

though waiting for the inevitable developer's tractor to shave the land bare. The only change was the long line of some dozen automobiles, engines at idle so that the drivers could run the heaters. Like participants in a racing contest, they waited for a signal from Noseworthy. He, too, waited, his teeth chattering into the radio held to his mouth.

Some sixty yards away Vincent Imperateri positioned Gertrude Forbes in the exact area where she claimed to have been that day. He looked at her now, dressed in a heavy coat and scarf and wearing those ridiculously thick eyeglasses. He shook his head almost imperceptibly, and hoped that his idea wasn't going to be an expensive waste of time. He also thought of how she had reacted when he'd called on her again, apologizing for the visit and stressing the importance of her testimony.

"Young man," she'd said, sounding very much like the schoolteacher she once was, "you said that you weren't going to pester me again. You were not completely candid. I suspect that you have no moral fiber. I suppose one should expect that sort of behavior from people of your kind."

Her words had stung him. He'd wanted to tell her off, bawl her out, threaten her with a subpoena, even lock her up for obstructing justice. But he needed her.

Integrity, moral fiber, he thought. The old WASP bitch would know the dictionary definition, but never the working meaning. His grandfather, he was a man who knew, without ever going to school or picking up a book.

The old man had refused charity, handouts, dishonesty, guile, as long as he'd had a working muscle in his body. And even when he didn't.

During slack periods in the construction trades, old Dominick, already in his seventies and wracked with arthritis, pushed a three-wheeled cart, handling up to five thousand pounds of ice a day. Sweat poured through his skin, the long johns he wore year-round, and his clothing as he scored ice blocks with tongs, chipped with a pick, and then lifted the split block to carry it up eight flights of stairs.

178

Always honest, always charging not one penny more than what the ice and his labor were worth. And in the winter, when demand for ice was small, he carried a pulley-driven grindstone on his back, walking miles with it and ringing a bell to let the neighborhood know the knife-sharpener had arrived.

Vincent Imperateri imagined he could hear the tinkling of the bell now, ringing as it had then, carrying far in the cold, brittle air. He shook his head as if to clear it of his thoughts. Then he lifted the radio to his lips to contact Noseworthy.

"Okay, Nose. Let loose with a couple of cabs first. Let's get them out of the way."

The taxi pulled into a predesignated spot marked off by posts. Mrs. Forbes shook her head. "No, Officer Imperateri, I am afraid it looked nothing like that."

Imperateri picked up the radio. "Nose, skip the other cab. Let's start the fuzz wagons."

The Virginia contingent led off. First came the Alexandria patrol car, all white with blue-green lettering on the doors marked with the *City of Alexandria* riding over the city crest, a ship on water.

Mrs. Forbes squinted, peered intently, moving her neck and head forward like a giraffe reaching for vegetation. Finally, she shook her head. "Definitely, no, Officer Imperateri."

Next came the Arlington County cruiser, blue and white with a triangle declaring its jurisdiction. The Fairfax County car, with similar colors but with a white hood, followed. On both, Mrs. Forbes made negative sounds by clucking her tongue and shaking her head.

When the last Virginia entry, a state trooper cruiser, was vetoed by her, Imperateri was convinced that he'd indeed made a futile move in gathering up the vehicles. All that time and effort wasted on a silly hunch that this woman could provide the slightest of leads. Already knocking on the door of dotage, she was probably one step away from being declared legally blind in both eyes. But he'd come this far, and now had to go through with the rest of it.

Imperateri thanked the departing Virginia police over the radio for their cooperation, and then called Noseworthy to continue with the Maryland delegation. Led off by a state trooper patrol car, the nearby counties of Montgomery, Prince Georges and Howard briskly rolled forward for inspection, only to be clucked away by Mrs. Forbes. Aside from a few private security cars similarly equipped with dome lights, only the Washington cuiser remained.

"Nose, let's have our own finest and get ready to go home."

The District of Columbia patrol car rolled into place. Imperateri held his breath. This was the last police vehicle. If the old lady couldn't make positive identification, he'd be back at the very beginning.

Gertrude Forbes scrutinized the white cruiser with its wide blue strip running on the sides and the gold lettering *Police* curved over a badge with a drawing of the United States Capitol building. She slowly shook her head and began to cluck. The sound was broken by a gasp.

"That's it. I remember the picture of the Congress."

TWENTY-ONE

The day after his return from Boston, Julian Stone found himself running late for his daily visit to his hospitalized patients. He was late to begin with, having had to give in to Lois in order to leave. She had argued that she was completely recovered, and that the day nurse he'd hired for home care was no longer needed. He finally agreed.

Behind schedule as he was, he still took precious minutes to detour through the downtown area. His destination was a stand selling out-of-town newspapers. There he braked to a stop and raced to buy a copy of the *Boston Globe*. Back in the car, he used still more time to glance at the paper, suddenly sucking in his breath as an article on the front page caught his eye. It was about the emasculation of Charles Warren.

There was considerably more information than in the article about Larry Wilson. Here nothing was left out. The article played up the storm of controversy following the reversal of the Warren conviction, and the possibility that an angry citizen had taken the law into his own hands. The term *vigilante* was used.

Stone turned the ignition and pulled away, a smile on his face. The publicity was a secondary consideration with him now that he had it. He liked it, enjoyed the idea that the public would surmise that the emasculation arose out of necessity.

Of more importance to him was the fact that no longer would Charles Warren traumatize or murder a helpless woman. Let other paroled rapists know that the someone was not going to let them continue their violent, disgusting acts.

As Stone drove, a new concern developed in his mind. The

181

publicity, while alerting the public to the mockery of criminal punishment, may also make future operations more difficult for him.

He realized that he could not operate in the New Jersey area where his action would be front page news. The police would know that a medically trained person was involved. It wouldn't take long before anyone who knew of his personal tragedy would put two and two together.

And even if he would scatter his operations, the news would have a cumulative effect, eventually making front pages and lead television news items everywhere. The rapists would be on guard, slashing out wildly at anyone they'd suspect was out to hurt them. And the police would be under strong pressure to stop the vigilante. It would cut short his campaign. That wouldn't do.

As Stone saw it, he had only one choice. It was to strike out fast, hitting as many rapists as possible before they could react to the widespread publicity which was sure to follow.

His mind made up, he skimmed over possible obstacles. Lois was no problem. She spoke of returning to school, starting all over again, even going to exercise classes.

Carl Miller was another possibility. The psychiatrist would recall having brought up the subject of castration as a punishment or a treatment. But Miller was now in Europe, far away from everything, at least for a while. Imperateri? A strong possibility. Yet the sergeant, with all of his local cases, may not bother following national crime news too closely. Also, he might not link the physician aspects and the vengeance motives to the New Jersey doctor whose daughter had been raped and murdered so many weeks ago.

As Stone drove on to the hospital grounds and to the physicians' parking area, he tried to recall the listing he had studied last night in the *Journal of the American Medical Association*. It was of upcoming medical meetings which were scheduled in almost every major city.

Though he usually attended conferences dealing with his own pediatrics specialty, he occasionally traveled to other meetings when he could spare the time and when they promised something interesting or new in medicine.

The American College of Radiology was going to meet in New Orleans in January. Chicago was to be the site a few days later for the annual ophthalmologists' meeting. And the surgeons had scheduled Los Angeles also that month, right before the neurologists would gather in San Francisco. He could easily make one trip to the West Coast and catch both of those meetings.

The schedule he'd follow was simple. After arriving at an airport and renting a car, he'd go to the main public library. There he'd repeat his newly-acquired skill in perusing old newspapers.

Julian Stone parked and jumped out of his car with the agility of a teenage boy. Buoyant and filled with renewed energy, he glanced at his watch. He was very late, but most eager to complete his hospital calls. He had other things on his mind, not the least of which was telling Betty Gruff to pick up flight tickets to New Orleans and return via Chicago. After this, he'd handle his own travel to California. It was best not to let his receptionist know too much.

Both Betty Gruff and nurse Eva Barlow would wonder about his frequent traveling to meetings in which he'd had no interest before. He'd have to make up stories. For Chicago, he'd lie about having to attend a special session on children's eye problems. Of course, he wouldn't tell them that even if there were such a session, he'd have no time for it.

Julian Stone felt more than the usual apprehension as he drove along North Marine Drive to the Lake Shore hospital. The difference between the Arctic-like winds blowing in from Lake Michigan and the warm humidity of New Orleans was absolute. In the Louisiana city, the good weather had made it seem like a vacation. He hated to leave after only one day, most of which was spent in the hunt for a patient and a subsequent successful bilateral orchiectomy.

Now when he asked himself what was bothering him, he realized it was not the sudden change of temperature, but whether he would be doing the right thing in castrating still another patient. As if to steel himself for the task, he brought to mind the article he had read in a month-old edition of the Chicago *Sun-Times* in a library only hours ago.

There had been no need bothering to clip out the article. The details so angered him that he couldn't help but commit them to memory.

Twelve years ago, Fred Watkins, then age twenty, gained entry to the black ghetto apartment of two very young sisters by identifying himself as a building inspector. The mother was not home at the time, leaving the sisters, Louella, eight, and Denise, ten, to care for themselves.

According to the prosecutor, Watkins tied the girls with belts and ransacked the apartment for money and valuables which he collected in a pillowcase. He then turned both a television and radio on loud and forced both sisters to perform oral sodomy with him.

After failing to have intercourse with Louella, he attempted to enlarge her vagina with a broomstick. She bled to death, and her body was found when the mother, Mrs. Jolene Harris, came home from her job as a cleaning woman. Denise was missing.

The prosecutor charged that Watkins took her to a vacant building and raped her repeatedly before strangling her and leaving her body, which neighborhood boys later found. Also found was his wallet and identification, dropped behind in his haste to leave.

Watkins was apprehended, tried, and given a mandatory sentence of thirty years to life for the kidnapping, double rape and murder.

Julian Stone realized that the act, horrifying though it was, was that of a sick man. Yet what angered him was the lead, or beginning paragraph of the article. It reported that a circuit court judge had released Watkins, who had served only eleven years of his sentence.

The judge said he acted on the recommendation of an Illinois state psychiatrist who advised that Watkins needed intensive treatment for psychiatric and drug abuse problems. The judge then placed Watkins on five years' probation with the requirement that he be treated at the inpatient residential facility at the Lake Shore psychiatric hospital.

The advising psychiatrist wrote that Watkins was mentally unstable and was a multiple drug abuser who had been pushed at the time of the rape-murders by his drug use of PCP and amphetamines. *Mr. Watkins does not come across in my examination as a basically anti-social person,* the psychiatrist stated.

Therefore, from my point of view as regards his disposition, I would think the emphasis should be on the psychiatric treatment rather than simply incarceration, the psychiatrist's report concluded.

"Bullshit!" Julian Stone shouted as he recalled the conclusion. He immediately realized that his shout was to give himself renewed conviction and courage. After all, the Fred Watkins operation was to be a distinct departure from Stone's established rules for selecting a patient.

Watkins just didn't fit all of Stone's criteria. Though the convict during the course of one evening had murdered two girls, raping one and attempting to ravish the other, he couldn't be technically called a repeater, a multiple rapist with record to show.

Stone pulled to a stop and opened his medical bag which held his disguise as well as his operating equipment. He pasted the mustache on and fitted the wig. With the glasses and mouth padding, he examined his face in the rear view mirror and enjoyed a brief laugh. He looked like a goddamn psychiatrist.

Exiting from the car, his mind was still full of doubts. Suppose Watkins could be rehabilitated. If so, it would be an inhumane act to castrate him, cutting away forever that which God had given.

Stone paused and looked at the hospital, its facade dark and dull brick, old-looking probably even when it had been new. He breathed deeply and moved forward slowly. He needed time to think, to make up his mind. Maybe if he had a chance to spend time with Watkins, look into the man's eyes, talk with him, maybe then some decision could be made.

Beyond a set of squeaky revolving doors a receptionist's desk stood. It was occupied by a middle aged lady with frosted hair who read a movie magazine and munched on a candy bar.

"Good afternoon," Stone said boldly. "I'm Dr. Forest. I'm here for a consultation on a Mr. Fred Watkins."

The receptionist looked up, irritation at being interrupted clearly evident on her face. She turned to her Rolodex wheel file, flipped through it, and them smirked triumphantly. "You'll have to check in first at the nurses' station on Eight West."

"Could you tell me his room number?"

"Against regulations," she replied, her eyes already back to the magazine.

Stone turned towards the elevators, not wishing to argue or spend more time with her. She undoubtedly would be questioned by the police.

The police.

They would come only if he operated, and he hadn't yet decided whether to go through with it. He had to see Watkins, see for himself whether the man gave off an aura of the predicated felon, the repeat offender, the rapist who would use his prick as though it were a weapon.

Stone now believed that he was endowed with a peculiar sense that enabled him to detect that lust-murdering instinct in certain men. He believed that they were possessed of a sure look and attitude that indicated they would kill whenever the urge overtook them.

This is what Julian Stone believed.

The old doors creaked open with the screeching sound made only by very old elevators, like that of a subway train just beginning to roll. Stone stepped out and began to walk purposefully towards the nurses' station.

Act as if you're being put upon, he ordered himself. He repeated his consultation story to a somber-faced nurse at Eight West who cocked her head to the side, as if deliberating how to tell him his request was out of order.

"Dr. Ferguson didn't leave any instructions . . ."

He cut her off at once, before her words could become hard and fast. "Can you telephone Dr. Ferguson while I go through Mr. Watkins's file?"

She shrugged a shrug to indicate a fair enough trade-off and handed him a metal clipboard which hung among others on the wall.

He sat down while she dialed, wondering what his next move ought to be when the good doctor expressed ignorance of the consultation. He gambled that she wouldn't be able to contact Ferguson right away. Few psychiatrists were ever immediately available. In the meantime, he still didn't know whether to go ahead with Watkins.

Skimming through the hospital blue and white sheets which summarized physical and mental examinations, he found Dr. Ferguson's report and discovered that he was the state psychiatrist who had recommended releasing Watkins. Stone didn't bother reading the report since it repeated information already covered in the newspaper story.

What attracted his attention now was a report that hadn't been publicized. It was a dissenting statement by another psychiatrist whose own recommendation was apparently ignored by the judge who had released Watkins.

Based on lengthy examinations over a long period of time, the dissenting psychiatrist had observed that Watkins was a classic sociopath and one of the most amoral men seen in some thirty years of psychiatric practice.

Watkins seemed to have no respect for the dignity of human life. After long and tiring sessions which bored him greatly, he admitted raping and committing forced oral sodomy many times, so many that he could not recall even an approximate number. His official criminal record does not bear this out, suggesting that the rapes, occurring within the black ghetto, were not reported by the victims to the authorities. This could be attributed to threats by Watkins, distrust of police by the victims, or a stoical attitude towards rape within the ghetto.

Perhaps realizing that he would have to show repentance and/or a capacity for rehabilitation, Watkins repeatedly referred to an "inner force" which had driven him to these acts, and which he would certainly control in the future. As for the past, he constantly compared himself to a bird with wings who had to fly, no matter what.

Watkins was observed to be a scheming and manipulative man, cynically enrolling in prison education and drug programs in the hope that they would impress a parole board and win for him an early release. He enrolled in these programs and began attending church services only after he had served one-third of his minimum sentence and discovered that he was eligible for parole.

The nurse interrupted Stone's reading. "Dr. Ferguson is with a patient and will call back in half an hour."

Stone shook his head gravely. "Well, nurse, I have my own patients to look after, and I don't have that kind of time to waste."

"Doctor, I have strict orders. Mr. Watkins is under a security watch. All visitors . . ."

Stone cut her off. "Are you authorized to accept an additional charge for my services?"

She stared blankly, then glanced at the telephone. She was obviously unwilling to call Ferguson again, to be caught in the middle. She looked at Stone and shrugged.

He was winning, but now had to lessen the attack. He smiled, his voice coming warmer, jokingly conspiratorial. "Look, I'll tell you what. I'll conduct a brief preliminary interview with Mr. Watkins and then will call Dr. Ferguson and square the whole thing."

"Mr. Watkins is in room eight-twelve."

Lying stretched out on the hospital bed, the black man's legs projected so far over the end that they resembled an unfinished cantilever bridge. He was enormous, dwarfing everything else in the room, the bed, a chair, a table. He lay barechested, his pectoral muscles standing out like superfluous slabs of marble on a Greek statue. His upper arms were the size of a young girl's waist.

"Mr. Fred Watkins?" Stone asked, swallowing his anxiety. Here was a patient to be wary of, a man of considerable strength and violence.

The man glared through swollen, sullen eyes. "Yeah, What's happenin'?"

188

"Dr. Ferguson has asked me to chat with you for a little bit. Maybe examine you."

"Shit. That's all you dudes been doin' since I been here."

"They treatin' you good here?" Stone asked, lapsing into the vernacular.

Watkins grinned. "The food ain't bad. All I got to do is stick around here a few weeks. Then they let me go and then I come back about once a week."

"You mean you'll actually be free? You'll come back here voluntarily?"

"That's what the judge say," Watkins replied, and then with a look of sincerity, gazed into Stone's eyes. "I could walk out right now if I had a mind to. But maybe I stick around."

"Mr. Watkins, I hope you will. We're here to help you. Now, Dr. Ferguson mentioned that you were driven by some 'inner force' to rape and murder those two little girls. There was something you said about being a bird who had to fly, no matter what." Stone pictured in his mind a two hundred and sixty pound black bird piercing a small girl as though she were a worm.

Watkins sat up, his brows beetling, his musculature rippling like wind-driven reeds. "Who tol' you that?"

"Dr. Ferguson, like I said."

"Oh, yeah, that's right. I didn't mean to do it."

"You didn't mean to stick that broomstick into that poor little girl so that you could make her hole bigger?"

"Shit, man. I don't wanna talk no more about that."

Stone nodded and opened his medical bag. "Well, Mr. Watkins, I have some bad news to tell you. We've come up with a touch of gonorrhea that you apparently caught in prison." Stone guessed that Watkins must have indulged in sodomy and homosexual activity while locked up.

Watkins pulled himself up to sit on the side of the bed. His face showed puzzlement mixed with concern. "What you say?"

"The clap. Bad blood. But nothing to worry about. I'll just give you a little shot which should take care of it." Stone locked the door. "I don't want anyone coming in while I shoot you in the ass. Now, pull those trousers down, please."

Watkins grinned and showed two huge, black mountains of solid flesh. Moments later, the giant of a man was asleep.

"It isn't necessary to lock you up forever or to hang you if you rape and kill again, Mr. Watkins," Stone whispered. "I'm just breaking your wings. You're never going to be able to fly again. Never."

TWENTY-TWO

Detective First Class John Bork was a young man, in his late twenties, with the swagger of the uniformed beat patrolman still evident in his walk. Vincent Imperateri envied him, the athletic build, the thick crop of hair, the Hollywood leading man features. But most of all, he envied his youthful enthusiasm, and within a short time of Bork's being assigned to the lust-murders, excused the younger man's lack of homicide experience.

At first, Imperateri couldn't find enough for him to do. Usually, two detectives were routinely assigned to a homicide. Where serial murders were involved, investigatory power mushroomed to over a couple of dozen detectives.

Imperateri felt, however, that given the lack of clues, the lust-murder cases wouldn't be helped by assigning more detectives. He believed that the case was one of those that would be solved by a fluke, not by another one hundred cops duplicating efforts and blindly stumbling over one another.

Yet with the Gertrude Forbes's disclosure, it now seemed that it was back to leg work, the interviews and checks, for which he'd use John Bork.

"Johnny," Imperateri said after briefing him, "we'll need the motor pool log of every precinct in the city. I want to know who had what patrol car out at the time the old lady sighted the killer."

"Alleged killer," Bork corrected, smiling and showing the most even set of white teeth that Imperateri had ever seen.

"Suspect," Imperateri countered, also with a smile. "And we'll want to match the approximate times of all of the other homicides against who had what patrol car out."

Imperateri didn't have to tell the younger man to move fast. Neither man was going to allow a lapse of time to permit the killer to strike again. And this time they were lucky. When a break came, it was usually at the expense of another tragedy.

Nor did he have to tell Bork what next to do with suspect patrol cars. Forensic experts would be called to vacuum up anything, bits of clothing dust fibers or hair, that could be compared with samples from bodies of the victims.

Before Imperateri could say anything else, Bork was off and literally running out of the squad room, pulling on his jacket and topcoat almost at the same time. Imperateri watched, again with a feeling of envy at Bork's energy and zeal.

For Bork, solving the case was a matter of trying to look good as a rookie detective. For Imperateri, whose zeal was tempered by the veteran's sense of pacing, ridding the streets of a homicidal maniac was more than being an important job. It was also personal. He had a daughter, and he wanted to make the city safer for her.

The telephone rang for him. It was Sergeant Tom Gibson, informing him that he was scheduled to appear before the trial board hearing tomorrow.

Now Imperateri added a third reason. Like Bork, it would now be a matter of trying to look good, especially after tomorrow when his world would fall around him.

In his office at home, Dr. Julian Stone studied his itinerary once more before slipping it into his briefcase. The trip would be his longest so far, a flight to the West Coast with visits to San Francisco and Los Angeles. Suitcases were packed and arrangements made to attend to two medical meetings scheduled a day apart. He anticipated no trouble in finding suitable candidates in at least one of the cities.

Though he was pleased at the prospect of being able to perform two castrations within a short time, his pleasure was not without some uncertainty. The fear plagued him even more that someone might notice the parallels between his trips and the operations. But what could he do to avoid such suspicion?

The solution was obvious as well as unacceptable to him. He would not decrease his activities not even postpone them as precautionary measures. To do so would allow dangerous criminals to roam at the whim of liberal courts and judges.

Suddenly from the den rose the sound of barking commands over a background of rock music. Counting cadence, the shouts ordered to stretch, jump, or twist.

Stone stepped to the doorway of the den. Lois, dressed in plum-colored leotards and tights, presented a pleasing figure as she swung her arms freely, following instructions from the phonograph recording. Wearing her mass of black hair coiled in a pony tail, she now seemed much younger than her mid-thirties.

He felt himself becoming aroused as she dropped to the carpeting and lay arching her back. She lifted her hips and buttocks to the pulsating music, emulating a sexual climax.

Recently, they had made love again, several times within a short period of time, after a long abstinence following Susan's disappearance. Lois had somehow seemed to erase their daughter's tragic death from her mind. But if it was only dormant, waiting to resurface, he was grateful for her return to life.

Lois turned her head and noticed him. She stopped her movements. "If you're going to ogle," she said, "come in for a front row seat."

He laughed. "No, I've got some more things to do for the trip."

"Come in, anyway. There's something I want to talk to you about."

Her voice, cool and businesslike, bothered him. "Something the matter?"

She switched the recording off and turned face-to-face. "You're darn right. I know what you've been doing and I don't like it."

He felt a strong premature contraction wrench his heart. "Doing?" he whispered hoarsely, trying to arrange his thoughts. How did she ever find out? Did the police get to her?

"Yes, doing." She stared at him. "Julian, what's the matter? You're as pale as a ghost."

He shook his head. "I'm fine. What do you mean, doing?"

"I want to know why you have to go on all those trips. You never did before. What's happened that made you want to run away from me?"

A strong sense of relief filled him. He grinned and patted her on the shoulder. "Believe me, Lois, I really have to attend those meetings. I've neglected keeping up with the latest advances because of what happened . . . and the office kept me so busy."

"Why haven't you asked me along?"

Stone again smiled, stalling while he thought of an answer. He'd had no idea that she had wanted to accompany him.

"Of course you can come along," he said. "I never asked you because I just thought it would be boring for you while I'm at meetings."

She smiled and shook her head.

"Okay," he said, "I'll make the arrangements. We'll make it a long overdue vacation."

"Oh, Julian, it'll be so nice to get away."

He was pleased. It would be no trouble having her along. In fact, she might even be helpful as a cover, a front, an alibi. It was strange that he hadn't thought of it before. He could sneak out on a mission while she slept at night. And during the day he could slip out of meetings while she busied herself shopping or sightseeing. It would be perfect.

"Of course," she hesitated, "you might not want to be seen with a pregnant woman of a certain age."

He felt another contraction in his chest. "What do you mean? Don't joke about something like that."

"I'm not joking. I didn't tell you, but I stopped taking the pill. I'm way past my period. And, well, it may have been a long time ago but I recognize the symptoms."

He grabbed and kissed her. "We'll call Gerry Gelman. He's the best OB-GYN man I know."

"I've already an appointment with Delores Rice."

"Who's she?"

"She's the best OB-GYN, ah, man. Uh. person. New in town, but some of my younger friends are just crazy about her."

Stone laughed heartily. He hugged and kissed Lois over and over, whispering that they were going to have a new beginning, a new life.

Later, alone and staring at the packed suitcases lying on the floor, he regretted that long ago time when they had decided to have only one child. He had been too busy with his education and then later with his practice. And Lois had wanted a career in art and had thought that more than one child wouldn't allow any degree of freedom.

Now he wondered whether his joy over her pregnancy masqueraded nothing but pure selfishness. Was having a new child a salve for an old injury? One dies, another is born. A future human being guaranteed to lessen past suffering, present memories. Property to replace that which was lost, stolen or destroyed. No, life was too precious. Yes, life was too precious.

He admitted to himself that he wanted the child as a new Susan. And he swore that he would do anything within his power to make sure his new child would face a safer world. That was why it was so important for him to go to California and anywhere else where sick minds destroyed helpless innocents.

Although the thought had crossed his mind that Mary Ann would make a good girlie for him, William Crawford quickly dispensed with that idea. She worked where he did and if anything happened to her, there would be questions and investigations of all of her co-workers. He couldn't risk that, especially since he guessed that she had probably told a few of her office girl-friends that she was interested in him. And then, she irritated him to no end with her constant female pursuit. It wasn't right. It was against the laws of nature that a woman should do that.

Nevertheless, he kept putting her off until she insisted upon cooking dinner for him one evening. He accepted, if only as a convenient way to let her know in the privacy of her apartment how he felt about their relationship.

From the very first moment that he sat in her living room he felt uncomfortable. The heat in the overly-warm apartment penetrated his skin and seemed to melt through to his bones like acid.

During dinner she chatted incessantly. Later they returned to the living room where he continually crooked a finger to pull at his collar while she appeared as cool as a Southern belle in the shade of some antebellum mansion porch. She even wore a fluffy white cotton dress with long, cuffed sleeves to heighten that impression.

Snuggling close to him on the couch, she said, "Take off your tie, Billy. You'll feel much better if you do."

"It's all right. I was just getting ready to leave anyway." Now was the time, he thought, to tell her that their relationship could go nowhere.

"Eat and run?"

"I appreciate your Southern hospitality, but I have a few chores to do."

"This late in the evening, Billy? What could you possibly do that couldn't wait until morning?"

He glanced around the apartment, trying to fix an eye on something that might summon an excuse. A picture of an English fox hunting scene with horsemen and hounds hung across the wall.

"My dog," he explained finally. "I have to walk him." He didn't have a dog, but she'd never know that, she with her forward behavior and silly posturing.

"I didn't know you had a dog, Billy."

He was tempted to say, *I don't*. "The subject never came up."

"Tell me about him."

Again he looked around the apartment, at the shag carpeting, the potted plastic plants, the odd, polka-dotted design on the lampshade. "His name's Spot. I got him for protection. There's been a lot of break-in's in the neighborhood."

"I'd like to meet Spot, Billy."

"Ah, look, Mary Ann. Nobody calls me that. Bill is okay."

She smiled and stuck a finger against her chin in the fashion of a cute five-year-old girl trying to recollect something. "How does that go? 'Sister calls me Will, mother calls me William, father calls me Bill . . . ' Oh, that's not right. You know, I had an uncle William. He traced our family way back. Would you believe we had the largest plantation and the most slaves? Tell me about your family, Bill."

It was torture for him even to sit and chat. It won't be long, he promised himself. "Not much to tell. Hardworking, honest folks." He didn't know where his parents were, if they were dead or alive, nor did he care. After he had been sent to the prison hospital, he never saw them again.

"I'd really like to meet them, Bill."

He rose to his feet. He'd tell her goodbye and good luck while standing. There was probably a psychological advantage to that, he believed.

Before he could say anything, she reached out and jerked hard on his arm, forcing him down once more. Emboldened by her own surprise move, she pressed her lips against his and held him close. He couldn't catch his breath. Gasping, he pushed her away. She leaned over again and bit his neck tenderly, murmuring his name over and over again.

For a few moments he did not resist, though he loathed being the object of her aggression. When she unzipperd his trousers and slipped her hand into his fly, he twisted away and jumped to his feet as if stung by a bee.

A look of hurt and puzzlement appeared on her face. "What's the matter with you, Bill?"

"I don't like women making sexual advances towards me," he said, angrily zipping up. "I like to do things my own way."

She turned her head away, partly in shame, partly in anger. "I never had a *man* treat me like that before. Might be that's what's wrong with you. You're not a *real man.*

He started to answer but held back. If she thought he was homosexual, all the better. Now maybe she'd leave him alone. And so would all of the other hungry women in the traffic division. The more he thought of the idea, the more he liked it. When he spoke, his voice was contrite, apologetic.

"I'm sorry, Mary Ann. I tried to make it plain at first without embarrassing either one of us."

197

She threw her head back and laughed. "Wouldn't you know it?" she said, shaking her head. She kicked off her high heeled shoes and wriggled a finger in an ear. It seemed as if her feminine, seductive exterior had collapsed with his disclosure.

He visualized how she would look in a few years after marriage, a dumpy housewife in a faded bathrobe with pink rollers in hair dyed either jet black or white-blonde. Even now that she had stopped smiling, small indentations under her eyes became visible.

"Ain't that the goddamndest shits?" she repeated several times.

"We could still be friends, Mary Ann," he said, masking his delight. "That is, if you'd like to."

She looked at him in a disinterested way and shrugged. He could have danced with joy.

"Don't get up, Mary Ann. I'll let myself out." He felt a tinge of sorrow, not because he had disappointed her, but because she'd never know how much of a man he really was.

TWENTY-THREE

The name amused Julian Stone. He repeated it several times, coming down hard on the consonants, rolling the r's and pronouncing the w like a v in the German manner.

"Dieter Warrenholtz. Dieter Warrenholtz."

The owner of the name lived in a rundown section of Los Angeles, far away from the Hilton where the American Academy of General Practice was holding its annual convention and where he and Lois were registered.

Stone didn't mind the long drive. It gave him time to turn over in his mind how he would handle any of a number of situations which might present themselves before he could remove the balls of Warrenholtz.

Stone knew from the newspaper article read and re-read only the night before that his latest patient was resident in a minimum security halfway house for paroled felons returning to society. The prospect of easy access to Warrenholtz intrigued Stone, but it was the convict's act itself that caught the doctor's interest. He now realized the facts of the article.

Am immigrant from Germany, Warrenholtz settled in Los Angeles, earning a good living as a chef in a fashionable restaurant. He had a wife and two teenage children. A success story in itself, except for a bizarre twist.

Dieter Warrenholtz had a history of sex offenses, beginning with the fondling of small girls and ending with a rape murder, for which he was tried and convicted.

Six months ago while driving aimlessly in a quiet neighborhood, he spotted Mrs. Libby Matthews, a young housewife, sunbathing in her back yard. He stopped the car, stealthily approached and ordered her into the house at knife point. In a second floor bedroom he tied her to the bedposts after stripping off her swimsuit.

According to a confession made to police, he then removed one wire from a night table lamp socket and inserted the plug back into a wall outlet. With the switch completing the circuit with the attached wire, he stuck the striped-back, live end into the woman's vagina.

He raped her before and after administering the electric shocks. Although shocks from a lamp cord are not considered strong enough to kill a person, Mrs. Matthews was found dead by her children returning from school some hours later. An autopsy failed to show the cause of death.

A neighbor saw Warrenholtz and called police. After being charged with the crime, his previous sex crimes were revealed. In Germany, he served a ten-year term for rape. Upon release, he lied to U.S. immigration officers about his record so that he could enter the country.

For the rape and murder of Mrs. Matthews, Warrenholtz was sentenced to twenty years. He also received five years for falsifying his immigration application.

Stone found it curious that rape and murder were only three times more serious than lying on a visa application. He surmised that a first degree charge was probably dropped when the prosecution couldn't prove that the rape and electrical current were what killed Mrs. Matthews.

Instead of being sent to a state penal institution, he was brought to a pre-release detention center upon request of the Los Angeles county sheriff. A controversy stormed. Newspapers charged that Warrenholtz was being catered to in a country club. The sheriff replied that the convict was a good cook and a responsible inmate and by being put to work was saving the county's money and not wasting it.

When questioned by reporters about the possibility that Warrenholtz could walk away from the minimum security installation, the sheriff said that the prisoner is aware that any escape attempt would throw him into the state prison system. "He'd be a fool to try anything."

Inmates at the detention center where the sheriff maintained his living quarters are allowed out every day to work but have to return in the evenings. Warrenholtz, however, is confined to the building at all times. There were no guards at the facility. *No guards.*

Was it going to be that easy? Stone had a premonition that the apparent clear course was actually an omen of danger and disaster. But what could happen? He would walk through the door, find Warrenholtz, identify himself as a prison doctor to perform an annual examination, and then suggest Warrenholtz's room for the checkup.

And then the needle. Within a short time Stone could be heading back towards downtown Los Angeles and a nice quiet dinner with Lois. What would she say if she knew? He had been on the verge of telling her several times but thought better of it.

Suddenly, the sky turned the shade of a blackboard, and a cold, blustery gust of wind shook the car. Stone shivered. He saw dozens of black people scurrying for cover as rain began to pour. Caught in the downpour, many became drenched, their hair scraggly wet, their clothing clinging.

This was the Watts section of Los Angeles where the detention center was located, amidst an abundance of empty and boarded-up buildings and a large, impoverished black population. Locating it anywhere else in the city would have brought petition drives and demonstrations from an outraged citizenry. Here, the people were accustomed to the presence of the law and lawbreakers and were too preoccupied with daily survival to care about the center.

The center building itself was off a main intersection and stood three stories high. Victorian in design, it was built of faded red brick, and had a crudely ornate cornice and long narrow windows. It had clearly once been a school or municipal building, transformed by need into a halfway house for rehabilitated felons returning to society.

Inside the building it was shabby and dim and smelled oddly

of mothballs. Bare, low-wattage light bulbs failed to illuminate the entrance foyer and the hallway ahead.

A black man dressed in uniform sat at a desk near the front door. Stone paused and drew back. There weren't supposed to be any guards, much less armed ones. The man's holstered weapon was clearly in sight.

Stone sucked in air, as if for courage, tapped his wig and mustache to check if they were in place, and strode forward, his medical bag bounding against his thigh.

"Good afternoon, officer. I'm Dr. Ferguson. Has Health Services called you yet?"

The strong black face squinted. "Who?"

Stone signed deep irritation. "They asked me to give Dieter Warrenholtz his annual checkup here since he's not in the prison system."

"We got our own doc . . ."

"Yes, I know, officer. But he's not with the State. He's county."

The guard shrugged. "You want Warrenholtz, he's down in the kitchen."

Warrenholtz, a wiry man with deep eyes, was dressed in baggy white trousers and a sweatshirt. As Stone explained the visit, the German constantly passed a hand over the long, blond hair slicked back in the European style.

"Your room would be the best place for the examination," Stone said.

Warrenholtz hesitated. "Nobody tell me nothing about this. I just had examination."

"Look," Stone said, his voice rising, "they're paying me for this visit. If you don't want it, that's okay with me, too."

Warrenholtz nodded and then motioned with his head for Stone to follow him. They passed by a recreation room with a table tennis set. Several residents sat watching mid-afternoon soap operas on a color television set.

"This is my room," Warrenholtz said, entering a narrow, windowless space. "Not much, but better than prison. There, the nigger boys, the spics, they gang-rape, especially fine blond boy like me."

"Just remove the sweatshirt for now, Mr. Warrenholtz."

Shirtless, the German turned to look suspiciously at Stone, holding a syringe. "What you do, what you want to stick me now?"

"Purely routine. An immunization shot."

Warrenholtz shook his head and curled his fists. "You don't stick me."

"Mr. Warrenholtz, it's required. If you don't get it here, you'll get it in the hospital with two orderlies holding you down."

Warrenholtz continued to shake his head, backing away as he did.

Stone ruffled through the medical bag, touching the Beretta. He didn't want to produce it, except as a last resort. "Now, come on, Dieter. Don't be difficult. There's a lot of VD going around, and the shot will protect you."

Stone couldn't understand why he mentioned VD, except that it worked with the rapist Watkins. Warrenholtz, however, might just know that there was no immunization available for venereal disease.

"What you think? Only men here. With men I fuck? You crazy ass-fucker!"

Stone advanced to touch his shoulder in a comforting way, but the German, believing he was about to be injected, pushed him angrily. Off came one side of the false mustache, hanging like a broken mast.

Warrenholtz gaped in surprise. "Who are you? What you want, you devil!"

Stone, feeling both ridiculous and angry over the mustache, pulled it off and flung it at Warrenholtz. "Devil? No. An angel, maybe. Here to make sure you don't ever harm another woman as long as you live."

Stone dug into the bag and pulled out the Beretta, leveling it at Warrenholtz. "How did you kill that young woman, you bastard? Why did you? How could you be so goddam cruel to do such a thing?"

"What you talk about? It was accident."

"The electric wire. You jammed it into the poor woman. Why?"

With a lightning-like move Warrenholtz lashed out and knocked the gun from Stone's hand. It clanked on the hard wooden floor and bounced under the bed. Warrenholtz then lunged forward, speed and surprise substituting for strength and size.

Stone, caught off balance, landed on the floor in a sitting position. Now the wig and eyeglasses scattered on the floor. His disguise was gone.

Warrenholtz stared at the fallen false items, then glared at Stone. "You hide your face, like murderer. You come to kill me for the woman."

He aimed a kick at Stone, who caught the blow on the forearm, sending an electric-like pain throughout his body. Again a kick lashed forward, this time smashing against the doctor's face.

Stone, unable to rise, groaned with the pain and shut his eyes, opening them a moment later to see still another kick coming. He twisted to the side, avoiding the blow. Finally, he scurried to his feet and faced Warrenholtz, now advancing slowly with arms positioned in front like a television wrestler.

"*Verflucter hund!*" the German thundered.

Stone had never had a boxing lesson, nor had he ever watched a prizefight, except for a few minutes when switching television channels. He nevertheless imitated a fighter, raising curled fists in a protective stance and keeping the chin tucked in tightly against the chest.

Warrenholtz was not intimidated. He threw a karate-like chop from the shoulder and struck Stone in the neck, sending him reeling backward. The doctor clutched wildly for support, found nothing to stay his descent, and went sprawling on the floor again, this time almost half under the bed. He reached blindly for the Beretta.

Warrenholtz lifted a heavy oak chair and rushed towards the prostrate Stone, who clutched the weapon and threw it instinctively at his attacker. As the gun left his hand, he instantly regretted using it as a missile. But it smashed against the bridge of Warrenholtz's nose, stunning and forcing him to cover the injured area with both hands.

Stone scrambled to his feet and bolted for the hypodermic syringe which he had dropped on the bed. He jabbed his patient in the upper arm. Feeling the shot, the German lashed out wildly, punching blindly at the needle which punctured a hole between his knuckles.

Within seconds, Warrenholtz succumbed. He shook his head and rotated his jaw like a cat tasting something unpleasant, and then fell backward on the bed.

Stone's breath came in gasps. Perspiration covered his face and his hands shook. He knew he could not operate this way.

With pain suffusing his body from the beating, and with his right hand rapidly swelling from a well-directed kick, he decided to call the whole thing off. And as if to lend support for his decision, a new fear entered his mind. Someone was sure to have heard the fracas. The police could well be on their way.

He gazed at Warrenholtz lying peacefully on the bed, and for a moment felt an urge to kill him. The German's death would remove a rapist once and for all. It would also stop him from giving a complete description of Stone to the police.

The doctor opened the door and looked up and down the corridor, listening carefully. There was not a sound to be heard. Could it be, he wondered, that the guard had already called for police reinforcements?

He hastily shut the door and looked once again at Warrenholtz.

Kill him, something inside him ordered. It would be so easy. Do it for yourself. For the young woman.

He shook his head. No, he wouldn't become a deadly avenger. That was not to be his role.

Working rapidly, knowing he had but a few minutes, he dragged Warrenholtz to the bed and unbuckled his trousers, pulling them off.

The German wore no underwear. His penis was incredibly

small, almost the size of a worn pencil. Even the testicles were miniatures, not much larger than a child's play marbles.

Who could tell what effect the size of Warrenholtz's organs may have had on his mind? Stone wondered. That was something for the psychiatrists to ponder. He recalled once reading that Hitler had one undescended testicle.

Stone began the operation, working faster than he liked to, and finding that the smallness of the testicles made everything more difficult. Several times he was tempted to amputate the whole scrotum rather than take precious time to remove its contents.

What seemed to Stone to be ages came when he dabbed the wound with antiseptic, dressing it moments later. He replaced his disguise and wobbled out of the room, hoping he could make it safely out of the building.

TWENTY-FOUR

Too impatient to wait for the elevator, Vincent Imperateri took the steps two at a time to the fourth floor editorial offices. He puffed with the exertion at the landing, and stopped to catch his breath before entering the huge, modern office.

He was mildly surprised. There were no clacking typewriters and copyboys scurrying from desk to desk. Instead, people sat quietly at dozens of computer terminals with electric cables running to video screens. The only sound was the humming of the terminals' cooling fans.

It had been some time since he had visited a newspaper office and he guessed the news business had caught up with the computer age, just as police had in recent years.

In the old days cops spent all of their time knocking on doors and sifting through telephone calls from witnesses who hadn't witnessed anything but who wanted to become involved, and from eccentrics who were only too willing to confess to crimes they hadn't committed. Now there were computer terminals. You give them a name, and they caught up a bunch of numbers, along with a criminal record if one were in the data base. If there were a record, the mug shots, fingerprints, associates' and relatives' names were also quickly available. Leads and tips combined with suspects and pieces of information could be shifted and juggled. Most often, it was a process of eliminating possibilities rather than moving forward. Sometimes bits of the puzzle came together. All too often, though, the bits did not, and it was back to the nuts and bolts, the knocking on doors, the face to face questioning. Ninety-nine percent of what police did was negative, wasted time and wasted effort, despite the advent of computers.

Reminded of his mission, Imperateri began looking for Marie. He was bursting with news which he had to tell her. At his ten minute appearance before the Internal Affairs hearing he had substantiated her version of the encounter with Anderson. He was deeply ashamed to think now that the idea of lying to advance his career had even crossed his mind. She'd had no inkling of it, despite his teasing her at the opera about his options. They hadn't seen each other since that night, mostly because of this heightened investigation of the lust-murder case, but partly due to his biting words about her headache being Anderson.

He spotted her, typing busily at one of the computer keyboards hooked up to a video screen a foot away. With eyes fixed on the green letters dancing on the black screen, she edited and transposed words to write her news story.

Her telephone rang. Seemingly without missing a tapped keyboard beat, she swept up the receiver and accommodated it between shoulder and slightly tilted head.

A wave of affection swept over him. His attitude had changed, and now it was time to get her to change hers.

"Could I help you?" A thin man with rolled-up sleeves interrupted his thoughts.

Imperateri pointed with his head towards Marie. "I just wanted to see her."

She greeted him coolly, destroying for the moment his desire to tell her how much she meant to him. He engaged in small talk to cover his disappointment.

She drummed her fingers on the desk and constantly looked at a large clock on the wall as he spoke. After a few minutes, she cut him off.

"Listen, Vinnie, I'm really on a tight deadline. Why don't you just drop by after work?"

Stung by her abruptness, he tried to mask his hurt with good humor. "But, Marie, you forgot. I work all of the time."

"Take an hour off at seven. I promise you a treat you won't forget."

All the way back to headquarters, Imperateri sang over and over the first few lines of *La Mattinata*, all that he could recall.

L'aurora di bianco vestita,
gia l'uscio dischiude al gran sol
di gia con le rosee sue dita
carezza de' fiori lo stuol."

Upon reaching the building, his singing turned to whistling, but that ceased when Noseworthy passed him in the hallway with barely a nod. Imperateri thought nothing of it until he entered the squad room amidst a sudden silence. The five detectives in the room turned away from him. He immediately guessed the problem, but still felt too good about Marie to let it get to him. There was no reason, however, in letting bad feelings drag out endlessly.

"Okay, police detectives, how about gathering around," he shouted in a friendly fashion.

The detectives looked at each other, wondering who would take the first step. Finally, Bork shrugged and moved forward. Then Perkins stepped up, followed by the three others.

Imperateri tried to look each one in the eyes as he spoke. "You have it in for me because I testified. Right?"

Noseworthy, standing by the door, entered and spoke first. "Vinnie, we're not proud of what you did."

"And I wouldn't be proud if I'd done what Anderson had wanted me to do. And what apparently everyone else here wished I had done. That was to tell a lie. But I followed my own conscience. I did what I thought was good for the whole department, not just for one man's ass. If you guys want a liar for a friend, I'm sorry I can't be it."

Noseworthy shook his head. "You made me and Perkins out to be liars. We backed Anderson all the way. How the hell do you think we feel?"

"The same way I would've felt if I'd have lied. Look, Anderson made a mistake. He tried to cover up. I'm sick of all that kind of crap. If I've been disloyal to one man, I've been loyal to the truth."

Imperateri paused, surprised at the strength and feeling of his own words. "I didn't mean to make a speech," he continued, "but if any of you can show me I did the department harm, I'll gladly resign now and forfeit my pension."

Robert Barnett, a burly ex-athlete, laughed. "You certainly didn't do us any good. The whole press is going to pounce on us about morale and corruption in the detective bureau."

Imperateri shook his head. "Negative. The public will blow kisses at us. They'll know from now on that whenever there's a question of right or wrong involving the homicide division, loyalty won't be a factor."

The men exchanged long looks. Imperateri now knew that he'd won.

The *blue code*, that unwritten tradition of never testifying against a fellow officer for the benefit of an outsider, had long ago begun to crumble. Whistle-blowing on corruption and bad behavior was encouraged by department higher-ups as well as by the mayor and city council.

Anderson was not the most popular man in the department, and it showed. Just then the captain walked in, beaming a smile on a face flushed with drink.

"What's this," he shouted, "a show of support for your captain? Well, thank you, men, one and all. You'll be interested to know that I got both good news and bad news. First, the bad news. The trial board has just issued a verdict of guilty against your captain, thanks to the testimony of one of you who shall go nameless since you know who that individual is. Your illustrious captain got himself a goddam reprimand which shall be a part of his personal record 'til the day he dies."

Anderson screwed up his face like an elementary schoolboy feigning pain or disappointment. Then he laughed and continued.

"Now, the good news. I'm taking Detective Sergeant Vincent Imperateri off street duty. Seems that the job got to him. He can't remember things too good. Needs a rest. He's being reassigned to the blotter battalion."

Imperateri turned away without saying anything. He knew it

would be useless. The captain was drunk. He returned to his own desk and stared at a printed form under the glass top which read *Rights of the Arrested.* On top of the glass was his current *Report of Investigation* on the rape cases.

A damn clerk's job, he brooded. Handling administrative matters, booking, keeping track of assignments, reports. Anderson was either trying to humiliate him, provoke him into doing something stupid, or maybe even forcing him to retire. Maybe all three.

He wondered whether to complain to the brass that his transfer was a punitive action, that he was being made a scapegoat. But such a move might splinter the department and enable the press to charge that the bickering was hampering police work. It was a no-win situation.

Yet if he kept quiet and sat at the desk for a short time, there was a chance he could return to investigations. After all, desk work wasn't that bad. There were plenty of guys on active duty who'd give anything to sit, to get away from the beat, from any kind of danger.

He smiled to himself as he recalled graduating from the academy and delighting in the walking of a beat. He was young and he believed he was going to change the world. He didn't have anything of value to lose, not his possessions, not even his life. It was a young man's game, as was investigatory work.

Now there'll be no more pressures to make arrests, to get convictions. There'll be no more fulfilling that unwritten obligation to close thirty percent of all of the cases assigned to him. His ulcer would heal, his nerves improve. No, he wouldn't bitch and moan. And when he got tired working the desk, he'd retire and go back to college for computer courses. But that never did sound too exciting for him after a career in police work. He could always sell shoes, become a security guard, or work for a private detective agency. A lot of cops do their twenty years and then got security jobs in hotels or chain stores. But that also held little appeal for him. He thought it was a comedown. What then?

He now felt free, liberated, excited. Whatever would be,

would be new. He'd have a new career and a new life, with Marie. The thought of her, and of seeing her in a few hours, quickened his pulse and brightened his mood.

Feeling no compulsion to stay late anymore, he left at five o'clock for home to shower and change. At precisely seven, he rang at her apartment. The door swung open.

She was dressed in a clinging red dress with a hem that crept and danced above her knees. Welcoming him with a kiss, she led the way inside where he was greeted by a familiar aroma. The smell, what was it? That hot, spicy, mouth-watering pleas- antness that used to send his stomach rumbling juices when he was a kid. It came to him suddenly and he blurted it out.

"Sicilian eggplant! Marie, where did you get it? I didn't know you could cook Italian."

She laughed. "Relax. It came frozen from the deli. But that's not all."

She grasped his hand to lead him to the kitchen. There, arranged like a picnic, complete with a checkered red and white table cloth and a bottle of wine in a basket, were plates of lasagna, pasta salad and mozzarella.

"Lovely lady!" he cried. "Now I know what I'm going to do when I retire. Open up an Italian fast food restaurant with you."

In between mouthfuls of wine and pasta, he apologized for barging into her office earlier in the day. "Suppose I was in the midst of a hot lead and you marched in, Marie. I wouldn't even look at you, much less indulge in conversation." He paused. "Well, maybe just to look."

She smiled and pushed the pasta plate closer to him. "What was so urgent?"

He slapped his cheek playfully. "So urgent that I almost forgot about it."

With tongue loosened by the wine, he told her of the trial board slap-on-the-wrist punishment meted out to Anderson but didn't mention his own reassignment. He also asked her not to write anything until a formal announcement was made by the department.

"At least the bastard got some comeuppance," she said.

"When they called me to testify, I brought my tapes because I couldn't trust your fellow officers to tell it like it was."

"Tapes?"

She got up, returning a moment later with her briefcase, from which she pulled her tape recorder. "Here. This kept everyone honest. I've got it all down. I switched it on as soon as Anderson began popping off."

Imperateri's eyes narrowed. "Why didn't you tell me you had us bugged?"

"Call it journalistic privilege. If I had told you, you'd have told Anderson to shut up."

"No, I mean later, when we got to know each other."

She paused a few moments before answering. "I couldn't take a chance afterward. I didn't really know you. All I knew was that cops were like doctors. They could hardly be trusted when it came to a member of the club."

Seeing his hurt reaction, she sighed and repeated herself. "I just didn't know you well enough, Vinnie."

A frown settled on his face. "That was downright dirty. I was willing to overlook that sneaky number you did on Anderson with that article the next day. But this shows me that's your style. How the hell do I know you wouldn't pull something like that on me some day?"

"Oh, Vinnie, I won't. Not unless I tell you first."

Shaking his head, he pushed himself away from the table. "Tomorrow morning I could pick up the paper and find a story by you of how I leaked the trial board's verdict."

"You're being a complete ass."

"The sorry fact is that you'd sell your soul for a good story."

"That's not true," she replied, her voice low and trembling, "and I want an apology."

"You'll get one when you deserve it. I love you, Marie, but I can't trust you." Saying that, Imperateri left as quickly as he could.

As he drove away, he felt his stomach roiling, threatening to erupt in a peptic ulcer attack. He knew it wasn't because of the wine and pasta.

TWENTY-FIVE

A smoke-like vapor blew into the cabin, immediately raising excited voices from the passengers on the United Airlines eastward bound flight from Los Angeles. The four flight attendants, each with a frozen smile, walked up and down in an attempt to calm fears. Yet their stilled, rehearsed movements only served to heighten anxiety rather than to reassure of safety. It was not until the captain's bored and muffled voice came over the intercom that the passengers finally grew silent.

"We have a malfunctioning air conditioner. The vapor is not toxic. We are, however, going to make an unscheduled stop in Pittsburgh to change the machine's pack valve."

Julian Stone tilted his head back on the headrest and closed his eyes to feign sleep so that he would not have to engage in conversation with his seatmate. He didn't feel like talking. Pain racked his body and his ribs felt as though they were being constantly rubbed with sandpaper. He was glad Lois had decided to stay an extra few days and go down to Laguna Beach with some doctors' wives she'd become friendly with.

It was typical of his bad luck on the trip, he thought, momentarily opening his eyes to look at the vapor seeping through the cabin vents. Who would have thought that Dieter Warrenholtz would fight back and almost end the whole business?

Stone tried to convince himself that the two California castrations were successful, despite Warrenholtz's struggle. Yet the thought of the German constantly gnawed at him. He knew he had to perform another operation, and soon, else he would be terrified into inaction. He compared himself to a driver who had

214

to get behind the wheel immediately after having an accident in order to overcome an anxiety that could only worsen with each passing day.

The need for immediate action was given added impetus by his belief that Warrenholtz was now probably giving police a full description of him. It would be a matter of a short time before police all over knew what he looked like. If he were going to strike again, the sooner, the better.

It was not until the Boeing 727 began the descent that the idea struck him. Pittsburgh. Why not?

He could change his ticket for a return flight later to give him time to hunt up a bonus patient. He smiled at the thought. There was no doubt that he would find one. Every city and hamlet had them. The problem was tracking one down and cornering him, alone, helpless.

Within minutes of landing, he arranged to fly to Newark on US Air Flight 357 at seven Wednesday morning, giving him two days in the Steel City. He rented a car, checked in at a nearby motel and then bought some toiletries to replace those left in a suitcase on the United flight. He would reclaim it later.

His medical bag he had carried with him, and in the motel cleaned and checked the equipment and disguise before starting out to locate a library. There he would set upon a now-familiar task.

As he suspected, it wasn't difficult finding a prospective patient. One danced in front of his eyes on the front page of a recent edition of the *Pittsburgh Press*. The rapist's name was Theodore Williams and he was twenty-four years old. A photograph showed a wild-haired man with large eyes and thick eyebrows, giving him a jack-in-the-box expression.

Williams had been convicted of five rapes, the first when he was fourteen years of age, the last just two years ago. What prompted the recent article about him was the picketing of the state corrections office by a local women's rights group.

It seemed that Williams was included in a work-release program after serving a minimum amount of time for his last conviction. The program was designed for inmates serving the last portion of their sentences, and was intended to help ease their eventual transition to civilian life.

One of the woman picketeers was quoted in the article. *"It's one of the most frightening things I've heard of. That man's a walking time bomb."*

Maybe it was time to defuse the bomb, Stone thought. He returned to the motel, called Betty Gruff in his office and explained that he was delayed and asked her to inform the physician filling in for him. Then he called the local state corrections office.

"Good afternoon. Steve Thompson of the AP. We're doing a story on the work-release program and would like to focus on the Williams controversy. Can you tell me something about the program and where he works?"

The office was most cooperative. Elated, Julian Stone prepared for sleep, instructing the desk clerk to ring him at five-thirty in the morning.

A half-hour after being awakened, he was shaven and dressed, and soon driving through the fresh snow already peppered with smokestack grime from nightworking steel mills. He found his way to the south side of the city to a blue collar neighborhood. There, he breakfasted on a coffee and doughnut, and then returned to his car where he waited for about fifteen minutes.

At six forty-five, a green prison bus dropped off a hatless passenger dressed in a Mackinaw jacket. The man waved to the other inmates still on the bus, and began to thread his way on the snowy streets.

Stone waited until the man reached the end of the block before starting the car and following. Despite his anxiety, he was pleased. So far, the corrections office had been right about the bus drop-off location. The man with the wild hair and features had to be Williams. He even headed for a bar on East Carson Street where the corrections people said he was employed.

Promptly at seven o'clock, the bar opened to cater to the night shift of steelworkers coming out of the nearby mills. Tired and thirsty after eight hot and sweaty hours, they trudged into the bar for drinks before heading home.

For a long time Julian Stone sat patiently in the car, watching and waiting and thinking. It would do more harm than good by entering the bar dressed the way he was, a stranger in a dark business suit and topcoat. He'd stand out among the steelworkers. He couldn't go in for a casual drink, but he could certainly enter to make a telephone call. Any excuse would do. He was from out-of-town, lost while driving, and now calling a destination to apologize for being late.

Minutes after putting on his disguise, he pushed open the doors to the small, dark bar, one of several in a row. Loud hillbilly music blared from a jukebox. At the bar sat several foundry workers, some still wearing their hard hats. Even with their thick, down-filled jackets, he could tell they were muscular, tough, men not to antagonize. On the other side of the counter under a wall decorated with dozens of miniature liquor bottles were two bartenders. One, old, grizzled. The other, Theodore Williams, rapist.

Stone curled his fists in an effort to stop his hands from shaking. How to make an absolutely positive identification of his patient? he asked himself. He would have to play a game.

He squinted, looking for the telephone, saw it in the rear, and advanced. Eyes turned to look at him, the stranger, as he passed the tables with their padded plastic chairs on chrome frames.

Dialing on the wall telephone, he spoke to no one for a minute and then hung up, shaking his head for the benefit of the eyes still on him. At the counter, he sat down.

"Anything I can help you with, buddy?" Theodore Williams asked.

Closer up, Stone could see the meanness in the large eyes, the angry look in the tightness of the jaw. Again for the benefit of the on-lookers, Stone sighed. His voice came slightly muffled through the mouthful of cotton.

"I was looking for Legation Street but a whisky would make a fine substitute."

The men laughed. Williams shook his head. "Ain't no Legation Street around here."

"What about that whiskey then?"

The steelworkers laughed again. To a man, their calloused hands each gripped a drink, a shot of whisky in one and a mug of beer in the other.

"Just in from Chicago," Stone continued. "Rented me a car and started looking for a woman. Somebody told me Legation Street."

A white-haired foundry worker guffawed. "Just ask old 'Terrible Teddy' here," he said, pointing to Williams. "He knows all about women."

"Yeah, but he never puts out money for it," another said. "He just shoplifts."

They all roared with laughter, including Stone, although he felt sick with rage. He now knew without any doubt that the man was Williams. What bothered him was that the men, rather than abhorring his past crimes, took sort of a *macho* pride from them. He detested them all and wondered how they related to women in their own families. Contemplation of their own wives and daughters being ravished might fix an awful image in their mind's eye.

He downed the whisky, shivering from its impact. He was not accustomed to a drink so early in the morning, and a near-empty stomach didn't help, either.

"Yeah," the white-haired man said, winking, "just ask Teddy here. He don't pay and he don't say. He just takes, whether they want to be took or not. Right, Teddy?"

Williams smirked, and by way of reply began making sucking sounds through pursed lips, and then whistling and trilling like a canary.

The other bartender jabbed with a finger at the counter. The cue was for Williams, who made an obscene gesture at the older man but nevertheless wiped the bar. Then he hustled empty glasses to the back for washing.

Soon some of the men, elbows moving in unison almost like a violin section, wiped their mouths with the backs of their hands. When the last man left Stone as the only remaining customer, the bartender called out to Williams, still in the rear.

"Leaving now, Teddy. See you for the big one."

"What's the big one?" Stone asked.

"Lunch trade. Guys come in from the mills for a little libation." He put on his coat and looked at Stone suspiciously. "Say, ain't you supposed to go somewhere?"

Stone glanced at his watch and shook it for effect. "Yeah, but first I've got to make another telephone call." He got up, repeated his performance at the telephone long enough to watch the bartender leave.

No doubt the bartender as well as the foundry workers would be questioned later by police. They would describe Stone as having a mustache, glasses, and puffy cheeks. Stone patted his wig. And having bushy hair.

As he turned over in his mind what approach to make with Williams, a teenage youth and a girl entered and sat down at one of the booths, dropping their books on the seat. A moment later another man came in and sat at the bar.

Williams came out and served the man coffee and then waited on the teenagers.

"You're always this busy?" Stone asked.

Williams nodded. "School kids. Coffee trade. I take me a nap on this here counter right before lunch. Quiet as shit then."

Stone had no choice. He left and returned to the car, driving around aimlessly, stopping only to have coffee and read the paper. At eleven-fifteen he returned to the bar. It was empty. Williams was not happy to see him.

"You back again? I was just ready to take me a nap."

"Just a quick whisky and fix yourself one."

Williams rodded towards the door. "That son of a bitch boss'll be here soon. Smell my breath. Make me pay, and then turn me in to the . . . " He stopped, as if wondering why he had to explain to a stranger.

Stone winked and laughed. "I got something in the car guaranteed to kill bad breath. I'm a traveling drug salesman."

"What are you waiting for?"

On the way to the car Stone realized that neither he nor Williams could afford to drink. He had to operate with a steady hand and Williams shouldn't be mixing alcohol with an anesthetic. He returned with his bag and reached in for a package of paraldehyde capsules, handing several to Williams, enough to sedate him for a quiet injection.

"You have to take this before you start drinking, or else it won't work."

"First time I heard anything like that," Williams said, swallowing the capsules.

A few minutes later, Williams, his eyes glazed over, sat down heavily on a bar stool, resting his head on the counter. Stone locked the entrance and lowered the door shade. He then prepared for an injection, lessening the dosage to conform with the oral paraldehyde.

Next he cleared the bar counter of cocktail napkins, coasters, and empty bottles and glasses, and then struggled for several minutes lifting the patient on top of it. Its height and length made for a good operating table.

It was now eleven-thirty. He had a half-hour before the lunch crowd, but the boss could arrive at any moment. He had to work fast, but not too fast and not carelessly.

As he was about to cut, he turned over in his mind once again the morality of his action. Was he helping Williams or punishing him? He thought of medieval times, when amputation of the hands was practiced to stop thievery. Was he turning the clock back?

He sighed, hand again poised in midair. What difference did his reason for castrating make? He was stopping a rapist, and that was all that mattered.

He recalled working as a young intern in a hospital emergency room. A young rape victim was brought in, vomiting great gobs of blood. Her nose was pulverized against both cheeks and her front teeth poked through her lips.

"Tell her about turning the clock back," Stone said aloud, making the first incision.

He worked quietly and quickly until a foghorn blasted atop one of the mills, signalling the hour of noon. He had just enough time to cleanse the skin and write a note calling for immediate hospitalization for Theodore Williams, the shoplifter.

Outside, new snow began falling. Stone turned the ignition in his car just as he saw the old bartender arrive. The car edged forward, its tires crunching against the sticky pavement. As the windshield wipers jerked back and forth, he asked himself whether his conscience was going to stop him before the police did.

Detective John Bork grinned sheepishly as he handed Imperateri one of the packets of pink sheets and carbon paper used to record telephone tips from informants. "I don't know if you still want these, Vinnie."

"Allow me to make a judgment on that," Imperateri replied with goodnatured mock importance. He glanced at the packet on which were written numbers and dates, filling most of the page.

Bork with an audible sigh, plopped on the chair next to the desk. "It's the scout car and cruiser report, Vinnie. Since you've been reassigned, I thought . . . " Bork didn't finish the sentence.

"What do you mean I wouldn't want these? Just because I'm off a case doesn't mean I'm not a cop anymore." He pushed the packet aside. "Just tell me what the numbers mean."

"I checked out each of the seven precincts. It adds up to three hundred and four marked patrol cars used at some time during the night or day of each holiday."

Imperateri shook his head slowly. "That's a lot of suspects to look at."

"All cops, too, Vinnie. Should be fun."

"Turn this over to Noseworthy. He's top-dogging the rapist now. And something else. Go back to the precincts for a recount. Eliminate all team patrols. Get me—ah, I mean Noseworthy—the names of everyone who drove a one-man cruiser on those dates."

Bork shrugged. "You sure it's okay for me to do this, you being off the case and not my official team leader and all that?"

"I'll cover for you, John. You know that." Imperateri knew that his testimony before the trial board, although damaging to a fellow officer, had enhanced his integrity, swollen his stature. If he told the detectives he could walk on water, they'd believe him.

And Anderson's attempt to humiliate him before the squad had backfired. Since that day, all of the detectives went out of their way to show some kindness.

Bork, however, was still incredulous. "Something I don't understand, Vinnie. If you're officially off the case, how come you want to break ass when it's not your plum anymore?"

"John, listen. If you ever get to the point where you don't bust tail to help some poor little girls, if you ever find that doing that doesn't mean anything to you, they you'd better quit."

Bork raised an upward palm of surrender. "I understand all that. I'm just thinking about you losing this plum."

"I don't care if a smelly sanitation inspector in a brown uniform breaks this case. I hope a mailman with swollen feet breaks it. I'm not looking for glory. I just want a solution."

As Bork left, Imperateri pulled out the *Report of Investigation*. The idea of the murderer being a cop fit everything in the case. No sane girl would talk to a strange civilian. And the killer had enough presence of mind to dump the bodies in different police jurisdictions. But, he wondered, if a District of Columbia police car were involved, wouldn't it stick out like a sore thumb in any of the other jurisdictions? Not necessarily. He'd often seen out-of-jurisdiction cruisers rolling about for one reason or another. Old Mrs. Forbes had seen that cruiser that day. What was the reason for it being there, a cross-jurisdictional mission?

He shrugged and looked up at the wall calendar. The sixteenth of February, George Washington's Birthday, was coming up in a few weeks. He'd have to get Noseworthy to call a meeting of all area detectives working on the case to map out some plan, bearing in mind that some cop may be the killer. Noseworthy might also check out what cruisers went on a mission to Maryland the day Mrs. Forbes saw the murder car.

Imperateri poked at the *Report of Investigation*, staring at it, and then suddenly remembering the promise made to Dr. Julian Stone about keeping him informed. Well, there were a couple of developments. Old lady Forbes on the case and old man Imperateri off it.

He lifted the telephone and asked for long distance. In a moment, the voice from Newark spoke.

"I'm sorry, but Dr. Stone is in Albany for a consultation. He'll be back tomorrow."

"I'll try then," Imperateri said, hanging up.

TWENTY-SIX

The seedy Schenectady motel was a duplicate of every other neon-lit lodging in suburban strips across the country. With their musty-smelling lobbies loaded with vending machines, and rooms mixing odors of stale air conditioning, cigarette smoke and unventilated toilets, they seemed to spawn copies of each other. A room in Schenectady resembled one in Chicago, cheap shag carpeting, laminated table tops and black and white television sets with worn knobs and pictures that never quite focused.

Julian Stone could not be bothered with the surroundings because he had no intention of staying long. He merely needed a place to arrange his disguise and wash up before heading back to his Albany hotel to rest up a bit, check out, and head home.

Now he looked at his watch, decided that he had plenty of time, and lay down on the bed with a newspaper he had purchased.

He was pleased at the way things were going. After returning from California, he had told the office that he needed a brief winter vacation and that he was going to combine it with a consultation. Reservations were made for Albany, ostensibly for skiing. He guessed that city had ski facilities. Though he had invited Lois along, she refused, saying that she preferred Florida this time of year.

By pure effort of will, he managed to subdue, at least temporarily, his misgivings, his picky conscience. And as far as descriptions of him were concerned, his fears were unfounded. Apparently the patients had been too much in shock to give an accurate portrayal of their attacker. Nor had the Pittsburgh bartender and his patrons been of much help to police, at least not publicly. Still, the papers were full of the new cases, two on the West Coast, and the one in Pittsburgh.

He picked up the newspaper and re-read an article for the third time.

Federal and local law enforcement officials have warned that paroled or released convicted rapists could be targets of a roving avenger dubbed "Jack the Snipper" who has performed more than half a dozen illegal castrations nationwide.

The FBI and the local authorities admit they are bewildered by the apparent random choice of the victims. An FBI spokesperson revealed that the only common threads linking the attacks were that the victims were convicted rapists on parole, and that a surgeon may have performed the castrations, possibly as a lone, self-styled vigilante.

"This is the first time that we have had this type of thing," said the spokesperson. "We're looking for either one person, or several medically-trained persons with the same method of operation."

The rest of the article traced the meandering course of the
vigilante across the country, from Maryland to Boston to New Orleans and Chicago. A composite drawing showed a middle-aged male with horn-rimmed glasses, a full head of hair and a mustache. In no way did it resemble Stone.

A switch in appearance was necessary, Stone thought, laying the paper aside. He doubted, though, whether his next patient read much of the newspapers. He was a recently released leader of a Schenectady gang which had gang-raped and robbed several young women during a month-long spree four years ago.

With plans already mapped out for the abduction of the rapist, Stone closed his eyes. He was tired. The four hour, hundred and sixty mile drive would have to be repeated in a few hours for the return trip.

He could not nap, and instead switched on the television set and was immediately transfixed by a talk show program in progress. The host discussed with a psychiatrist the wave of emasculations. Another participant on the show, a woman whose celebrity Stone vaguely recognized, also listened as the host questioned.

"Doctor, how do we know if the surgical vigilante is only one man? It could be several are involved. One deranged man reads about the emasculations in another city and decides to try it in his own."

The psychiatrist shook his head. "The evidence shows that a highly trained medical person, no doubt a physician, performed the delicate operations, all in the same manner. It's hardly possible that there are vigilante doctors all over the country who are similarly deranged."

"What kind of person would do that? Can you give us a psychological profile of this man?"

The woman sitting next to the psychiatrist bristled, lifting a finger and waving it. She was a heavy-featured brunette, and Stone now recalled that she was a leader in the women's rights movement. Her voice was strident, her expression one of wary angriness.

"How can you be so sure she wasn't a woman?"

"Few women are capable of such mutilation," the psychiatrist replied, a sad smile on his face.

The woman guffawed. "Nonsense! A moment ago you described it as a delicate operation."

"It could be that and still be a mutilation. You misunderstood me."

"I understand perfectly well that a woman is just as capable as a man as far as surgery and motive are concerned. A woman thirsty enough for vengeance could certainly do it. I know I could without even knowing how to operate."

The audience cheered and applauded loudly. The host, obviously enjoying the exchange, broke for a commercial and begged the viewing audience to remain tuned.

Julian Stone sighed deeply and sat up on the side of the bed. He had mixed feelings about watching any more. He liked the woman's argument, but knew that the psychiatrist would soon come up with uncomplimentary Freudian mumbo-jumbo.

On the screen a young beautiful woman expounded the virtues of a vaginal spray. Moments later, the host returned, beaming widely as he re-introduced the subject.

"We're talking about Jack the Snipper, the mysterious mutilator of former rapists . . . "

The woman interrupted him. "Former? The passage of time doesn't change their action or guilt. That's like saying a former murderer."

The host held up a hand by way of indicating that he didn't want to debate the term. "All right, but what of this man, or woman, who has taken it upon himself or herself to ignore responsible legal administration of justice in favor of the do-it-yourself kind? Are his or her deeds just too barbaric for our enlightened society to perform? Doctor, what do you think?"

The psychiatrist cleared his throat several times and then clasped his hands. "The emasculator is living out a vicious exercise in vengeful paranoid fantasy and aggressive wish-fulfillment."

"Gobbledegook!" the woman shot back. "She or he is a hero to women who've been assaulted, battered and raped. And I count myself among them."

Many in the audience gasped. A few people applauded her courage and revelation. She continued in a lower voice.

"If the armchair critics of emasculation could see the physical and psychological aftermath of rape, they wouldn't weep so many tears for torn testicles."

Loud laughter mixed with cheers and applause again filled the television studio. The woman, encouraged, pointed a finger at the psychiatrist.

"You say that emasculating rapists is wrong? Try convincing their victims." Now she turned and looked directly into the camera. "Whatever you are, vigilante, male or female, black or white, you're a hero to the women of America."

The psychiatrist, cheek muscles rippling, waited for the applause to subside. He moved forward to the edge of his chair and spoke with a voice quivering with emotion.

"I hold that the mutilation suspect is not only a male, but a demented doctor intent on seeking vengeance against rapists. Something has happened in this man's life to account for his emerging from a cocoon into an efficient mutilating machine."

Now it was the psychiatrist's turn to stare directly into the camera. "If you are watching, doctor, I appeal to you, as one physician to another, to seek help before it is too late."

"Too late for whom?" the woman countered. "The convicted rapists still roaming our streets at will?"

Stone reached out to switch off the set. He had heard enough, especially of the words *demented* and *deranged* to describe him.

He asked himself whether he were actually unbalanced, insane by whatever standards the courts used. He was well aware that his actions were illegal, but were they those of someone who had lost touch with reason? How could he tell or be certain?

He realized that some might say his mind had snapped when his daughter was murdered and that he had sought either vengeance or solace by his actions. If apprehended, such an argument could result in his psychiatric confinement for an indefinite period at best, or at worst, for the rest of his life.

Was it better to come forward and explain in a rational way why he had done what he had done? To do so, maximum attention would be given to castration as a means of thwarting sex criminals.

That he was a hero to many amused and filled him with elation. For a moment now he felt compelled to reveal all, confess that he was indeed the one called Jack the Snipper, and was ready to accept whatever praise or punishment due him.

Perhaps later, after he had performed a few more operations. Just as a clinical researcher might wish to add patients to increase the validity of a study, so would he add to his record of accomplishment.

The realization came to him that he would have to exercise greater care, however. The publicity, the pinpointing by the psychiatrist and conceivably by police identifying the castrator as a grief-stricken doctor was just too close to offer comfort.

If either Eva Barlow or Betty Gruff kept a record of his absences and matched it with the times and places of the castrations, he would be in serious trouble. If they wouldn't think to link him with Jack the Snipper, routine police investigations certainly would. He would have to cover up somehow, go to places without telling his office, and go to other cities and meetings and not perform castrations, just to throw investigators off the track.

Now, however, he was in Schenectady with a patient already selected. It would be a shame to let this one slip by.

He would not.

Noseworthy shook his head from side to side and then pushed the packet of papers on Imperateri's desk. The top sheet showed lists of names in separated squares, with arrows denoting that the names had been cross-referenced.

"A real dead-end, Vinnie. A good idea, but it didn't pan out."

"Bork's cross-checks?"

Noseworthy nodded. "He followed your instructions. Every lone driver on holiday duty when there was a lust-murder was checked against other murder holidays. During the second or third murders they teamed with a passenger officer, or weren't riding squad at all. So it looks like none of them could be called suspect material."

Imperateri stared at the ceiling and spoke as if to air his thoughts rather than to address Noseworthy. "It's unlikely that two officers could team up to kill, with one or the other acting singly at other times. But crazier things have happened." He looked at Noseworthy. "How many suspect partners do you count?"

"Thirty-seven."

"I hope you're going to put them under surveillance."

"Are you kidding? Where are we going to get the manpower? Besides, that's hard to do, putting one cop on two others. They'd spot a tail."

"Nose, for one day, Washington's Birthday, you can do it. Get Anderson to request help from vice and robbery. Even drug and bunco."

Imperateri paused, noting Noseworthy's pained expression, and then continued in a harsher tone. "Look, Nose, I'm not

229

even supposed to be working this gig. If you don't want to carry out a logical operation, don't come crying to me about lack of progress."

Noseworthy nodded wearily. "If that's what we have to do."

"Something else. Bork hasn't had time to push for dust and chemical analyses on the suspect cars. Find some excuse to pull them in from the precincts. My guess is that there should be plenty of latent prints all over those cruisers. It's going to take time and effort."

"Anything else?" Noseworthy asked in a sarcastic tone.

Imperateri smiled. "If you still have time I've got a couple other ideas." He watched Noseworthy dance away and then got up himself for a stretch.

One of his desk jobs was to check and file regional and national crime reports coming over the national police network teletype. He paused at the ticker just as the machine began to spew out details of the latest castration less than an hour after it had occurred in Schenectady. The transmission gave a description of a white, male, well over six feet tall, between the ages of forty and forty-five, with a shock of black hair, and with mustache and glasses. An advisory noted that the last three features may have been an attempt at concealment. It also stated that the castration-mutilation was probably done by the same doctor involved in a series of similar acts.

Imperateri read the report once and then again. He smiled to himself. Dr. Julian Stone, you crazy son of a bitch, you.

It was coincidental, circumstantial and probably doubtful. All Vincent Imperateri knew so far was that Julian Stone was in Albany at the same time a castration took place in Schenectady, some fifteen miles away. That and the belief that the criminal castrator was probably a doctor or some medical technician. Add to it the fact that Stone's daughter was murdered by the cannibal rapist, a pathological killer so insane that he'd have given Sigmund Freud nightmares.

The missing ingredient to a clear case was whether Stone could indeed have been motivated enough to do it. No,

Imperateri thought, not motivated, but made mentally unbalanced enough to avenge the rapes of other women.

Imperateri hastened to the file containing printouts from the FBI's National Crime Information Center computer, and pulled out the list with the dates of each castration, location, and victim's name. All of the castrations occurred after Susan Stone's murder, none before. In the intervening weeks after Susan's death, could time have compounded the damage of that savagery? Imperateri wondered. Could the initial numbing effects have worn off, and the psychological pressure on the survivor, Stone, intensified beyond his control?

The platitudes say that time heals and life goes on, must go on. But instead of returning to obscurity and eventual recovery, Stone reacts differently. He seeks vengeance. It could happen to anyone.

The question of what immediate steps to take frustrated Imperateri. He couldn't alert the New Jersey police or the FBI until he was sure of what he had. He owed that much to Stone. There was no need to let the doctor suffer through the publicity and humiliation an interrogation would bring. At least not after what he'd been through. And what was the basis for such questioning? A strong suspicion but not a shred of evidence. After all, there was the possibility that Stone indeed was legitimately in Albany on a consultation.

Imperateri knew that his choice was clear. He'd have to go up to New Jersey at once, while Stone was still in Albany, or Schenectady, or wherever the hell he was. And he'd have to travel on his own time and expense. Anderson would not give him official approval, certainly not now and not on a case that wasn't local. Imperateri wouldn't even bother asking for one of the headquarters cars.

The thought of the cruisers assigned to headquarters struck him suddenly. He should have asked Bork to check out holiday off-duty drivers on those, as well. No, Imperateri decided. He'd do that himself when he got back from Newark.

The waiting room was empty of patients, Dr. Julian Stone being out of town. Only a receptionist now stood behind a counter which separated the room from her work area. She looked up from her accounts ledger book and envelopes to be mailed. A wide smile lit her face.

"You must be the police detective. I wasn't expecting anyone else."

"And you must be Miss Gruff," Vincent Imperateri said, opening his wallet and flashing a badge at her. He hadn't dared to tell her that he wasn't a local cop when he'd made the second call. Nor did he now give her a chance to read the *District of Columbia* raised lettering on the badge, instantly snapping the wallet shut. Nothing could be gained if she were to alert Stone to a Washington policeman's visit. He'd also had this in mind when telephoning and giving a fictitious name and making up a story about drug thefts from doctors' offices.

"As I've mentioned, Miss Gruff, we're investigating any possible break-ins around the area. Have you noticed anything missing?"

As she glanced up and down the office as if to jog her memory, Imperateri looked her up and down. A bit on the thin side, he decided, but definitely a pretty face, upturned nose, big brown eyes. If he weren't so wrapped up with Marie, he'd have made a gentle pass.

Betty Gruff slowly shook her head. "We haven't had anything like that, Officer. Eva Barlow, our nurse, is off today, too. That's because doctor isn't in. She keeps track of drugs. But you have to realize that this is a pediatric practice, and we just don't carry the sort of drugs addicts are interested in."

"Miss Gruff, an addict sees a doctor's shingle on the door and doesn't care what kind of practice it is." He paused, preparing to toss the next question. "Now you say the doctor is out of town?"

"Albany. He had a consultation on his way back from the coast."

Imperateri smiled and winked. "Hey, doctors have it made, don't they, traveling all over like that with expenses tax deductible?" He gambled on winning her confidence. She must be perturbed, having to work while the nurse had days off with pay probably, during the doctor's many trips.

"I'll say," Betty Gruff began, obviously eager to find a sympathetic ear. "He's been gallivanting all over. And guess who's got to work? Someone has to stick around and mail out bills and answer the telephone."

Imperateri nodded sympathetically. "Is that so? Gallivanting all over. Mostly medical meetings?" He hoped at the very least for a dossier by memory, but Betty Gruff did better. She flipped over pages of a desk calendar.

"All medical meetings. For starters, he's been to Boston. That was early in the month, the second and third. He was also gone from the office the fifteenth through the eighteenth, I don't know where. I guess he handled his own travel arrangements." She looked back at the calendar. "Also in January, the twenty-third, there was Cleveland."

As she continued, Imperateri itched to jot down the dates and places but knew he couldn't without arousing suspicion. Stone had to be kept in the dark until it was time to make a move.

Turning to leave, he forced a laugh. "It looks like I'm in the wrong business."

"Oh, I don't know," she said, looking at him as if for the first time and smiling flirtatiously. "You boys seem to get around."

"Mostly in circles, Miss Gruff." He winked at her over his shoulder.

Outside, back in the car, he compared the FBI printout with his memory. Everything matched except one or two gaps. California, for example. But Stone could have been there without anyone knowing.

As Imperateri drove south on the New Jersey Turnpike, he thought about bringing in the Jersey police. They had enough to put a tail on Stone, bring him in for questioning, but not enough to lock him up unless a search proved something. Could they get a conviction?

"Imperateri," he addressed himself aloud. "It's a case in futility."

"No, it's not," he replied. "It's all circumstantial. But what's there is good. Everything fits. It's got to be him."

"Just put it up for indictment. If they don't indict, they don't indict."

"I don't put him up, friend. It's the Jersey fuzz that do."

Imperateri nodded in agreement with himself. If only Stone were down in my territory. I'd come down hard on him. I'd freak him out with a set of plastic balls in the mail. I'd put him on the polygraph and watch it go wild.

As if to register an abrupt reversal in his thinking, he tamped down hard on the pedal. No, you wouldn't do that. Not to Stone, after all he's been through. You'd talk to him. You'd tell him that a court would look favorably on a plea of insanity brought on by his daughter's brutal murder.

Imperateri lit a cigarette and decided that the first thing he'd do when he got back was to call both the FBI and the Jersey authorities. But still the thought did not sit well with him. He deemed that it wasn't fair, giving away a plum collar to those guys. It had to be a good collar, sure to attract national attention and make a hero out of the arresting officer. Didn't he deserve it, a blaze of glory to throw in Captain Anderson's face?

Yet there was only one right choice to make. Either he was a cop or he was a publicity hound. He'd go home, put together what he knew and ship it off to Newark. Let them worry about presenting it to a prosecutor.

"Imperateri, you've got your own worries. Like finding the killer of the girl whose father you want to hurt."

TWENTY-SEVEN

Back at headquarters Vincent Imperateri put the Julian Stone matter temporarily aside when he saw the pile of administrative papers someone had dumped on his desk, probably on Captain Anderson's orders. And in keeping with Imperateri's new duties, his message spike was empty save for one note. It was from John Bork who reported negative results so far by forensic experts looking at the precinct cars, even those logged out for personal use. Less than half of the precincts had been checked so far.

Imperateri chafed over the slow pace of the dust and fabric collectors. His vexation waxed by thoughts of how he had to hide from Anderson what he was doing. He was also irritated with himself for worrying about Julian Stone's escapades rather than concentrating on the vampire killer in police clothing.

He took another look at the pile of papers, shook his head, and turned on a heel. He was glad that he'd taken it upon himself to check out headquarters cars. It was something worthwhile to do.

Sergeant Ben Tolson in traffic operations was a wiry black man with wide, pleasant eyes. He was cooperative, although a bit suspicious at the visit. He provided the logs to Imperateri, mentioning that they even included personal use time. When questioned about that, he immediately went on the defensive, carefully explaining the department policy of allowing off-duty cops to drive patrol cars.

"It's a known fact, Vinnie. The increased visibility cuts down on street crime."

"I'm aware of that Ben. I'm not questioning policy." Imperateri spoke quietly and with no intention of giving the true reason for the inquiry. He didn't want to tip off anyone that a probe was underway within the department and thus panic the possible killer.

Nevertheless, Tolson remained wary, anxious to defend his turf from criticism by the criminal investigations division.

"I don't have to tell you, Vinnie, about our manpower shortage, what with the hiring freeze and all those retirements. We had every uniform out on the street, on overtime, too. Didn't do much good until we came up with the off-duty idea. Lives have been saved because an off-duty officer has been in a cruiser."

"Yeah, Ben, I know. Do you keep good records on what officer gets what car?"

"Sure, do, Vinnie. But let me tell you this. Did you know that off-duty officers using the cruisers must have their radio on and have a weapon with them and must respond to calls? That's if they're in the cruiser at the time."

"Yeah, I know, Ben. Say, what about headquarters cars on holidays?"

"Holidays? We only have seven or eight a year. How come you're not asking about weekends?"

"Okay, tell me about weekends."

Tolson waited a moment before answering, as if to think of the implication of his words before they were spoken. "Weekends, sure. Those guys that can put the two days together. Not many like that. Only thing we ask is that they pay for what they use. We keep a close watch on gas for personal use. Saves the city a lot of money that way. Wear and tear on the vehicles during personal use, well, that's something else. We're talking about the city absorbing that."

Imperateri let him continue in that vein, hoping to give the impression that criminal investigations was looking at vehicle misuse. "Now, what about the holidays?" he asked again.

"The one day? Nobody wants to bother checking out for one day because they're not allowed to take it out of town. But we got a couple regulars who make use of it."

"Who?"

"Both in testing. Bob Lipsky and Bill Crawford."

Imperateri feigned indifference by covering a forced yawn. "Okay, thanks, Ben. Looks like everything's okay."

Tolson beamed and took Imperateri by the arm. "Hey, why would Homicide be interested in my cars?"

"Haven't you heard?" Imperateri asked with a look of surprise. "I've been shafted. No longer in Homicide. Been put on administrative duties, like checking cruiser use."

Tolson smiled again and punched Imperateri playfully on the arm. "Hey, Vinnie. Square with me. I know why you're down here."

"Oh, yeah?"

"For the Internal Revenue Service. I heard they're asking cops to pay taxes for the free use of the cars."

Imperateri shrugged. "I can't talk about that, Ben."

"Just don't forget to tell them about visibility and the cut down in crime."

"If they should ask, Ben. Ah, say you couldn't get me the numbers of the vehicles used by Lipsky and Crawford, could you?"

Vincent Imperateri watched Robert Lipsky from a distance as the testing officer marked off a scoring sheet attached to a clipboard. The man was tall and good-looking. Was that a plus or a minus on the suspect rating sheet? Imperateri shrugged to himself.

Lipsky certainly couldn't be desperate for women, not with his looks. But, then, there have been rapists who were downright handsome. And there was the belief that rape was not an act of sexual gratification but one of pure violence. Finally, the police weren't dealing with an ordinary rapist, but with a madman. Anything can happen, and usually did. There were no rules, no parameters, no limits. Looks, marital status, occupation, church work were of no consideration.

He recalled the case of Theodore Bundy, the convicted lust-rapist. A handsome, charming law student, he was active in politics and was destined for a great future. The only flaw in his personality was a penchant for raping, bludgeoning and slaughtering young women.

Imperateri turned to leave. He wouldn't bother checking to see what the other man, Crawford, looked like. Another face, another mask hiding present thoughts, covering past deeds.

So far he had two possible suspects. Now he needed more evidence on one or the other before sticking them in a line-up for Gertrude Forbes and Marcie Simkin. He was that close.

Back in the office, he read their personal files from cover to cover, carefully absorbing each detail and taking notes. When he was through he sadly concluded that he had learned nothing that would make one man more of a suspect than the other. It was possible that neither man had anything to do with the killings. It was also possible that a janitor, a carpool mechanic, a building handyman could have borrowed a cruiser for those fateful days.

He looked at his notes. Both Lipsky and Crawford were bachelors and apparently lived alone. Lipsky was thirty-three. Crawford, twenty-seven. Both came from out-of-state to join the motor vehicle department.

He couldn't help believing that the records were inadequate, obsolete, dead. They told him nothing. Of course, he admonished himself, there would be no criminal record. If they had had one, they wouldn't have been allowed to join the department. That is, if the department had known about it. There was a possibility that either man had somehow managed to hide a rap sheet from some other state.

Again opening both files, he stared at the set of fingerprints attached to each man's official ID photograph. For what it was worth, he'd ask the FBI to run a fresh fingerprint check. Now it was time to get back to the flesh and blood.

He returned to the motor vehicle department where William Crawford was pointed out to him. Nothing spectacular, Imperateri decided, thinking that the man looked like an average guy who was balding, a bit on the thin side and tense with quick movements.

Leaving the testing lot for the building, he struck up a conversation with a clerk, a young woman who mailed out license plate applications. She seemed to be pleased and flattered to be seen talking with a detective. Imperateri sensed this, and made sure he held his jacket open to reveal a holstered .38. Though he realized he was a bit too old to be showing the swashbuckles, he reminded himself that he had a job to do.

Now he joked about the many single pretty girls in the motor vehicle section and asked if there were as many bachelors. She laughed and then mentioned both Lipsky and Crawford. Then she passed gossip that Bill Crawford had been seeing Mary Ann Austin, in the cashier's office.

Mary Ann Austin had a vacuous, open-mouthed look, one cultivated by imitators of young actresses. She was more than honored to be taken into confidence in an investigation of William Crawford.

"Me, oh my! What in heaven's sake did he do?"

"Well, we're just considering him for another position. Is there anything about him that you think might reflect in a bad way on the department?"

She hesitated a few moments before answering. "I guess I could tell you. These days everybody seems to be proud of it. So I don't suppose Bill would mind."

"Mind what, Miss Austin?"

"Me telling you he's gay. Homosexual through and through. Why, he'd no more go to bed with a woman than you would with a camel."

Noseworthy trudged into the squad room. Imperateri saw his glum face and leaned back in his chair in anticipation of bad news.

"The shit said hello to the fan," Noseworthy said, his voice sounding like someone who had just shouted his way through a long argument. "Anderson found out about the surveillance on Lipsky and is raising hell."

"Did you tell him why you're doing it?"

"Of course. But he said it sounded like one of your half-ass ideas."

"And at that point you told him you were capable of your own half-ass idea, right?" Following a smile from Noseworthy, Imperateri continued. "Nose, we have to keep watching that guy. Can't you cook up some story for Anderson?"

"We've been looking at Lipsky for a week. A crazy stud is what he is. He likes singles' bars and married women. We found nothing in his apartment but a supply of rubbers. Anderson was particularly exercised that we broke into Lipsky's place and car."

"I didn't like asking you to do it, either, Nose. But a warrant may have sent him packing for Kamchatka."

Noseworthy shrugged. "The vacuumings from his own car and from the cruisers he used showed zilch. My question is, how long do we have to keep this up?"

"Until after the holiday. Three more days."

Noseworthy shrugged again and shuffled away without promising anything, yet Imperateri knew that the twenty-four hour surveillance would continue. Noseworthy would find some way.

After eliminating Crawford as a suspect, Imperateri no longer cared who was to garner what glory for the final collar. He just wanted to see Lipsky in custody.

The lack of Lipsky's prints at any of the murder sites could be explained by his use of rubber gloves. As far as no implicating hair or fibers in any of his cars, he could have used the police body bags. His clean apartment? Why, he took the girls to some other place. There was an answer for everything.

Satisfied with his thoughts, Imperateri pulled out a chart of Robert Lipsky's movements during the past few months. The date of Kitty Burns' murder was the first entry on the upper left of the desk-blotter-sized chart. Below were the dates and names of the subsequent victims. Across the top were the dates Lipsky had used the cruisers. Near that were scribbled the beginnings of a record of places and times where he had been on the murder dates, according to friends and associates.

There were a lot of holes yet to be filled in, Imperateri knew. But he'd just started the chart. Now he considered it nothing more than a visual aid, much better than a notebook of barely legible notes written on the run.

One main worry was to keep a step ahead of Anderson. Despite the captain's edict, Imperateri was determined to continue working on the case.

A lot of interviewing of Lipsky's acquaintances still had to be done. A difficult task, for it required confidentiality, demanded that they not tell their friend he was being investigated by his own colleagues.

Imperateri lay the chart aside for a moment and studied the artist's two renditions of what the suspect looked like according to Marcie Simkin and Gertrude Forbes. The composite portraits showed a common-faced man with no outstanding features. The pictures in no way resembled Lipsky. Maybe by a slight stretch of the imagination, they could be said to recall the smallish features of William Crawford.

Crawford, Crawford, Crawford.

Imperateri tossed the pictures aside and slapped the top of the desk with the bottom of his fist. When would he learn? When would he know not to take the word of one person as the gospel truth? Still, Mary Ann Austin was a friend of Crawford's, and she had no reason to lie. She had no idea why police were really interested in him.

On the other hand, Imperateri couldn't go by an artist's composites. They were not photographs, just a fourth party's conception of a third party's vague description. Too often in the past the difference between a composite and the apprehended was striking.

He took out a cigarette and looked at it as he tried to think of what next to do. He rolled the cigarette in his palm for a few moments and then returned it to the pack. He would not smoke. He was strong enough without it.

At that moment, Noseworthy rushed up to his desk. His voice sounding more strained than before.

"Vinnie, it looks like we're going to drop the Lipsky stake-out. Another girl's been reported missing. Two days. Unless Lipsky has a double somewhere, he couldn't have possibly done it."

Imperateri reached for the cigarette, this time lighting it.

241

The men stood with the small of their backs pressed to the bar, watching the dancers and making cracks to the passing women. "You girls look like you need a man."

"Know one?" one young woman finally shot back.

William Crawford, sitting at the bar, watched the scene but soon turned his head away in disgust. He loathed disco music and despised people who thought so little of themselves as to frequent singles' bars. He considerd the mating moves demanding, more appropriate for the chickens on his father's farm than for thinking, civilized beings. Yet he realized that he had little choice if he wanted a new girlie for himself.

There were few places besides bars where it was possible to pick up a female, especially since all the publicity about the rape murders. It was getting so that almost all women traveled in pairs, even older ones in whom he had no interest. And when a lone girl had to take a taxi by herself, a friend saw her off after obtaining the cabbie's name and license tag number. No longer did one see hitchhiking girls or women standing by themselves at bus stops or walking on empty streets, unless they were police decoys armed with weapons and supported by backup officers. The city was like a state under siege. It was panicked into a togetherness it had never known before.

Yet with all that, the news was that another girl was missing and presumed to be a new victim. Upon hearing about it, William Crawford had experienced mixed emotions. He hoped that the girl was safe and that her abductor would soon be found and punished.

What bothered him had been the possibility that his own plan not to wait for the coming Washington's Birthday may have been placed in jeopardy. Then the thought had come that perhaps he ought to act immediately. The fact that another girl was missing might give him an advantage. No one would expect another attack until the next holiday. Guards would be lowered. In keeping with his new tactics, he would not use a police car, either as a pick-up or a drop-off.

He believed that he was still one step ahead of the police, despite his earlier anxiety. It was ludicrous the way he had panicked into trying to kill Imperateri. All because of a newspaper story which he now guessed the cops had planted in hopes of getting new witnesses or shaking up informants.

Nevertheless, William Crawford reluctantly came to the conclusion that the time had come to move on to another city. He didn't believe in riding out a streak of successes, but looking for better opportunities elsewhere. Tonight would be the last time for him in this city, he decided. And then he'd move on, perhaps somewhere in the South to escape the cold weather.

But now he suffered through loud rock and disco music which battered his eardrums while the flashing lights assaulted his eyes. For almost half the night he had watched as men in open-necked shirts framing medallions dangling from chains danced with women in skin-tight, satiny body suits. Several times he had tried to strike up a conversation with different women, but when they learned he had no interest in dancing, they shrugged and looked for someone else.

He just could not bring himself to kick and sway and force his body to perform such bizarre movements. It was indecent and unnatural.

Sadly he realized that he had to abandon his mission for the night. Gulping the rest of his drink, he prepared to pay and leave when he saw her. In an instant he knew that she'd be the next girlie.

She was a petite girl with long brown hair and she sat quietly at the far edge of the bar. Too young to be a police officer, or decoy, he decided. He knew by sight most of the headquarters female officers, and she didn't look at all familiar. Still, she could be from one of the precincts. He had to be careful.

He elbowed his way through the crush of bodies and plopped down on the stool next to hers. "I'd ask you do dance," he began, "but I don't know how."

"Don't know how to ask or to dance?"

He forced himself to laugh at her silly, stilted reply but stopped short when he saw that she didn't even crack a smile at her own joke. A tough cookie.

Closer now, he examined her. Her face was flushed and her

hair wisped damply against sunken cheeks. Her head bobbed a little, in a manner of one who had had too much to drink. Good. His job would be that much easier.

"Nice music," he said.

"Uh, uh."

"Come here often?"

"Maybe."

"I haven't seen you here before." He'd never been there before, but he felt it wise to have her think he was a regular.

"Haven't you? You ought to keep your eyes open."

"So you come here a lot?"

"That would be telling, wouldn't it?"

"Hey, you're too sharp for me. I'm just a country boy." He was ready to play that role, if need be.

"Go hump it, cowshit," she said, twisting to look at the dancers.

He shrugged and turned to leave. She laughed and called out.

"Hey, dude boy. Only kidding."

He liked her spirit. She reminded him of . . . what was her name. Susan?

"Hey," he said, "someone once told me never to expect conversation from disco girls and never attempt any because it frightens them off."

"Climb off it."

"I'm serious."

"I'm not. You look like a slick dude ready to spin a good rap. Forget it. I'm not in the mood."

He shook his head. "Oh, I'm nothing like that. Would you believe I noticed you a while ago and I've been asking myself how I could approach you?"

She roared with laughter. "Say, you're for real. No shit."

"Do you really come here often?"

"That the most-asked question every stud asks. So you're not so different after all."

"Different enough to realize I don't like this place. I've been here two times now, first and last."

She studied him. "I thought you said you've been here before."

Careful, he thought. She's not all that drunk. "Oh, just checking if you're paying attention."

She glanced around the crowded dance floor. "I guess it could get on your nerves if you're not used to it. On weekends, I used to drink and boogie all night and then go outside and see the bright morning sunshine. It really flips you out."

He nodded sympathetic understanding. "I prefer a quiet evening at home with good food and wine and soft music." he paused, and then as if thinking of the idea for the first time, continued. "Say, I couldn't interest you in that, could I?"

"I don't know you," she said after a few moments of silence. "You could be the cannibal killer."

"I could, but that'll make things easy for me because I happen to be looking for him." He pulled open his jacket to the label where he had pinned the badge from his uniform.

"A detective! Wow! You really are different."

He nodded and stood. "Now let me pay for your drink and take you to a really nice place. I've just installled a new stereo and bought a new French wine. I'm dying to try them both with someone I like very much."

She cooed and grabbed his arm. "My name's Kim. But that's not my real name. I'll tell it to you if I get to like you."

"Whatever you say, Kim. Shall we go now?"

The houses were all identical, red brick with picture windows and one-car garages. William Crawford's house was the only one with a lawn that did not have a child's toy, an overturned bicycle, a ball, or a doll scattered about. Nor did his house shine a front light rebounding off the lawn and hedges and welcoming visitors. It was almost as if his world were closed off, dark and cold with no life within it.

After ringing the doorbell and making sure that Crawford was not at home, Vincent Imperateri parked a block away and walked back to the house. He entered through a rear kitchen window by breaking glass and turning a latch. It was easy, but he reminded himself that he'd have to steal something to make it look like a real burglary.

The two-story house had a living and dining room on the first floor and three bedrooms upstairs. Why Crawford, a bachelor, needed so many rooms mystified Imperateri. He recalled the story of Bluebeard and his many wives and the mysterious, locked room upstairs.

Imperateri found no similar arrangement. Using only a small flashlight, he swept through the house in less than ten minutes. He knew exactly what he was looking for, evidence of a struggle, of blood and a girl's clothing, or even the victim herself, either dead or still alive. But there was nothing to indicate any villainy on the part of William Crawford.

If anything, the only violation he seemed to have committed was one of excessive neatness, of going against normal patterns of bachelor untidiness. The bed was made with military-like precision, sharp, taut. Everything was in order. Books, magazines, bric-a-brac were neatly stacked and arranged, and clothing put away with care. A silver-plated urn on the hallway table reflected Imperateri's flashlight as he passed to the basement door.

If the upstairs were orderly, the basement was not. Old furniture was scattered in all corners. Rotting lumber, cardboard boxes, newspapers were tossed about with abandon. It was a junk yard. Whatever tragedy might have occurred, whatever horror might have dwelled there was masked by disarray.

From the outside came a squeak of a car braking to a stop in the driveway. Imperateri hastened up the stairs to the kitchen window, squeezing through with the silver urn he scooped up along the way.

As he came to a halt in the driveway, a small beam of light from the hallway danced through a window and caught his eye. He turned off the ignition and peered into the darkness of the house. The light was now gone. He guessed it had been a reflection from the headlights.

"See something?" Kim asked.

"I thought I did," William Crawford replied. "Nothing, though. Let's go in."

There was no need to pull the car into the garage and enter through the side kitchen door, as he had done with his other and unwilling guests, away from the prying eyes of neighbors. This one was quite willing to enter, and didn't have to be carried to the door, or forced in by the edge of a knife.

"It's dark. Watch your step," he said solicitously.

Inside the kitchen he felt something wrong immediately. It was not until the cool draft struck his face that he knew what it was. The window was broken. He ran his finger along the broken edge of glass and cursed.

Kim came up behind him. "What's the matter?"

"Burglar broke in. I've got to check around." He went in and out of all the rooms, followed by Kim.

"Nice place you got here. Sure looks like it got a woman's touch. You sure you don't have a chick stashed away somewhere here?"

His eyes darted towards her. "Shut up!"

"Well, excuse me!" she shot back, tilting her head to the side.

He noticed the empty space where the silver urn had stood. "I knew it. The best thing in the house. It was only silver-plated, but it cost a lot."

"Aren't you going to call the police?"

He said nothing in reply.

"Answer me. Why don't you get the cops?"

For several moments he remained silent. When he spoke, his voice was tight, angry. "I don't want them here. I mean, you forget I'm a police officer myself. I can handle it my own way."

She accepted that and now he thought that it was time to play with her. He patted her shoulder. "I'm sorry I lost my temper. It was the silver urn. I said it was the best thing in the house. I was wrong. You're the best."

She moved closer and snuggled against him. He drew back.

"Not here," he said, pointing to the basement door. "Downstairs. There's a special place."

She shook her head when she saw it. "It's so dirty down here. Can't we go upstairs to a clean bed?"

247

"Later. Look, here's a mattress and it'll be just as good." He nodded towards an air mattress. Next to it was a steel upright beam, around which a thin chain was looped.

She shuddered and began removing her clothing. While she did and before she realized what was happening, he slipped the chain around her neck and fastened it with a latch.

"Oh, you're one of those, huh? Well, just don't make it so tight. It hurts."

"Kim, I'll loosen it in a bit."

He did not. Instead he quickly secured her hands with a rope.

"I don't think I'm going to like this, ah, say, I don't even know your name."

"Sister calls me Pill, mother calls me Grill, father calls me Kill."

He laughed.

Early the next morning Vincent Imperateri knew that there would be an urgent meeting the moment that he saw the early newspaper. The story about the missing girl was featured prominently on the top half of the page. Her name was Joan Marchi, and she was a high school student who had not been seen since leaving cheerleading practice two days ago.

Next to that story was an article about the police trial board hearing on Captain Anderson. Written by Marie Mackay, Imperateri could see it lacked objectivity and painted the board decision a whitewash. Further below and to the side, an editorial referred to the two stories and lambasted the department for ineptness, low morale and jurisdictional squabbling.

The summoning of all criminal investigation heads and detectives came at nine in the morning. The night watch and day duty rosters attended, and an effort was made to call in off-duty and vacationing officers.

Minutes before the meeting Imperateri attempted to talk with Captain Anderson about William Crawford, but the captain would not see him. It was then that Imperateri made up his mind to go it alone.

The only odd puzzle piece was the missing Joan Marchi. If not at Crawford's house, where was she? Had he already killed and dumped her body, or was he as innocent as Lipsky?

Imperateri pushed his thoughts aside as the chief marched in with his coterie. Little was known about him, except that he was newly-appointed and that he wore his uniform to social functions, including church.

The detectives and uniformed officers in the packed auditorium hushed like schoolchildren in the presence of a martinet principal. As the chief began speaking of efforts to solve the rape murders, his voice sounded curiously soft and high pitched for man of his barrel-chested bulk.

"The press is taking potshots at us. We're being held up for public ridicule. I say, we're not going to take it."

Applause sounded, the the chief didn't want it. He immediately raised a hand and frowned.

"We're taking some drastic steps. As of now, all leaves are cancelled. All detectives are to be assigned to Homicide. Captain Anderson, who has my respect and confidence despite a smear attempt, will head up the investigation. He will run a joint command post. He will coordinate the work of all jurisdictions involved."

Imperateri squirmed in his seat. "We did that after the second murder," he whispered.

"Each day," the chief continued, "he will begin with a critique meeting on the previous twenty-four hours' activity. He will then allocate leads to street teams. One last word. We will use our friends in the media, if we still have friends. . . "

Laughter interrupted him, and this time he smiled.

"We will use them to appeal to all women, old and young, black or white, single or living alone. . . "

"Oh, my God!" Imperateri said to Noseworthy and Bork flanking him. "He's hitting the panic button."

" . . . to keep their doors locked, to have truck with no stranger, to report all suspicious persons. In short, to alert our womenfolk to the homicidal maniac stalking them."

Imperateri shook his head in despair. Ever since the second or third murder, almost all women took precautions. Now only the most foolhardy ones placed themselves in any danger. A new and hysterical alerting campaign aimed at the general population won't succeed in reaching them any more than previous ones had. To place emphasis on a lunatic preying on all women could demoralize the city, with its sizable female population.

The chief said little more, other than to introduce Anderson before parading away as brusquely as he had arrived, followed by his assistants in lock-step.

Anderson mounted the stage steps. When he spoke, his voice huffed and puffed from the climbing exertion.

"We're pulling out all the stops. We're going to check out every known sex offender, everyone released from mental institutions during the past year."

Imperateri whispered to his neighbors again. "Also done. Second murder."

"We're going to set up an emergency number for this case and this case alone."

"Second murder," came the whisper.

"We're going to use roadblocks, helicopters, tracking dogs . . ."

"What about the Strategic Air Command?" Imperateri's murmured heckle came loud enough to elicit chuckles from the surrounding rows.

"We're going to make this a group project with all the talent we can muster. We're going to leave no stone unturned."

How about looking in your own back yard, Captain? Imperateri said to himself, thinking of William Crawford.

Suddenly, as if he somehow guessed that Imperateri was ridiculing him, Anderson pointed and addressed him by name.

"Sergeant Imperateri, you have gone against my express orders not to continue on this case. I know about your visits to the motor pool, the lab and motor vehicles, where your bungling caused an innocent fellow officer to suffer humiliation. If it weren't for the urgency of my new tasks, I'd have filed insubordination charges against you. I will repeat once more for the benefit of all here. You are no longer on this case. I am ordering all components to cease further cooperation with you."

250

Anderson waited a few moments for his words to impress the non-Homicide divisions who did not know him. Then he dismissed the gathering.

"That's it for you, friend," Noseworthy said.

"I'm too poor to quit and too old to be hurt," said Vincent Imperateri, knowing he was only half lying.

"Morris Cohen here," the gruff voice roared over the telephone in the manner of a hard-of-hearing person who thinks all people have the same problem.

"That's no way for a famous forensic pathologist to talk. First of all, get a secretary. Then when you answer, say, 'Dr. Cohen speaking. How may I help you.'"

"Vinnie, don't they keep you busy so that you wouldn't be a curse in my old age?"

Imperateri laughed, his tone then turning serious. "Doc, I need your help. It has to be on the sly. I'm on Anderson's excremental roster."

"So I heard from the chief M.E. What can I do, providing it's legal, and if it ain't, you won't tell anybody?"

Without mentioning Crawford's name, Imperateri spoke of lab work needed to tie a suspect in with the killings. "Anderson would only sabotage me if I went through him. I could get Bork, one of the guys in Homicide, to provide you with the material."

Morris Cohen was enthusiastic, Imperateri ecstatic.

"Doc, if I were sixtyish, Jewish and female-ish, I could fall for you."

"I'm already married, Vinnie, but thanks for the compliment."

All Imperateri had to do now was to beg or cajole Noseworthy and Bork for their help.

TWENTY-EIGHT

For Vincent Imperateri now, it was all in the waiting for the telephone to ring. He remained at his desk, emptying his cigarette pack, one by one. As he watched wisps of smoke curl and rise to disappear near the ceiling, he worried how long he could get away with his new scheme. Once Anderson found out, there was no doubt of a suspension from the force. What then? A trial board hearing, a decision to strip him of rank, privileges, job, pension?

He looked at the telephone, as if willing it to ring, hoping to hear from Bork that the headquarters cars in question had been gone over, vacuumed, and the pickings given to Morris Cohen. A good sign had been the willingness of Bork to cooperate, despite Anderson.

First, Bork had to determine which of the hundreds of cars in the employee parking lot belonged to William Crawford. That was easy. The parking permit office would tell him that. But breaking in, picking it clean, and getting away with it as Imperateri had done with Lipsky's car was another matter. Suppose Crawford chanced upon the scene, or Anderson heard about it, as he had about Lipsky? On top of that, no laboratory technicians could be used and Morris Cohen had to dust. Imperateri wondered how good a fingerprint expert the medical examiner was.

If the fingerprint dustings and the vacuumings pan out, he'd have enough to go to the D.A. In a matter of minutes, Crawford could be socked. Under the lights, he'd tell soon enough what he did with the latest victim, little Joan Marchi.

The telephone rang. Imperateri burned a finger on a cigarette. It was John Bork, brief and to the point, as if the young detective didn't want to spend too much time with the blacklisted older one.

"All done, Vinnie. Dr. Cohen has it all. He says he needs a couple of hours. I even got Crawford's blood type from the personnel file."

Hanging up, Imperateri stared at the telephone. *Crawford.* Would he be the missing piece to the whole puzzle?

Even the fire-bombing attempt seemed to fit. Imperateri recalled it had happened a day after Marie Mackay had published the story about him being close to an arrest. Crawford had apparently panicked, thinking Detective Sergeant Vincent Imperateri was on the verge of closing the case.

Imperateri also recalled being puzzled how anybody besides a few close friends had known where he lived after the separation and divorce. He had an unlisted telephone number. The probability, he now realized, was that Crawford had simply strolled into headquarters personnel office just as Bork had done, and looked up his address. Nobody but a department employee could do that. William Crawford.

The telephone rang again. This time it was from Chris Daley in Missing Persons.

"Vinnie, I know you're not active on this, but I just wanted to let you know that we found Joan Marchi."

Imperateri held his breath. "Alive?"

"And well. But she's a regular sperm bank now. The boys on the football team chipped in for a motel room out of town and kept her there. All voluntary. We're going for statutory rape."

Imperateri thanked him for the call and now knew why Crawford's house was clean. Joan Marchi was just a red herring, one of many in a detective's life.

A hunger pang reminded him that he'd skipped breakfast and that the lunch hour was long over. He thought of the Sicilian eggplant he'd had at Marie's. How long ago? A week? They hadn't seen each other or communicated since then. He now felt he'd been too paranoid, too quick to accuse.

253

Wearily he trudged to the snack bar, punched the cheese sandwich slot in the vending machine, and then drew black coffee from another vendor. Returning to his desk, he half-hoped he'd find her sitting there, just as she had been the first time he laid eyes on her.

Only a message that Dr. Cohen had called now greeted him. His fingers couldn't dial fast enough. Morris Cohen answered.

"Vinnie, bad news is that I can't find transfers of dust or fiber, anything that could connect one victim with another, or to the killer. Too much passage of time, maybe. Or maybe the killer just cleaned, washed the bodies too well."

"So, Doc, you're telling me we don't have a case."

"Didn't say that. We vacuumed up all kinds of pubic hairs from the trunk of the suspect's own car. We found them to be microscopically indistinguishable from pubic hair specimens from a few of the victims. Kitty Burns, for example. We could also match samples of Susan Stone's hair with that found in one of the cruisers that your suspect used."

"What does that mean?"

"It's a hair match, but it's not like a fingerprint. You know it won't hold up in court as strong proof of identification. Now, we also picked up Susan Stone's O-type blood in the trunk of the cruiser, but O also happens to be your suspect's type."

"How do you know that?"

"Your man, Bork gave me Crawford's file." Cohen paused for a moment, as if reading. "William Crawford, right. Well, Crawford's lawyer could always say the boy cut his finger changing a tire. We could break the blood down further, fractionate it for better identification, but it'll take time and nothing may come of it."

Imperateri heaved a deep sigh. "At least we tried."

"Wait a minute, sonny. I'm not through. You've got probable cause for a search warrant."

"He's got nothing to hide in that house, Doc."

"I'm talking about his mouth. I want an impression of his teeth."

"To compare with the bite marks on the victims?"

"You're getting smarter, Vinnie. That's completely admissible evidence in a court of law. You'll have to bring the whole bastard in."

Imperateri thanked the doctor once more and hung up. It was almost over. Suddenly, a bee in the back of his mind buzzed. This could be a two-fer. Crawford could also be used as bait. For Jack the Snipper. Dr. Julian Stone.

Upon hearing the doctor's voice over the telephone, Imperateri experienced a twinge of regret about having to deceive the man, already tormented beyond words. For a moment, Imperateri felt a strange alliance with the doctor. After all, wasn't Stone, if he were actually Jack the Snipper, helping society to be rid of criminals? But the law was the law, and Imperateri found his voice.

"We've got a bit of good news, doctor. We're about to make an arrest in your daughter's case."

For a few moments there was silence at the end of the telephone, and then Julian Stone's voice came labored and hoarse. "Who is it?"

"I'm ashamed to say that he's an employee of the police department. A driving test examiner."

"But you haven't arrested him yet?"

"No, Dr. Stone. We're working up an arrest warrant and nailing a couple of points for the prosecution people. I thought I'd let you know before we do anything but you'll have to keep quiet about it."

Imperateri paused, praying that his bold and ridiculous lie would hold and that Stone, in his obsession, would fall for it. "We expect to make the arrest early tomorrow morning," the detective continued, thinking that this would give Stone time to drive down by tonight. "We're all keyed up. This case is really screwed down tight."

Stone said nothing, and now Imperateri feared that he saw through the flimsy scheme. But then Stone cleared his throat and spoke.

"How do you know he won't get away?"

255

"He doesn't have the faintest idea we're on to him. We're not even bothering to watch his house," Imperateri added. Stone had to be assured that the way would be clear for him.

"I still don't understand why you're not arresting this menace at once."

"As I've said, doctor, I'm waiting for a warrant. Early tomorrow's soon enough."

"It just seems so strange that you're not . . . "

"I admit it does, doctor," Imperateri interrupted, "but you know the killer strikes only on holidays, for reasons which we hope to clear up soon. Washington's Birthday is not until the day after tomorrow."

"Sergeant, would you mind telling me a little about him? Who he is, what does he look like?"

"I understand your curiosity, doctor. The suspect's name is William Crawford. He's about six feet, slim build, light hair, a little bald. As I've mentioned, he works for us and had access to police vehicles. It seems that he used them to pick up all of his victims, except in your daughter's case."

Again there was silence from Stone's end of the line. When Stone spoke once more, Imperateri could detect a tone of forced nonchalance.

"That's very interesting. Tell me, does he live alone?"

"Yes, in his own house in Anacostia. That's a little section of Washington." Imperateri tried not to sound too eager to relay information, and did not volunteer the exact address. Stone's suspicions might be aroused. The doctor could always look up the street number in the telephone book.

"And you're absolutely sure Crawford's your man?"

"No question about it. He checked out police vehicles on the holidays preceding reports of missing victims. Hair samples found in the cars match those of the dead girls. In your daughter's case, he used his own car to pick her up, and a cruiser to dispose of the body. We've managed to get samples without his knowledge. Everything checks out. As soon as we pick him up, we'll have Marcie Simkin and Gertrude Forbes in for a line-up. We should get a good, solid conviction on this one."

Imperateri heard Stone thank him and hang up. As Imperateri replaced his own receiver, he knew that the trap had been set. Tonight he would collar both the cannibal in his cave and Jack the Snipper with his shears wide open.

Julian Stone stared at the telephone for a long time after hanging up. It was not until the intercom buzzer sounded that he awakened to his surroundings.

"We have Mrs. Dolan and her son in the first examining room, doctor."

"Thank you, Betty. I'll be right out. Oh, by the way. Something came up. Don't take any more drop-in's or emergencies. Send them to Dr. Cooper. I'll ask him to cover. I've just learned I've got to leave early and maybe come in late tomorrow."

Betty Gruff was by now quite accustomed to his leave-takings. He guessed that neither she nor Eve Barlow could figure them out, and that both receptionist and nurse suspected his behavior and something to do with his change in personality following Susan's death. Such a change, the moodiness, the daydreaming, was natural. Even the strange and sudden departures and disappearances, sometimes for days at a time, were understandable. Betty never questioned him and merely relayed the annoyance of parents whose appointments were suddenly cancelled and rescheduled.

He would have to tell Lois the usual story about a medical meeting at the hospital. It would be a late conference. She shouldn't wait up. He would have no problem with her.

What bothered him now was the sure knowledge Sergeant Imperateri would have once the rapist Crawford was castrated. There would be no doubt in the detective's mind that he, Julian Stone, was indeed the perpetrator, the man who took vengeance for his daughter's murder and who tried to teach the criminal justice system a lesson.

He again thought of what might happen to him after being caught, for now he was certain that he would be. The mitigating circumstances certainly could be argued. Stone, a grief-stricken father driven to acts of desperation. Crawford, a madman rapist,

257

bloodthirsty, brutal. The force of public opinion would pull for the poor doctor.

Stone believed he would not serve long if convicted. If they parole murderers and rapists, they would certainly release him early, especially since his wife was to be delivered of a new baby. The baby, another mitigating factor in his favor. And his new baby would be born in a slightly better world, free of some half-dozen rapists.

Realizing the inevitability of his arrest and conviction, Stone was now determined to ensure that the public learn his side of the story. What better way than by going directly to the press?

He recalled the name of Marie Mackay, the reporter who had interviewed him and who had seemed to be so understanding. He would call her, indicating that he had a good story and suggesting that they meet at a certain time. The place would be Crawford's house. The time, after the operation.

Again the buzzer sounded, heralding Betty's impatient voice. "Doctor, are you ready now?"

"Yes, I am ready."

At about half past five in the evening, Vincent Imperateri dialed long distance directly to Dr. Julian Stone's office. A woman's voice on a taped message answered, informing that the doctor was out until Wednesday and referring the caller to a Dr. Cooper.

Imperateri hung up, still not satisfied. He needed more reason to believe that Stone had left and was heading for Washington.

He checked his telephone listing and dialed again, this time to Stone's residence. It wasn't until after the first ring that a minute measure of misgiving struck him. He hadn't the vaguest idea of what excuse to offer for the call.

The second and third rings sounded as thoughts raced through his mind. Of course, he concluded, he could inquire after Mrs. Stone's health.

"Stone residence," a raspy female voice answered.

"Is Dr. Stone in? This is Sergeant Imperateri calling." Stupid to give his name, he thought. He'd just called Stone earlier and would seem strange making another call a few hours later to ask about his wife. Stone was no fool. He'd suspect something.

"He's gone to the hospital for a long meeting or something. He said he'd be back late, real late."

"Is this the maid?"

"Housekeeper."

"How long ago did he leave?"

"He drove away about three o'clock. Who did you say you was?"

"Never mind. I'll see him at the hospital."

Imperateri replaced the receiver and drew a deep breath. He looked at his watch again. Stone would probably arrive before seven. A comparatively short wait. For a detective, waiting was eighty percent of the game.

In his jacket pocket was a warrant for William Crawford's arrest. With Morris Cohen's help, he had no trouble getting a Superior Court associate judge to sign it. Imperateri had the power to bring Crawford in so that x-rays and impressions could be made of his teeth.

Imperateri checked his .38 and patted the pair of handcuffs on his belt. He'd leave now, grab a hamburger and coffee on the way, and then wait in the car. He deliberated taking along Noseworthy or Bork for backup. Help might be needed for the double arrest of two nationally-known criminals, the cannibal killer and the castrator-mutilator.

He shook his head at his own thought. This was going to be his show, his double collar, especially now since his very job was in jeopardy. He didn't want any glory-grabbing by another cop, and he didn't want Anderson giving the credit out of spite to another cop.

As Imperateri rose to leave, Noseworthy entered the squad room and shrugged out of his coat, rolling it into a ball and throwing it on a chair. "Shi-it!" he cried, looking around the room before spotting Imperateri. "Vinnie, break out the Valium. Ol' Let 'Em Go Joe's done it again. He let your boy, Andre Jones, out on bail."

Imperateri grimaced. "Don't joke, Nose."

"I just testified at the arraignment. Let 'Em Go said Andre's Constitutional rights have been violated."

Imperateri plopped down in his chair, shut his eyes and rolled his head from side to side several times. "What the hell's the goddamn use? You tell me that, would you?"

"Lets make the streets safe for the animals," Perkins piped up from his corner desk. His normally ruddy complexion was now a deep red from unexploded anger.

Imperateri stood and addressed Noseworthy. "What Constitutional rights? The son of a bitch confessed to a dozen other felonies."

"That just it, Vinnie. The statement that Andre gave us about those half dozen rapes and robberies, well, that got published in the press."

"So what?"

"So it doesn't count, according to Let 'Em Go. That's because a prospective juror might remember reading about it and be prejudiced against Andre in the rape-homicide. What that means is that Let 'Em Go won't consider the confession and won't hold Andre under preventive detention. The judge says there isn't strong evidence that Andre'll be convicted or that he'll commit another felony while out on bail."

"Oh, God!" Imperateri shouted, slapping a cheek with an open palm. "Listen, Nose, Anderson won't listen to me, but you've got to convince him to assign someone to watch Andre. That boy's an uncaged tiger."

"Fucking lawyers, fucking judges," Perkins said. "They want to teach cops a lesson in law. But at whose expense? The citizens on the street, that's who."

Imperateri pulled on his coat. "I've got to run out on a case."

Noseworthy jerked his head back. "What case? You're on paper patrol."

Before Imperateri could offer up a lie to cover his tracks, Perkins called out to him. "Vinnie, wait a minute. Your wife, ah, ex-wife is on hold and the Captain wants to see you right away."

"Tell her I'll call back in a few minutes."

"She says it's urgent."

Imperateri hesitated. Another complaint from her about a late child support payment. Or maybe she's had another fight with Judy. Or maybe she wants to bitch that the postage stamps she bought didn't have enough stickum.

He glanced at the other officers, each trying to look busy so as not to appear interested in another domestic squabble. "Tell her that anyway," he said, keeping the irritation out of his voice and exiting the squad room.

Anderson was waiting for him, his jaw muscles tightened so that they balled up at the cheeks. Imperateri could detect that the older officer had been drinking, so clearly evident by a flushed face above an open top button on his shirt and a necktie askew.

"Sergeant, can't you get it through your thick wop skull that you're off the street? What's this shit I hear about you getting a warrant? Who gave you the right to . . . "

He paused, sputtering for words to complete his sentence. Unable to, he continued on another tack. "That settles it. You're on sixty-day suspension without pay."

Imperateri betrayed no emotion. He stared directly into Anderson's face, forcing the captain to look down on the desk. When Imperateri spoke, his voice came cool and deliberate.

"Number one, I don't even allow my friends to insult my ethnic heritage. Number two, you can't suspend me because I'm filing for retirement. You'll get my letter of intent in the morning."

Saying that, Imperateri reached for his wallet, unpinned the badge and tossed it on the desk. "Here's my tin. Up asswards shove, with the pin open." He spun around and marched out.

Anderson called after him. "Come back here, you bastard! Nobody quits unless I say so!"

He shouted to an empty doorway.

Back in the squad room, Imperateri said nothing to the other detectives about his retirement. They'd learn about it soon enough from Anderson. Tomorrow it would be official. And tonight he'd wrap up Crawford and Stone and go out in a blaze of glory.

Again he put on his coat, feeling the .38 press against him but missing the lump of the badge in his rear pocket. After so many years, it was like walking on the street without shoes.

"Hey, Vinnie," Perkins again called to him. "What's going on here? The captain wants to see you again and your ex is back on line four."

"I'll take it. Tell the captain I left a minute ago."

Beth was sobbing so that he could barely understand her. "Judy," the words finally came through, "she's missing."

He listened to Beth but said nothing, fearing that an interruption would stop the flow of information, vital news that he'd need to bring a swift halt to whatever danger faced his daughter.

Judy was several hours overdue. None of her friends knew where she was. Beth continued, "She was supposed to be home by four, after some school club meeting. She'd asked me to pick her up. I couldn't because I'm trying to save money on gas."

"Don't lay that guilt crap on me, Beth. Just tell me what you know."

Beth gasped. "If you were a *real* father . . . " She paused and began again. "Since I couldn't make it, she decided to hitchhike."

"How do you know that?"

"From Nancy, her friend. She called to tell me that."

It couldn't happen to his own daughter, Imperateri thought. The odds, what were they in a situation like this, where the paths of cop and criminal cross in a coincidental, personal and fatal way? The population of the Washington metropolitan area was more than three million. The odds were incredible. The possibility that Crawford ensnared Judy was unreal. Like so many kids her age, she'd merely taken off for a couple of hours without telling anyone. People were so paranoid now. Maybe she'll turn up like that cheerleader girl.

Beth's voice broke into his thoughts. "What should I do?"

"Have you called the police?" he asked, an inevitable question made ridiculous, he suddenly thought, by his asking. *He was the police.* "I mean, did you call anyone before me?"

"Just Judy's friend, Nancy. You've got to come over right away."

He hesitated, looking at his watch. Even if he'd rush over, he'd barely have time to make it then to Crawford's house before Stone. Besides, what could he do at Beth's apartment to help Judy? What could he do alone with one pair of eyes while driving the neighborhood streets looking for a car no one could identify and for a driver no one could describe?

"Look, Beth, let me get back to you." He hung up without giving her a chance to respond and checked his telephone listing again, this time for Crawford's number.

"Hello," a mellow voice answered.

Imperateri cleared his throat. "Ah, Mr. Crawford? Mr. William Crawford? This is Johnny Roberts from the Home Insulation Company. One of our insulating experts is in your neighborhood and we'd like him to drop by for a free home inspection and estimate."

"Not interested."

"But this offer is absolutely at no cost . . . " Imperateri jerked the receiver away and looked at it, his ear ringing from the force of Crawford's hanging up.

The detective now had heard what the suspect sounded like, and had learned that he was at home. But Imperateri still didn't know where Judy was. He couldn't very well have asked Crawford that question. The odds, he thought once more, were on his side. But even a gambler never fully trusted odds.

TWENTY-NINE

Julian Stone drove up the dark, empty street and located the house within moments. He parked, not bothering to take precautionary moves, either to circle the block several times or to observe the house closely. Eager to get at William Crawford, he cared little for his own safety. Nor did he care that when Imperateri and his police arrived to arrest a castrated Crawford, they would know immediately who the castrator was.

Nevertheless a shiver ran through his bones. His muscles ached, as though with fever. He couldn't believe the moment which he'd waited for so long had finally come. Crawford wasn't just a rapist, an unknown name from a long-forgotten crime plucked like the others out of old newspapers. He was the last person to see Susan alive. He was the cause and instrument of her death.

What kind of person was he? Did he really exist, this monster, or was he but an imagined quarry, a convenient scapegoat for outrage and vengeance?

His anticipation keyed up to a high pitch, Julian Stone sucked in a deep breath. He could feel his pulse throbbing, his heart skipping beats.

Opening the medical bag lying on the seat, he reached in to feel the cool hardness of the scalpel, as if drawing strength and confidence from its touch. He also felt the roll of strong twine he knew would be needed.

Stone opened the car door and got out, bending in to pick up the bag. As he did, his fingers shook as though palsied. Now his legs wavered under him. When he tried to move them, they felt rubbery, recalcitrant. It was as if he were in a dream, unable to summon movement.

He gulped the chilly night air and thought: I'm living out a fantasy. I'm on a high few people ever realize. How many have ever confronted the killer of their child? How many have wished they could?

The vengeance was part of him, like his own flesh. It possessed him. To take it away would be like tearing out a part of himself.

A flood of purpose coursed through him now, thrusting him forward, energizing his body in a way over which he had no control.

The apartment smelled of stale smoke, which was not surprising to Vincent Imperateri. Beth was a chain-smoker, and had been one long before they had married. He always smoked more around her.

Tall, with fluffy light blond-streaked hair and an oval face, she was not an unattractive woman, even barefooted and dressed in an old, large kimono and dragging on the ever-present cigarette. For several minutes they smoked, frowning at each other with mutual dislike while she repeated what she had told him over the telephone. When at last he rose to leave, she angrily snuffed out a cigarette and lit another, shouting at the same time.

"What do you mean you have to go now? You just got here!"

"I told you, I called in about Judy on the car radio. Every patrol car in the city has got an eye out for her, a cop's kid. There's nothing I can do waiting around here."

"I know what you can do. You can talk to me. We can help each other through this."

"Not now, I've got a big case going." He edged towards the door. She followed, her voice now thundering.

"You haven't changed a fucking bit! Still putting your job ahead of everything, your family, your daughter!"

"Beth, Judy's all right. I know she is. Let's just relax on this."

"Don't you ever dare tell me to relax about anything, do you hear? A killer rapist is running loose and your daughter is missing. And what the hell are you doing? You're off maybe to bust some pimp for beating on his whore?"

Imperateri didn't want to tell her that the big case was Crawford. She would get hysterical, maybe even plead to go with him.

Driving almost recklessly, he regretted taking precious seconds to stop off at Beth's. Suppose Crawford did have Judy. He cursed himself for not arresting him right away, for playing a cat-and-mouse game with Stone.

A sudden, sharp pain struck him between his navel and breastbone. "Oh God, no!" he cried. It had to be a heart attack, he was sure. The cigarettes. The rich food. "Not now. Not now."

And then he remembered the aching soreness which had bothered him for the last couple of hours. It was his goddam ulcer, now burning as if a hot liquid had been poured directly into his stomach.

With one hand on the wheel, he dipped into a pocket for a box of pills. The container was empty, holding only particles of the antacids. He threw the box aside and snapped open the glove compartment to search blindly with his free hand. Then he recalled that the spare pill box was discarded weeks ago.

Now he'd have to stop at a drugstore and lose more valuable time. No, he would not.

He again picked up the empty container and tapped the residue into his mouth, gulping down whatever dropped in, but the pain increased in intensity.

I won't stop, he thought. Judy's life's at stake.

He'd read somewhere that a severe ulcer attack if left untreated may result in perforation of the stomach. That meant peritonitis, and he knew that could be fatal.

He felt faint. The sweat was pouring off him. He realized he couldn't continue. But he had to push himself. Suppose Crawford had Judy.

Just then, Noseworthy radioed him.

"Vinnie, we found your daughter okay. She was with some boy and lost track of time. We called your wife. We're taking her home."

"Thank God. Oh Thank God. Nose, hey, listen, can you get down to the station and stand by?"

With Noseworthy's reassuringly affirmative reply lingering in his ears, Imperateri suddenly reversed direction, heading towards Providence Hospital where he knew the night ER crew. They'd give him something quick and easy for the pain.

He also knew that whatever else it was for Julian Stone, it wasn't going to be quick and easy for him this time.

William Crawford, his naked body painted a pastiche of perspiration, chicken fat and human blood, heard the doorbell ring. His head jerked and his eyes darted up the basement steps towards the sound and then fell to the floor where the body lay on the mattress. Finally, his eyes turned to his own body. He couldn't answer the door looking like this.

He had no idea who it could be, but imagined it had something to do with the call he'd received a short while ago about home insulation. Did they dare come bother him after he'd said no?

No matter. He wouldn't answer. But then he remembered that burglars often rang on one pretext or another to learn if anyone were home. It would be ironic if a housebreaker found the dead girl and collected any of the numerous rewards for turning in the lust-killer.

The buzzing continued, persistent and steady. Crawford took his time washing his body at the basement sink, hoping the caller would grow tired and leave. But the bell persisted and he put on the robe and slippers he'd brought down with him. Before ascending the stairs he took a yearning look at the body, in the manner of a person forced to cut short a favorite pastime.

She had turned out to be the best of the lot, a tough street type who cursed and struggled until the very end. He thought she might be a prostitute, though she hadn't asked for money before she willingly undressed.

For her, he had taken the day off from work, and had regretted having had to kill her, but it was in keeping with his new program of change, of keeping the police off balance. They'd find her body before she'd be declared as missing.

267

As he reached the top step, the bell rang once again. He carefully shut the basement door and then peeked through the front window.

A man, dressed in a windbreaker and holding a small bag, stood impatiently. No doubt it was the insulation man, Crawford guessed, and no doubt he was anxious to make a sale. Or was it someone else?

A danger signal sounded in his brain. Strange things were happening. First, the breaking and entering of his car, right on the damn police parking lot, of all places. He didn't report it because nothing was taken and he didn't want to raise a fuss.

And then there was the break-in and theft of the silver urn and then the insulation telephone call. And now, this visitor. Well, there was only one way of determining if there was any connection.

"Who is it?" he shouted through the door.

"Gas company. Our computer shows you have a leak."

"I don't smell anything."

"That's what they all say, until it's too late."

Crawford reluctantly opened the door a crack. "Look, can you come back tomorrow? I'm entertaining. You know, a guest."

Julian shoved the gun through the crack into Crawford's stomach. "Open the goddamn door!" He pushed his way in before Crawford could react.

Julian Stone locked the door behind him and motioned William Crawford further back with the Beretta. "Where's your guest?"

Crawford shot a glance towards the basement door and smiled weakly. "No guest. I just didn't want to be bothered tonight."

Stone looked around the foyer and then into the living room, all the time keeping an eye on Crawford. The place had a closed-in smell, one mixed with a strange sweet-sour odor. He pointed to the living room. "Inside."

"What do you want?" Crawford asked. He was starting to shake.

"Let's say I'm a burglar and I'm going to help myself to your jewels."

268

Crawford blew air through compressed lips. "Look, I don't have any jewelry but take anything else you want. Say, you the one here the other night. Well, you took the only thing of value already."

"Shut up and listen. Lie face down on the floor, hands clasped behind you."

Stone watched as Crawford assumed the position which would make it difficult to strike back or resist. Then he pocketed the Beretta, freeing both hands to bind Crawford's with the twine he pulled from the bag.

"Now get up and lie down on the couch. This time on your back."

Not having his arms for support, Crawford struggled to his knees, aided by Stone who then led him to the couch. Crawford lay face up, eyes on Stone, willing him to ransack the house and leave quickly. He tried not to think about the body in the basement, as though thinking about it would tip this man to go down there.

But the man only went upstairs and came down immediately. Just too quickly to check what valuables were available. Crawford could not understand. Maybe the man was indeed looking for someone else in the house.

But the intruder now appeared satisfied that they were alone. He stared at Crawford for a full minute before approaching and fumbling with his robe, untying the belt.

Crawford's eyes bulged. "Hey, what are you trying to do?"

"You'll see," Stone said, flinging open the robe. "No trousers, no underwear? That's convenient."

The shriveled penis lay over a wrinkled scrotal sac which hung tightly. Stone knew that the man's fright triggered the scrotum's muscles to contract instinctively, drawing the testes closer to the body for protection.

Crawford wanted to talk, ask questions, scream, but he gagged, unable to make a sound.

"I'm going to rape you."

Crawford's eyes flickered, then remained fixed and disbelieving. Again he tried to talk but his mouth opened and closed soundlessly.

"It's not that bad. Haven't you ever been raped before? Or maybe you raped a couple of times yourself. It's an unforgettable experience."

Shaking uncontrollably Crawford finally managed to blurt out, "I'm afraid you're making a stupid mistake. I happen to be a police officer."

"I know."

"You do? Who the hell are you anyway?"

"Someone who's going to save you from what you are," Stone said in an almost caressing tone.

Crawford's eyes darted sideways to the black bag lying on the floor. He looked at Stone. He tried to smile. "Please . . . Please . . ." was all he could get out.

Stone, silent, reached for the bag and pulled out the scalpel. It flashed reflected light from a lamp. He gently rubbed it back and forth on a thumb, as if to test the sharpness of the stainless steel blade.

Crawford was almost hypnotized by it. "Jesus," he rasped. "I know who you are. You're the guy the police are looking for. I don't know what you want with me. Let me tell you, you're making a big mistake. I never harmed anyone. Check with the police, with anybody." His voice was now a high-pitched whine.

"The police told me about you."

Crawford was hysterical, almost incoherent. "They told you what? It's a damn lie. If it's true, why haven't they come after me?"

"You murdered my daughter," Stone said, leaning over, brandishing the scalpel. "Even after you killed her it wasn't enough for you. You had to go and tear apart her body like a jackal."

Crawford lashed out suddenly with a foot, kicking Stone fully in the chest. Stone reeled back, dropping the scalpel and gasping for breath. Crawford, handicapped by his arms tied beneath him, nevertheless scrambled to his feet and charged with lowered head as a battering ram.

Stone stood surprised and motionless. He caught the charge on a shoulder. Like an enraged bull, Crawford turned for another pass, but this time Stone parried by pushing him aside. Again he charged. Stoned balled up a fist and struck him full smack on the bridge of the nose, the impact of the blow increased by Crawford's lunge.

Stone felt cartilage give and then saw blood gush from the nostrils with faucet-like force. Crawford, groaning, fell to his knees. His tongue hung from his mouth, amid red spittle and a thread of saliva.

"Back on the couch!" Stone snarled.

Like a spastic child on his knees, Crawford crawled back, leaving a trail of blood in his wake.

Now Stone gathered more twine to tie Crawford's spread-apart legs, anchoring each to a leg of the old-fashioned couch. He then retrieved the scalpel. Kneeling, he held it under a buttock and slid it across the skin, drawing a thin, red line.

Crawford whimpering, winced. "Stop. Please."

"That hurt? Shouldn't. Just a simple defilement of the body. Not like rape at all."

Stone now held the blade against the penis, teasing it from one side to the other. Now there came the look that Stone had been waiting for. An indescribable look of abject terror. Stone did not disappoint. He nipped ever so slightly the opening of the member, sending a few dark red droplets trickling.

Crawford twisted his head from side to side. Animal, unrecognizable sounds coming out of him.

"How many have you killed? Tell me how my daughter suffered."

Crawford licked away the blood still dripping from his nose. He willed himself to stare unblinkingly at the scalpel and said nothing.

"You just don't remember which one she was, do you? I'll remind you. Her name was Susan. She was a beautiful young lady with a lovely soul and with everything to live for."

A picture of Susan came to Stone's mind, changing suddenly as though through film special effects to show her body as it looked when found. Her skin, the color of ochre clay. What flesh, sunken here and bloated there, had not been vio-

271

lently disfigured by Crawford had been torn apart by field animals.

Julian Stone shook the image away. He picked up an edge of the scrotal sac with the dull side of the knife and levered it upward.

Crawford shuddered and jerked his legs. Simpering, he begged in a barely audible voice, "Please, oh please!"

"Tell me how you killed my daughter."

"I didn't do anything to anybody."

Stone pulled out a cigarette lighter, lit it, and held the edge of the scalpel over the flame. "Must sterilize," he whispered, trance-like.

When the metal turned bluish-red, he raised and swung it like a whip, sounding a slight hiss in the air. Crawford remained transfixed by the sight and sound. He drew back as much as he could when the scalpel drew closer.

The penetration came in the pubic area, singeing hair and crackling skin. Flesh bubbled and closed over the scalpel's tip. As Crawford's wail mounted to a shriek, Stone jerked the blade out with a single movement.

Crawford choked with rage. The folds around his drooping, blood-smeared lips gave his face the mask of a circus clown. "You're going to die for this!"

"You don't want me to sterilize?"

"You fucking bastard!"

Again, visions of her body came to Stone. Caked with dried blood and dirt, it was lifted from its makeshift grave. He imagined the head jerking and bent, rigid arms jumping like those of a puppet.

Stone now clamped the scrotum with one hand and made a slight cut in the bag, through which blood oozed. Crawford howled. He sucked air through his teeth, flared his nostrils, and again wiped his tongue over a contorted mouth.

"Oh, please don't!" Was he saying it aloud? Did the man hear him?

The vision: Now of her once lithe and vibrant body as it looked before her death and disfigurement. She struggled as she tried to defend herself. Her convulsed face over a chained, bleeding neck. Pleading. Crying. Her body, heaving and contracting, shaken by agonizing shudders. Finally, stillness. Blood, at first sticky, then dried and blackish. Globs of coagulated blood. Her eyes, oozing holes.

Stone, still grasping the genitals, wanted to slash away at them, blenderizing them into bits and pieces. Instead he aimed an inch away and jabbed at the flesh of the top and innermost thigh. A jet of bright, red blood splattered his hand.

"This is how it feels to be raped!" he shouted.

Crawford howled. His eyes rolled back, revealing only the whites between half-closed lids. He was crying uncontrollably, great heaving sobs. "I really didn't mean to do it! Not to any of them!"

Stone now played with the scalpel around the sac, rubbing against it as if sharpening on a strop. With each stroke, the testes stood out in bright and purplish outline against the membranous covering.

"Nooo . . ." Crawford sobbed.

"I must."

Crawford began pounding his head on the arm of the couch. Veins danced along his temples. Below, rivulets flowed, blood, mucus, spittle, sweat, tears. "Please put me out before you operate," he cried. "I don't want to feel the pain."

"You didn't want me to sterilize before and now you want a painkiller. Make up your mind." Stone squeezed the sac to receive a deep incision. "No more fooling around, rapist. Here it comes."

But Crawford did not hear him. He gurgled, froth foaming at his lips. Muscles in his face contracted and spasms shook his arms and legs. Then his body arched from heels to neck and he passed out.

With aluminum hydroxide turning the volcano in his stomach into a mild bubble, Vincent Imperateri reached the home of William Crawford. There was a car out front with an M.D. license. It had to be Stone's.

273

Imperateri approached and gazed through the window. Crawford lay naked and bloody and tied up while Stone hovered over him with a scalpel ready to cut off his balls. Or was he? He was talking to Crawford. Teasing him with the scalpel.

A strong feeling of futility came over the detective. He'd have to take Stone into custody. As for Crawford, also an arrest, but then most probably rescue from punishment by some legalism, a crime in itself. Crawford may well be freed in time, the responsibility for his misdeeds shaken off by cockamamie shrinks and lawyers.

He tightened his fists so that the veins looked like swollen rivers flowing to the gorges of white knuckle mountains. It wasn't right that bastards like Crawford escaped with impunity while a guy like Stone could be driven to such a stupid act and have the book thrown at him for it. He had to talk to the good doctor. But what he saw now made him jump. Stone was lowering the scalpel, ready to cut.

Imperateri pulled out his revolver, dashed to the front door and kicked it open. "Just hold it right there!"

Stone nodded wearily. "I didn't expect you so soon."

"Put that sticker away, would you?"

Stone raised the scalpel in a dejected manner and dropped it into his bag.

Imperateri holstered the weapon and looked at Crawford's nose. "Looks like you castrated the wrong end."

Stone shrugged and then looked straight into Imperateri's eyes. "Well, Sergeant, I guess now you're ready to manacle me for the dungeons. I expected as much and I am ready."

A noise from the front door caused both men to jerk their heads toward the sound. Imperateri moved cautiously to the foyer and returned a few moments later, shaking his head. "Have you looked around?" Without waiting for a reply, he headed for the hallway. "Let's hit the basement first."

With the light switched on, he hunkered down on the top landing, hoping to view the basement without trudging down the flight. After all, he'd seen it only the other night. He drew a deep breath and stood immediately, his voice suddenly coming dry and grim. "Doctor, you'd better get your bag."

Before descending the last few steps, Stone knew it was useless. Nobody could lose so much blood and survive.

Covered with blood, parts of the basement floor looked as if a bucket of cheap red paint had been accidentally tipped over. Clumps of red-outlined footprints made a trail from the body to the stairs, on the bottom step of which rested a doormat, also darkened by red splotches.

The body of the girl lay cut up, with chunks of flesh torn from the buttocks and inner thighs as though by a wild animal. Breasts, mostly severed, hung precariously from the torso, ready to drop loose like wax from a melting candle. Bits of chewed-up flesh lay scattered about the body.

Imperateri resisted an urge to throw up. "Son of a bitch bastard!"

Stone gasped and began to choke. "Never, never . . ." was all he could say, shaking his head wildly as though the movement compensated for the lack of words.

"You could have left your bag upstairs, Doc. Nobody can help her anymore. Let's get back before our friend wakes up."

Crawford, however, was still unconscious.

"I feel like shooting his damn head off," Imperateri said, turning towards Stone. "Maybe I should have let you do what you wanted to." He perched on an arm of the couch and continued speaking as he gazed at Crawford.

"Maybe he'll be sentenced to a couple of consecutive life terms. But he'll be a model prisoner, mostly because there'll be no young girls to rape and murder. He'll take college courses, go to church, spill his guts to some shrink. Then he'll be back on the streets in seven years, four months, and three days. Doc, let's admit that we've lost and the bad guys won."

Stone nodded, held out his hands and curled his fists. "Come, Sergeant, the handcuffs."

"What for? You didn't do anything here tonight. And I've no proof you're Jack the Snipper." He rose and pulled off the handcuffs attached to his belt. Then he rolled Crawford over and re-moved the twine, replacing it with the cuffs.

"Besides," he continued, "I've only got one pair of these. That means I'm going to have to let you go."

"You can't be serious."

"Maybe it's wrong, but so what? This time I'm doing what's right according to my lights. The courts do it all of the time. Now do me a favor in return. Get the hell out of here. Go back to Jersey. Go lance your boils and treat your diaper rash. If anybody turns you in for being the Snipper, it won't be me."

Crawford stirred, his eyelids fluttering open. Stone, picking up his bag, leaned over to an ear. He spoke in a low and raucous voice, so different that he himself was astonished by the sound of it. "Next time I'll send you through the gates of hell!"

A shaking Crawford began babbling incoherently.

Imperateri nodded a farewell to the departing doctor and picked up the telephone to call Noseworthy. As he relayed information, he stared with disgust at his prisoner and wondered what reason could be given for his beat-up condition.

"Oh, Nose," he said, "the suspect resisted arrest. Might have to drop by the ER for patch-up."

But what about the story Crawford's sure to tell about Stone, Jack the Snipper? How to squelch that?

"Also, Nose, our boy's gone over the edge. Keeps ranting about someone trying to cut him. The wounds look self-in-flicted."

Imperateri hung up after a few more moments and then heard a noise in the foyer, the sound of the front door opening and closing. He rushed out but saw nothing. Then he heard a car start from around a corner and listened to it roar off into the distance.

From afar now came the sound of sirens. He retraced his steps to Crawford, his bloodied face grotesquely distorted.

"He didn't cut me, did he?" Crawford asked with slurred speech.

"Who? There's nobody here."

"The man with the knife. The mutilator. Who everyone's talk-

276

ing about." He had become strangely lucid, almost articulate.

"I told you, there's nobody here except what's in the basement. You want to talk about that? Who is . . . was she?"

Crawford sat up trying to look at his genitals. "Did he do it? I can't tell. There's so much pain."

"Never mind that, you son of a bitch. What about that woman downstairs?

"Woman? I don't know. I came home and that man attacked me."

Imperateri sighed. "You not-guilty-by-reason-of-insanity-bastard, listen. I am Detective Sergeant Vincent Imperateri. You are being placed under arrest pending further investigation of the homicide of the subject on your premises and other subjects who will be named. You are also being taken into custody pending questioning concerning the attempted homicide of a police officer."

Crawford was not listening. "That man," he began, "he tried to . . ."

"You have the right to remain silent. You are not required to say anything or to answer any questions. Anything you say can be used . . ."

"That man who cut me, he was the one who did it to the girl downstairs."

Imperateri nodded, continuing with the Miranda ritual. He wanted to make sure that Crawford wasn't going to beat him in court, at least not on that technicality. As he finished, he heard the sirens squeal to a stop outside.

Crawford also heard them. He smiled. "They'll believe me. I'm a cop myself."

"I've got something good to tell you, Crawford. About your dues to the Fraternal Order of Police."

"What?"

"They'll be returned to you."

Vincent Imperateri hesitated for a moment before turning the key to his apartment. He couldn't think of anything else he'd rather not do than to enter the dark and lonely rooms and eat some cold leftovers. There was always the all-night cafeteria, or, better still, the fish food joint where they always gave him a discount because he was a cop. Better take advantage of that, he reminded himself. After retirement, there'd be no more fringe benefits like that.

Turning away from the apartment, he began to make his way back down the hall but stopped short. It really would be better to throw a steak under the broiler and grab a hot shower, watch some television and get a good night's sleep.

Though filled with elation at wrapping up the Crawford case, he ached for Marie Mackay. He wanted to apologize with all his heart for walking out on her. But she was nowhere to be found. Her apartment answering machine received his message and her office said she was out. Was she out only for him?

An emptiness gnawed at him as he thought of her. Why did he have to let her go? Why was he always playing the role of an unforgiving, unrelenting jackass?

Shrugging, he retraced his steps and let himself into the apartment. He stopped in his tracks. The lights were on. Sounds came from the kitchen. Tinkling, scraping, scratching.

Gun drawn, he crouched and advanced slowly. Just as he was about to rush in with weapon held high, a familiar odor struck his nostrils. He grinned and put the gun away, entering the kitchen.

Marie smiled at him, holding out like an offering a dish of Sicilian eggplant. "If you don't want to eat it," she said, "you could always rub it on your aching back."

"I could pull you in for breaking and entering." He glanced at the door. "How did you get in?"

"The custodian. He's a real cupid." She gently touched his cheek. "I'm back, Vinnie."

"I tried to get you all evening."

"I left the office early and didn't go home."

"Marie," he stammered, "I'm sorry about what I said."

"Forget it. It didn't hurt because I knew it wasn't true. I'm not a cold-blooded bastard, and I can prove it. I was hiding out at Crawford's and I heard everything."

"So I did hear something!"

She nodded. "Stone had called me and wanted to meet at Crawford's about some hot information. The door was open."

He rolled his eyes. "I busted it."

"After I left, I did some thinking. Decided to write the story but to leave Stone completely out. He's been through enough."

"Nobody else knows?"

"May I and my video display terminal be turned into a pillar of salt if I let a word be known. All I ask is that you give me details on Crawford."

He laughed. "At least one of us will be working."

When she asked why, he told her of his retirement plans and the rift with Anderson. She listened quietly, but anger flashed in her eyes. When he was through, she spoke in a loud but quivering voice.

"I thought you were tough, but now you're talking cut and run. Don't you know you're a goddamn hero? That's what my story's going to say. Listen to me, Vinnie. You're not quitting. And you're going to get that promotion. Let's see what foul mouth Anderson says about that."

He laughed again and took her into his arms, raising her off the floor and spinning her around.

"I missed you," he said.

Julian Stone succumbed to curiosity. The drive to the suburban Washington town of Rockville, Maryland, would be worth it to see Larry Wilson. Stone felt that he had to see what the rapist looked like, what changes had occurred since the castration more than six months ago.

Though impelled by his inquisitiveness, he realized that a visit carried grave risk. Suppose Wilson recognized him and took counter vengeance right then and there. Yet at the time of the castration Stone had worn a disguise and had masked·his voice. He also doubted that Wilson could now identify him after the long passage of time. On the other hand, the physical and psychic trauma Stone had wrought had been great, perhaps leaving the rapist with an indelible impression of his attacker's most minute characteristics, the tilt of the head, the walk, the inflection of the voice. It was possible that Wilson prayed for the day when his attacker would show himself once again.

Leaving the Baltimore Harbor Tunnel with its gritty white tiles, he turned to the Washington Parkway, a leg of Route 1 going south. Every few miles a sign proclaimed the distance to the capital city.

As he drove, he pictured in his mind the way Lois had looked before he left. Her face had blossomed into a new freshness, and her abdomen protruded with a healthy mid-term roundness.

A new life to substitute for what had been lost, he now thought. Would it ever replace the old?

Of course, the lady obstetrician had performed amniocentesis, because of Lois's age. Not only was the fetus perfectly normal, but it . . . she, was a girl. A girl. In their joy they'd already chosen a name. Eve, the first-named of women.

He smiled to himself, but the sudden approach to the outskirts of Washington brought a shudder to his body. The city was full of nightmares for him. Yet he knew he'd have to face up and overcome them sometime.

He looked up at the rearview mirror, met his eyes, and spoke aloud. "I've mourned enough."

Near the end of the Parkway he headed west on 495, the Washington Beltway. Entering Rockville, he concentrated on the streets, trying to recall the lay of the land and hoping that he hadn't missed the garage where Wilson worked. Suppose he were no longer there?

Rising at the next intersection was the familiar lot where he had spent hours last winter. And across the street was the gas station, so cold and dirty-looking in the bright light of day. He drove in, parking at the side of the station rather than at the pumps or service bays.

He got out and strode over to the bays. Wilson was nowhere to be seen. In the office, a man dressed in a clean uniform used an adding machine to tally up a pile of slips.

"Excuse me," Stone interrupted. "My name's Jackson. I'm an old friend of Larry Wilson's, just passing through. Last contact I had he said he worked here."

The manager, a thin man with a pinched face, nodded. "Sure does. But he don't come on 'til four."

Of course, Stone recalled. Wilson had the late shift. "Yeah, I'd like to see him. It's been a few years."

"I'll tell you, Mr. Jackson. Larry's been a little sick. You wouldn't recognize him. We don't know what happened, but we think it's his glands. He was hurt bad, cut up in a holdup. He don't talk about it and gets mad when we ask. He gets out of his new character."

"What do you mean?"

"I don't know how well you knew him. He used to have a trigger temper. A fly would set him off. Now, nothing bothers him, except talk about his sickness." The manager looked at his watch. "You've got some waiting to do."

"Oh, I'll go get something to eat. Would you have him do a lube job on the car. And I'd appreciate it if you don't tell Larry whose it is. I'd like to surprise him."

At four-fifteen, Stone returned. The manager was gone and the only person at the station was a man in one of the bays lubricating Stone's car on a lift.

It had to be Wilson. His back was to Stone, but it was clear that the physique had taken on the soft lines of femininity. A role of flab bounced above the belt. Gone were the trim, hard hips and narrow buttocks, replaced by soft, bulging flesh.

Stone stepped forward, took a deep breath, and spoke. "Got much more to do on that?"

The man turned slowly around. It was Larry Wilson, though bloated and changed beyond the recall of memory. The eyes were soft and pleading like a doe's no longer hard and angry. The masculine, youthful face was also gone. Instead, there was a strangely puckered image with many small wrinkles on a sickly, sallow skin.

"Almost done, sir," Wilson said. "I'll have it in front in a minute."

His voice was pitched in a higher register than Stone could recall, but still within the normal range for an adult male.

As he paid the bill, Stone managed another close look. Smallish breasts pushed against the blue work shirt, but they were not too noticeable to the unscrutinizing eye because of the general weight shift.

Later, driving home, he couldn't help erasing images of Wilson from his mind. All of the changes, he mused, were a small price to pay. A small injustice as punishment for a great one, and a preventative for even greater ones. It couldn't be any worse than spending a lifetime in jail, if indeed Wilson and the others ever were to serve full sentences. Few ever did. He thought of the whimpering mass that was Crawford as he'd last seen him.

A thousand years it took to rise from barbarism to a more gentle and civilized society, now only to fall to legal savagery. He clucked his tongue, frustrated in his anger, rapidly turning to rage as he thought of how Crawford, so far, hadn't been brought to trial as his attorneys sought delay after delay on one technicality after another.

Julian Stone felt helpless. What could an insignificant citizen do about all of those do-gooders intent on emptying the jail of monstrous criminals, no matter what? The soft-hearted judges, psychiatrists determined to prove a theory, probation boards eager to meet a quota, publicity-hungry lawyers knowing of their clients' guilt but pressing for a courtroom victory. If only they could be made to understand the consequences of their actions.

He recalled the old joke about the definition of a conservative: A liberal who's been mugged.

Now he smiled to himself. Suppose that a liberal judge could be forcibly taken and locked away in a secluded place. And suppose a criminal recipient of that judge's mercy would likewise be abducted and brought to the same hideaway, to be shackled cheek-by-jowl with his benefactor. What would happen?

It could be done, he mused. The logistics presented no insurmountable difficulties. The leasing of an isolated cabin and the purchase of food, manacles, shackles, portable toilets. The actual abductions? No more difficult than the stealth and daring required for the castrations. After all, he would only do it once or twice, sufficient enough to make a point and attract national attention.

He would leave the pair alone for several days, either returning himself or tipping the police off where they could be found. The results would be interesting.

For a woman psychiatrist or psychologist who paved the way for a rapist's release, Stone would ensure her that rapist's company. For her male counterpart, any homicidal subject would be a suitable match.

If any harm came to anybody it would be compensated many times over by the good coming from the ensuing publicity.

Stone reasoned that there was a distinct possibility that nothing could happen, for both captives might concentrate on escape. Even so, the lesson wouldn't be lost, for again the media would learn of the event.

Lois would be busy with the baby. And as far as his practice was concerned, well, his staff and patients were by now well accustomed to his frequent absences.

It could be done.